"I need to wind this inv  **next forty-eight hours, you've become a distr**

"Is that what I am to you," Ford said, grinning.

"I'm serious. Please go home so I know you're safe."

"I can't do that." He held Hitch's gaze. "I came here to save Rachel if I could. Instead I find myself getting involved with you."

"I wouldn't say we're involved."

"Wouldn't you?" He cupped her cheek, drawing her face up to his own. "Tell me there is nothing between us and I'll walk away right now."

She parted her lips, but no words came out. He pulled her into his arms. He could feel her heart pounding in her pulse. "Last chance," he said.

B.J. Daniels is a *New York Times* and *USA TODAY* bestselling author. She wrote her first book after a career as an award-winning newspaper journalist and author of thirty-seven published short stories. She lives in Montana with her husband, Parker, and three springer spaniels. When not writing, she quilts, boats and plays tennis. Contact her at bjdaniels.com, on Facebook or on Twitter, @bjdanielsauthor.

Books by B.J. Daniels

Harlequin Intrigue

Cardwell Ranch: Montana Legacy

Steel Resolve
Iron Will
Ambush Before Sunrise
Double Action Deputy
Trouble in Big Timber

Whitehorse, Montana: The Clementine Sisters

Hard Rustler
Rogue Gunslinger
Rugged Defender

The Montana Cahills

Cowboy's Redemption

Whitehorse, Montana: The McGraw Kidnapping

Dark Horse
Dead Ringer
Rough Rider

HQN

Montana Justice

Restless Hearts
Heartbreaker
Heart of Gold

Visit the Author Profile page at Harlequin.com.

New York Times and USA TODAY Bestselling Author

B.J. DANIELS

TROUBLE IN BIG TIMBER

&

TWELVE-GAUGE GUARDIAN

HARLEQUIN
INTRIGUE

HARLEQUIN®
INTRIGUE®

ISBN-13: 978-1-335-21400-3

Recycling programs
for this product may
not exist in your area.

Trouble in Big Timber & Twelve-Gauge Guardian

Harlequin Enterprises ULC
22 Adelaide St. West, 40th Floor
Toronto, Ontario M5H 4E3, Canada
www.Harlequin.com

Printed in Spain

CONTENTS

TROUBLE IN BIG TIMBER

This book is dedicated to anyone still hung up on an old love. If you saw the person again, would it ignite those old sparks? Or would the fire have burned out? Or, would you realize that they were never quite as amazing as you remembered?

Chapter 1

The narrow mountain road ended at the edge of a rock cliff. It wasn't as if Ford Cardwell had forgotten that. No, when he saw where he was, he knew it was why he'd taken this road and why he was going so fast as he approached the sheer vertical drop to the rocks far below. It would have been so easy to keep going, to put everything behind him, to no longer feel pain.

Pine trees blurred past as the pickup roared down the dirt road to the nothingness ahead. All he could see were sky and more mountains off in the distance. Welcome back to Montana. He'd thought coming home would help. He'd thought he could forget everything and go back to being the man he'd been.

His heart thundered as he saw the end of the road coming up quickly. Too quickly. It was now or never.

The words sounded in his ears, his own when he was young. He saw himself standing in the barn loft looking out at the long drop to the pile of hay below. Jump or not jump. It was now or never.

He was within yards of the cliff when his cell phone rang. He slammed on his brakes. An impulsive reaction to the ringing in his pocket? Or an instinctive desire to go on living?

The pickup slid to a dust-boiling stop, his front tires just inches from the end of the road. Heart in his throat, he looked out at the plunging drop in front of him.

His heart pounded harder. Just a few more moments— a few more inches—and he wouldn't have been able to stop in time.

His phone rang again. A sign? Or just a coincidence? He put the pickup in Reverse a little too hard and hit the gas pedal. The front tires were so close to the edge that for a moment he thought the tires wouldn't have purchase. Fishtailing backward, the truck spun away from the precipice.

Ford shifted into Park and, hands shaking, pulled out his still-ringing phone. As he did, he had a stray thought. How rare it used to be to get cell phone coverage here in the Gallatin Canyon, of all places. Only a few years ago the call wouldn't have gone through.

Without checking to see who was calling, he answered it, his hand shaking as he did. He'd come so close to going over the cliff. Until the call had saved him.

"Hello?" He could hear noises in the background. *"Hello?"* He let out a bitter chuckle. A robocall had saved him at the last moment? he thought.

But his laughter died as he heard a bloodcurdling scream coming from his phone. "Hello?" he yelled. "Who is this?" The scream was followed by a woman's desperate pleas.

"No, please, don't hurt me anymore." Another scream and the sound of breaking glass.

"Hello?" He was yelling, frantic, having no idea who was on the other end of the call—just that she was in trouble. Had the woman meant to call 9ll? Maybe it was a pocket dial and she hadn't meant to call anyone—let alone a stranger.

"Tell me where you are!" he yelled into the phone, but his voice was drowned out by another scream, this one filled with pure terror—and pain. He knew both too well.

The sound of something hard hitting soft flesh was followed by a choking sound. Choking on blood? The woman was being attacked. By an intruder? Or someone she knew? He'd never felt more helpless as he listened to more breaking glass and the woman's screams.

"No! Please, Humphrey, you're going to kill me! Please. Stay back. Don't make me…" The gunshot sounded deafening—even on the phone. Then there was no sound at all coming from his cell.

Ford stared down at the phone in his hand, shock shuddering through him. The woman on the other end of the line had called the man *Humphrey.* His already pounding heart thumped against his ribs, making his chest ache. It couldn't be. He stared at the name that had come up on his phone. No. He tried to call the number back. It went straight to voice mail. Someone must have found the phone and shut it off. Or declined the call.

His heart was pounding. For a moment, he was too stunned to move, almost to breathe, at what he'd just heard, what he'd been unable to stop. Rachel. The call was from his former college roommate's wife, Rachel Westlake— now Mrs. Humphrey Collinwood.

He'd only recently added her number to his contact list after she'd sent him a friend request on social media and they'd exchanged cell phone numbers.

His pulse pounded so loud that he couldn't hear himself think. Fumbling in his fear and panic, he hit 911. It couldn't be true. He knew Humphrey. They'd been roommates most of their time in college. His former friend wouldn't hurt anyone. Humphrey idolized Rachel. But from what he'd heard on the call...

Outside the pickup, the wind howled in the pines. A gust blew dirt over the cliff and into the abyss, reminding him how close he'd come to making that same descent. The only thing that had stopped him was the phone call. Or would he have hit the brakes on his own? He would never know.

The 911 operator came on the line. "What is the nature of your emergency?"

"I think I just heard someone being attacked and possibly killed on what I suspect was a pocket dial." His voice broke. "Her name is Rachel Westlake. Sorry, it's Collinwood now." He listened as the dispatcher asked him a question. "No, I don't know where she lives exactly. A ranch north of Big Timber. That's all I know. We only recently reconnected. That's how she had my number. Please, you have to find her. She might still be...alive."

Chapter 2

Dana Cardwell Savage looked out her kitchen window at the row of black clouds gathering over the mountains. She'd awakened this morning with one of her "bad" feelings. Her husband, Hud, used to joke about them. He still didn't necessarily believe in her foreboding "sixth sense." But over their many years together, he'd learned to acknowledge her premonitions with caution, if not take them seriously. Unfortunately, she never knew what was coming—just that something was.

At the sound of a vehicle pulling up in front of the main house on Cardwell Ranch, she squinted into the morning sun to see her cousin Jackson climb out. From the worry etched in his handsome face, she knew even before she opened her front door—someone was in trouble. She ushered him into the kitchen, a place where everyone knew they could get a mug of hot coffee and a kind word—if not advice. Good listener that she was, Dana dispensed it all—and usually with some warm homemade cookies fresh from the oven.

Jackson brushed a lock of hair back from his forehead as he took a seat at her kitchen table. It was large and marred like the floor under it from years of cowboys pulling up a chair and resting their boots under it and their arms on it.

She noticed her cousin's salt-and-pepper hair and felt a shock at how much they had all aged. She didn't feel her age most days. It was only when she looked in the mirror or thought about everything that had happened over the years, the good and the bad.

As she poured her cousin a mug of coffee, she could tell that something was bothering him. She hadn't seen him for a while, but knew that her cousin's barbecue restaurant with his brothers was doing well, so that wasn't the problem.

"Ford's back," Jackson said as he took the mug from her.

Dana brightened as she joined him at the table. She remembered the first time she'd seen the boy when he was about five and Jackson had brought him to the ranch. Such a sweet child. She said as much to his father.

"We'll have to have a party," she said, a part of her brain already making plans. She did love getting all the family together here on the ranch. When Jackson didn't respond, she looked at him closer.

He was holding the mug in his large hands, staring down at the steaming brew in a way that made her heart drop. "What's wrong?"

"Ford's not the same," Jackson said after a moment. "The war, losing his men in the plane crash..." He looked up and she saw fear in his eyes. "I'm worried about him."

She'd heard that Ford had gotten a Purple Heart for his bravery and that he'd saved most of his crew when his plane had crashed. "He wasn't injured, I heard."

"Not physically. But a lot of his crew died. He can't seem to get past it. Why did he survive and not so many others? It's his mental attitude that worries me. He seems…lost. He has a degree in engineering, but doesn't seem interested in pursuing anything. I told him we can find a place for him in the barbecue business…"

"You know he's welcome here on the ranch," Dana said quickly. "In fact, we could really use him. Please tell him that."

Jackson nodded. "As much as he loves the ranch and working here in the past, I doubt even that would help right now."

"Is it PTSD?" she asked.

He shrugged. "Probably. He's been getting help. I just think being over there in that war took the life out of him. He saw too much death, too much pain, just too much." His voice broke and he took a sip of coffee. "I just got a call from him. He's on his way to Big Timber. Seems this woman he knew in college…" He looked up at her. "I shouldn't bother you with this."

"You know I'm here in any way I can help. Ford's family. Why are you worried about this woman?"

"Ford was in love with her. She married his best friend. It wasn't anything he told me, but I have a feeling that this woman did a number on him years ago," Jackson said. "Her coming back into his life right now…"

"She called him for help?"

Her cousin scoffed. "It's much worse than that. She was in a domestic dispute with her husband apparently. For all Ford knows, she might even be dead."

After calling 911 and relating what he'd heard, Ford had called his father. He'd given him the abbreviated version of what had happened as he'd driven out of the mountains. He left out the dumbass thing he'd almost done. Just hearing his father's voice was a reminder of the pain he would have caused if he hadn't stopped. He felt embarrassed and guilty.

"I'm on my way to Big Timber now. All I know is that she lives north of town on a ranch. I'll call you when I know something more."

Now he concentrated on the highway in front of him. He was down the east side of the Bozeman Pass when he got a call from the Sweet Grass County sheriff, Charley Cortland.

"You the one who placed the 911 call?" the sheriff asked. His voice was gruff and he sounded like an older man.

Ford explained what had happened—and what he'd heard. "Did you find her? Is she…?" He couldn't bring himself to ask what had happened, fearing she may be dead.

"She's alive. Your call got us to her in time." The sheriff said he'd gone out to her ranch himself and gotten her to the hospital.

He breathed a sigh of relief. On the drive he'd kept remembering a young Rachel in a yellow sundress, her head tilted back, laughing at him and Humphrey. She'd been so beautiful. In his memory, she and Humphrey had looked so happy and so much in love. So what had happened over the past fifteen years to change that?

"How do you know Mrs. Collinwood?" the sheriff asked, pulling him out of his thoughts.

"We were friends back in college. Her husband was my roommate all four years. I was best man at their wedding."

"I see," the sheriff said. "You said you're on your way here? I'm going to need a statement from you. I'm at the scene, but will be returning to my office soon. One question. Why did she call you instead of 911?"

Ford explained what he suspected had been a pocket dial and how he'd only recently gotten her number and vice versa. "Can you tell me if Humphrey...? Is he...?"

"I'm afraid that's all the information I can give you now. We'll talk at my office. How soon did you say you would be arriving in town?" the sheriff asked.

Ford explained that he was driving from Big Sky, but was now only about an hour away, then disconnected.

Rachel was alive. But how badly injured? As far as he knew, there was only one hospital in Big Timber. Unless she'd been flown to Billings. But that would mean that her injuries were too critical to be taken care of at the local hospital. He knew he had to see for himself that she was all right—and that what he'd heard on the phone had really happened. It felt surreal. He knew Humphrey. They'd been like brothers. And Rachel... He shook his head, not wanting to admit even now the crush he'd had on his best friend's girl.

He passed Livingston, the Crazy Mountains growing closer and closer as he drove. With the speed limit being eighty, he was making good time. The thought of seeing Rachel had him both anxious and excited. He'd hated the way they'd left things for the past fifteen years.

The truth was, he'd never expected to hear from her again after her wedding to Humphrey. After what had happened, the three of them had gone their separate ways. Humphrey had reached out a few times, but Ford hadn't responded. Now he felt sick about that. If Humphrey was gone, he'd never get to make amends.

Then there was Rachel, the woman he'd compared other women to for all these years. Strange how fate worked, he thought now as a chill moved through him. If Rachel hadn't pocket dialed him when she did…she might not have gotten help in time. And Ford…well, he might be at the bottom of a cliff right now.

Chapter 3

"I know who you are," the sheriff said after the medical examiner introduced herself at the crime scene. He hoisted up his tan uniform pants over his protruding belly and rocked back on his boot heels. "I've heard stories about you. You go by Hitch, right? Well, we don't really need your help. George here can handle it just fine."

State medical examiner Henrietta "Hitch" Roberts smiled at the sheriff and the elderly man standing next to him in the entryway of the Collinwood home. "I'm sorry, Sheriff, but the governor himself asked me to handle this one personally. I believe if you check your emails, you'll find one from him."

"Is that so?" Sheriff Charley Cortland tucked his thumbs into the pockets of his pants and narrowed his blue gaze at her. A large fiftysomething man with a robust laugh and a belly to match, Charley had been the law for years. He liked to say to anyone who would listen that he'd seen it

all. "George here is our local coroner and I've already assessed the situation. The wife was getting the hell beaten
out of her. She grabbed a gun and shot her husband before
he could kill her. It's cut-and-dried self-defense, the way I
see it. Shot him right in the face."

"Does seem that way at a glance," Hitch said. She'd dealt
with her share of rural law enforcement and already heard
about Charley Cortland. As state medical examiner, she
was brought into those areas that lacked access to more
than a local coroner. On this one, she was lead investigator. "My job is to try to find out what really happened here,
if at all possible."

She'd already called the Department of Criminal Investigation. By now they would have arrived at the Big Timber hospital and taken photos of the wife's injuries. They
would have also collected the clothing she'd been wearing,
checked under her fingernails and run gunpowder residue tests on her hands and wrists, as well as getting blood
samples to see if she had been under the influence of alcohol or drugs at the time of the shooting—as Hitch had
requested. They would have also gotten a video statement
from her—if she was able—of what led up to the altera-
tion and subsequent death of the husband.

"We already know what *really* happened," the sheriff
snapped. "Got proof. She called someone during the fight
and he heard the whole thing. I just got off the phone with
him. He's on his way to give me a statement that will back
up what I just told you." She listened to the sheriff describe what the caller had related to him. "So she definitely
thought he was going to kill her if she hadn't shot him." He
had a so-there smug look on his ruddy face.

She pulled out her notebook. "What is the name of the
man she called?"

"Ford Cardwell. She married his best friend. He was in the wedding party."

Hitch looked up at him. "He told you that?"

"He did."

"I'll need to talk to him, as well as see the video statement you take from him," she said, pocketing her notebook and pen. "Also, did you document what you saw at the scene on your arrival?"

"I called an ambulance and got the poor woman to the hospital, if that's what you're asking," the sheriff snapped.

"No, I'm asking if you documented the scene." Law enforcement was trained to document everything, including the time of arrival, the location and condition of the body, and determining the identity of the person involved. "Did you observe any vehicles leaving the area?"

The sheriff looked put out. "No. There was just the two of them. Look here, young lady. You're trying to make more out of this than what it is."

"I'm trying to get to the truth," she corrected him. "And you can call me Hitch. Did you observe anything at the scene that seemed out of place?"

He laughed. "Practically anything breakable in the kitchen, I'd say." The coroner he called George laughed with him. "If you just look in the kitchen, you can *observe* for yourself that they had one hell of a fight, with her pleading for him not to kill her."

Hitch could see that she wasn't getting anywhere with the sheriff. He hadn't documented anything and had, in his mind, already solved the case. She glanced past the large living area to the kitchen. Even from here, she could see all the broken pottery and glass on the floor, along with blood and other matter from the body still lying in the middle of it.

"Someone was angry and took it out on the decor, that's

for sure," she said. She'd seen this kind of fury before. It often ended in bloodshed.

"Looks like the damned fool had it coming to him," Charley said. "The wife's in the hospital. Beat the hell out of her." He shook his head. "Got to wonder what the two had to fight about, though. Look at this place. Can't even imagine living on a spread this large, let alone in a house like this."

"Guess it proves money can't buy happiness," Hitch said distractedly as she noticed where the sheriff and the coroner had walked through her crime scene. "DCI should be here soon to process the scene. We'll know more after that."

"Seems pretty obvious what happened here," the sheriff was saying. "Self-defense, plain and simple. Can't see why the state crime department had to get involved." He motioned to the body in the other room. "No judge would put her in prison for killing the bastard after what he did to her."

It certainly appeared to be a case of self-defense, but she preferred to wait until all the evidence was in. She said as much to the sheriff again. "So if you don't mind letting me do my job, Sheriff, I'd appreciate it if you would secure the crime scene and make sure no one else tromps through."

The sheriff said something under his breath that Hitch was glad she couldn't hear.

"Why don't we step outside, George, and leave the lady to her...work," the sheriff said.

"It's Hitch. Or Dr. Roberts. And, George, I won't need your coroner van to transport the body to the morgue. The DCI unit will take care of that for me," Hitch said.

Both men nodded sourly and left. She closed the door behind them and took in the scene before reaching into her satchel for her booties and gloves.

The victim lay on his back on the kitchen floor among

broken glass and debris that had apparently originated from the couple's quarrel. The only heads-up she'd been given on the case was an urgent appeal for her to get to the Collinwood Ranch north of Big Timber as soon as possible and take charge of the case. Apparently, there'd been some concern of the crime scene being contaminated.

Fortunately, she'd just finished a case not far away. Otherwise, she was sure George, the local coroner, would have already removed the body. He and the sheriff had already walked into the kitchen. One of them had left a boot print in the blood and then used a paper towel to wipe off the sole.

Along with the urgency of the matter, she'd been told that she would be dealing with what was believed to have been a domestic dispute that had ended in gunplay—and that the wife had been taken to the local hospital with multiple injuries. She hadn't needed to be told that this was a sensitive case because of who was involved. None of that mattered to her. She treated all cases the same.

But she also knew that because the name Collinwood meant something to someone in power, this one would be under the media microscope, so she'd better make sure she left no stone unturned.

Carefully approaching the body through the broken glass, she could definitely tell there had been a violent argument. As she squatted next to the deceased, she could see that he had been shot in the face at close range. The single bullet had entered a half inch off center of his left eye and exited the back of the skull, taking a lot of brain matter and bone with it.

The husband had been so close… Had he been trying to take the gun away from her? Daring her to pull the trigger? Had he been that sure she wouldn't shoot?

Hitch rose to take her camera from the bag slung over

her shoulder. She wanted to shoot photographs of the scene before even the state lab unit arrived. As she did, she considered the mess in the large, normally white kitchen. It was a cook's delight with its latest stainless-steel appliances, copper ranch house sink and white marble countertops. The tile floor was also white like the cabinets. It would make the crime scene investigators' jobs even easier, she thought. The perfect crime scene from a forensics standpoint.

At the sound of another vehicle, she looked out to see two DCI vans pull up. The sheriff and coroner had apparently managed to stretch some crime scene tape across the railing on the front deck and outside the door. The sheriff now leaned against his patrol SUV, watching the DCI team emerge from their rigs before he climbed behind the wheel and took off in a hail of dust and gravel.

Sheriff Charley Cortland swore as he roared out of the Collinwoods' ranch, the coroner eating his dust behind him. How dare that young woman treat him as if he didn't know how to do his job. He rubbed his neck with a free hand as he took a turn in the road. He was going too fast, but Hitch, or whatever she wanted to call herself, had gotten his temper up. Coming in like she had and finding fault right away with the way he did things.

Had he documented everything? she'd wanted to know. He thought about the notebook and pen he kept in his patrol SUV. He was sure they were still in his glove box. Glancing in that direction, he almost missed the next turn and finally forced himself to slow down.

What he hadn't realized, but was becoming abundantly clear now that he thought about it, was that this was going to be a big case. The kind of case that could make or break a career. He should have realized that. Hell, he knew the

Collinwoods had money once he'd seen the spread—let alone that humongous house they'd had built for themselves.

But lots of rich people bought up the ranches in the area. What made these two so special that the governor would call in the state medical examiner and the DCI?

As he reached the main highway, he stopped and dug out his notebook and pen. From this point on, he would do this one by the book. He could remember well enough the scene when he had arrived, right? He'd put it all down.

The one thing he wouldn't do was let that woman make him look bad again.

Turning on his lights and siren, he raced back toward Big Timber. Just outside town, he called his office. "There a fella waiting to see me?" he barked into his phone. "Tell him I'm on my way."

He disconnected, smiling and nodding to himself. Ford Cardwell had heard the whole thing on his phone and was now cooling his heels in the office. Charley would get his story. If that didn't prove what he was saying about this case, then nothing would. All his years of experience had to account for something, he told himself. Even as he thought it, he found himself questioning his assessment of what had happened with this case.

It was a slam dunk, wasn't it? He couldn't be wrong about this one.

Ford had no trouble finding the sheriff's department when he'd reached Big Timber. He'd been told to take a seat. Ten minutes later, the sheriff arrived in a flurry of movement. A large, heavyset man with a flushed face, the sheriff waved him back into his office. The room was small, unlike the rotund older man who took a chair behind the desk. He had a head of graying hair beneath his Stetson, which he removed and tossed in the direction of a hook on the wall as Ford entered the office.

"Sheriff Charley Cortland," the man said as he shifted his weight, making the chair groan under his considerable bulk. "You say you're Ford Cardwell, right? Let's get your statement while it's still fresh in your mind." He reached for his phone and called in a young man who set up a video recorder, turned it on and left.

"State your name, the time and the date for the record," the sheriff said, and Ford did.

Charley rocked in his chair and nodded. "So you heard the whole thing," he said, urging him on.

"I wouldn't say that. It actually felt as if I had come in toward the end. I heard what I believe was the last of the argument. At first, it was just background noise and then a scream."

"Can you describe from the start of the call everything you heard?"

He took a moment, reliving it, knowing now how it would end. He went through it, finishing with, "At the time, I thought the call had just been random. I didn't know the woman was Rachel Westlake—I mean, Collinwood."

"Right. You knew her in college. So when was the last time you saw her?"

"It's been years—fifteen, actually. Like I told you on the phone, I only recently reconnected with her on social media and we exchanged phone numbers. I haven't seen her since college."

The sheriff nodded, studying him. "But you knew her husband?"

He caught the past tense. "Humphrey? Yes, we all knew each other at college. Wait—so he is…?"

"Deceased."

He had heard the booming report of the gunshot on his phone. "Humphrey's dead?" He felt an anxiety attack coming on and had to concentrate on his breathing for a few moments. His plane crash came back, filling his mind with horror just as it had when he'd realized they were going down and there was nothing he could do about it. Just as there was nothing he could do but save the few men he'd been able to drag from the wreckage before it exploded.

The sheriff's voice brought him out of the flashback with a shudder.

"He was killed this morning during the phone call you overheard. In fact, I believe you heard the shot that killed him."

Ford closed his eyes for a moment. Flashes of light radiated behind his lids. He opened them, chasing away the flames to face a different kind of horror. Rachel had shot and killed Humphrey.

"You said that he was your best friend."

"In college." He couldn't make sense of this. Humphrey and Rachel? This couldn't be happening. "Humphrey and I were roommates all four years. Look, if that's all, I'm anxious to find out how Rachel is doing." She must be devastated, he thought, not to even mention her physical injuries.

"Cardwell. Why does that name sound familiar?"

"My family owns a barbecue restaurant in Big Sky. My aunt owns a ranch there. Cardwell Ranch." When the sheriff's expression hadn't changed, he added, "Her husband is Marshal Hud Savage." Why was this man avoiding telling him Rachel's condition? "Sheriff, is Rachel all right?"

"I'm waiting to hear from the doctor, but she sustained multiple injuries from the beating she got." The sheriff picked up his phone and called to tell the young man who'd set up the video that they were finished. He said nothing until the man exited with the equipment. "Appears there were only the two of them home. We'll know more once she can tell us her side of the story. But at this point, it seems clear that it was a domestic dispute that turned tragic."

Ford's head reeled. He kept thinking of the call. Of Rachel's screams. Her pleas for Humphrey to stop. And the gunshot just before the line went dead. That had to be when she pulled the trigger and killed Humphrey. *Oh my God, Rachel, how did this happen?*

Chapter 4

Hitch did what investigating she could on the premises until she had the body on the examining table for the autopsy. She'd worked with this team of investigators before, so while they processed the scene, she did an inventory of the house. Putting on fresh gloves, she wandered around in fresh paper booties, trying to get a feel for the people who had lived here while she waited for the team to release the body.

All on one level, the house seemed to go on forever. She peeked in each room, not sure what she was looking for. Answers, always. Like the sheriff had said, this one seemed cut-and-dried. Mitigated homicide. So what was bothering her? She couldn't put her finger on it. Just that something always nagged at her when a case felt…wrong.

She found the master suite and stopped in the doorway to take in the breathtaking view before entering. A wall of windows looked out on rolling hills lush with grass and studded with pines. She tried to imagine the couple waking up to this each morning. Stepping to the bed, she checked the side tables, curious if the two were still sleeping together before everything went south.

There was a book lying facedown on one side of the bed. From the title, she guessed Rachel slept on the right. She pulled open the drawer. It seemed a little too empty, as if someone had gone through it, knowing that detectives would be doing the same thing soon.

Stepping to the other side of the bed, she found a notebook and pen. From the writing and what was written there, she guessed it was the husband's notes about a work appointment. She photographed the notes. There was much more in his drawers, though nothing that sent up any red flags. Except for the extra clip of cartridges for a .38 pistol. She photographed everything in both drawers, then hesitated.

If Humphrey Collinwood kept the gun in this drawer, how did it end up in the kitchen, where he died? Which one of them took the gun to the murder scene?

She thought of the .38-caliber weapon lying on the floor of the kitchen earlier. By now, the lab techs would have bagged and processed it. The question was, when did the wife take hold of the gun? Was it always loaded? Had she ever fired it before?

There were always more questions than answers at this point, Hitch thought. When the woman had gotten the gun could indicate premeditation, so it was important—and probably hard to prove since only one person knew the truth. The other one was dead.

So, she thought, studying the king-size bed, it appeared they had been sleeping together. But that didn't mean that things had been copacetic. The bed was huge.

They wouldn't even have to touch each other if they didn't want to.

She checked out the his-and-hers walk-in closets, as well as looking in the chests of drawers. She found a lot of expensive clothing on both sides. She took more photographs, not sure which ones might prove important.

It was the small, seemingly trivial things that solved a case, she thought as she checked out the bathroom. She saw expensive beauty products and what appeared to be a container of birth control pills, most of the pills already taken, lying on the floor in the back corner, almost out of sight as if dropped there. Or thrown there? That was interesting. At least one of them wasn't interested in having a child.

As she started to leave the bedroom, she realized what she hadn't seen. The woman's purse. She checked the walk-in again. Lots of empty purses, but not one the woman had apparently been using. Nor had she seen one in the living room or the kitchen. As she wandered through the house, she kept looking. At the entry into the kitchen, she called to the techs.

"Have either of you seen her purse?" Hitch was curious if it was large enough to hold a handgun. Also, if it wasn't here, then where was it? The sheriff was so sure that no one else had been here. Would a ranch this size have some kind of hired help?

"Not in here," one of them called back.

She turned and headed down past the bedrooms again toward the garage. Living this far from civilization, maybe she'd left her purse in her vehicle. Just as Hitch had expected, none of the vehicles were locked. She opened the first one, a Range Rover that smelled of leather and men's aftershave. This would have been his car.

After searching it and not finding much of interest other

than a few receipts, which she took photos of with her phone, she tried the next vehicle. It was a BMW convertible and smelled of the same perfume scent she'd picked up in the master bedroom. No purse, though. No receipts either.

The purse wasn't in the large SUV or the older-model pickup.

"You can have the body now," one of the techs called.

On her way back through the house, she had a thought and checked the powder room by the door to the garage. The moment she opened the door, she pulled up her camera and took a few shots of the room—and the large designer purse lying on the floor in front of the sink. The purse was made of soft leather and had more than enough room for the .38 now lying next to the body in the kitchen.

What had caught her eye was where it lay—on the floor as if it had been dropped there. Also, the large zippered compartment was open, the woman's wallet partially hanging out, as if Rachel Collinwood had been in a hurry and that was why it was open and lying on the floor like that.

Hitch stared at the purse, imagining the woman coming home from town. It was a fairly long drive. Had she come in, headed straight for the powder room and then heard a garage door open, signaling that she was no longer alone? She would have known it was her husband. Had she dug in the bag for the gun? And for her phone, or both, since both were found in the kitchen on the floor next to the body? She'd apparently picked up the phone after shooting her husband and called 911 for help. Hitch had already photographed the phone, covered with bloody fingerprints, lying next to the body.

Then hearing him enter the house, had she dropped the bag and followed him into the kitchen with the gun and phone? Or hurried into the kitchen to wait for him?

After picking up the purse, Hitch spread out a clean towel and dumped the contents onto the counter by the sink. A small box of handgun cartridges tumbled out. She inspected them. They were .38-caliber cartridges, the same caliber as those used in the handgun that had been on the kitchen floor not far from the body—and was assumed to be the murder weapon.

She put everything back into the purse and returned it to the spot where she'd found it, before going into the kitchen and telling the techs what she'd found. "Definitely want prints on that birth control container," she said.

The investigators put the deceased into a body bag and loaded it into a van. One of them would follow her into town to the morgue and return to finish processing the scene.

"You know who he is, right?" Bradley Mar asked her. She'd worked with the young investigator before on other cases. He was smart, cute and definitely not her type, with his crooked grin and his bedroom brown eyes.

"Humphrey Collinwood," she said. "Is that name supposed to mean something to me?"

"The family is from back East. Old money. The father and grandfather are still powerful politically, and Humphrey was the heir apparent. There was talk that he might one day be president. This case will probably garner nationwide media coverage. Even if she had probable cause to shoot him, I wouldn't want to be in her shoes right now."

Hitch knew what Bradley was saying. Even if it was self-defense, the Collinwoods could probably want their pound of flesh. She was sure DCI had been warned to be especially careful with the evidence in this case. Any mistakes could cost them all their jobs. The DCI unit was always thorough, but with this one, they would make sure they dotted every *i* and crossed every *t*.

Closing the back of the van, she watched the other investigator return to the house. Lori Stevenson was about the same age as Bradley, but much more serious. Hitch hoped that Lori hadn't already fallen for Bradley's charm. The young man was a heartbreaker. Unfortunately, Hitch knew the type. It was one reason she hardly dated.

Climbing behind the wheel of her SUV, she started the engine and drove away from the huge house set against a backdrop of rolling hills and pasture with mountains off in the distance. As she did, she considered how isolated it was. The drive out was a good two miles to the paved highway. From there, it was another twenty miles into Big Timber. That kind of isolation could get to a person, she thought. Anything could have caused the altercation and subsequent shooting.

In her experience, money was usually the big issue in most marriages. After that it was infidelity. She thought about the rambling house, the two separate walk-in closets filled with expensive clothes and jewelry, the four-car garage with luxury vehicles, the ranch itself with its beautiful vistas.

For most people, this would be paradise, and yet one of the residents was dead and the other in the hospital facing possible homicide charges. So what had happened?

The purse on the floor in the powder room bothered her. It suggested that Rachel Collinwood had been somewhere and had just come in from the garage. Was the husband already home? Or had he just entered the house from the garage, not knowing she was in the powder room? Had the wife known her husband would come home angry? Had she felt she was in danger?

But if the gun had been in her purse along with the .38 cartridges, when had she taken it from her husband's bedside table? And why would she take the gun and her cell phone and go into the kitchen if she was afraid for her life? Why not get back in her car and get out of there?

The sheriff had said the man she'd accidentally dialed had heard it all—including the gunshot before the phone call ended. So had Rachel Collinwood attempted to call 911 for help in the middle of the altercation and accidentally dialed Ford Cardwell instead?

Hitch was anxious to talk to both Mrs. Collinwood and the man she'd called. Her cases often intrigued her, but none more than this one. She tried to put herself in the woman's shoes in that powder room, knowing it was all speculation at this point. But the wife had been in the powder room. The purse proved it. After returning from town? So where was the husband? Just driving in? Or waiting for her in the kitchen?

What had been her state of mind? Panic? Or cold-blooded calm? The purse could have been dropped in terror at the sound of the garage door opening. Rachel could have been in a hurry to reach the kitchen before her husband. Had the husband been looking for her as he moved through the house? Had the argument started somewhere else? Where had they been before the argument? A larger question was also more than relevant. Had there been prior abuse? Was that why she had the gun? Assuming it had been in the purse and not hidden somewhere else in the house.

All simple conjecture until she had more evidence. The real question for Hitch was, what had been going through the woman's mind when she'd taken the gun from her husband's bedside drawer in the first place—if she had? If Rachel Collinwood had been terrified of her husband, why hadn't she simply gone to the garage, gotten in her car and driven to safety?

In her mind's eye, Hitch could see her standing in the kitchen amid all the debris from the fight. What had she done with the gun? If she'd had it from the start of the argument, she hadn't used it. Had she threatened her husband with it? Or had she come in, dropped the purse in the powder room and hurried into the kitchen to hide the gun, hoping she wouldn't have to use it, until she'd felt she had no choice?

The moment the wife had armed herself, she had made up her mind that she was going to pull that trigger—whether she realized it or not.

At the hospital, Ford waited until the doctor received permission from the sheriff for him to see Rachel. He'd been warned that it would only be for a few minutes.

"She's going to be groggy," the doctor said. "Also, the sheriff has asked that she not be questioned about what happened."

Ford thanked him and headed down the hall to where a uniformed guard sat outside her door. Seeing the man sitting there gave him a shock. At first, he'd thought it was for Rachel's protection. But from whom? Then he realized with a start—the guard was there to keep Rachel here. Had she been arrested?

He felt sick to his stomach at the thought. But she'd killed a man. And not just any man. A man they had both loved. He couldn't imagine being pushed that far, and yet he'd heard enough of the fight on the phone to be terrified for her. That was why he had to see her and make sure she was all right. While he wouldn't ask anything about the incident as the sheriff had ordered him, he desperately needed to know at some point what had happened that the marriage had ended like this.

As he stopped at her hospital room door, he kept replaying what he'd heard on the phone over and over in his head. He still couldn't believe any of this was real. The scenes in his head kept overlapping with his own tragedy, blurring the lines.

He'd thought he'd known Humphrey. He never would have expected this of him. And Rachel… How long had the abuse been going on that she had to stop her husband with a bullet?

The guard at the door double-checked with the sheriff and then gave Ford a nod. Pushing open the hospital room door, Ford hesitated, not sure he was ready to see the beautiful woman he'd known and loved in whatever state Humphrey had left her.

After taking a breath, he let it out and stepped in. She lay in the bed, her eyes closed, her face as pale as the pillowcase beneath her head—except for the lacerations, stitches, bandages and bruising that made the woman he'd known almost indistinguishable. The extent of her injuries shocked him. He'd just assumed that the quarrel hadn't been going on long when he'd first gotten the call. But Humphrey couldn't have done this much damage in that short amount of time before the gunshot.

All Ford could figure was that at some point, Rachel had tried to call for help and either dropped the phone after accidentally hitting his number or Humphrey had knocked the phone from her hand.

The violence he saw mirrored in her injuries made his chest ache. He felt perspiration break out over his body. He grabbed the metal rail of the bed to steady himself as he felt another anxiety attack coming on.

* * *

The rattle of the bed rail awoke her with a start. Rachel let out a cry. She'd forgotten for a moment where she was. She shrank back from the dark figure beside her bed.

"I'm sorry. I didn't mean to frighten you," Ford said as he quickly took a step back.

She recognized his voice. It was low and soft and soothing, always had been. As her gaze focused on him, she tried to smile, but her cut and bruised mouth hurt too much. "Ford." His name came out a whisper. She felt tears rush to her eyes at just the sight of a friendly, familiar face in the middle of all her pain.

As she held out her hand, he moved closer and took it in his two large, warm palms. It had been years since she'd seen him, so she shouldn't have been shocked that he'd changed. His body had filled out from the lean college boy he'd been. If anything, he was more handsome. She'd heard what had happened to him during his time in the military and wondered how an experience like that would change a man like Ford. She could see now that there was a hardness to him that was only partially due to muscle and physical strength. There was also a darkness in his pale blue eyes.

"*Ford?* I'm so glad to see you, but what are you doing here?"

"I heard what happened to you," he said. "Are you all right?"

She shook her head, tears rushing to her eyes again. "Humphrey." The word came out choked on fresh tears.

He nodded and squeezed her hand. As he looked down at her fingers entwined with his, she thought about earlier when two state crime investigation officers had stopped by to take her fingerprints and take swabs of her skin around her hands and wrists. When she'd asked, they'd told her they were checking for gunpowder residue, and that brought it all back. The deafening sound of the gun. The damage the bullet made an instant later.

But more than anything, what she kept seeing was the shocked, disbelieving look on her husband's face. She would take that look to her grave.

Ford squeezed her hand gently. "I'm here for you." She looked at him, knowing he meant every word of it. She'd forgotten this side of Ford and felt her throat tighten.

"I can't believe any of this has happened," she said, wiping at the tears with her free hand as she focused on his face. To think she had actually thought about marrying this cowboy, she told herself, then pushed the thought away as her pain threatened to overwhelm her again.

"What about you? Are *you* all right?" she asked when she gained control again. "I heard about your accident... I'm so sorry."

"Don't worry about me," he said quickly. "I'm fine. It's you I'm concerned about. But I'm here for you. Whatever I can do. I'm not going anywhere."

At the sound of the hospital room door opening, she glanced toward it and saw a man in uniform and star enter. She swallowed the lump in her throat at just the sight of the sheriff's grim expression. Only hours ago she'd been standing in her kitchen with the gun in her hand and her finger on the trigger. She closed her eyes but felt fresh tears on her cheeks as Ford let go of her.

She heard him step away from her bed as the sheriff said, "I need to talk to Mrs. Collinwood. Alone. But don't go far, Mr. Cardwell. I'll need a word with you, as well."

Rachel smelled peppermint on the sheriff's breath as she heard him pull up a chair beside her bed. She heard Ford's boots on the hospital room floor, the slow, deliberate gait of his walk and the swish of the door opening and closing.

"Mrs. Collinwood, you remember me? I'm Sheriff Charley Cortland. I'm the one who called for an ambulance for you. The doctor said you might be a little groggy, but I need you to answer a few questions if you feel up to it."

Rachel opened her eyes, turning her head to look at the man. What she saw made her relax a little. There was kindness in his weathered face rather than accusation. She wiped her eyes and said, "I'll tell you everything I can remember."

The hospital room door opened again. This time a young man came in with a video recorder. He set it up next to her bed. She touched the bandage on her cheekbone and realized she probably shouldn't be thinking about her appearance at a time like this.

"Don't worry—you look fine," the sheriff said. "We just need to get your statement while it's fresh in your mind so everyone knows what happened."

Chapter 5

Hitch looked up as a distinguished older man in a suit burst into the morgue. He had a head of salt-and-pepper hair and keen gray eyes with deep crinkles around them. His skin appeared ashen under his tan, and his hand shook as he clutched the doorknob and looked around the autopsy room.

"Where is the medical examiner? I want to see my son," he demanded.

She'd been expecting Bartholomew Collinwood. "I'm the medical examiner. Henrietta Roberts," she said. "If you give me a few minutes, you are welcome to make an identification for the record."

He stared at her in surprise and then what might have been slight embarrassment. He seemed to check his anger as she asked him to please wait outside the autopsy room. "I'll have someone show you where you can have a seat." She thought he would object. But then he looked past her to where the body bag was being unloaded from the state investigators' van.

The realization made him stagger a little before he caught himself and turned back into the hallway, letting the door close behind him.

She hurried to help roll the body into the morgue. Once she had it on the examination table, she went to find Mr. Collinwood. He was sitting on a bench outside, his head in his hands.

"If you'd like to come with me now," she said quietly. She never got used to the amount of grief she witnessed. She hoped she never did.

It took him a moment to rise from the bench. He was a man who clearly carried himself with unsparing confidence, and she saw that he was now struggling to maintain it. She often saw this kind of debilitating grief and felt it clear to her core. In these rural areas of the state, she was often alone in these duties of telling friends and family of their loss.

The hardest part was asking them to identify the bodies. Usually, that fell to the local coroner unless she'd been called in on a case.

If the dead man hadn't been Humphrey Collinwood, killed by his wife, Rachel Collinwood, then right now George would be doing this, she thought as she led Bart Collinwood into the morgue to identify his son.

Ford wondered why the sheriff wanted to see him again, but he stayed around the hospital. Down in the cafeteria, he got himself a cup of coffee. At the smell of the evening meal, he realized he hadn't eaten all day. No wonder he felt weaker than usual. But he suspected he wouldn't be able to get a bite down right now.

Back up on Rachel's floor, he parked himself in the waiting room and sipped his beverage. It was hot and bitter, which suited him just fine. He thought of Humphrey, but quickly pushed his image away. Instead, he tried to remember how it had all started and realized that would have been the moment he first saw Rachel. The moment Humphrey also saw her and Ford lost her.

It had been in the park near the university. He and Humphrey had been sitting on the grass under a large oak tree like they usually did after their chem class when a woman had caught Ford's eye. She was a vision in an orange-and-white polka-dot sundress that accented her slim, sun-kissed form. She was trying to feed a squirrel a scrap of bread from her lunch. He watched her for a few minutes, amused by her patience. Humphrey had been lying back on the grass, smoking and staring up at the blue sky overhead. Ford had been leaning back against a tree, watching the world go by.

He remembered that carefree feeling with his whole life ahead of him. It had felt as if anything was possible. That was when Rachel had caught his eye. She and the squirrel chattering at her from a nearby tree. What fascinated him was the way she could hold so perfectly still, kneeling on the grass, her arm extended, the scrap of bread pinched between two fingers. He'd been impressed by her perseverance, her naive belief that if she waited long enough the squirrel would come to her.

He hadn't been able to help himself. He'd pulled out the cell phone he'd gotten for Christmas and snapped a photo of her. The movement caught not just her eye, but also that of the squirrel, which took off up the tree.

Getting to her feet, she'd mugged a face at him as he'd

gotten up and walked over to her. "I'd almost had him convinced to take the bread." It was a rebuke.

Ford had laughed. "That squirrel was never going to take that bread."

"How do you know that?" she'd demanded, glaring at him.

"I heard what he was saying to you." He'd grinned. "He doesn't eat white bread."

Her face had softened into a glorious smile, one that would haunt his dreams for years to come. "You understand squirrels?"

"Clearly better than you," he'd joked. "I'd be happy to teach you, though. I'm Ford Cardwell, squirrel whisperer."

Her smile had broadened as she said, "Rachel Westlake. You do know that has to be the worst pickup line I've ever heard." Her gaze had shifted to Humphrey, who had spotted the two of them and gotten up to join them.

Ford had taken one look at his friend's face and known that he'd been as captivated by the woman as Ford had been. The difference was that Rachel had been looking at Humphrey with that same expression.

Rachel and Humphrey used to joke that it had been love at first sight. Ford knew it had been for him, not that he'd ever told anyone, especially the two of them. Rachel and Humphrey had started dating after that, the three of them often together. He thought of all the photos with Humphrey with one arm around Rachel and one around Ford. Humphrey always said that he couldn't live without either of them. It had been like that right up through graduation and their wedding.

Now in the waiting room, he felt that old guilt and pain. What hurt was how much he'd missed his best friend the past fifteen years and now Humphrey was gone.

As the waiting room door opened, Ford started. He'd expected it to be the sheriff. Instead, it was a man he'd only met a few times but recognized at once. Bartholomew "Bart" Collinwood walked in as if he owned the hospital. He certainly could have bought it if he wanted to, Ford knew. Humphrey and his father had had a tense relationship back in college. His friend always felt that he would never live up to his father's expectations. Ford wondered if that had changed over the years.

Bart stopped short in the middle of the room and frowned as he stared at him. "Ford, isn't it?"

"Ford Cardwell." He was a little surprised the man even remembered him.

"I recall you saying it was an old Texas family name, right? Or was it Montana?" The shock of his son's death wore heavily on the man. He seemed confused and unsure of himself for a moment. Then his gaze seemed to clear. "You know, you're the reason my son bought the ranch out here. All those stories you used to tell about ranch life."

He heard accusation in the man's tone. Did he believe that if his son hadn't bought a ranch in Montana he'd still be alive? Ford didn't know what to say, so he said nothing. The man was grieving. He was probably also looking for someone to blame.

"You two were good friends, roommates," Bart continued. "Had a falling-out at the end of your senior year at college, right?"

Was that how Humphrey had explained it? "I joined the military," Ford said.

"That's right." The man shook his head. "I'm surprised my son didn't follow you right into boot camp since he wanted to do whatever you did. Rachel knew how much he admired you. She must have stopped him. She wouldn't have allowed him to do anything but make more money for her to spend."

Ford shook his head, recalling that Bart had never been a fan of Rachel's. "Humphrey loved her."

The man let out a bitter laugh that almost sounded like a sob. "And look what it cost him."

Ford started to argue that Humphrey hadn't been the only victim in what had happened, but Bart cut him off.

"So you're here for his wife."

Was that an accusation or just Ford's guilt making him hear it that way? "It isn't like that."

"It sure looks like that."

The sheriff stuck his head into the door of the waiting room, drawing both of their attention. Bart moved swiftly to the lawman and grabbed his arm as he began demanding justice for his son.

The sheriff shook him off. "I thought you might be here wanting to know how his wife is doing after being severely beaten almost to death by your son," Charley Cortland said. "She's recovering nicely."

Bart huffed. "I want to see her."

"I don't think that's a good idea," the sheriff said. "You're just going to upset her and she's been through enough."

"*She's been through enough. She killed my son!* I was just at the morgue. She shot him in the *face!*" Bart's voice broke with emotion. "I *will* see her. She *will* look me in the eye and tell me the truth."

At the raised voices, a security guard pushed open the waiting room door.

The sheriff turned toward the uniformed man. "Hal, show this gentleman out of the hospital. If he comes back, let me know so I can arrest him."

"You have no idea who you are dealing with," Bart said angrily. "You'll be lucky to be the dogcatcher when I get through with you."

Chapter 6

Back at the morgue, dressed and ready for the autopsy, Hitch studied the corpse lying now on the metal table. After Mr. Collinwood had left, she'd gone online. It had been easy to find information about Humphrey Collinwood and his wife, Rachel. He'd been handsome, wealthy and a successful businessman. There were dozens of shots with him and his wife at gala affairs and fund-raisers before they'd moved from New York City to the ranch north of Big Timber, Montana. The two had been photographed at every party they attended as the VIPs they were.

That had been until about a year ago, when they'd bought the ranch and moved here, from what Hitch could tell. Was that the beginning of the end?

She'd also done research on Ford Cardwell. A cowboy turned hero flyboy who'd received a medal of honor after his plane had crashed because of a mechanical failure in war-torn Afghanistan. Miraculously surviving the crash, he'd fought to save his crew, rescuing some but losing others when the plane exploded. He'd only left the military a few months ago. Interesting, she'd thought. Before that, it had appeared he was making the military his career.

But what intrigued her more was how he'd gotten involved in Humphrey Collinwood's death.

Pulling up her mask, she turned on her video recorder and began the autopsy.

Cause of death: a single gunshot wound. She went through the steps, documenting each into the camera.

She frowned as she noticed the deceased's hands. If he had been beating his wife, there would have been bruises, abrasions, some sign of trauma.

Carefully, she removed first his wedding ring and bagged it. Then the ring on his other hand. His right hand. It was large, gold and heavy with a diamond at its center. She noted the blood and skin that had been caught in the design before taking a sample and bagging the ring. If he'd been right-handed, then this was the hand he would have used to hit his wife.

Still, the lack of abrasions or bruising on his hands bothered her. She took photographs of each hand. But until Hitch saw the extent of her injuries, she wouldn't know if he had used something other than his fists.

The sheriff had already decided it had been a case of self-defense. But she knew most were never as simple as that. Had Rachel Collinwood feared for her life? Had she used the proper amount of force based on that fear? Had she shot to stop the man or kill him? Hitch recalled one case where the location of the gun had been a deciding factor in whether or not the woman had planned to kill her husband—and whether she was exonerated.

Rachel had a witness of sorts already waiting in the

wings. Hitch couldn't wait to meet Ford Cardwell and hear how it was that his old friend from college just happened to call him at one of the most tragic times of her life.

"How long are you going to be in town?" the sheriff asked Ford after the security guard left with Bart in tow.

"I'm not sure yet," Ford told him. "I'm not leaving right away. I want to be sure that Rachel's all right. Truthfully, I also would like some answers. I still can't believe any of this. Humphrey was like a brother to me. This just doesn't make any sense."

"People change," the sheriff said. "Either that or he was always like that and just hid it well."

After being told that Mrs. Collinwood was down in X-ray and he wouldn't be able to see her again until to-morrow, Ford left. He'd just walked out the front of the hos-pital when he saw a woman etched against the last of the sunset. She stood off the sidewalk, at the edge of the deep shadows that had settled in around the hospital. It had been a long day, so no wonder he thought he was seeing things. The woman resembled someone he used to know. He was about to turn toward his pickup when the woman spotted him and called his name.

"That is you, isn't it?" she said as she stubbed out her cigarette and moved from the shadows so he got a good look at her.

"Shyla?" He couldn't help his surprise. Like with Ra-chel, it had been years since he'd seen her best friend from college. He frowned. How had she known about what had happened and gotten here this quickly? "What are you doing here?"

"The same thing you are, I would imagine," she said.

"Have you seen Rach? Is she okay? The guard wouldn't let me in to see her."

"I mean, how did you get to Montana so quickly? Did you fly in with Bart?"

"Bart? Good Lord, no! I live here now. I guess you haven't heard. My last name's Birch now. I married a cowboy." She laughed. It was high-pitched and loud—just like it had been in college. Like Humphrey, Shyla had come from old money. It was no surprise that she'd said at college that her family considered her the black sheep. "I know. It was my dream, right?"

"How long have you lived here?" he asked.

"I was out here visiting Rach a year ago and…" She waved a hand through the air. "It just kind of happened. Listen, if you aren't doing anything right now, I could really use a drink. Think we can find a bar close by?"

Ford had to smile. Shyla Earhart hadn't changed in the least. Brash, abrasive, loud and completely without filters. He didn't want or need a drink, but he needed to know about Rachel and what had led up to today's tragedy.

"I'm betting that you already have a bar in mind," he said.

She laughed again and looped her arm through his. "You know me so well. So how have you been, Ford?"

"Just dandy," he lied as they walked to his pickup.

The bar Shyla chose was small and dark and surprisingly quiet. It definitely wasn't a cowboy bar. He wondered idly about her husband and how they'd met, but after getting them two drinks from the bar, he asked about Rachel.

"So what happened with Rachel and Humphrey?" he asked.

Shyla mugged a face. "He turned out to be a real bastard." She quickly raised a hand as if she thought he would argue and rushed on. "I know he was your friend, but he'd changed." She grimaced. "You have no idea how bad it got once they moved out here. Rach didn't want to move here, you know. She hated living out in the sticks. Like he cared. He was often gone to the big city on business, so she was out there, terrified in that big house, all alone. That's why I came out to stay with her for a while and ended up meeting my cowboy and getting married. My family had multiple heart attacks over it." She laughed and picked up her drink.

"Did you know he was abusive to her?" Ford asked as Shyla drained her glass and signaled the bartender for another. He hadn't even touched his yet.

"Sure, I knew. I mean, I'd seen the bruises a couple of times. She always had a story. Walked into a wall. Got hit by a tree branch. Fell off her horse. The usual." Shyla rolled her eyes. "I knew something was wrong."

"Why didn't she leave him?" He took a sip of his drink.

"Why do you think? His father forced her to sign a prenup before they got married. Divorce was out of the question unless she wanted to live like a pauper."

"She could have gotten a job."

Shyla laughed. "Rachel? She majored in psychology at college and hasn't worked all these years. You want fries with that?"

"But if he was abusing her—"

"He traveled a lot and it didn't happen all the time, but I had suspected it was getting worse when he returned to the ranch. When they first married, she'd wanted kids. He didn't. You knew about the miscarriage, right? Then they moved out here and he decides he wants kids. She reminds him that she can't get pregnant. Something about that miscarriage after their wedding. He wants to adopt. At thirty-two, she felt like that ship had sailed."

"A lot of women are having babies later in life," he said.

"Not with a husband who is abusive," Shyla said, leaning toward him. He could smell cigarette smoke and her cloying perfume mixing with the booze she'd drunk. "He was a spoiled rich kid and he wasn't happy, so he took it out on her."

He didn't remember that about Humphrey. Sure, his friend came from wealth, but he'd seemed almost embarrassed by it. Ford reminded himself that he was getting only one side of the story: Rachel's, as told to Shyla. But then again, that might be the only side he was ever going to get now.

"She might go to prison," he said.

Shyla's eyes widened. "How is that possible? For killing the bastard when he was trying to kill her?"

"I heard a lot of it while it was happening," he said.

She froze. "You *what*?"

"Rachel called me. I heard her screaming and pleading with him not to hurt her—"

"Wait. You two have been talking?"

"No. She contacted me on social media recently. We exchanged phone numbers. That's all it was. I never planned to call her…"

"She called you for help?"

He shook his head. "It wasn't like that. I think she pocket dialed me by accident. Anyway, I heard all of it right up to the gunshot before the call ended."

"You told the sheriff this?" He nodded. "Then there is no way she's going to prison, Ford. Clearly, it was self-defense, right?"

"It sure sounded that way," he said as he finished his drink and she downed her second one.

Her cell phone rang. He could hear only one side of the

conversation but it seemed pretty clear. Her husband was reminding her that she was supposed to be cooking dinner and she needed to get home.

"We should go," he said, although Shyla had told her husband that she'd be home when she was good and ready and it was high time he learned to cook.

She smiled almost sheepishly. "He really is a good guy. Just a little too much sometimes."

He took her back to the hospital where she'd left her car. "Are you going to try to see Rachel again?"

"Tomorrow," Shyla said as he walked her to her car. It had gotten dark while they were in the bar. She opened her car door and turned to look at him. "Is it bad? What he did to her?" Ford nodded. "She was lucky he didn't kill her. You asked what happened between them. She thought he was having an affair. And get this—it was with a local woman who works as a waitress at the Corner Café in town. Emily Sutton."

"You know her?" he asked.

She shook her head. "Rachel only told me a couple of days ago. She'd just found out. I went by the café after that, but Emily wasn't working, and the next thing I knew, I heard about what had happened out at the ranch earlier today. Thanks for the drinks." She climbed into her car and drove away.

Ford watched her go. Shyla was out here in Montana married to a cowboy. He couldn't believe that any more than he could that Humphrey was having an affair, had beaten Rachel and she'd felt forced to kill him. But as the sheriff said, people changed. Ford wondered if the alleged affair was what the two had argued about. Or was it about adopting children?

His cell phone rang. He pulled it out, saw that it was his

father and realized he wasn't in the mood to explain everything that had happened today. Or how he found himself involved again in Rachel's life. He knew his father wouldn't have thought it was a good idea. Jackson had met Rachel and Humphrey back in college. And while his father had been taken with Humphrey, he hadn't been a fan of Rachel's. Or maybe what his father hadn't liked was Ford's obvious infatuation with the woman who was clearly more infatuated with Humphrey than his son.

Ford wasn't getting involved with Rachel. But he didn't want to argue the point, so he texted back, saying he was fine and would be away for a few days. Not to worry. Then he went looking for a place to stay.

Hitch was just finishing up the autopsy when the sheriff stuck his head in the door.

"About done?" he asked, sounding impatient and out of sorts.

She looked at the clock on the wall in surprise. She hadn't realized how late it was. Behind the sheriff, she could see through a far window that it was dark outside. She'd lost track of time—as she often did. But she had needed to get on this one right away.

"I should have the report to you by tomorrow afternoon," she said. "Do you have a minute?"

He had started to leave. She could tell he wanted nothing to do with the autopsy room. After shrugging out of her garb, she washed her hands and stepped out into the hallway with him.

"Tell me it's a slam dunk," he said. "Gunshot to the face, I don't really need to ask the cause of death."

"I was wondering about the woman's injuries. You were the first one on the scene, right?"

"Like I told you, I found her in the kitchen, sitting on the floor, leaning against a cabinet, looking terrified. She was still holding the gun in one hand and the phone in the other. She dropped both when she saw me and tried to get to her feet. The floor was slick with her blood and his. I had to help her up." He grimaced as if recalling the scene. "I could see that she was in bad shape and that he was dead. I could see what happened. What more is there to say?"

"There is no doubt that she fired the fatal kill shot," Hitch said as she pulled out her phone to consult the report DCI had sent her. "The techs found gunpowder residue on her hands and wrists along with the clothing she was wearing at the time." Slacks, blouse, heels. Dressed like a woman spending the day on the ranch? Or one who'd been to town?

"That seems pretty obvious since there was just the two of them in the house," the sheriff said sarcastically. "She fired the gun and killed him. It wasn't like he shot himself in the face."

"Did she say anything to you about what had happened?"

"Like confess? She was hysterical, in pain, bleeding. I handed her my handkerchief."

"The lab will want that if you still have it," she said, making him roll his eyes.

"You're just going to beat this one like a dead horse, aren't you?" He shook his head. "Let the state get involved and they'll blow this up for no good reason... Fine." He pulled out the soiled handkerchief from his pocket. She could see only a few spots of blood and something dark. Gunpowder residue? As he tried to hand it to her, she made him wait until she grabbed an evidence bag, getting her another eye roll.

"So she didn't say anything about shooting her husband?" Hitch asked again as she sealed the bag.

"No. She just cried. Clearly, she was in a lot of pain." His jaw muscles clenched and unclenched. "I interviewed her at the hospital. Before you ask, I videotaped her statement."

"Thank you, Sheriff. Oh," she said as she started to turn away and pretended to change her mind. "I'll need to see any statements you've taken, including the ones from Ford Cardwell and Rachel Collinwood."

"I'll call my office and tell them to send you both video interviews." He didn't move for a moment and she could tell he was chewing on something. "I'm damned good at my job, I'll have you know. It's why I've been in this office as long as I have." With that, he turned and left.

She felt the weight of the day. Often she worked late rather than eat alone at some restaurant before going back to an empty motel room. If she didn't love her work so much...

Turning out the light, she started to leave when she looked out to see a pickup parked outside. The lights were on and the engine was running, but she couldn't make out who was behind the wheel.

As if the driver had seen her staring out the window, he sped off. Was it a male driver? She'd just assumed so. She watched until the taillights disappeared around a corner, surprised by the anxious feeling she'd gotten. The driver had just been sitting out there as if watching her. She didn't spook easily, but being alone this late here at the morgue and seeing the driver of the pickup just sitting there...

She shook it off, telling herself it had been nothing. Just a long day and the violent case she'd found herself embroiled in. Tomorrow she would be getting a call from the governor wanting answers. She hoped she had some by then.

Chapter 7

After a rough night filled with nightmares, Ford showered and drove down to the Corner Café Shyla had mentioned for breakfast. He was curious about the kind of woman his old friend would jeopardize his marriage over. If true. His head ached from the images that had played in his mind and kept him from sleep.

He kept seeing Rachel's bruised and battered face. But it was Humphrey, once his best friend, who haunted his nightmares the worst. In them, the man had been pleading with Ford to forgive him, as if it had been Ford who'd pulled the trigger on that gun.

He took a seat in an empty booth and waited. The café was busy. He saw there were several waitresses scurrying around. One had short dark hair. The other, long blond hair tied back. Humphrey had always preferred blondes. He figured this one had to be Emily Sutton. When the woman came to his table with a menu tucked under her arm, a glass of water and pot of coffee, he got his first good look at her and felt a start.

She could have been a young Rachel with her big blue eyes and bee-stung mouth. "Coffee?" she asked, smiling. He could only nod, still taken aback. She righted the cup in the saucer that was already on the table and poured, commenting on the beautiful summer day outside, then said, "I'm Emily. I'll give you a minute to look over the menu. But don't worry—I'll be back." Her smile was devastating in its beauty and innocence—just as Rachel's had been all those years ago.

Humphrey would have seen the similarities between the waitress and his wife. Would it have been like falling for Rachel all over again?

Ford opened his menu, surprised at the impact the realization had made on him. What had happened between Rachel and Humphrey? Had he just been looking for a newer model? How deep had the rift between them gotten that it had led to such a catastrophic ending?

He tried to concentrate on his menu. He hadn't been hungry for a very long time. Loss of appetite was only one symptom, he'd been told. As if he didn't know the rest of them. He was apparently the poster boy for post-traumatic stress disorder. He had it all, from the flashbacks, memory loss and nightmares, to the severe anxiety, the emotional numbness and feelings of hopelessness—right down to the despondent suicidal thoughts.

He started to close the menu, thinking he should go back to Big Sky. Rachel didn't need him. Anyway, there was nothing he could do to help her. Other than what he'd already done. His cell phone rang. He saw that it was from the hospital and quickly picked up. His heart rate did a little bump as he heard Rachel's voice on the other end of the line.

"Are you all right?" he asked as he hurried to take the call outside.

"I'm much better, thank you. I was hoping you were still around."

"I am."

"I'm so glad to hear that. I need to see you." The café door opened as several people exited. The clatter of dishes and laughter followed them out, along with the smell of bacon. "You're having breakfast. Please, finish eating. They're taking me down to X-ray again, but then I should be back in my room in the next hour. Come see me?"

"I will." To his surprise, when he disconnected he felt like going back inside the café. The smell of food that had nauseated him earlier now made his stomach rumble. He sat down and the waitress hurried right over.

"Have you decided?" Emily asked. On closer inspection, she wasn't as pretty as Rachel.

He nodded and ordered the special, flapjacks and bacon.

"Good choice," she said and hurried off.

Ford picked up his coffee cup and took a sip. Rachel wanted to see him. What was it he'd heard in her voice? Fear and something else, something he remembered from a very long time ago. He heard her words from fifteen years ago at the wedding. "It should have been you, Ford." And then her mouth and hands were on him and he was kissing her—the woman who'd just married his best friend.

That memory had always come with guilt like a weight around his neck. This morning it didn't feel so heavy. Maybe even just hours after the wedding, Rachel had realized the mistake she'd made.

He felt lighter. He'd been wrong. Rachel *did* need him. He hadn't realized how much he'd needed her right now, he thought. She'd saved his life on the mountain. Not that he would know if he would have gone through with it. But he felt as if she had literally pulled him back from the brink. Maybe he could do the same for her. At least for the moment it would give his life meaning.

Back from X-ray, Rachel itched to get her bandages off, head home and soak in a hot bathtub. She had a slight concussion. Her ribs were cracked, not broken. Same with her cheekbone. She felt dirty, grimacing when she saw the dried blood still under her fingernails. Emotions, hot and fierce, bubbled to the surface. Was it her blood? Or was it Humphrey's? The thought of his blood made her wince.

She closed her eyes, wishing for sleep. Last night she'd lain awake, haunted by the memory of her husband's face— and what she'd seen in those blue eyes—that instant before she'd pulled the trigger. Where once there had been such love, such admiration, such gratitude, she'd seen— She couldn't bear to think about it or what their lives had come to.

At college, Humphrey had been the shy, wealthy young man who studied hard, partied little and dated even less. She'd expected him to be cocky the first time she met him after finding out who he was. Instead, he'd been sweet. It didn't surprise her that Humphrey and Ford were good friends. They'd been a lot alike. Ford hadn't even seemed to notice how wealthy his friend's family was. But that was Ford. Money had never mattered to him.

Ford. Of course, he'd been there when she'd needed him. If only she had married him, she thought, then remembered what he'd said when she'd asked him what he planned to do after graduation.

"Maybe work in the barbecue business with the family. Although I think I'd like to work on Cardwell Ranch with my dad's cousin Dana first. I've spent a lot of time there growing up over the years. It holds special memories for me."

Rachel had been shocked at how little he'd wanted. "You must have another dream. Aren't you majoring in engineering?"

He'd actually laughed and said he didn't need to set the world on fire. He just wanted to have a simple life and give his kids what he'd gotten growing up, an appreciation for Montana living and family. "What I've learned would come in handy on the ranch."

"But didn't I hear Humphrey say that he could get you a job with his dad?" she'd said.

Ford had looked shocked. "That was nice of him, but that's not the life I want."

Was that when she'd been glad that she hadn't set her sights so low? Ford was nice, but she needed more. She needed his roommate because she'd dreamed of the nicer things in life.

She cringed at the memory. Humphrey was dead, while it had been Ford who'd come to her rescue. She had a flash of memory of her lovely kitchen covered in shattered glass and pottery, with Humphrey lying in the middle of it. That vision now served as a nightmare snapshot of her shattered dreams. She closed her eyes tightly, trying to wipe it all away.

At the sound of someone coming into her hospital room, she opened her eyes and braced herself. This waking nightmare wasn't over any more than the ones that ruined her sleep. In fact, she feared the horror was just beginning.

Ford had started down the hallway toward Rachel's room when a female voice called after him. Turning, he saw an attractive brunette woman wearing jeans, boots and a Western shirt headed toward him.

"Mr. Cardwell?" she asked when she reached him.

The title felt wrong. "I'm Ford Cardwell."

She held out her hand. She had pale green eyes under dark lashes. "Henrietta Roberts, state medical examiner. Most people just call me Hitch. I'd like to ask you a few questions, if you don't mind. The doctor said we could use his office down the hall, if you'll please follow me." She didn't wait for an answer. Everything about her said she had authority, from the steel in her spine, to the tone of her voice and the no-nonsense look in those eyes. He gathered that she was a woman used to giving orders and having them followed.

He hesitated, though, anxious to see Rachel. She should be back from X-ray. She would be waiting for him. "I was just going to see—"

The medical examiner stopped to look back at him, seeming almost amused. "She isn't going anywhere. I promise you. This way."

In the doctor's office, she closed the door behind them and told him to take a seat. To his surprise, she didn't go behind the desk and take the doctor's chair. Instead, she pulled up the second one in front of the physician's desk. Their knees were only a few inches apart.

Taking out her phone and notebook and pen, she said, "I'd like to record this, if it's all right with you."

"You do know that I already did this at the sheriff's office, right?"

"Yes, but if you don't mind, I'd like to hear it directly from you." She set up her phone to record on the edge of the desk so it was facing him. "I understand you know those involved. Can you please explain?"

He did, going over his relationships with Humphrey and Rachel and then the phone call and what he'd heard.

"So you never heard the victim say anything."

"Is that what you're calling him?" Ford asked. "What does that make Rachel?"

"At this point, they're both victims. I'm trying to find out what happened so I can sort this out. So voices. You heard…"

"The only person I heard was Rachel. I thought at the time that she was being attacked by an intruder. I could hear glass breaking and her screaming…"

"Humphrey never spoke before she called him by name?"

"No."

"Did you hear anything else in the background other than breaking glass?"

"Not that I can remember."

"When you knew Rachel in college, do you know if she owned a gun?"

"No. I mean, no, she didn't. She hated guns."

"Did she learn how to shoot one, that you were aware of?"

"I have no idea. I hadn't seen her for fifteen years until yesterday." He remembered telling her goodbye the day he'd left. More memories hit him like typhoon winds, making a rushing sound in his ears.

"It's clear to me that you care a great deal about her."

Was he that transparent? He started to deny it, but decided to save his breath. "I was half in love with her way back when. I was young. We all were young, that is. But like I said, that was years ago."

"Humphrey Collinwood was your roommate and your best friend, you said. Did the friendship survive the years?"

He didn't know how to answer that. He could feel her

studying him with those sea green eyes that seemed to notice everything. "We drifted apart."

She nodded. "You said the last time you saw her was at her wedding to Humphrey?"

He realized he must have told the sheriff that and now she was making too much out of this. He nodded, wishing he'd denied having feelings for Rachel.

"Did Humphrey know how you felt about her?" Those eyes widened. "Did you ever consider getting back at him?"

The accusation caught him flat-footed. He glanced at her phone. Was it still recording? "What are you suggesting? Yes, I had a crush on Rachel years ago, but I wasn't… jealous, not like that."

"I find it interesting that it was your phone number that she called during the altercation with her husband."

"I explained that—"

"So just a few weeks ago, she contacts you out of the blue on social media. Whose idea was it to exchange phone numbers?"

He shook his head. "I don't remember." But when he thought about it, he did. It had been Rachel's.

"Also, you drove right here, making really good time apparently, after the call."

"I was worried after what I'd heard. I knew the sheriff would want to talk to me." He couldn't believe what she was insinuating. "Wouldn't you have done the same thing after hearing something like that involving old friends?"

She didn't answer. "You don't find it a little odd she just happened to call *you*?"

"I explained that. It must have been—"

"A pocket dial, right. Making you a defense witness. Was Rachel surprised when you showed up here?" She didn't give him a chance to answer. "I didn't think so. She knew you would come to her rescue after the call since you were old friends. She had to have known how you felt about her. Even though you'd lost touch for fifteen years, she'd known you'd come when called."

Ford didn't like where this was going. "You'd have to ask her. Look, if we're about finished here…" He stood.

The medical examiner turned off the video on her phone. "I'm assuming you're planning to stay around for a while?" She again didn't give him a chance to answer. "Good. But I can always find you back in Big Sky. If I need to."

He felt a chill run the length of his spine. All those days of feeling nothing but an emotional numbness were gone. Like a bucket of ice water poured over his head, he was now wide-awake as he realized what this woman was accusing him of—and Rachel, as well. She thought he was somehow involved in Humphrey's death? Because of a phone call?

With a silent groan, he thought about what had happened between him and Rachel at the wedding all those years ago. He hated to think of what the medical examiner would make of that.

Chapter 8

Ford felt so shaken after his encounter with the medical examiner that he didn't go right to Rachel's room. Instead, he went outside and walked around town for a little while to clear his head. Big Timber was a small Western ranch town set in the middle of several impressive mountain ranges along the Yellowstone River.

The views would have taken his breath away if he wasn't already short of breath from what the medical examiner had accused him of doing. That he'd always wanted Rachel and had helped her kill her husband out of jealousy and was now her…defense? That was insane. How could she think such a thing?

By the time he returned to the hospital, he was still shaken but more in control. He'd come here to help Rachel. That Hitch—as she called herself—thought Rachel might have planned the whole thing so she could kill her husband was even crazier. Had the woman seen Rachel's face? The doctor had just taken her down to X-ray. Clearly, she'd been beaten.

If the medical examiner believed that was what had happened, then Rachel needed him even more than he'd thought. He had to see her again and he'd kept her waiting long enough. But he felt off balance as he found the doctor and got permission. The guard at the door let him in. As he stuck his head around the corner into her room, he did his best not to let her see how upset he was. He wondered how much of it was guilt over what had happened all those years ago.

"The doctor said you can have some company for a few minutes."

She waved him in. "I must look awful," Rachel said and touched the bandage at her cheek.

"You couldn't possibly look awful and you know it," Ford said as he pulled up the chair next to her bed. "Since you're fishing for compliments, you must be feeling better."

She chuckled even though it seemed to cause her pain. "That's what I always loved about you, Ford. You tell it to me straight." Her expression softened and he felt a slight electrical charge in the room. It was dated and weak, but still he felt it. "I'm so sorry." She began to cry. "The sheriff told me that I called you and that you…heard. I can hardly face you. Now I've involved you in all this."

"Rachel, really, it's all right."

"No, it's not. I never wanted anyone to know and now…"

He reached for her hand, thinking they all had things that they never wanted anyone to know. "When I got your call, it caught me at a really low point. The truth is, Rachel, your call saved my life."

She wiped her eyes. "Ford, you don't have to say that."

"I'm not." He hesitated, but only for a moment. "When

you called, I was driving toward the edge of a cliff. I'd planned to end it."

Her blue eyes widened. "No," she said, looking horrified.

He nodded. "But then you called. So I'm the one who should be thanking you."

She studied him for a long moment and then laughed. "Look at us. Who would have ever thought this is where we would end up." He squeezed her hand.

For so long he hadn't felt anything and thought he never would again. Yet when he'd gotten her phone call yesterday and realized who it was, he'd felt as if his numbed emotions had been touched with a cattle prod. He'd known he had to come to Big Timber. Her wrong number had brought him back into her life. If that wasn't fate, he didn't know what was.

After his interview with the medical examiner, it was clear that Rachel needed him—even if she didn't know it yet. "How are you doing?" he asked.

"You've been through something like it, so I suspect you know."

He did know. Their situations were nothing alike except for the feeling of horror at where life had landed them. He hated to think what she must be going through. Seeing her again, it felt as if no time had passed since they last saw each other. He wanted to ask if she'd been happy at least some of those years with Humphrey, but didn't want to remind her about her marriage. She must have loved her husband. At least until the abuse began.

"Do you want to talk about it?" he asked.

She shook her head. "He just wasn't the man I thought he was. I really thought when we married that we would live happily ever after. Silly, huh?"

"I think that's the way most people go into a marriage."

Rachel picked at the edge of the sheet, her eyes downcast. "He was so sweet, so caring, so generous. At first." She looked up. "You know, he bought the ranch because of you."

"That's what his father told me." Ford remembered what Shyla had told him about how miserable Rachel had been at the ranch. Bart had even wanted to blame Ford for Humphrey's buying the ranch and dying here.

"Bart's here?" she said, her voice breaking. "You know, he hates me. Always has. He'll do everything in his power to get me sent to prison for life."

"We won't let that happen."

Eyes shiny and bright, she smiled up at him, taking him back to that day in college—those few precious moments in the park before she saw Humphrey.

Hitch had watched Ford Cardwell from the hospital window as he'd left earlier. He'd had his hands in the pockets of his jeans, his head down. She'd obviously upset him. Because it hadn't been true? Or because it had?

She had seen how anxious he'd been earlier to see Rachel Collinwood. At the window, she'd decided to wait him out, knowing he would be back once he'd calmed down. The fact that he'd been so upset told her how deep his feelings apparently went for the woman in question. Sure enough, he'd come back and gone straight to Rachel's room.

From down the hall, she now watched him exit the woman's room. It was time to take this to the next step. Hitch put in a call to the sheriff, then headed down the hall toward Rachel Collinwood's room. As she walked, she mentally processed what she'd learned from Ford Cardwell. If Rachel needed someone she could depend on, well, then she'd certainly made the right call—so to speak—when she'd hit Ford Cardwell's number.

Hitch pushed open the hospital room door, already knowing what she was going to find. Still, she stepped in and stood for a moment studying Rachel, who lay in her bed, eyes closed. Hitch was curious what kind of woman inspired the kind of loyalty the flyboy hero had for her.

Rachel Westlake Collinwood even in her current condition radiated that kind of beauty that few women possessed. Though bruised, lacerated and swollen, her face still had the heart shape so popular on magazine covers. The woman's eyes, she knew from her online search, were big and deep blue. Those eyes now opened in surprise to find Hitch studying her with speculation. Hitch saw the woman's guard come up. Had the sheriff warned her about the female medical examiner?

"Rachel Collinwood?" she said, stepping to the bed. "I'm state medical examiner Henrietta 'Hitch' Roberts." She pulled up a chair beside the bed. "I need to ask you a few questions about what happened yesterday. You don't mind if I video this." She set up her phone so it was aimed directly at the woman, not waiting for her approval. "So, Mrs. Collinwood, why don't you tell me in your own words exactly how this all happened. I know the sheriff already took your statement. You don't mind going through it for me, though, do you, just for the record?"

Rachel glanced at the phone, then at Hitch. Her eyes instantly filled with tears. "He's dead, isn't he?"

Hitch met her watery gaze. "He is. Why don't we start with what happened before you got home." She caught that moment of surprise, just a flash in the woman's eyes. Rachel hadn't mentioned that she'd just gotten home from town when she'd been questioned by the sheriff.

"Or do you want to start with the argument that began before the two of you returned to the ranch?" Hitch asked.

Rachel Collinwood swallowed and seemed to be buying time. "This is very hard to talk about. I've suspected for some time that my husband's been having an affair. When he said he had to go into town to pick up some part or another, I followed him. I caught up with him outside the woman's house and we argued. I went home, upset, and he followed me."

From there, Hitch noticed that this was the same story she'd told the sheriff on video, almost verbatim. She'd learned that interrupting the speaker often changed their account because they were so used to telling it in order, they would forget where they were. She didn't intend to get the same exact story from Rachel Collinwood if she could help it.

"That two-lane highway into town doesn't get much traffic," Hitch said, stopping the flow of the woman's words. "It must have been difficult to follow him into town since he would know your vehicle."

"I took the pickup. I figured he'd expect me to take my car."

"Your car being…"

"The BMW. Anyway…" She picked up her water glass next to the bed, adjusted the straw and took a sip. "When I got home, I heard him coming. He'd been angry in town. I was suddenly afraid for my life."

"Why would you go back to the house if he'd physically abused you before?"

"He had, but never like…that day," she said, dropping her gaze to her hands lying on the sheet as she toyed with the space where her wedding bands had been. The hospital staff normally removed jewelry for safekeeping. But in this case, the DCI investigators had taken all of her jewelry as evidence.

"But you had to be expecting trouble, right? Otherwise, why carry the gun in your purse? Unless you planned to kill him."

The woman's gaze shot up to hers in surprise. "I... I want a lawyer. And turn that thing off." She made a swipe at the phone, but Hitch got hold of it before Rachel could knock it to the floor. "I have nothing more to say to you. You're trying to twist my words. After everything I've been through, I can't believe..." She glared at Hitch. "I would think another woman would understand. He could have killed me! He would have, too, if I hadn't..." She clamped her lips shut and looked away. "Please go. I have nothing more to say to you."

"I need to inform you that you are under arrest pending the results of this investigation and a possible trial," Hitch said. "Once you are able to leave the hospital, you will be taken into custody until a hearing before a judge, in which case you will either be allowed bail or put behind bars."

"You can't be serious!" the woman cried. "He would have *killed* me. He told me he was going to kill me!"

"In the meantime, you will be fitted for an ankle bracelet that requires you to stay on this floor of the hospital." Hitch pocketed her phone as she heard the sheriff talking to the guard outside the room. "If you'll excuse me for a moment," she said and stepped out.

The sheriff lumbered toward her looking angry and upset.

"Sheriff, I need you to inform Mrs. Collinwood of her rights and make sure she understands she is under arrest for the death of her husband."

"That's why you got me down here?" he demanded angrily. "You got me away from my lunch for this?" He shook his head. "You are one heartless woman."

"I'm just doing my job. Isn't that proper procedure in a domestic homicide? I see no reason to let this run the full seventy-two hours. Mrs. Collinwood has admitted to shooting her husband with the intent to kill. Sheriff, if you prefer, I can call—"

The man growled. "I don't need you calling anyone," he snapped.

Minutes later, after the sheriff had read Mrs. Collinwood her rights, she was fitted with an ankle bracelet. Hitch stood at the door and watched. Rachel Collinwood lay in the bed, her face turned to the wall, quietly crying.

Hitch's cell phone rang. She took it on the way out of the hospital.

"I thought you'd want to know. Two shots were fired from the weapon that killed Humphrey Collinwood," Bradley from DCI told her.

She stopped just short of her SUV. "How many casings did you find?"

"Only one in the kitchen on the floor."

"Were there any slugs found in the wall?" she asked, frowning as she tried to understand when and where the other shot might have been fired.

"Negative. But both shots had been fired close to the same time."

Hitch swore under her breath. "We have to find that other slug and casing."

"Have you seen the size of that ranch?" he asked.

"Let me see what I can do. That casing is somewhere out there, and I have a theory that the first shot was a practice one."

Chapter 9

Hitch couldn't get the news off her mind as she drove out to the Collinwood Ranch. Pulling up to the house, she thought she saw movement inside but realized it was only the reflection of the crime scene tape flickering in the breeze.

After getting out of her SUV, she stepped under that tape and entered the house with the code the sheriff had given her. The first thing that struck her was the absolute silence, followed almost instantly by the smell of cleaning supplies.

The kitchen shone white—all signs of the violence gone. She stepped in and looked around. The DCI unit had been thorough; she didn't doubt that. Which meant the second casing hadn't been in this room. Just as the slug wasn't embedded in any of the walls. Glancing around, though, she knew that the other shot hadn't been fired in here.

Her gaze went to the sliding glass door from the kitchen out onto the deck. She carefully opened the door. The breeze brought the sweet scent of pine and summer as she stepped out. Had Rachel stood here, with the gun in her hand? Rachel Collinwood wasn't the kind of woman who left things to chance, right?

Because of that, she would fire the gun to make sure it worked. To know how it felt, how much it kicked in her hand, what it would do when the time came.

Hitch walked to the edge of the deck and leaned her elbow on the railing to take aim. She spotted the closest pine tree and pretended to fire. Then she glanced down at the thick shrubbery below. The weapon would have ejected the casing.

But before Hitch went digging in the shrubs, she wanted a look at that pine.

A dozen yards from the deck, she stopped in front of the tree. She didn't see it at first. The bullet hadn't skinned much of the bark. Instead, it had lodged in the soft wood and was nearly covered by a piece of bark. She walked back to her vehicle for her satchel, took a few photographs, then pulled on latex gloves and went to work with her pocket-knife.

As the slug came out, she dropped it into an evidence bag. Hitch told herself that anyone could have fired the weapon from the deck. But Bradley had said the two shots had been fired close together.

Holding the slug up in the sunlight, she knew it didn't prove that Rachel had orchestrated the murder of her husband. But then again, it did add to growing evidence that she had.

Putting down her satchel, she bent at the edge of the deck. If she found the empty casing… She had been looking in the shrubbery directly off the deck railing when something farther back under the deck, closer to the house, caught her eye. The casing lay next to the house and the door out to the deck.

Goose bumps rippled over her skin. She'd thought that Rachel had taken the first shot as target practice so she knew how the gun would react when she pulled the trigger. She would have put her elbows on the railing to take aim because she wasn't used to firing this weapon.

But Hitch knew now that it didn't happen that way. Rachel Collinwood had fired the shot that hit the tree standing at the open kitchen doorway. She had practiced with the gun long before the day of the shooting.

It explained why Humphrey Collinwood's voice was never heard on the phone call to Ford. Because he was already dead from the first shot fired—before Rachel had "accidentally" made that alleged pocket dial.

While Humphrey Collinwood lay in a pool of his own blood, his wife had taken the phone, made the call, acted out the attack and then stepped to the open glass doors and fired the shot that Ford heard before she'd disconnected and called 911.

That would explain why Ford Cardwell hadn't heard Humphrey Collinwood say a word.

After taking a photo of where the casing had landed in relation to the house, Hitch put her camera away to leave. But as she did, she felt an icy chill and turned quickly, unable to shake the feeling that someone was watching her. Her gaze took in the sliding glass door into the kitchen. For a moment, she'd expected to see someone standing there.

But the doorway was empty. So was the yard. So was the land that ran from the house to the rolling hills to the mountains in the distance. Behind her, the breeze stirred the boughs of the pine tree, making an eerie moaning sound.

Hitch laughed at her foolishness, but it sounded hollow. She didn't spook easily, but this wasn't the first time she'd felt…something that raised goose bumps across her skin. She doubted it would be the last, given her job. And yet, as she climbed back into her SUV to leave, she found herself staring at the house, unable to shake what felt like a warning.

When Ford visited Rachel again later that afternoon at the hospital, he was glad to see that she seemed in better spirits. Her face was badly bruised, but several of the bandages had come off. Also, she seemed glad to see him.

"You look as if you're feeling better," he said, going to her bedside.

"Looks can be deceiving," she said, meeting his gaze. "I'm scared, Ford. I'm under arrest."

"My uncle's a marshal in Big Sky. I talked to him earlier. He said that it's police procedure. What does your lawyer say?"

"That we'll fight it. The problem, he says, is that self-defense claims are fairly common. Because of the amount of force I used…well, it could complicate things. If I hadn't killed him, only wounded him…" She met his gaze. "He was so close. I knew that if he got his hands on me again…" She looked down at her own hands knotted together on top of the sheet. "I was holding the gun. You heard me tell him not to come any closer or I would shoot him." She closed her eyes. "He wouldn't listen. I had no choice. I pulled the trigger."

He placed his hand over hers, surprised someone had told her not only that she'd accidentally called him, but also what he'd heard her say before the gunshot. "What can I do to help you?"

Rachel opened her eyes and wiped them before she

turned that high-wattage smile on him. And he'd been so certain just forty-eight hours ago that he'd never be able to feel again. There was a time that her smile would have filled him with so much joy. He told himself the reason he didn't feel that joy now, couldn't because of everything that had happened to them both. He realized Rachel was still talking.

"I don't know what I would have done if you hadn't been here," she was saying. "It's crazy, it's like fate, but I'm so thankful that somehow I hit your number. What are the odds?"

What were the odds? he thought.

"So just your being here is enough," Rachel said. "I can't tell you what it means to me."

"I'm sure your lawyer will get you bail and fight this," he assured her.

"I don't know. He says we have to prove that I was defending myself and believed I was in imminent danger."

"Your injuries should prove that."

She nodded. "It's just hard to prove when there was only the two of us there." She brightened. "But I guess it wasn't just me and Humphrey. You were there." She looked away. "I can't believe any of this is happening."

He knew the feeling. "How is your head?"

She grimaced. "It hurts. The pain pills help. I can't believe what he did to me." She began to cry. "The doctor is releasing me tomorrow, and if I don't make bail, I'm going to jail."

"Do you have money for bail?"

She nodded. "I was afraid all our assets might have been frozen until the outcome of the investigation. But thankfully, they weren't. The thing is, Humphrey always handled the money. I have no idea how much I will be able to raise."

"I'll help what I can," he said.

"I know." She flashed him that smile again. "I knew I could count on you. Oh, Ford." She took his hand in her two. "I'll never be able to thank you enough."

"I should have known you would be here," said a female voice behind him. He turned to see Shyla come into the hospital room. She moved to the bed to give Rachel an awkward hug and a kiss on the cheek. "How's our girl?"

Ford looked to Rachel and smiled. "She's doing okay, under the circumstances." A silence fell over the room. "I'll leave you two alone so you can visit."

"Don't run off on my account," Shyla said, even though he got the feeling that she was anxious to talk to Rachel alone. Because she would be more honest with her than she'd been with him?

He realized that he was letting Hitch get to him, her and her suspicions. "I've got to go anyway," he said, as if there was anywhere he needed to be. But maybe he should see how much money he could raise on Rachel's behalf if she needed more bail money. "But I'll be back."

Rachel grabbed his wrist as he started to turn away. "Thank you," she whispered.

Ford stepped out into the hall, closing the hospital room door behind him. He stood in the hallway for a moment. Why had this visit with Rachel left him feeling…not so sure of her? The medical examiner had him questioning everything Rachel said, and he hated her for doing that to him. He shook his head and reached into his pocket for his pickup keys. Empty.

He swore under his breath and turned back to Rachel's room, remembering putting them down on the side table when she spilled her water.

But as he pushed open the door, he froze as he overheard

Rachel's words. "I should have married Ford." He started to ease the door closed and stopped.

Shyla laughed. "Oh, please. He wasn't even in the running and you know it. His father owns a barbecue joint with his brothers."

"They have a dozen barbecue joints, as you call them, and were worth a bunch even back in college."

"You ran a financial on him?"

Rachel's laugh was like a fingernail down a blackboard. "Why does that surprise you?"

"Actually, nothing you do surprises me," Shyla said. "I know you, Rach. Ford told me how you two met. A squirrel? Really. You just happened to be there feeding a squirrel? You went after Humphrey and you used Ford to do it."

Silence, then Rachel's voice, stronger than it had been when she was talking to him earlier. "I wanted to marry someone who could take care of me in the way I wanted to become accustomed. What's wrong with that?"

"*Really?* Have you noticed how that turned out? You're on your way to jail when you get out of here."

"Maybe. We'll see. I'll make bail. Ford's going to help me."

"Of course he is."

Ford saw his chance and said "I forgot my keys!" as he pushed the door all the way open. Both women turned in surprise as he hurried in, grabbed his keys and waved an apologetic goodbye as he left again.

He reached the door and stopped just out of their sight around the corner at the edge of the hallway. The deputy was no longer outside her door since she'd been fitted with an ankle bracelet. Ford didn't let the door quite close.

"Do you think he heard us?"

Shyla laughed. "Even if he did hear, Ford's still so in love with you he'd forgive you anything. Oh, don't give me that look. This comes as no surprise to you. So tell me. How is it that you just happened to call his number?"

"I have no idea. But he saved my life."

Ford closed the door softly behind him. He stood in the hall trying to catch his breath. His stomach roiled with what he'd heard. He tried to still it, assuring himself that he hadn't heard anything he hadn't already known. He'd seen how Rachel felt about money even back in college. She'd been at the university on loans and small scholarships. She'd hated being poor and had made no bones about it.

Yet he couldn't help but think about the medical examiner's suspicions. He felt sick to his stomach. Worse, Hitch thought he and Rachel had planned this whole thing to get rid of her husband. He'd come running to save her—even though he hadn't forgotten what had happened at her wedding.

What had she gotten him involved in this time? Murder?

Chapter 10

Hitch decided since she was already at the ranch that she would see if she could find the hired hands. If Rachel Collinwood was being abused by her husband, then someone must have noticed.

According to the sheriff, the Collinwoods employed only two young men who lived in the old ranch house several miles from their employers' home.

As she approached, she could see horses in a pasture and a corral and several outbuildings next to a large barn. The house was a modest two-story farmhouse with a wide porch complete with a swing. Hitch wondered about the former owners of the ranch. Had they moved to Arizona? One of them died? Why had they sold to the Collinwoods? Often it was because there was no one who wanted to keep the place and work it. But in this case, maybe they'd been made an offer they just couldn't refuse.

Hitch parked in front of the house, and before she could

get out, two young men headed toward her from the direction of the barn.

Both men appeared to be in their early twenties, tall and gangly and green behind the ears. She introduced herself. The more handsome of the pair was Pete Baxter. He was also the more cocky of the two. Clayton Mandeville was the more talkative of the two.

"So what does a state medical examiner do?" Clayton asked, grinning. "Cut up dead bodies?"

"That and investigate for the state," she said. In this case, she had been given carte blanche from the governor. Which was flattering, but she could feel the weight of it on her shoulders. The message had been clear: don't screw this up. "Can we step inside and talk for a few minutes?"

The house was homey, though dated. Once seated in the living room, she asked, "So the two of you live here?" They nodded. "What is it you do here on the ranch?"

Pete laughed. "We look after things."

"Does the ranch run cattle?"

"It's not a real ranch, if that's what you're asking," Clayton said. "The only animals are the horses."

"I saw a tractor out there," Hitch said. "Does the ranch grow anything?"

They shook their heads. "So you basically take care of how many horses?"

"Six. When the boss wants to ride, we saddle one of them up for him," Clayton said. "We muck out stalls and exercise the horses."

She nodded, looking from one man to the other. Clearly, they had a pretty good setup here. "What about Mrs. Collinwood? Does she ride?" They both shook their heads. "So you don't see her often?" More head shakes. "Where were the two of you yesterday?"

"We had the day off," Clayton said without hesitation.

"Was it your usual day off?"

She asked the question of Clayton, who scratched his neck before saying, "I had some extra time coming. The missus told me to go ahead and take it off."

She looked to Pete, who added, "It was my regular day off."

"So you were both here at the house?"

Clayton shook his head. "I went into town for a while. We were out of a few things."

"He went to see his girlfriend," Pete said with a chuckle.

"And you?" she asked Pete.

"I was here all day. I took one of the horses out for a while and then did chores since someone has to muck out the stalls." He elbowed Clayton.

"So you usually both don't have the same day off. Why yesterday?"

Pete shrugged. "Clayton wanted to see his girlfriend. I didn't mind filling in for him. It isn't like we have a lot to do around here."

"So the Collinwoods don't really know what the two of you do here," she said and hesitated since she wasn't sure how to ask the next question. "Have either of you seen any trouble between Mr. and Mrs. Collinwood?"

Clayton started to speak, but Pete cut him off. "We shouldn't be talking about our employers," Pete said.

"One of them is dead and the other arrested," Hitch pointed out. "I'm not sure how long you're going to be employed. What I need to know is if you had reason to see the two of them together since she didn't ride any of the horses."

"We'd get called up to the house sometimes to do a chore for the missus," Clayton said.

"Did you hear them fighting? Ever see him hit her?"

"Never," Clayton said quickly. "They argued. You know, like old married couples do. Like my parents. He got annoyed with her, but I could tell he loved her. Can't see him raising his hand to her, though."

She looked to Pete, who was studying his boots. "You disagree?"

"I don't like telling tales out of school, but I'd seen her a few times in tears and noticed some bruises on her. I also saw him looking at her a few times like he wanted to kill her."

She studied the ranch hand, curious why his story was so different from Clayton's. "*Like he wanted to kill her?* What kind of look is that?"

Pete shrugged. "You'd know it if you saw it."

"So what happened yesterday doesn't surprise you?" she asked, sure they both had heard all about it.

Pete shook his head. "Not everyone can take living out here in the middle of nowhere. She wasn't raised for this kind of living. Like her husband cared."

Hitch could hear the sympathy in his words. It was clear which side he was on. "She ever talk to you about how she felt?" He looked at his boots again, confirming it. Rachel had complained to the older of the hired hands, the one closer to her own age. There was nothing illegal about that—unless she needed his sympathy for when she killed her husband. Or worse, had been hoping to get him to help her.

"Well, it shocked *me* what happened," Clayton was saying. "I can't imagine what might have set that off, but I never thought he'd do something like that, let alone her ever shoot him. I would have doubted that she even knew how to fire a gun."

Pete merely stared at his boots and said nothing more.

As Hitch drove away from the ranch, she considered the differences between their opinions. Rachel had gone to Pete with her complaints about living on the ranch—and about Humphrey. But Pete didn't seem like the type she would trust as her accomplice. He seemed to Hitch like the kind of man who would have bled her dry for the rest of her life.

That was what had been bothering her, Hitch realized. Rachel couldn't have pulled this off without help. But who had she turned to? She needed a man who was more than sympathetic. She needed one who'd get involved with murder.

She thought about the man who'd allegedly come running the moment he heard the gunshot, Ford Cardwell. After pulling onto the two-lane paved highway, she hadn't gone far when she looked back and saw a pickup behind her. It had one of those large cattle guard grilles on the front. With the sun glinting off the windshield, she couldn't see the driver at this distance. Had the pickup come from the Collinwood Ranch? She didn't think so. Wouldn't she have noticed if either Pete or Clayton had followed her?

The pickup appeared to be the same color as the one that had been sitting outside the morgue last night. She sped up. The pickup driver did the same. She slowed down. The pickup driver did the same.

She told herself that it didn't mean anything, but she was glad when she neared the outskirts of Big Timber and looked back to see the truck gone. It wasn't like her to feel this jumpy. But she couldn't remember ever having a case like this one. Since the first day on this case, she'd had a bad feeling she couldn't shake that things would get worse before they got better.

At the back of her mind was always that one big question. What if she was wrong? What if Humphrey Collinwood's death was exactly like what it appeared to be and Rachel Collinwood was innocent?

Her cell phone rang. She quickly picked up when she saw it was coming from the DCI lab.

"We found something interesting when we began checking the broken shards of glass and pottery found on the floor of the kitchen at the crime scene," Bradley told her. "Fingerprints."

She frowned. "*Fingerprints?* Of course there would be fingerprints."

"Yep, of the lady of the house. But what's missing are the fingerprints of the deceased. If he had broken up the kitchen—"

"You'd have found his fingerprints on the shards," she said and felt that light-headed feeling she always did when a case began to come together.

Ford hadn't wanted to go back to the hotel right away. He kept replaying what he'd heard Rachel and Shyla talking about. Rachel had planned the whole meeting with him—and Humphrey. She'd already staked out the man she planned to marry. That day with the squirrel... She must have known that he and Humphrey often came to that spot in the park after chem class. The woman had done her homework.

There was something so cold and calculating about that. He knew Rachel had been driven, but clearly there were things about her that he'd missed. He shook his head, feeling off balance. Was it possible she'd set this whole domestic homicide up for the money?

He refused to believe she would do something like that even though he knew what money meant to her. Once at a party, the two of them had struck up a conversation outside.

That was back when she'd smoked. He'd found her standing at the deck railing. When he'd joined her, he could see that she'd consumed more than she usually drank.

She'd opened up to him about growing up living hand to mouth and her fear of being poor. "My father used to call it the snake pit, saying it was hard for people like us to climb out. That we could never feel like we belonged, even if we made a whole lot of money. No one like us gets out of the snake pit, he used to say."

"Rachel," he'd said that night on the deck. "Look at you. You're going to an Ivy League university. Your father was wrong."

She'd looked at him with tears in her eyes. "Are you sure about that?" She'd scoffed. "What if we have to be born into a family like Humphrey's with real old wealth to ever be one of them?"

He'd forgotten about that conversation until now. Rachel had married into money, but had she still not felt as if she belonged or ever could?

"Ford?"

He turned to see Shyla come out of the hospital.

"Are you all right?" she asked, smiling oddly at him. "You were just standing here on the sidewalk as if you didn't know which way to go."

She was joking, but she had no idea how true that was.

"Just enjoying this beautiful day," he said.

Shyla lit up a cigarette. As she let out a cloud of smoke, a sheriff's department car pulled up. The deputy on the passenger side put down his window. "Hey, baby," the officer behind the wheel called. Ford couldn't see him without stooping down. He didn't. The officer on the passenger side was studying Ford openly and making him nervous. "We were just going to the drive-in for lunch. You wanna come?"

"Sure. I'll catch up to you." Shyla turned to Ford. "You want to join us?"

He declined and her husband took off, making the tires squeal on the cruiser. "You go on ahead. I have some things I need to do. I thought you said you were married to a cowboy?"

"Don't let the uniform fool you," she said with a laugh. "He's all cowboy. You should see his Wild West fast draw. He could be a movie star," she said as she stubbed out her cigarette on the sidewalk and headed toward her car.

Ford watched her go, wondering at how people changed. The lawless young woman who Rachel had bailed out of jail back in college had married a cop cowboy with a fast draw? He shook his head. Wasn't it possible that if Shyla could change, Humphrey could have turned into a man who'd tried to beat his wife to death?

Chapter 11

Hitch got the call from Lori Stevenson from DCI on the way back into town. "Those phone records you asked about? I'm emailing them to you. We're still checking out the numbers. Only one call jumped out at us. Didn't you tell us that Rachel Collinwood believed her husband was having an affair with a woman named Emily Sutton? Well, Mrs. Collinwood called her cell phone number at ten the morning of the shooting."

"She called before she went into town?" Hitch said, frowning. "How long was the call?"

"Four minutes."

"*Four minutes?* She wasn't simply checking to see if the woman was working. She'd actually talked to her that long?" Hitch had two quick thoughts. How had she gotten Emily's cell phone number? And why had Rachel left that part out of her statement? "Okay, thanks. Anything else?"

"Bart Collinwood wants his son's body so he can have

him flown home and buried. He's called everyone, from what I can tell, including the governor."

Hitch was surprised the governor hadn't called her. Yet. "Great. I need to run a few more tests," she said. It wasn't quite true, but she wasn't ready to turn over the body. She had a feeling that she'd missed something. "I'll let Mr. Bart Collinwood know." She disconnected and drove to the morgue.

Once in the autopsy room, she pulled Humphrey Collinwood's body out of the cooler, that niggling feeling growing. She was certain the reason the deceased hadn't said a word during the fight was because he was already dead. But what if he was unable to speak for another reason? She began to search the body for injection marks.

The sheriff stood at the foot of Rachel Collinwood's hospital bed, Stetson in hand. She was so pretty and sweet and looked so shattered and afraid. "I have some good news for you." At least he hoped she'd see it as that. "A bail hearing has been scheduled for tomorrow, the day of your hospital release. That means, if you can make bail, you won't have to even spend one night in my jail behind bars."

Her smile was weak, but it still warmed his heart. "Thank you so much, Sheriff. You've been so kind. I can't tell you how much I appreciate it. I know this is just standard procedure, that you aren't responsible for me being arrested."

"No," Charley quickly assured her. "I don't understand why a woman like yourself has to be put through this. It makes no sense to me. Anyone can see that you feared for your life. Justifiable use of force. That's what it was."

"Unfortunately, not everyone feels like you do. That woman, the medical examiner, for one."

"Hitch Roberts. I know," he said with a shake of his head. "You'd think as a woman, she would be more understanding."

"My father-in-law is even worse. Not that I blame him. His son is dead, but he *raised* him. That's why Bart doesn't want to believe what really happened. It would reflect on him and the Collinwood name."

All the sheriff could do was nod for a few moments. "You got yourself a good lawyer?"

"I hope so. If I do get out on bail, will I be able to go back out to the ranch?"

"I don't see why not," Charley said. "They're through with your house. I had someone go out there and clean things up for you. I hope you don't mind."

"Sheriff, that is so sweet." Tears filled her eyes. "Thank you so much. That is so thoughtful. But I doubt I can ever go into that kitchen again."

"She never went in there much anyway," Bart Collinwood said behind the sheriff as he came into the room. "It wasn't like she was much of a wife to my son."

The sheriff turned on him. "I told you, you aren't allowed in here. I won't have you badgering this woman."

"You told me a lot of things, Sheriff, but I just talked to the governor and he said I have every right to face the woman who killed my son."

"In court. In the meantime..." Charley pulled out his phone to call Security as Collinwood took a step toward the bed.

"You will pay for what you did," Bart declared, pointing a finger at her. "If I have my way, you'll rot in prison."

"Security is on the way," the sheriff said. "Unless you want me to arrest you—"

"On what charge?" Bart demanded. "Anyway, I'm leaving. I've had my say." He looked again at his daughter-in-law. "You might have fooled this local yokel with your crocodile tears, Rachel, but you have never fooled me. You married my son for the Collinwood money. I'll kill you myself before I'll let you spend a dime more of it."

With that, the man stormed out, pushing past the hospital security guard on his way through the door.

"I hope you heard that, Sheriff," Rachel said, her voice breaking. "He just threatened to kill me. Father like son." Then she burst into tears.

Emily Sutton squirmed in the chair as the video recorder was turned on. She looked so young in her jeans and T-shirt. Hitch had asked to sit in on the interview with the waitress who was allegedly having an affair with Humphrey Collinwood.

The sheriff grumbled and complained but agreed. After introducing herself to Emily, Hitch had taken a seat and pulled out her notebook and pen.

"State your name and occupation," the sheriff said after giving the date and adding that the state medical examiner was also here.

As soon as Emily finished, he asked, "Were you having an affair with Humphrey Collinwood?"

Her eyes widened in alarm. "No." She shook her head adamantly. "We were just friends."

"Friends?" the sheriff asked mockingly.

Hitch shot him a warning look. "Would you please describe your friendship, Miss Sutton?"

"He came into the café a lot of mornings."

"Without his wife?" the sheriff said.

"He said she wasn't an early riser." Emily smiled. "He said he liked to watch the sun rise and that he loved the café's waffles. He always ordered the same thing. He said his wife didn't cook."

"What else did he say about his wife?" Hitch asked.

Emily shook her head and looked away for a moment. "Nothing bad. He just seemed...lonely. I got the impression he needed someone to talk to." She smiled. "I'm a good listener."

"You aren't going to tell me that he didn't talk about his wife, are you?" the sheriff said, ignoring Hitch's look.

"It wasn't like he complained about her. He didn't. I just got the feeling that they didn't have a lot in common. He'd been looking for a horse for her birthday. She loved pintos and paints. My cousin up in Malta raises them, so I put him in touch with Tom."

"We'll need your cousin's contact information," Hitch said.

"I can give it to you. He'll tell you."

"Did Mr. Collinwood buy a horse for his wife's birthday?" Hitch asked. "I understand she didn't ride much."

"He did," Emily said. "He showed me a photograph. It's a beautiful horse. He was hoping that his wife would love it and that they could ride together. He'd hoped it would encourage her to ride more."

"Humphrey ever come over to your house?" the sheriff said, drawing her attention to him again.

"Just to drop off a thank-you present, that's all. It was my day off and he said he had to fly out the next day for a board meeting. He wouldn't even come inside."

"What did he give you?" Hitch asked.

She beamed, clearly pleased with the gift. "It was a miniature carousel. I'd mentioned once that one of my happiest memories was riding a paint horse on a carousel." She blushed, her joy in the gift from Humphrey reddening her cheeks.

Hitch studied her for a moment, seeing her embarrassment and so much more. "You liked him."

She nodded. "He was nice. He reminded me of my father." She looked to the sheriff. "My father died in Afghanistan. He was a marine."

"You more than liked Humphrey Collinwood," the sheriff said.

Her head came up, eyes widening. "No. He was just nice to me. He was married. He would never have…" She shook her head and lowered it again. "He told me how much he loved his wife. That's why he wanted to surprise her with the horse. He said he was trying to find a way to make her happy in Montana."

"Tell me about the phone call you got from his wife, Rachel Collinwood," Hitch said, surprising both Emily and the sheriff. "She called you the morning of the shooting."

Emily nodded, tears in her eyes. "She thought we were having an affair. I told her we weren't, but she wouldn't listen. She was upset and wouldn't believe me." She paused for a moment. Then said, "Tell me that isn't what they argued about, what…got him killed."

"It wasn't," Hitch said before the sheriff could speak. "You aren't to blame." She stood. "I think we've heard enough."

"Maybe he didn't have an affair with the waitress, but he wanted to," the sheriff argued after Emily Sutton left and Hitch had returned from making a call out in the hallway.

Hitch shook her head at him. "You heard her. Humphrey Collinwood loved his wife. He was buying her a horse for her birthday. I called Emily's cousin. Humphrey Collinwood paid for the horse. It was going to be delivered on his wife's birthday next week. Does that sound like a man who's having an affair?"

The sheriff clearly refused to give an inch. "Sounds like a guilty conscience to me."

Hitch sighed and left before she said something she'd regret.

Back in her hotel room, she watched the videos the sheriff had sent her again of both Ford Cardwell's statement and then Rachel Collinwood's. She was even more suspicious of why Humphrey Collinwood hadn't said a word during the altercation. Ford had heard only Rachel's voice. It was almost as if the husband hadn't been there. And yet she hadn't found any needle marks on the body.

"What are we looking for?" the lab tech asked when Hitch called to request more tests to be run on the samples.

"Run the whole drug spectrum," she told her. There had to be a reason Humphrey Collinwood hadn't spoken at all during the time Ford had been listening in on the alleged pocket-dialed phone call. If he wasn't already dead, then he had to have been drugged or incapacitated in some way.

"Can you put a rush on it?" Hitch asked. "I'm worried that my suspect will make bail tomorrow and that might be the last time we ever see her."

"You're that sure she's a flight risk?"

"If she thinks she might be doing time, she'll run."

The lab tech asked, "Anything in particular you're thinking you're going to find?"

"Something that would debilitate a two-hundred-pound male. Or possibly enrage one. I'm betting it's the first—if there was a drug in his system at the time of his death. Look for something…unusual." Rachel wouldn't have used anything she thought would show up in a normal drug sample taken during the autopsy.

"That is the whole spectrum," the lab tech said with a laugh. "I'll see what I can do."

Hitch disconnected and sighed. She doubted she was going to be able to sleep. She'd talked to the doctor earlier. Rachel Collinwood would be released from the hospital and arraigned tomorrow. If the judge gave her bail, then the woman would be free. Rich, as well. The judge would confiscate her passport, but any fool knew how easy it would be for a woman with her resources to get one in another name and slip the loop.

Except Hitch was determined that wasn't going to happen if she had anything to do with it.

The question was, where did Ford Cardwell fit into all this once Rachel was free?

She'd seen the haunted look in his eyes. After what he'd been through, what was it doing to him being this involved with an old flame suspected of murder?

Hitch guessed she would know tomorrow. What would Ford do once Rachel was out on bail? Go back to Big Sky? He was Rachel's defense, her proof that she feared for her life. Would she want to keep him around? Now that he'd given his statement to law enforcement, she really didn't need him anymore.

All Hitch's instincts told her that the woman was through with Ford. He'd played his part and now he needed to walk away. But would he? It would depend on how deep he was in all this.

Either way, if Hitch was right, Ford was in a very dangerous place. She wondered if he was beginning to realize it. Pulling out her phone, she called his cell phone number.

"It's state medical examiner Henrietta Roberts. Hitch? Where are you?"

It seemed to take him a moment, as if he had to place her name. "At the hospital."

Of course he was, she thought. "I need to talk to you again."

"It's late. Can't this—"

"No, it can't wait," she said. "I'm on my way. How about we meet in the waiting room on Mrs. Collinwood's floor?"

It took her longer to get there than she'd planned. When Hitch pushed open the door to the waiting room, she stopped cold with the realization that she'd caught Ford in an unguarded moment. He looked so miserable that she knew instinctively that it had more than something to do with this case. She couldn't imagine the trauma he'd gone through when he was overseas with the military. She knew a little about survivor's remorse and wondered if that wasn't playing a part in this.

Did she still believe that he'd been in on this with Rachel? The woman had needed an accomplice to pull it off. She hadn't beaten herself and neither had Humphrey Collinwood. Whoever had helped her kill her husband had to be as cold-blooded as she was. Or he'd gotten himself into something he now regretted. As miserable as Ford looked, she feared he might be that man.

Right now, sitting there in this room alone, he looked like what she realized he was. A broken man. Her heart hurt for him. She wanted to go to him, take him in her arms, mend every broken part of him. The emotions surprised her, especially with him so deeply involved in this case.

But she pushed those emotions down. She had to come at him again. It felt cruel, but she had to do her job. He was involved one way or another. Maybe it had only been when Rachel had "accidentally" called him in the middle of her life-and-death situation. Or maybe long before that.

Either way, Hitch had to get to the truth.

She cleared her voice and Ford looked up, a shield coming back up as he quickly rose to his feet. "Why don't we step into the doctor's office again? It will be more private."

He looked as if he'd rather have a root canal, but he came with her.

Again, she turned on her phone to record their interview. After she'd entered the date, time and who was in the room, she said, "I'll tell you what's bothering me. It must be bothering you, too. Why didn't Humphrey speak during the phone call?"

"I have no idea, like I told you. The call wasn't that long."

"It was actually longer than you think. During that time, the only voice you heard was Rachel's. Where were you again when you got the call?"

"I was up in the mountains." He glanced away. He was definitely hiding something.

"What were you doing in the mountains? Hiking, fishing—"

"Just driving around. It's been a long time since I've been back in Montana. I just needed some time to myself."

"So you were alone." A nod. "What was your first thought when you heard—" she checked her notes "—a scream?"

He seemed to think about it. "I realized it was a woman in trouble, but I had no idea who it was. I hadn't checked to see who the call was from. I tried to get her to answer me."

"But she never did?"

"That's when I realized it must have been a pocket dial."

Hitch gave it a minute. "You didn't recognize her voice?" He shook his head. "Once you heard her say her husband's name, you must have been shocked."

"More than you can know," he said. "I couldn't believe it was Rachel and that the man she was begging not to hurt her was Humphrey. I still can't believe it."

"Neither can I," Hitch agreed. "What would you say is your relationship to Mrs. Collinwood?"

"I don't have a relationship with her."

"Because you hadn't seen or talked to either of them for fifteen years, since their wedding, right?"

"No. Not until we reconnected through social media a few weeks ago." He looked as if he wanted to say more but had stopped himself.

She raised a brow. "I believe you said in your statement that he was your best friend, and yet the three of you went fifteen years without talking or seeing each other. Something must have happened. Did he realize you were in love with his wife?"

He opened his mouth, closed it and opened it again. "Are we back to this?"

"You dropped everything to come running when she needed you. This sounds like your feelings run deeper than that of an old friend from college whom you hadn't even been in contact with for fifteen years."

His laugh was edged with bitterness. "I didn't have a lot going on when I got the call."

"You still care about her."

"That's not a crime. Look, she called *me*. Check her phone records. I was miles from here."

"Can you prove that?"

He started to say something but stopped and shook his head. "I told you. I was up in the mountains outside Big Sky."

"Did anyone see you?" she asked.

"Not that I know of."

"Then you raced here to save a woman who you hadn't seen in fifteen years."

"If you must know, she saved me." He looked away, then met her gaze. She saw his jaw muscles bunch. "I was about to drive off a cliff." He must have seen her shock. "I'm apparently suffering with PTSD—at least I have all of the symptoms. It was stupid and I regret even considering what I almost did. But I was only yards from the edge of the cliff, driving too fast in my pickup, when I got the call." He exhaled gruffly. "Happy?"

For a moment, she didn't know what to say. "You think she saved your life."

"That's what I thought at the time." He shook his head. "I don't know if I would have hit the brakes or not if my phone hadn't rung." He looked away again.

"I'm sorry." She realized this explained so much. If he thought she'd saved his life that day… "Do you still feel that she saved your life?"

"I don't know how I feel. All of this…" He raked a hand through his hair.

"Do you deny you have feelings for Rachel Collinwood?"

He chuckled. "I care what happens to her. But none of that has anything to do with what happened. I told you. I only recently reconnected with Rachel. That's how she had my number."

"When was the last time you reconnected with Mr. Collinwood?"

He looked down at his feet. "Years ago, just like I told you."

"At their wedding?"

He nodded, a muscle in his jaw tightening.

There was something there she couldn't put her finger

on. Whatever had happened at the wedding, though, was the key. "When you and Mrs. Collinwood reconnected recently, did she mention any conflict in her marriage?"

"It wasn't that kind of *reconnection*," he said. "We didn't share anything more personal than phone numbers."

"She was the one who contacted you? So you're on social media."

"One of my nieces insisted on signing me up. I hardly pay any attention to it."

"Until you saw a friend request from Rachel. But after you shared your number, you didn't call her?"

"No. I doubt I would have. She was married and a lot of water had flowed under that bridge."

Hitch nodded, confirming her suspicions about whatever had happened at the wedding. But did it pertain to the murder? It could be simply because Ford Cardwell had never gotten over the woman and had to distance himself from the two of them. Had Rachel known about his crush on her? Of course, Hitch thought. That was why she'd called him. "But here you are, coming to her defense."

"I came here to tell the sheriff what I heard during the phone call, that's all."

"You also said you came to Big Timber to make sure Rachel was all right."

When he didn't answer, she stared him down until he said, "Why are you trying to make something more out of this than it is?"

"Because Humphrey Collinwood is dead and I want to know why." She studied him openly for a moment.

He sighed, sounding worn out. "I want to know, as well. Maybe I want to know more than even you do. But other than the phone call, that's my only involvement in all this."

She wondered if he actually believed that. "Have you

ever heard of a case of domestic homicide involving a husband's shooting where the wife put the gun outside the house because she was afraid he would use it on her?"

"I'm not familiar with any domestic homicide cases," he said impatiently.

"The wife got off because it appeared she hadn't planned to kill him. And yet she ran outside, knowing the gun was there."

Ford shook his head. "You really do think that Rachel took a beating so she could kill her husband. That would mean that she set this all up."

She heard something in his voice. The idea wasn't a new one for him. He was wondering the same thing, but afraid to admit it. "Humphrey Collinwood is a very wealthy man, but I think you know that. Did you also know that Rachel signed a prenuptial agreement that she couldn't benefit from that wealth if they divorced?"

"I didn't know anything about their...marriage arrangements."

"Dead, she walks away with everything the two have accumulated since the marriage, which is no small amount. Had she divorced him, she could have gotten half of whatever their high-priced lawyers didn't take. In other words, a whole lot less, and it could have been years before she got her share if there was a long legal battle, since his business is tied up with his father's."

She watched him grind his teeth but he said nothing. "Here's what bothers me. Other than the huge coincidence of her pocket dialing you in particular, you didn't hear him threatening her on the phone. Normally in an argument like the one you thought you overheard, the husband would have been saying something as he attacked his wife. Also, why did she have the gun with her in the kitchen? If she was really afraid for her life, why not leave? Why not call 911? Because she needed him dead to get the money."

He shook his head. "What if it was exactly what it seems and Humphrey was beating her?"

"Do you really believe that?"

"I don't know what to believe, but I'm starting to wonder if Bart got to you. He wants his brand of justice and he has the money to buy it. And if I know him, which I do, he wants Rachel to pay for shooting his son. Did she really believe that Humphrey was going to beat her to death? I don't know. You're the one with all the answers. Not me." He got to his feet. "This interview is over." With that, Ford Cardwell stomped out.

Chapter 12

Ford walked away from his interrogation by the medical examiner feeling angry, scared and confused again. As if he hadn't been all of those since he'd answered his phone and heard a woman screaming. All of this felt...complicated. Complicated like Rachel herself.

Since the phone call, seeing her, overhearing her and Shyla talking earlier, one thing had become clear to him. Love was often blind. His certainly had been. This had made him see Rachel more clearly than he ever had before. The thought almost made him laugh. The shine had definitely come off those old feelings he'd had for her back in college.

Did he have his doubts about her story? Hell, yes. He kept remembering how completely awestruck Humphrey had been with her. Even though Humphrey had known that she'd married him for his money, he'd still loved her passionately, blindly, unconditionally. So what had happened?

Whatever it was, it had destroyed not just their marriage, but their lives.

He'd come to the hospital to see Rachel. But after his interview with Hitch, he didn't feel up to it. As he started out of the hospital, though, he received a text from her. Need your help. Rachel. XOXO. Hugs and kisses, followed by a smiley face.

As he pushed open her door, he heard her on the phone. She sounded...happy. The moment she saw him, she quickly disconnected.

"You're in a good mood," he said to her, hating that the medical examiner's suspicions had only made him aware of his own. Her injuries aside, her cheeks were flushed and she was the old Rachel, the one who turned heads when she walked past. It was as if she'd forgotten what had happened not all that long ago, ending with her killing her husband.

"That was my attorney on the phone," she said, smiling. "He said I will be booked tomorrow, but once I'm arraigned, he thinks he can get me bail so I won't have to spend any time in jail. That is such a relief."

"I'm so glad to hear it," Ford said. If her attorney really thought he could get her bail, then he must think the evidence to support her case was sufficient. Did that mean she was innocent? Would a jury see it that way?

"What can I do to help?" Ford asked, noticing that the bruising on her face was more pronounced even though her cuts and abrasions appeared to be healing.

"The sheriff took my clothing as evidence," Rachel said. "I can't show up in court in a hospital gown. I need something to wear."

Ford hadn't thought of that. Of course she would need clothes. He'd been feeling so helpless since he'd arrived here. Now there was actually something he could do to help. "I can buy you whatever you need."

"No, that's really sweet, but I prefer my own clothes since you can't get anything decent to wear in this town. Would you mind going out to the house?"

This was definitely the old Rachel, he thought, feeling more of the shine come off his infatuation with her. He didn't want to see her house, where she and Humphrey had lived until…it ended.

She gave him a pouty look he remembered so well when she'd wanted something. "It's a terrible inconvenience, I know."

"I don't mind." It felt like the least he could do.

Brightening, she smiled a wide smile, even though it seemed to hurt her to do so. How many times had she turned that smile on him back in college? The medical examiner had asked if Rachel had known how he'd felt about her all those years ago. He looked into her blue eyes. This time when his heart ached, it had nothing to do with an old crush. Of course she knew. Wasn't that why the medical examiner questioned why she'd called him even accidentally?

"I just want to look my best tomorrow in court." The smile instantly disappeared, replaced with tears. "I look awful enough after what Humphrey did to me."

It was so like Rachel to worry about her looks at a time like this. He wanted to laugh at how he'd romanticized coming to her rescue. Had he really thought that her call had been fate? That she'd saved his life? That if anyone could bring him back to life, it would be this woman he'd fantasized about for so long?

"Ford, I don't know what I would have done without you," she was saying. She held his gaze for a long moment before she reached for the pad and pen on the nightstand next to her bed. He wondered why she hadn't asked Shyla to do it for her. Then he felt guilty for even questioning it. Hadn't he told her he would do anything for her?

"I've made a list of what I need from my closet. I put the passcode on there so you can get in."

"That won't be necessary." He turned to see Hitch had come into the room. "I'd be happy to take Ford out to the house to get what you need. They've finished cleaning for your return and I have the passcode to get inside."

"I don't need you to come along," he said quickly. "I can handle it."

"I want to check something out there anyway," the medical examiner said. "We can go now. Unless you have something else you have to do," she said to him.

She knew he had nothing he had to do. "No. Now's fine." He shifted his gaze back to Rachel in time to see dislike written all over her face. Her jaw was tight. Ice glittered in her blue eyes. She quickly changed her expression.

"Perfect," she said and handed him the list before grabbing his hand. Her hand was as cold as her eyes as she smiled up at him and said, "I owe you. Thank you again."

"I'll wait for you in the hallway," Hitch said and left.

Rachel let go of his hand as she stared after the medical examiner. "That woman." She shook her head. "She scares me."

Ford nodded. "She scares everyone."

"No, she has it in for me. I can tell. She's questioned me repeatedly. Is that her job?"

"I think in this instance it is." He wasn't sure if he should tell her Hitch's suspicions. But didn't she have a right to know what she was up against? "From what I hear, she has free rein. The governor apparently asked her to look into your case. At least that's what I overheard when I was down at the sheriff's office."

"Bart's doing, no doubt." Rachel's jaw tightened again, muscles bunching before she unclenched it. "If he gets his way, I'll go to the electric chair."

He could have told her that Montana didn't have an electric chair, but the state still had lethal injection—though it hadn't been used for a while, as far as he knew.

"It's so unfair." She touched the small new bandage on her cheekbone and winced. "It doesn't matter what his son did to me, not just that night but others." She looked away as if embarrassed.

"Why didn't you leave him?" Ford asked impulsively. "If he was hurting you…"

When her blue eyes met his again, they were swimming in tears. "Because I loved him and I thought…" She shook her head. "He was always so sorry afterward and so sweet for a while until…he wasn't." She covered her face with her hands for a moment. "I still can't believe he's dead. All of it just seems like a bad nightmare. I keep waiting to wake up."

"I know." He felt the same way. "I better go. I'll get everything on the list," he said, carefully folding the paper and putting it into his shirt pocket. "I'll bring the clothes back tonight so you'll be ready in the morning."

"I'll never be ready for what I'm going to have to face tomorrow. Why do I have to prove anything? Can't they look at me and see…?" She shook her head. "How could this be happening? I'm the real victim here. Our judicial system is so messed up that a woman can't defend herself against a husband who's trying to kill her?"

He didn't know what to say. "You rest. I'll see you later."

Out in the hallway, Hitch was leaning against the wall, waiting for him.

* * *

On the drive out to the Collinwood Ranch, Hitch could tell that Ford was still wary of her as if she was the enemy. She'd seen enough from the doorway of Rachel Collinwood's hospital room, though, to see how the woman manipulated him. The question was, how long had she been playing him?

As the huge rambling house came into view, Hitch saw that all the lights in the entire house must be on. She suspected a person could see it from space. The cleaners must have left the lights on. Hitch knew that she hadn't turned them on.

The crime scene tape had been removed since the last time she was out here. The sheriff had told her that he'd hired cleaners with Rachel's permission. Hitch parked and glanced over at Ford. He was staring at the house, looking a little dumbstruck. "Nice digs, huh."

He said nothing as he opened the passenger-side door and stepped out. She followed, curious what he was going to think of this house and the way Rachel and Humphrey had been living.

Once inside the house, she asked, "Would you like to see where it happened?"

"No," he said, glancing toward the kitchen and then looking away as he removed his Stetson.

She saw that he had the list Rachel had given him in his other hand. He seemed to be in a hurry to get this task finished. "You've never been here before?"

His gaze shot back to her. "No. I already told you—"

"It was just a question."

He shook his head. "No question is just a question with you, State Medical Examiner Roberts, and we both know it."

"Please, call me Hitch."

"Are you always so suspicious of people's motives, Hitch?" he asked.

"It comes with the job. Getting to the truth isn't always easy."

"Whom are you kidding?" he said. "You've already made up your mind about this case."

"What makes you think that? Just because I'm suspicious?"

"No," he said with a laugh. "You were suspicious of Rachel right from the very beginning. Admit it."

"Not right from the very beginning."

"Then when?" he demanded.

"If you must know, it was the phone call. I have trouble with coincidences."

"They happen."

She smiled and nodded. "But did it happen this time? The fact that it wasn't just any number she happened to call has to make a person wonder. Calling a man who she knows is still in love with her—"

"I'm not still in love with her."

He sounded adamant about that. "No?" she asked in surprise.

"Can we please get this over with?" he asked, his voice cracking with anger. "You're wrong about me. Humphrey was my friend. If I thought for a minute that she'd somehow set the whole thing up so she could murder him..."

"What would you do, Ford?" Hitch asked. "Walk away?"

"Yes," he said. "And not look back—after I was sure that justice had been done."

She studied him for a long moment. She thought of what she knew about his military career, the man who'd risked his life to save the men on his plane. She believed him. "I suppose we'd better get to that list of yours," she said, turning to lead the way down the hall to Rachel's massive walk-in closet. "I figured you'd need my help to find whatever she's planning to wear tomorrow."

"I think I can manage, thank you."

She laughed. "You haven't seen her closet yet."

As they reached the master bedroom, Hitch walked in and stopped to look back so she didn't miss Ford's reaction. He tried to hide it, but she could tell from his expression that he was taken aback at the size and splendor of the place.

"The closet is this way. They also had separate bathrooms." She walked into the closet with its sitting area. The walls around it were full of clothes, shoes, purses, coats. It looked more like an upscale department store. Hitch wondered if a person could wear all of this apparel even in a year.

"Some people would kill to keep this kind of lifestyle," she said, baiting him in the hopes of getting an honest reaction out of him.

"So Rachel's guilty because she married well?" Ford said.

Hitch turned to look at him, pleased that she'd ruffled his feathers. "She's guilty if she orchestrated what happened here in order to kill her husband for his money. I'm suspicious for the same reasons you are."

"I didn't say I was suspicious." He raked a hand through his thick dark hair. He wore it longer than usual and wasn't used to it, she thought, because this wasn't the first time she'd seen his long fingers raking through it. It certainly wasn't the military cut she'd seen in the photos she'd found of him during his distinguished career.

"You didn't have to say you were suspicious," Hitch said.

He sighed. "What about proof? Don't you need that?"

She met his gaze. "Of course. Proof goes both ways.

She could still surprise me. The call could be a coincidence and she could have killed her husband in self-defense." She saw that he hadn't expected that. What she didn't say was that from experience, she knew that Rachel wouldn't surprise her. All her instincts told her that the woman was guilty as hell.

But she could use Ford's help, so she didn't share that detail with him. Rachel trusted him because she believed she could control him. It was Hitch's hope that the woman would lower her guard and make a mistake. Ford was an honorable man. He'd proved that. What would he do if he found out that Rachel had murdered her husband in cold blood? Walk away like he had fifteen years ago? Not until he'd seen justice done, he'd said.

Which was why Hitch was more worried about what Rachel would do if Ford suddenly became more than dispensable. If he became a liability... The thought made her shudder. If Ford found out the truth about Rachel, it could get him killed.

Rachel had no intention of going to prison for the rest of her life. And if Hitch was right, the woman had already killed once. To save herself...? Hitch had no doubt that Rachel would kill again.

"So let me help you with the list." Hitch held out her hand and waited until he handed the note to her. Rachel's handwriting was neat, the list organized right down to the smiley face on the bottom that was for Ford. Just like the small heart the woman had drawn on the smiley face's cheek. And the kisses and hugs. She handed the note back. "Why don't you read it to me and I'll find the clothes?" He seemed relieved to let her. "Let's see, first on the list. Was that a white suit with navy piping?" She moved to the suit area. "Nice that she has everything color coordinated. That will make it easier."

"I'll find the pumps she wants," he said behind her as she thumbed through a variety of white suit sets.

It took them a while, but they found everything on the list. As they loaded the items into the largest piece of luggage from the closet, as per Rachel's instructions on the list, Hitch said, "Tell me about Humphrey. You roomed with him for four years at college, were his best friend. Did you ever see any indication that he would do something like this?"

At first, she didn't think he would answer. But as they carried the luggage out to the car—a large suitcase and Rachel's makeup case—he said, "No, I never did. But that doesn't mean—"

"Did he know how you felt about Rachel?" She sensed the heat of his gaze.

"No. Maybe." He shook his head. "Apparently, I'm pretty transparent—at least according to *you*."

She slid behind the wheel and waited for him to climb into the passenger side. "Why do you think Rachel reached out to you on social media after all this time?"

"She'd heard I was back in Montana. She wanted me to know she was in Montana, too." He looked out his side window for a moment as she started the SUV's engine. Was that when the idea had come to Rachel, the beginning of a plan to kill her husband? "Maybe there was trouble in her marriage and she needed someone she could trust to talk to."

"She doesn't have a friend she could confide in?" Hitch started up the road that would lead them off the ranch. In her rearview mirror, the Collinwood house was dark again—just like the night around them.

"Look, I don't know why she contacted me. Maybe out of

nostalgia. Anyway, she has a best friend here. Shyla. Shyla Birch. She's probably the one you should be talking to. She's a friend of Rachel's from college. Shyla should know more about Rachel and Humphrey's marriage than I do."

"Another friend from college?" Hitch said, glancing over at him in surprise. "Did they also only recently reconnect?"

"You make me wish I hadn't said anything."

"You told me because you're worried about Rachel. Like me, you want to know the truth. You're also worried that I might be right."

He shook his head again. "Don't be telling me what I'm thinking, all right?"

"I'm not psychic, but I have good eyesight. Rachel knew about your accident and discharge from the service, didn't she? She caught you when you were…vulnerable, knowing she could count on you."

His expression said she'd hit the nail on the head.

He glanced away quickly and swore. "I understand you digging into Humphrey's and Rachel's lives, but I really wish you would stay out of mine." His voice was rough with emotion.

"I wish I could, but once you got that phone call? Rachel pulled you right into her mess."

"I don't know how many times I have to say this. She didn't mean to call me. She was probably trying to call 911."

"Glad you brought that up. She botched calling 911, but didn't have any trouble doing it after she killed her husband," she said as she drove away from the Collinwood Ranch.

"He was attacking her during the first call," Ford pointed out.

She glanced over at him. His eyes were dark with anger. Or was it worry? "You're right. It could have been just one of those strange coincidences. Then again, some might even call it fate."

"Not you, though," he said, an edge to his voice. "You only believe what you can prove."

She smiled. "Exactly."

Ford was glad when the ride out to the Collinwood Ranch was over. After seeing the place, he couldn't help but remember what Shyla had told him about how unhappy Rachel had been living there. It was isolated, but so grand. Rachel had once told him that she wanted one day to live in a palace and have so many clothes to wear that it would be hard to pick out something to wear. And yet she'd been miserable.

He couldn't understand it. Now Rachel was in more trouble than he felt she realized. If Hitch and Bart had their way, Rachel would be going to prison for life or worse. Hitch had done her best to make him doubt what he'd heard. Like her, he had his questions. And maybe, if he was being truthful, his suspicions.

Hitch had dropped him off at the hospital. She'd offered to help him with the luggage but he'd declined. "I can handle it, Ms. Roberts."

"Hitch. I'm sure you can," she'd said before pulling away in her patrol SUV.

"Did you have any trouble finding everything?" Rachel asked anxiously when he brought in her large suitcase and cosmetic bag.

"No. Hitch helped."

"Hitch? You're on a first-name basis with that woman?"

He looked at her, unable to miss the razor-blade sharpness of her tone, and saw that she was visibly upset. "What is it you're asking?"

"She wants to put me in prison. She'll do whatever she can to do that—especially if she thinks she can use you against me," Rachel snapped.

"Because I'm your defense?"

She started to say something, but apparently changed her mind, closing her mouth. Her blue eyes flashed with anger. He watched her try to gain control again. She hadn't expected him to stand up to her.

"I'm sorry," Rachel said quietly. "I know none of this is your fault. It's just that she keeps trying to dig up something against me."

"There's nothing she can dig up, right?" he asked.

"No. But she said she had to go back out to the house. What was that about?"

"I don't know."

"She didn't search the place or act like she was looking for something?"

"No, not that I saw," he said and felt himself frowning. "What would she be looking for?"

"I don't know," Rachel cried and busied herself smoothing the sheets over her. "All of this is so terrifying."

He said nothing, studying her. Even with the years that had passed, he realized with a start that he still knew this woman. While he'd definitely put her up on his own pedestal all those years ago, he didn't think she'd ever truly hidden her flaws from him. He'd just forgotten how she'd used her smile to always keep him on her side when she and Humphrey had an argument.

Ford thought of what Hitch had said, insinuating that he'd put all the blame on Humphrey—rather than Rachel— for forcing him to walk away from the two of them after the wedding.

"I didn't mean to snap at you," Rachel said into the heavy silence that had fallen between them.

"You're under a lot of stress."

"I am," she said, sounding close to tears. "I never thought my life would turn out like this."

"I'm sure Humphrey didn't either." He hadn't meant it the way she'd taken it. Her shocked look, the color that shot to her cheeks, the horrified widening of her eyes, made him regret it.

"You blame me, too?" she said, her voice breaking.

"No, no. That isn't what I meant. I don't know what happened that day. But I do know that Humphrey would never have wanted it to go so wrong."

She turned her head away, clearly dismissing him.

"I should go," he said and started to move toward the door. "I'll see you in court tomorrow."

As he stepped out of the room, he felt that familiar melancholy take hold of him. He fought to pull himself out of it. He had to see this through. But that thought didn't lift him back up—not the way it had at first.

He considered the woman he'd left in the hospital room as he left. Hitch thought he was a fool. She didn't think he saw through Rachel's helpless act. Rachel was scared, no doubt about that. But the woman had never been helpless. Was that why she'd had a loaded gun? When had she learned to fire it? Or had she just gotten lucky with that one shot?

Ford swore under his breath. Hitch and her suspicions had him doubting everything. Rachel had always used her feminine wiles to get what she wanted. But not all women did. The thought made him think of Hitch.

So what if Rachel loved the finer things in life. That didn't make her a murderer. And Humphrey? Ford couldn't help but remember when they'd been best friends. Like brothers. Had Humphrey turned into a violent man who'd done so much damage to his wife's face and taken a bullet for it?

With a start, Ford realized that if he were a juror at Rachel's trial, he might find her guilty of setting this whole thing up to kill her husband for his money. Never in his life would he have thought Rachel—the woman he'd once adored—could be a cold-blooded killer. Until now. And he hated himself for even considering it.

Chapter 13

The courtroom had a chill to it this morning, Ford thought as he took a seat on the hard wooden bench a few rows back. Bart was already seated in the row behind the prosecutor. Ford watched the two talking quietly. They separated quickly when Rachel was brought in to take her seat alongside her attorney.

Attorney Denton Drake was an elderly man with a pleasant smile and a fatherly attitude toward Rachel, Ford noted. He wondered if the lawyer was good at his job. Rachel needed all the help she could get, if the medical examiner and Bart Collinwood had anything to do with it.

But Rachel was a worthy opponent. In her expensive, beautifully cut white suit, she looked beautiful. Her blond hair was up, gold gleamed at her earlobes and her bandage had been removed. He noted that she hadn't used the makeup he'd brought to the hospital. Her attorney's idea to let the judge see the damage Humphrey had allegedly done? Or had it been Rachel's idea?

Ford saw Hitch drop off some papers for the prosecutor before she spotted him and, to his irritation, slid in beside him.

"Good morning," she said quietly.

"Is it?" He caught her scent, clean and understated, just like the woman herself. He scrutinized her more closely. All the other times he'd seen her, she'd been dressed in either canvas overalls and jacket with *Medical Examiner* stenciled on the back or jeans and a T-shirt with a jean jacket. Her auburn hair was usually pulled up in a knot at the back of her neck. But this morning she wore a nice-fitting gray suit with a white blouse that was opened at the neck. Her hair fell below her shoulders in a cascade of burnished curls. The woman was striking. He wondered how he hadn't noticed it before.

She turned those tropical green eyes on him and seemed to be taking him in with the same kind of scrutiny. He'd had to go shopping for clothes since he'd left in what he'd been wearing, so his jeans and Western shirt were new. His boots were old ones he'd left at his father's place years ago.

"Didn't get much sleep, huh," she said, studying him with that observant look of hers.

Before he could comment, she shifted her gaze to Rachel, who was talking animatedly to her lawyer. "Looks like she got more sleep than either of us."

"The sleep of the innocent," he said.

Hitch chuckled, but then turned serious. "Does that mean you aren't innocent? Or maybe you have more of a conscience?"

Ford shook his head. He wasn't up for another word battle with this woman. He was relieved when the bailiff called out "All rise!" and the judge came into the room. Her Honor signaled for everyone to sit. "Let's make this quick. I have a lot on the docket today."

Ford listened as the charges against Rachel were read. Deliberate homicide? The judge asked how she pleaded and Rachel said, "Not guilty, Your Honor."

Her attorney asked that she be given bail since this was a justifiable use of force. "She has already surrendered her passport and isn't a flight risk, Your Honor. She has agreed not to leave the state, but simply return to her home north of town."

The prosecutor rose from his chair. "Mrs. Collinwood has sufficient assets to get herself another passport in another name and disappear. I don't think the lack of her passport would stop her."

Rachel's attorney argued that she had no priors, had been a model citizen and that most of the assets were in her husband's name and not accessible to her due to a prenuptial agreement she'd signed. "Mrs. Collinwood is the victim here, Your Honor."

The judge banged her gavel. "Bail is set at five million."

Rachel gasped loudly. In the stunned silence that followed, she turned to look back at Ford, tears in her eyes. He felt that old familiar pull at his heart in spite of everything. But it was accompanied by nausea. He honestly didn't know the truth about her and feared he might never know.

"What will happen to her now?" Ford asked Hitch as Rachel was being led to a jail cell until she could post her bail bond. The courtroom began to fill again. They walked out into the deserted hallway.

"If she can raise enough liquid assets, she'll be released

until her trial," Hitch said. "Otherwise, she can post a property bail equivalent to five million dollars."

"If she can't?"

"Then she'll stay in jail until her trial."

"You're that sure this will go to trial?" he asked.

"She killed a man."

"Yes, but—"

"The law doesn't recognize…yes, but."

"What will happen to her if…she's found guilty?"

"During the trial it will be decided if she used justifiable force to stop her husband. If so, she could be charged with mitigated homicide and serve anywhere from two to forty years."

"Forty years!"

"But if the jury finds that she used extreme force that wasn't justifiable, then she could be convicted of deliberate homicide and could be sentenced to life, which is a minimum of thirty years."

He looked sick.

"Or, depending on the judge, she could get ten to a hundred years. We do still have the death penalty in Montana. Lethal injection, though there hasn't been an execution in years."

He clearly couldn't stand the thought. "How is that possible if she was fighting for her life?" Ford said angrily.

"It will be up to a jury and what evidence there is to the contrary."

"Evidence you're gathering against her."

"Only if the evidence is there."

He raked a hand through his hair, looking miserable. "No one is stupid enough to gamble their life for money." She raised an eyebrow, making him furious. "Rachel might be materialistic, but she isn't stupid." He got a smirk at that.

"You're wrong. She would have had to know that she might not get away with it."

"Not if she covered all her bets, including making sure you heard enough of the argument that you are now a very large part of her defense. I have to admit, the phone call was pretty brilliant. A medaled war hero just back home? You make a good witness because any jury would see that you're also an honest, honorable man."

He swore under his breath. "You're making Rachel out to be a mastermind criminal and me a saint."

"Most criminals think they're smarter than law enforcement." Her eyes twinkled mischievously. "And I don't think you're a saint. I just think you're a nice guy who fell in love with the wrong woman and has never let himself get over it or the guilt."

"I'm glad you have me all figured out," he said.

She could tell that he was having trouble getting his mind around all this because he didn't think like a criminal. In her job, she'd learned to do just that.

"You still believe she would do this knowing she might go to prison for years?" he said, sounding even more incredulous because he couldn't imagine doing anything like it.

"I'm still on the fence. But it isn't up to me to decide. Once I finish my investigation and provide what evidence I've found to the prosecutor, then it will be up to a jury to make the final decision." She didn't tell him that she'd talked the governor into letting her tap Rachel's phone now that she would be getting out on bail. Hitch couldn't wait to see whom the woman called over the next few days.

"Admit it—you want her to be guilty," Ford said.

"The way you want her to be innocent? No. I just want the truth."

"What makes you think I don't?"

She smiled. "You don't want to believe that she's capable of cold-blooded murder because even if you aren't still in love with her, Humphrey was once your best friend." Hitch started to step away. "Maybe sometime you'll tell me what happened at the wedding. In the meantime, be careful. We have your testimony about the phone call. Your job is done until the trial. Rachel won't be needing you anymore. I don't think you want to stay beyond your welcome or you're going to make her regret calling you."

He shook his head. "You think she used me." Hitch said nothing. "I'm not as blind when it comes to her as you think."

"I hope for your sake that's true, Ford. By the way, someone slid a note under my hotel room door this morning right before I left to come here. You wouldn't know anything about that, would you?"

Back in her room, Hitch considered the note she'd found and bagged as evidence. It was short and to the point: *You need to leave town while you still can.* It had been typewritten, probably on a computer, on plain white paper. She would have it checked for prints, but she wasn't hopeful.

She had ruffled someone's feathers—nothing new there. She didn't think the note was from Rachel, but from someone close to her. Now, who would that be? Not Ford. She'd seen his surprise when she'd asked him about the note.

Spreading out all the evidence she'd collected on her bed back in her hotel room, she went through it again. She was missing something. She could feel it. But she had someone worried. That gave her hope that she was getting close.

Picking up the photos of Rachel Collinwood's injuries that DCI had sent her, she studied them, wondering what it was that was bothering her besides Ford Cardwell.

He was a principled man who believed in right and wrong. Yet he still had feelings for Rachel Collinwood, no matter what he said. Hitch liked him, which made this case even harder. She hated that he was involved and might get in even deeper before it was over. Would he help Rachel cover up her crime, if she asked? Rachel wouldn't ask unless she was desperate, and that was what worried Hitch maybe the most. What would Rachel do if Ford turned her down?

Hitch tried to concentrate on the cuts, bruises and abrasions on Rachel Collinwood's face in the photos. Frowning, she noticed a distinct mark on the young woman's cheek that she hadn't before. Pulling out her magnifying glass, she took a closer look. It appeared to be an odd-shaped bruise, the kind an unusual ring might make. It definitely wasn't Rachel's husband's ring with the traces of her blood and skin on it.

Pulling out the photos she'd taken during the autopsy, she studied Humphrey Collinwood's ring again. Nothing about it would have made that distinctive bruise. Was there anything in the kitchen that could have made that kind of mark? She studied the photos of the items lying on the kitchen floor and counter. She was becoming more convinced by the moment that the bruise had been made by a ring—just not one worn by the woman's husband.

All along, she'd known that if the murder scene had been staged, Rachel Collinwood hadn't acted alone. The evidence seemed to be piling up. That was what she loved about criminals. They usually made at least one mistake—often more—even with the best-laid plans. If Hitch could find the person who had been wearing this unusual ring...

Her cell phone rang and she saw that it was the lab on the toxicology samples taken from Humphrey Collinwood.

"Tell me you found a drug in his system that would have made him immobile," she said into the phone, knowing it would be the last piece she needed to prove her suspicions were true.

Chapter 14

Ford wasn't sure that Rachel would want to see him. When he'd heard she'd made bail and had been released to return home, he'd called her.

"Ford, I thought you'd gone back to Big Sky," she said, sounding surprised he was still in town and annoyingly reminding him of what Hitch had said. "I appreciate everything you've done for me, but there really isn't anything anyone can do now until the trial. Not that you have to come back for that. I wouldn't want to put you through all of this again. It's bad enough I'm going to have to go through it."

She was dismissing him. Both the sheriff and the medical examiner had his statement. It was all Rachel had needed from him, just as Hitch had said.

"What will you do now?" he asked, hating these gnawing doubts that were haunting him. He knew he'd been listening to Hitch and had bought into her suspicions that he'd been a pawn in Rachel's plan to kill her husband. It wasn't a comfortable place for him—questioning whether the woman he'd once loved hadn't just used him, but instead had set him up so she could get away with the killing of his once best friend.

"There is nothing I can do but hope that all charges will be dropped and that it won't even go to a trial," Rachel was saying. "The sheriff seems to think I might have a chance of avoiding any more pain." The sheriff might feel that way. But not Hitch. She would keep digging. "Thanks for calling, though," she said, clearly trying to get off the line.

"You'll let me know what happens?"

"Oh, I'm sure you'll read about it in the newspapers."

And just like that, she disconnected. He knew he couldn't leave town feeling like this. He didn't think he could live with these doubts about her. She couldn't have involved him, setting this all up, knowing how he'd felt about her. He wanted to be wrong in the worst way. He had to see her again.

As he topped the rise, he spotted the ranch house sprawled below him in the evening light. He passed a side road that went back into a stand of pines. A stray thought hit him. What a perfect observation point. A person could park in those trees and see all the comings and goings at the main house.

He hated that he'd even thought such a thing as he drove down to the house. Given the way she'd been on the phone, he doubted she'd be happy to see him, but he couldn't leave until he put his mind to rest. This felt unfinished. Not that he knew what kind of closure he expected to get. Certainly not a confession.

A shadow passed quickly before a large plate-glass window as he pulled up in the front yard. Getting out, he walked up the steps to the massive deck that spanned across the front and side of the house. The views from here were incredible—all rolling hills and green pines and pasture all the way to the mountains. He hadn't noticed when he'd come out here with Hitch. He'd been too uncomfortable in her presence knowing that she was watching him every second.

He paused now, taking it all in, wondering if she appreciated how breathtakingly beautiful it was out here. After ringing the doorbell, he turned again to stare out at the expanse.

Where he lived in Big Sky was different but equally as beautiful. He just hadn't noticed it either since he'd gotten back to Montana. He'd been too much in his own head, too consumed with what had happened when the plane he was piloting went down. Coming here had forced him to feel again, he thought, telling himself he shouldn't have any regrets no matter how this ended.

It took Rachel a while to answer the door. He'd had to ring the bell several more times even though he'd seen her shadow pass that window when he'd driven up. He knew she was home. He'd almost think that she didn't want to see him. Too bad. He wanted to see *her.*

"Ford? What are you doing here?" she said when she opened the door only partway.

"I couldn't leave without telling you goodbye in person."

"Well, isn't that sweet. But you needn't have driven all the way out here." She was standing in the doorway, blocking him as if she didn't want him inside. It made him sad and all the more determined to see what she was hiding.

"I wanted to see for myself how you were doing. I don't like how we left things at the hospital yesterday." She started to say she was fine when he cut her off. "Why don't you invite me in? I promise not to take up too much of your time."

Rachel flushed as if just realizing how rude she was being since he was her alibi—her defense. A fluke, just as he'd thought? Or all part of a murderous plan?

"Of course. I'm sorry," she said, stepping back. "You had sounded on the phone like you were anxious to return home. Come in." She said it loud enough that he felt she was warning someone that they had company. It made him sick inside.

"Are you alone?" he asked, wanting to watch her lie to him.

"Why would you ask that? Of course I am."

He met her gaze, his disappointment in her making him feel even more nauseous. It was true. Over the past fifteen years and probably longer, she'd been the perfect woman in his memory. He'd always imagined her in that dress trying to feed that squirrel. The vision used to make him smile. But apparently the squirrel scene had been a well-planned scheme only to meet Humphrey. Rachel, it seemed, had a talent for staged plots.

"Why don't you come in here?" She motioned toward the kitchen—the same kitchen where she'd shot her husband. "I'll get us something to drink and we can take it out on the deck. It's such a lovely evening." As he followed her into the very white open room, he felt himself cringe. This was where it had happened. Right here. He found himself staring at the floor, imagining Humphrey lying dead there.

"You still like a cold beer, don't you?" she asked, her back to him as she grabbed up some dirty drink glasses and put them in the sink. He'd stopped in the middle of the room and was still staring at the floor, trying not to imagine the gruesome scene.

When she turned, she must have seen his expression. "Are you all right?"

He realized she was standing in front of him holding out a bottle of beer.

"You do still drink beer, don't you?"

He nodded and took it from her. "Rachel, isn't this where—"

Belatedly, she seemed to realize what was wrong with him. She flushed, cheeks hot with anger. "I can't think about that anymore. I have to live here. I can't leave the state. I have to make the best of it," she said, taking her glass of wine and heading for the glass doors. There were two chairs facing the east and a small table between them on the deck. He watched her pick up an ashtray from the table and empty it over the side of the deck railing.

"Are you smoking again?" he asked, feeling shaken by how insensitive she was about all of this.

She shook her head, her back to him. "One of the hired hands stopped by earlier. Nasty habit. Let me get rid of this." She moved past him to return to the kitchen. When she came back out, she had the wine bottle in her hand— a hand she seemed to be fighting to keep from shaking.

He sat down in one of the chairs and watched her slide into the one next to him, exposing a lot of thigh. She wore shorts and a sleeveless top, both in a pale yellow that accented her fresh spray-on tan. There were bruises on her arms that looked like dark fingertips pressed into her flesh. Were they from Humphrey?

"What happened, Rachel?" She looked startled for a moment before he added, "What happened with you and me?"

With a relieved look, she leaned back in her chair and took a sip of her wine.

"Nothing. We've always been good friends. It's my fault I let you walk out of Humphrey's and my life."

"You know I wanted to be more than friends."

She smiled over at him. It wasn't one of her smoldering sunshine smiles.

It held a note of pity that made his heart ache even more. "It was always Humphrey, wasn't it," he said. "From that first day with the squirrel."

"He said it was love at first sight."

"Was that what it was for you?" he asked, suddenly aware of the sweating beer bottle in his hand. He took a drink. It was cold and bubbled all the way down his throat. It was the first sip of alcohol he'd had in a long time.

"I suppose it was love at first sight," she said, not looking at him.

"When did Humphrey...change?"

"Change?" She sounded puzzled by the question as she looked at him and frowned.

Ford met her gaze. "Surely he didn't hurt you at first."

"No, you're right. It started when he was having trouble with his father, the business, you know. He would come home from New York in a bad mood and any little thing would set him off. He knew I wasn't happy here and that upset him. Things just kept getting worse."

"Why weren't you happy here?" he had to ask as he looked out at this beautiful country.

"Are you kidding? After New York City?" She shook her head. "It's duller than dirt out here. He brought me here to punish me."

"For what?"

She shook her head again and sipped her wine.

He looked away, trying to imagine this Humphrey Collinwood compared to the one he'd lived with most of their time at university. There had never been an easier-going man. "I thought I knew him, so it is so hard for me to understand how this could have happened."

"Why are you questioning me about this? Humphrey had a dark side that he hid from everyone else," she snapped. "It's typical of abusers. I suspect his father abused his mother. That's usually how it works."

"You've researched the subject, have you?"

She didn't answer, but he saw her stiffen in anger. Nor did she look at him. He dragged his gaze away, unable to look at her either.

After a few moments, he relented. "I guess most people hide their…dark sides," he said and finally glanced over at her again. "You're different than I remember."

Rachel flipped her hair back, her blue eyes sparking. "You're angry with me because I had to shoot him." She bit her lip. Tears welled in her eyes. "I'll never forgive myself. Is that what you need to hear? I should never have grabbed that gun. I thought that if he saw it, he wouldn't…" She looked away, wiping at her tears before taking a gulp of her wine.

At that moment, she made him doubt himself. Maybe Humphrey *did* have a dark side. Maybe she *had been* afraid he would kill her. Maybe she *was* here alone. The house was so huge, it probably did take her a while to get to the front door. And the glasses she'd put in the sink? Hadn't she said one of the hired hands had stopped by? It would explain the cigarettes in the ashtray on the deck, as well.

He hated mistrusting her, questioning everything about the young woman she'd been in college, comparing her to the one sitting out here with him right now. The beautiful warm summer Montana evening was like a caress. He realized that, if anything, Rachel had gotten more beautiful. Maybe she was the same young woman he'd known in college. Maybe he was the one who'd changed. Maybe Humphrey had, too. Ford reminded himself that he was a big enough mess without rewriting what had once been the sweetest part of his life, his friendship with Humphrey and Rachel.

And yet he couldn't seem to help himself. "You knew I was half in love with you," he said and met her gaze.

Her expression softened. "I know." She reached for his hand and squeezed it. "I always cared about you, Ford. I wanted the best for you. Humphrey and I never knew why you'd exited our lives like you had right after our wedding. Did you know he tried to reach you numerous times?"

He knew. "You know why I left like I did."

Her light laugh didn't quite come off the way she must have meant it. "You and I should never drink that much together." She turned back to him, something almost coquettish in those blue eyes.

"Neither of us were drunk, Rachel. You dragged me into one of the spare rooms and told me you wanted me to make love to you," he said.

Her lips quirked up on one side. "I believe you kissed me back, and as I remember, that was your hand on my—"

"If someone hadn't tried the door, would you have actually gone through with it?" Would he have? It was something he'd always wondered about even in his guilt over the incident. The memory of it filled him with shame. He'd kissed his best friend's girlfriend and he'd wanted to make love with her. If he could have, he would have stolen her away in a heartbeat. Knowing that, he knew he was no longer Humphrey's best friend and couldn't stand being around the two of them after that.

"We'll never know, will we?" Rachel took a sip of her wine and gazed out at the rolling hills of the ranch.

He put his nearly full beer bottle down on the small table. A breeze blew her long hair into her eyes, and for a moment, she looked like the girl he'd known. "I should go." Getting to his feet, he walked toward the end of the deck that led to where he'd left his SUV. He had no desire to go back through that kitchen.

"Ford!" she called after him.

He turned to look back at her. For a moment, in that soft pale twilight, she looked just as he'd remembered her.

"Thank you."

"I didn't do anything."

"You were here for me when I needed you most. I'll never forget that."

He nodded and started to say it was nice seeing her again. But that would have been a lie. All the pain he'd felt before that phone call seemed like nothing compared to this.

Behind him, he heard Rachel's cell phone ring. Once, twice… She picked up. "Shyla, hi. I'm glad you called." She rose, the chair scraping as she headed back inside the house.

As he passed the front window, out of the corner of his eye, he saw movement. Rachel had lied. She wasn't alone. He wasn't even sure that had been Shyla on the phone.

Chapter 15

"Tell me you found something," Hitch repeated into the phone. If there was a drug in Humphrey Collinwood's system, one that would have made him a walking zombie—

"We ran the entire spectrum of possible drugs," the lab tech said. "I'm sorry. We found nothing."

Nothing? Her mind whirled as she got up to pace her hotel room. She'd been so sure that in order to shoot her husband in the face the way she had, Rachel would have had to subdue him somehow. Otherwise, the reaction of a man who was beating his wife wouldn't have been to just stand there while she pulled a gun. Had he charged her and Rachel got lucky, getting a shot off before he reached her? The marks on his back showed that he'd fallen backward, landing on the broken pottery and glass on the floor.

"Thanks for trying," Hitch said into the phone, hating that she'd wasted the lab's time and her own.

"Wait a minute. Lori's here. She wants to talk to you." She handed over the phone.

"Hitch, I heard about the lab tests you asked to be done. Bradley and I both looked on her computer for anything that might need to be red flagged."

"I'm guessing she was too smart to look up How to Kill Your Husband and Make It Look Like Domestic Abuse."

"No, but something came up that you might find interesting. Mrs. Collinwood did research a common drug used on horses called ketamine."

Hitch sat up, feeling her pulse take off. Bingo. Hitch almost let out a *whoop*, before she caught herself. "But you didn't find it in the drug tests you ran."

"That's because it leaves the system quickly. It works as an anesthesia and is often used on horses. The drug would have been readily available on the ranch. Mrs. Collinwood would have had access to it." Hitch thanked her and quickly got off the phone.

She knew a little about the drug, but quickly looked up the symptoms, especially for large doses. The words leaped out at her.

Blocks sensory perception.

Distortion of environment.

Diminished reflexes.

Muscle rigidity.

Available in a clear liquid or powder form.

"I think I know how she did it," Hitch said to the empty room, unable to hold back her excitement. Unfortunately, it wasn't enough to convict Rachel Collinwood of murder. It was just another piece of a larger puzzle.

Her excitement waned. She had enough to confirm her suspicions—including that odd bruise on Rachel's face. But she didn't have enough for a conviction. Had there been a drug in Humphrey's bloodstream, she could have wrapped up this case. There had to be a way to prove deliberate homicide because all her instincts told her that Rachel Collinwood was lying. She couldn't bear the thought that she hadn't done a good enough job and the woman might get away with murder.

At a sudden pounding at her hotel room door, Hitch quickly opened it. Her mind was already wondering, what now?

"Are you going to let Rachel get away with murdering my son?" Bart Collinwood demanded as he pushed his way into her room.

"I'm still gathering evidence," she said and hurried to gather up the papers and photographs she had strewn across her bed. She finished and turned to look at him. His face was flushed with anger and grief. Her heart went out to him because she felt his frustration only too well.

"I know my son." He shook his head angrily, looking close to tears. "He would never have laid a hand on her unless…"

She felt her pulse jump. "Unless?"

Bart looked away. "He just wouldn't have."

She knew even before she asked the question. "He'd hit her before?"

"No, no," he said at once. "Not my son."

She saw him swallow and knew.

"My wife and I…." He couldn't meet her gaze.

"Your son saw abuse at home is what you're saying."

His head rocked up. "Not like you're thinking. I lost my temper and slapped my wife in front of him once. Humphrey was horrified. He never forgave me or believed it had never happened before or since."

She wasn't sure she believed him. "You're worried he might have done this," she said.

Bart looked ready to deny it with a vengeance. "You don't know what Rachel is like," he said instead, biting off each word. "She antagonized him, belittled him, did everything in her power to provoke him."

"You're saying she asked for it?" She couldn't keep the edge out of her voice.

"No, that's not what I'm saying," he snapped, looking like a man who wished he'd kept his mouth shut.

"Mr. Collinwood, domestic abuse is often generational."

He let out a curse. "I only lost my temper that one time. I've regretted it ever since."

"It's that attitude—"

"Oh, please. You're just looking for an excuse to let her off. She murdered my son. Humphrey never raised his hand to her. He didn't do this. I'm telling you. I don't know how she pulled it off, but that woman set this whole thing up."

"What if you're wrong and he lost his temper? What if he did do this?"

Bart Collinwood met her gaze and she saw the doubt that she knew had been lurking in there, the fear and guilt. What if he was more like his father than even Bart had realized?

Ford didn't feel better as he left the ranch after seeing Rachel. He thought about driving home to Big Sky, but it was dark and late enough that he knew he should wait until morning. Even as he thought it, a part of him wanted to see this all the way through. But rationally, how long was that going to take?

Hitch had her suspicions, but that was about all, from what he could tell. This could go on for weeks or even months before finally going to trial. He got the impression, though, that Hitch wouldn't be on the case that long if she didn't find something fairly soon.

Ford couldn't believe how naive he'd been. He'd thought that by seeing Rachel one last time, he could find some kind of closure. If anything, his visit had made him even more suspicious and upset about the part he'd inadvertently played in all this. Worse, he kept asking himself, "What if Humphrey wasn't an abuser? What if Rachel had lied about everything? Or what if Rachel is telling the truth but goes to prison for thirty years or more for only trying to save herself?"

He honestly didn't know what to believe, except that Rachel had lied to him. His faith in her had been more than tarnished. He'd come here to save her—and had, since his statement about the phone call was on record now. His work here was over. He could get up in the morning and go back to Big Sky. Back to… That was just it. He didn't know what he was going back to.

When he thought about what he'd almost done before her phone call, he felt foolish and embarrassed that he'd let himself fall that low. Maybe it was Humphrey's senseless death and its repercussions, but he knew he'd never try anything that stupid again.

Tonight, though, just the thought of going back to the hotel and packing what little he'd bought since being here was too depressing. He kept thinking about Rachel and the shadow he'd seen at the window. He'd tried to tell himself it had been his imagination. But he knew better. Rachel hadn't been alone. Who was in there with her that she hadn't wanted him to see? The accomplice Hitch suspected had helped Rachel stage the killing?

A set of bright headlights suddenly filled his rearview mirror. He flinched as his gaze went to his side mirror.

Only minutes before, there hadn't been another vehicle on this stretch of black two-lane. Not only did the driver have his high beams on, but he was coming up behind him way too fast. The damned fool acted as if he didn't see him. Was the driver drunk?

Ford touched his brakes, but the act seemed to have little effect. He felt his initial alarm grow into fear. The driver wasn't slowing down. He looked to the road ahead. There was no place to turn off the shoulder-less highway. Worse, the highway took a tight turn ahead as it dropped down through the hills and creek bottom.

He didn't realize he'd been holding his breath until the vehicle behind him went flying around him and kept going. His breath came out in a whoosh. He realized that his hands were shaking. He'd been so sure that the driver was going to hit him. Slowing down, he tried to make sense out of the panic he'd felt only moments before. Was this another flashback? No, the driver had wanted him to think he was going to hit him and force him off the road—if not kill them both.

Ford stared after the red taillights. It had been a pickup, but that was all he could be sure of. He hadn't even tried to get the license plate number. Pickups in this part of Montana outnumbered cars and even SUVs. It was probably some ranch hand anxious to get into town to see his girl.

But he knew that wasn't what was bothering him. Had he, for that split second, thought Rachel's accomplice was driving that truck? He had. Because of Hitch's suspicions or his own? He thought about the threatening note she said someone had slipped under her door.

Well, it hadn't been Rachel's accomplice—if there was such a person, he thought with relief.

Until he came around a corner and saw the headlights coming right at him.

Instinctively, he turned the wheel hard to the right and hit his brakes as he went off the road an instant before the other vehicle swept past, only inches from hitting him. He left the pavement, flying off the road and down into the shallow borrow pit.

Something slammed hard against the undercarriage and then he was back up onto the highway before he got his pickup stopped in the darkness. His thundering heart lodged in his throat. He had a death grip on the wheel and was shaking inside.

His gaze quickly went to his rearview mirror, expecting to see the other driver and vehicle crashed in the ditch. But all he saw were taillights before they disappeared over the next rise.

Ford sat for a moment, fighting to catch his breath. The near miss had a tight grip on him, but to his surprise, it didn't call up a flashback. He stared at the empty highway for a moment. His first instinct was to chase down the vehicle. Fortunately, he was thinking clear enough that he didn't. It was long gone. Or maybe it had only gone back to the Collinwood Ranch.

Whoever had come flying around him had been the same pickup that had run him off the road. But did that mean that the person was involved with Rachel? There was only one way to find out.

He did a highway patrol turn in the middle of the empty two-lane and headed back toward the ranch.

Chapter 16

It was getting late. Hitch had been parked in the pines on the mountainside overlooking Rachel Collinwood's house long enough that she'd seen Ford arrive and leave. Soon after that, she'd spotted a pickup kicking up dust on one of the back roads on the other side of the house. Had it come from the ranch house and she'd just missed it? Or had whoever had been driving it parked at a distance and walked up through one of the ravines to the house?

The pickup was so far away and moving at a speed that she doubted she could catch up to it. Had whoever was driving the rig been at Rachel's? If so, the driver had gone to a lot of trouble not to be seen. The accomplice? If so, there probably wouldn't be any more visitors tonight.

She was thinking about leaving her hiding place and going back into town for something to eat when she heard a vehicle approaching. She glanced toward the road into the ranch. No headlights. She watched the dark shape as it headed slowly in her direction. She reached for her weapon.

Setting the loaded Glock next to her right thigh, she waited, curious who was joining her on the side of the mountain. One of the hired hands? Was this secluded spot with the great view a make-out spot? She recognized the pickup even before she recognized the broad shoulders behind the wheel. Ford made several attempts to get his driver's-side door open and had to put one of those broad shoulders into it. What was wrong with his door? she wondered. It was the lawman in her that she noticed such things.

The bigger question was what he was doing here.

As he reached for her passenger-side door, she unlocked it and watched him climb in. "Couldn't sleep?" she asked.

"Probably for the same reason you couldn't," he said. She saw that he'd brought his own binoculars. Had he also brought his own gun? He glanced at hers lying against her thigh, then turned to look through the binoculars, glassing the house below them.

"Seems we both had the same idea," she said.

Without looking at her, he said, "Been here long?"

"Long enough," she said and studied him. "How was your visit with Rachel?" He looked pale even in the dim starlight and she realized there had to be a reason he'd come back after leaving. "Are you all right?"

"I had a close call on the way into town."

"How close?" she asked, feeling her heart do a little bump.

"Close enough to make me question what's going on." He sounded as if that was hard to admit.

"What happened?" She thought she might have to drag it out of him, but he continued after a moment.

"Rachel was acting…oddly. She said she was alone, but I don't think that was true. After I left, a pickup came roaring up behind me and then passed me and kept going over a hundred. I thought it was just some reckless kid until I realized that the driver had gone up the road and turned around and was coming right at me. If I hadn't taken the gully…"

Hitch couldn't speak for a moment. Hadn't she feared something like this might happen? "That's when you sprung your driver's-side door."

"Apparently, since it was fine before that," he said.

"Was it something you said to Rachel?" she asked. "Or something she said?"

He still had the binoculars up, watching the ranch house. "I might have asked too much about Humphrey and the past. Then I saw someone in the house even though she swore she was alone. As I was leaving, she got a phone call. Supposedly it was Shyla, but I'm not sure she was truthful about that either, especially since not too many miles down the road, someone driving a pickup ran me off the road. I know you don't believe in coincidence—"

"That's a lot of coincidences," she said. They were quiet for a long moment. "If Rachel thinks you suspect her and might do anything to recant what you'd heard on the phone…"

"I won't change my story, because it was the truth."

She nodded. "Still, if she thinks you aren't on her side anymore, it could get dangerous." Picking up her binoculars, she studied the house for a moment. Wasn't this what she'd feared might happen? "You need to go back to Big Sky."

He seemed to ignore that. "Is there another way into the ranch besides the main road?"

She lowered the binoculars for a moment to study his face. His binoculars were trained on the house. "Isn't there always, if you know the ranch well?" she said. "You think he came back here?"

"I didn't pass him on the highway."

"About the truck—I'm assuming you didn't get the license plate number."

He shook his head. "Just a set of bright headlights. But as it went flying by, I caught a glimpse of it. Dark colored. Large pickup. Probably a king cab. That's about it. Except it had a large guard grille on the front of it."

It sounded like the pickup that had been parked outside the morgue. "You didn't see the driver?" He shook his head. She could tell the entire episode—from his visit to Rachel, to him coming up here—had shaken him. He had wanted so desperately to believe in the woman he'd loved. Maybe still loved.

"We're probably wasting our time tonight," Ford said. "If you're right, Rachel planned all this too well. She'll know she's being watched. She's too smart to mess up now."

"Maybe," Hitch said. "But if we're right, her accomplice has already gone off script. Him and his recklessness is her Achilles' heel. I suspect it was his stupid idea to scare you earlier. She won't like it. All he's done is make you more suspicious. She can't have any mistakes at this point. She doesn't need a hothead trying to protect her—but then, that's how he would have gotten involved in the first place. He had to think he was saving her by helping her get rid of her husband. Why not get rid of you, as well?"

He lowered his binoculars to glance at her. "Which means the accomplice isn't as smart or as patient and composed as Rachel," he said.

"He's already made one mistake by running you off the road. I doubt it will be his last. Let's just hope that you're smart enough to get out of town before the next mistake the man makes kills you."

He chuckled at that. "I'm assuming that's the way you dispense advice? Did anyone ever tell you that you're a scary woman?"

She laughed. It felt good to laugh. She'd been worried about Ford because he was so dang trusting and because of how he felt about Rachel. After tonight, maybe his eyes were finally open. Hopefully now he would take her advice and go back to Big Sky, where he should be safe. He was a nice guy. She didn't want to see him hurt any more than he had been.

The dark night, the closeness inside her SUV, the slight summer breeze coming in her cracked open window all made her feel strangely vulnerable, as if she had more in common with this man than she could have ever thought. "You're not the first person to think I'm scary. My ex mentioned it on his way out the door," she said and laughed again. It didn't come off as light as she'd meant it. She could feel his gaze on her.

"I'm sorry."

"Don't be. It was for the best." She glanced at him. "What are you really doing here?"

"Same thing as you. I want to know the truth. I *need* to know the truth since Rachel dragged me into it. Now she wants me gone. I think it's because she's afraid I'm suspicious, and if I think she used me, I might be determined to discover the truth."

"Is she wrong?"

"No," he said.

She stared at Ford. She'd been so sure he was a sheep and Rachel was a wolf leading him to slaughter. She realized she was going to have to reassess what she thought of him.

Love could make you blind and stupid, she knew well. But the smart ones paid attention to the red flags. There were always red flags when a relationship wasn't right.

"So the driver of the pickup," he said, looking through his binoculars again. "I figure he's the boyfriend."

"What makes you think her accomplice is a boyfriend?" she asked, pretending that wasn't exactly her thought.

Ford chuckled. "For the same reason you do. If she orchestrated all of this, then she had to have someone she trusted to pull it off. It had to be someone she had wrapped around her little finger. That usually involves money or sex, in my experience. Sex is the cheapest."

She laughed. "You surprise me," Hitch said, leveling her gaze on him.

"I must look dumber than I am."

She shook her head. "Rachel thinks you're still in love with her and will do anything for her."

He chuckled. "Not after my visit this evening," he said with a grimace. "If she deliberately set Humphrey up to kill him…" Ford looked away for a moment, and she knew he was thinking of the consequences of Rachel's actions if true.

"You know what they say about secrets," Hitch said. "Two people can keep them, as long as one of them is dead. Her accomplice made a mistake tonight by trying to run you off the road. He best watch his back, because I'm betting his days are numbered."

Ford lowered the binoculars and looked at Hitch in the dim light. She had raised her binoculars and was watching the ranch house again. The lights were still on even though it was after midnight. There was a sweet innocence about her face that was at odds with her career choice, he thought, and that determined strength that made her indomitable. "I'm curious. How did you get into this line of work?"

"My dad was a cop. My mother was an attorney. They argued all the time because of their jobs, especially at the dinner table in the evening after work. My brother became a psychologist, my sister a schoolteacher, and I studied to become a medical examiner." She shrugged. "I always liked dissecting frogs in school."

Ford couldn't help but smile. "How does your family feel about it?"

"It makes for interesting discussions on Thanksgiving," she said with a laugh. "What about you?"

"Me?" He shook his head. "Nothing interesting. During my parents' divorce, Dad moved us to Montana. I was just a kid when he and his brothers opened a barbecue restaurant in Big Sky. My uncles, all of them, ended up moving to Montana. My dad's cousin Dana Cardwell Savage lives on a ranch, so I spent a lot of time there growing up."

"You went into the military after college?"

He nodded. "I'd majored in engineering. What I really wanted was to fly."

"And now?"

"Not so much." He picked up his binoculars and scanned the darkness around the house below them on the mountain, desperately wanting to change the subject.

"Have you thought about ranching?" she asked. "It sounds like you enjoyed that."

He hadn't thought about anything. For so long after the crash, the rehabilitation, the end of his military career, he had felt as if he was in a black hole. Rachel had yanked him out of it. He'd always be thankful for that even though he now suspected that she'd had her own reasons for reaching out to him.

Ford thought of Cardwell Ranch and the position his aunt Dana had offered him. He'd thought he'd lost all his enthusiasm for life. He'd been so down, so depressed, so despondent. The doctor's visits didn't seem to be helping the PTSD. But maybe they'd been doing more good than he'd thought.

Because he was beginning to realize that it had been more than Rachel's phone call that had brought him back from the brink. He'd had to hit bottom before he could climb back out. Now here he was.

"I might ranch." Even as he said the words, they surprised him. But he realized they just happened to be true.

Hitch fell silent, aware that something intimate had passed between them. She stared out into the darkness at the house down the mountainside for a few moments.

"You know what bothers me?" Ford asked. "Rachel doesn't seem that heartbroken about Humphrey being dead."

Hitch glanced over at him. "She wouldn't be if she was telling the truth and her husband beat her until she feared for her life and had to protect herself. She also seems to believe that he was having an affair—which he wasn't, according to the woman in question. But the alleged girlfriend did say that Humphrey seemed lonely. He was getting Rachel a horse for her birthday this coming week." She waited for his reaction.

"Doesn't sound like a man who would beat his wife."

Hitch laughed. "The sheriff thinks it made Humphrey look guilty."

Ford lowered the binoculars and looked at her. "He could have been trying to assuage his guilt and make it up to her if he really was abusing her."

"All possible," she agreed as she caught movement out of the corner of her eye and picked up her binoculars again. "Well, how about that? It appears someone is finally making a move."

Hitch pulled out her camera with the telephoto lens and aimed it at the man coming out of the house. Unfortunately, it was too dark to see his face. He'd walked out of the house and was now going around to the back.

She lowered the camera and started the SUV. "I want to see what he's driving." She punched the gas before Ford could move, forcing him to hang on.

"Do you always drive like this?"

"Usually. Am I scaring you?"

"I don't scare that easily," he said, and she sped up.

As they came around the last curve, she spotted the lights of a vehicle racing up the ranch road. "I think I can cut him off down at the highway," she said as she took a side dirt road and increased her speed. He'd asked earlier if there was a back road into the ranch. She'd already checked them all out online, so she had a pretty good idea where the pickup was heading.

They were flying along, bouncing over ruts and bumps. She glanced over at Ford from the corner of her eye. He looked a little green around the gills. "If you're going to throw up, please do it out the window."

"Throw up?" He scoffed. "I can take whatever you dish out."

She grinned at that. "I do love a challenge."

Not far down the road, she hung a right and came roaring up onto the paved highway before hitting her brakes. Looking both to her right and left, she saw no sign of vehicle lights.

"He could have gone the other way," Ford said just an

instant before a set of headlights topped a rise and shot toward them.

"Let's see if we can get a make and model of this car," she said as she pulled to the edge of the road and cut her engine and lights. "A license plate would be even better."

A dark-colored pickup sped past at the same time Hitch restarted the SUV and gunned the engine. Her vehicle jumped up onto the highway again, tires squealing as she went after the truck.

Ford fought back the nausea. He would rather die than prove Hitch right by vomiting. His stomach roiled, though. The wild ride was giving him flashbacks of his plane crash—as well as his recent race to the end of a cliff. He felt disoriented and out of control. Sweat broke out on his back as he struggled to separate the events and fight off the anxiety attack.

Taking deep breaths, he stared straight ahead at the two red taillights. The lights grew larger and larger as Hitch closed the distance. He saw that the back of the pickup was covered in mud, making it almost impossible to read the license plate.

"It's a Chevy half-ton pickup. Newer model. Dark blue or gray. Hard to tell with all the dust on it," Ford said, concentrating on the truck rather than the flashbacks that flickered like an old-timey movie in his head. He could smell the smoke, feel the flames licking at him as he fought to get his men out before the plane's gas tank blew.

"Can you read the plates?" Hitch asked.

"Starts with 40."

"Big Timber."

"I think it's 19 after that, but I can't read the rest," he said.

She turned on her blinker and passed the truck, getting

the SUV up to over a hundred. "You might want to duck down. If he sees you and recognizes you—"

"I'll take my chances, thanks." His head hurt and he still felt sick to his stomach. Given the vibration of the SUV, he estimated that she had to be pushing the SUV to over a hundred and thirty. They zoomed past the pickup.

"Well?" she asked as she whipped back into the right lane and kept going.

"He was wearing a cowboy hat, so I couldn't see much of his face." She shot him a look, making him more nervous. "The road," he said. "Also, aren't there deer out here at night?"

"Was the man behind the wheel the one who had tried to run you off the road earlier?"

He shook his head. Wrong pickup, he was pretty sure. His head ached. He could hardly think. But he was sure this wasn't the same driver or the same pickup.

"Well?" she asked.

He rubbed his temples. "I don't think so, but honestly, I don't know." He felt as if he had disappointed her.

"We should go back and get your rig," Hitch said, hitting her brakes and doing a highway patrol turn in the middle of the road. Once they were headed in the opposite direction again and slowed down, she said, "Tell me you can do better than that on a description of the man since you're about to get another look at him."

He looked out the windshield as the pickup sped past. "Strong jaw, straight nose. Dark designer stubble. Nice looking. Are we assuming this is the boyfriend? The age looks about right. Maybe a little young for her."

She chuckled at that. "I guess I'll find out once I know who he is."

Chapter 17

It didn't take long for Hitch to match the make and model of the vehicle the man had been driving last night to the partial plate number.

"Who is Lloyd Townsend?" she asked the sheriff when she walked into his office first thing the next morning.

Charley didn't look happy to see her. "Why are you asking about Lloyd?" She waited him out until he finally sighed and said, "He's one of our most respected businessmen in town. You don't want to go messing with Lloyd. Everyone in this town loves him. He's always the first to donate to any cause. Salt of the earth."

"Got it," Hitch said and turned to walk out.

"Hold up there a minute," the sheriff said. "Mr. Collinwood is on my back about his boy's body being released."

"He can take him today," Hitch said and saw Charley's surprise. "I think I have everything I need."

"To convict that poor woman?" the sheriff demanded, an angry edge to his voice.

"If she's guilty, then hopefully yes," Hitch said and left the sheriff's department. As she headed out the front door, she spotted Ford leaning against his pickup as if waiting for someone. She smiled, realizing she was that someone.

"Have you had breakfast?" Ford asked as he pushed off the side of the vehicle and stepped toward her.

"As a matter of fact, I haven't."

"Well, I'm hungry and I don't like to eat alone. Hop in. I'll drive."

He drove the few blocks to the café, neither of them saying anything. Once inside, they sat across from each other in a booth.

"Why do I suspect you have something on your mind besides breakfast?"

He nodded. "I had a lot of time to think last night. I'm not as convinced that Rachel had something to do with me being run off the road." Hitch nodded as if she wasn't surprised. "Did you find the man we saw last night coming out of her house?"

"Might have." She pulled out her phone, tapped in the name and came up with a photo of an elderly man with a thick head of gray hair. "How old would you guess the man was who you saw driving the pickup?"

"Forties maybe. He could have been younger. As you know, I didn't get a good look at him either time."

She turned her phone screen so he could see it. "Could he have been sixty-seven with gray hair and glasses?"

Ford chuckled. "My eyesight is better than that. Who's the man?"

"Lloyd Townsend," she said, putting her phone away.

"Clearly not the one driving last night. But it was his truck." The waitress brought them coffee, water and menus, and they both ordered quickly without hardly glancing at their menus.

Ford's mind was on the woman across the table and their surveillance adventure last night. He'd seen another side of Henrietta Roberts, one he rather liked. "I don't think that pickup and driver was the same one that ran me off the road. The more I've thought about it, I think it was just a drunk driver and I was being paranoid."

"That it was a coincidence that this driver showed up shortly after you left Rachel Collinwood's house? Like the coincidence of her pocket dialing you just before she killed her husband?"

He met her gaze. "What if you're wrong about her? What if we both are?"

Hitch leaned her elbows on the table, giving his question some thought. "Then the lack of evidence will allow her to either walk or get a lighter sentence. She did kill a man. If she truly was an abused wife, she needed to leave him—or in this instance do what she could to get away from him. If she'd hit him with a frying pan, well, she would have had a better chance of getting off. Having the gun makes it look as if she was laying for him."

"What if she was afraid to leave Humphrey?" he asked. "I've looked into this a little, and from what I've read, the highest risk time for a homicide is not when she's *in* the relationship but when she's trying to leave it."

"In order to prove self-defense, she has to prove that she was or at least believed that she was in imminent danger. The problem is that she had the gun. Did she have other alternatives other than to use what could be seen as unreasonable force? That will be up to a jury to decide. Why did she have the loaded gun handy? If she feared they were going to have a knock-down, drag-out fight, why wouldn't she get out of there?"

"Because she felt safe. She had the gun if things got out of control," Ford said. "If he'd beaten her up before, then this time she planned to stop him."

"We can't know what was going through her mind at the moment she pulled the trigger. We might never know."

The waitress brought their breakfast orders and they ate in a companionable silence, until Hitch pushed her plate away and asked, "What do you know about Humphrey's parents? Did he ever mention that they didn't get along?"

"You're asking if Bart was abusive." He frowned. "You found out something about Humphrey." He could tell that she didn't want to share the information with him.

"Bart let it slip that his son had seen him hit his wife. A slap. Bart swore it was the only time and that Humphrey had been horrified and never forgave him."

Ford groaned as he raked a hand through his hair. "You're thinking father like son."

"It could be that Humphrey mentioned what he'd seen to Rachel. It could have given her the idea. Or he could have been so angry with her…"

"This makes you have doubts," he said, shaking his head. "So your mind isn't completely made up after all." He smiled at her, liking her even more. Not that he wanted it to be true of Humphrey.

She looked at the time on her phone. "I have to go. Thanks for breakfast."

"My pleasure." He watched her leave, wondering how Lloyd Townsend's pickup played into all this.

Lloyd Townsend owned a hobby ranch on the Yellowstone River just a few miles from town. As Hitch drove up into the ranch yard, she spotted the pickup she'd seen last night and parked beside it.

Getting out, she walked over to the truck and looked inside, seeing nothing of interest.

"Can I help you?" asked a male voice from the front porch of the house. She hadn't heard anyone come out.

Turning, she considered the elderly man for a moment, before she stepped to the house, stopping at the bottom of the stairs. "I'm Hitch Roberts, state medical examiner." He seemed to be waiting for more. "I'm currently working on a local case. Were you driving this pickup last night sometime after midnight?" She waited, wondering what his answer would be. If he lied, he might be involved. If he didn't—

"No," he said, frowning. "You're sure it was my truck? After midnight?"

She nodded. "It was this truck. Who else might have been driving it?"

Lloyd Townsend rubbed his jaw for a moment before he said, "I suppose one of my sons could have taken it. What's this about?"

"I was hoping the driver of your pickup last night might be able to help me with the case I'm working on. Are your sons around?"

"I believe they're out by the corral behind the house working with one of the horses. You're welcome to go back there. It's just around the side of the house." He made a motion with his right hand and started to turn back inside.

The light caught on his hand from the movement.

"Excuse me—I just noticed your ring," she said as she climbed a couple of steps to take a closer look. Lloyd looked down at his ring and smiled as he held out his hand so she could admire it. "It's quite unusual."

"It's our family crest," he said with no small amount of

pride. "Both of my sons wear one. Rather a family tradition. Are you familiar with the history of the coat of arms?"

"I can't say I am," she said, her pulse having jumped when he'd told her that both of his sons also wore the same design of ring.

"Coats of arms were used for centuries to identify a certain family. They were created for the battlefield," he said, clearly warming to the subject. "Other knights couldn't tell who was inside of a suit of armor, so they created symbols to attach to the armor. Not to be confused with the crest, which is only a portion of the coat of arms that was worn above the helmet."

"Fascinating," she said, taking the steps back down the stairs. "Thank you for the information. Oh, by the way, what are your sons' names…?" As she went around the side of the house, she called the sheriff on her phone. "Meet me at Lloyd Townsend's ranch as quickly as you can." She hung up before he could argue. She figured he'd come racing out here, hoping she hadn't upset a town favorite.

As she reached the corner of the outside of the house, she spotted the corral. One of the sons was leaning on the corral fence, while the other was inside it with a large bay he was apparently trying to break.

As she joined the one outside the corral, she climbed up on the fence to watch. It was a beautiful bay being green broke by what appeared to be the youngest son, Paul. Out of the corner of her eye, she saw the cowboy next to her look over.

"You must be John," she said, turning toward him. His father had described him as the oldest and bigger of the two. "I'm Hitch. Hitch Roberts, state medical examiner." She held out her hand, he shook it and she went back to watching what was going on in the corral, even though her mind was on the ring on his right hand. "He seems to know what he's doing."

She was wondering if she could get any of Rachel Collinwood's DNA off it after all this time. The lab wouldn't need much, and with the deep grooves of the ring...

"Paul *should* know what he's doing. He's been at this most of his life. Not that he won't hit the dirt before the day is out," John said with a laugh.

What their father hadn't told her was that Paul was the more handsome of the two. In fact, he was gorgeous, from his muscled lean body to his chisel-cut jawline and the styled stubble covering it. With his hat on, he definitely appeared to be the man behind the wheel of the pickup last night. She could also see how he might turn the head of a married woman—and vice versa.

"You here about a horse?" John Townsend asked.

"Actually, I'm looking for whoever was driving your father's pickup last night north of town sometime after midnight," she said.

"Don't look at me," John said. "I was in bed by then."

She noticed the wedding band on his left hand. Married. So he'd have an alibi—if he were telling the truth. "Anyone else drive the truck besides you, your father and your brother, Paul?"

"Not that I know of."

"Well, that narrows it down, doesn't it," she said and watched as Paul finished putting the saddle on the bay. He led the horse around the corral a few times before he swung up into the saddle. His behind hadn't touched leather but for a moment before the bay began to buck.

Hitch and John jumped back as the horse tried to knock Paul off by putting him into the corral fence. To his credit, the cowboy hung on longer than she suspected most would have before he and the horse parted ways.

Paul was getting up from the ground and dusting himself off when the sheriff arrived. Hitch went to meet him away from the corral and the two Townsend sons. She could tell Charley was already upset from her call. He was about to get even more upset, she thought. "I need the rings both of the Townsend sons are wearing."

"What the hell?"

"One of them—I suspect the youngest, Paul—paid a visit to Mrs. Collinwood late last night."

The sheriff looked both surprised and confused. "Maybe he was just—"

"Giving her his condolences?" she asked.

Charley spurted for a moment before he demanded, "Why in the hell do you want their rings?"

"For evidence."

"Evidence of *what*?"

"Murder. You do realize, Sheriff, that this is what the case is about, don't you? Finding out what really happened at the Collinwood Ranch and why Humphrey is dead."

He stared at her, openmouthed. "What are you talking about? You think one of the Townsends—"

"I want to bring Paul in for questioning. The governor has given me the authority to do whatever I have to. But you know them, so I'd prefer you do the honors."

The sheriff let out an angry sigh and stared at his boots for a moment. "If you're wrong about this—"

"I'll take full responsibility."

Rachel stood in the middle of the kitchen trying to catch her breath. She'd never had an anxiety attack, but she thought this must be what one felt like as she tried to calm herself.

She hadn't recognized the number when she'd gotten the call. For a moment, she'd almost not taken it. "Hello?"

The moment she'd heard the voice, she'd snapped, "Shyla, why are you calling me from some number I don't recognize? I almost didn't pick up."

"I borrowed a phone. I'm at the sheriff's department. I just heard the craziest thing. That medical examiner? She and the sheriff just went out to the Townsend place and confiscated both Paul's and John's rings. Supposedly it has something to do with Humphrey's death."

That was when all the air in the kitchen felt as if it had been sucked out. She'd had to grab the counter to steady herself. "Why would she care about their rings?"

"Beats me. Apparently," she said, lowering her voice, "they're evidence. But evidence of what? Not only that the medical examiner knows that one of the Townsends came out to your place last night. You aren't still—"

"Of course not." She tried to catch her breath. "I thought I heard someone. I was in the tub. Why would he come out here?"

"Why do you think? What if he tells them about the two of you…?"

She groaned inwardly, still fighting the lack of oxygen. She felt as if a ton of bricks had fallen on her chest.

"Well, I thought I'd warn you," Shyla said. "Listen, it sounds like the medical examiner is building a case against you."

"I know. But she's wasting her time. There isn't anything to find."

"Are you sure about that? Rick thinks it isn't just the

medical examiner but Ford who's the problem. Did you and Ford have an argument?"

Rachel had to sit down and put her head between her knees. "Tell Rick that everything is fine and for him not to worry about me. You either. I have to go."

Chapter 18

Paul Townsend looked more amused than anything as he lounged in one of the chairs across from the sheriff's desk.

"The medical examiner wants to ask you a few questions," Charley said, sounding apologetic as he leaned back in his chair and made it perfectly clear that none of this was his idea. "I'm sure it won't take long."

Hitch tried not to grind her teeth. She'd worked with enough small-town sheriffs that this shouldn't come as a surprise. "I happened to see your pickup on the road north last night after midnight. Want to tell me where you were coming from?"

The cowboy seemed to lose some of his cockiness for a moment. "Just went for a ride."

"A ride? No place in particular?"

"Nope."

"Paul, I should advise you that I witnessed you leaving Rachel Collinwood's house not long after midnight. I took photos of you and then later of the pickup you were driving."

He sat up a little and shot an uncomfortable glance at the sheriff as if he expected Charley to bail him out. Hitch gave the sheriff a warning look, daring him to do so. "So what? I wanted to see how she was doing."

"At midnight? That's when you decided to stop by?"

Paul looked around the office for a moment. "What's this about?" He wasn't as cocky as he'd been earlier.

"How did you get the scrapes on your knuckles?" Hitch asked.

He glanced down at his hands as if surprised to see them. "I don't know. Working on the ranch. You saw me working today. I get beat up." He sounded proud of that.

"What is your relationship with Mrs. Collinwood?" Hitch asked.

His eyes widened. "We don't have a relationship exactly."

Hitch leaned toward him. "I know you didn't pull the trigger, but how were you involved in Humphrey Collinwood's murder? If you tell the truth—"

"Wait! What? I don't know what you're talking about," he said, shooting to his feet.

"I'm talking about you doing less time in prison by telling us what really happened out at the ranch the day Humphrey Collinwood died. Otherwise, you will go down with her."

"No, you got it all wrong. Yes, I went out there last night. I don't know what I was thinking. I just wanted to see if she was all right." Hitch cocked her head at him and waited. He hung his head. "I'd had something to drink, okay? Maybe too much. I got to thinking about her."

"How long have the two of you been having an affair?" she asked.

He wagged his head. "It isn't like that," he said as he sat back down looking deflated. "It was just a few times."

"When was this?" Hitch asked.

"A year or so ago. I tried to see her again, but she…"

"Was married."

"Yeah," Paul said, lifting his head. "Look, my father doesn't know." He glanced at the sheriff. "Does he have to find out?"

"When was the last time you saw her before last night?" Hitch asked.

"A year ago. I called a few times, and when she quit taking my calls, I gave up. But I swear, I just went out there to make sure she was all right, but she didn't answer the door, so I left."

"I saw you coming out of the house," Hitch said.

He nodded. "I know the passcode. Like I said, I was worried about her, so I went inside, but her bedroom door was closed. I knocked on it, thought I heard water running. I got to thinking that she might shoot me, too—you know, thinking I was a burglar or something—so I left."

"When you were involved with Rachel Collinwood a year ago, did you notice any bruises on her that might have indicated she was being abused?"

He shook his head. "But I could tell she was afraid he would find out, you know?"

Hitch thought she did. "Would you please remove your ring, Mr. Townsend?"

He closed his hand into a fist. "Why?"

"I'd like to take it for evidence," Hitch said.

Paul looked at the sheriff, then back at her. "You can't take my stuff without a warrant, right?" he asked, his gaze back on the sheriff.

"If you are unwilling to relinquish it and allow me to

take it as possible evidence, then I will have to ask the sheriff here to arrest you for conspiracy to commit murder, at which time your possessions, including your ring, will be taken and used as possible evidence in the case."

"But I just told you—" The cowboy looked like a trapped animal. "I want a lawyer."

She looked to the sheriff. "Would you please arrest Mr. Townsend for me, Sheriff?" Her look said, *Don't make me call the governor.*

"I'm sorry as hell about this, Paul," Charley said, lumbering to his feet. "Why don't you just give her the damned ring?" The cowboy covered the ring with his other hand and shook his head. "She's going to get it, one way or another," Charley continued. "You want to spend time behind bars over a stupid ring? Don't make me have to arrest you."

Paul angrily jerked off the ring, rose and threw it down on the sheriff's desk. As Charley reached for it, Hitch beat him to it, using her shirtsleeve to pick it up before bagging it.

"I want that ring back," Paul said angrily. "And a public apology."

The sheriff sighed deeply before saying, "You're free to go now and we'll make sure at some point that you get your ring back."

"But let me know if you decide to leave town," Hitch called after him as the cowboy stormed out and got on his cell phone. "I wonder who he's calling. Rachel Collinwood to warn her?"

"He's probably just callin' for a ride back to the ranch," Charley said, picking up his keys. "You might recall that he rode with me." The sheriff shot her an incredulous look as he walked out after Paul.

"I'm going to need his phone records," Hitch said to his retreating back.

She was anxious to check the ring against the photographs of Rachel's bruises before sending it to the lab. Back in her hotel room, she pulled out her magnifying glass. She studied first the bruise, then the surface of the ring. Tilting the ring this way and that, she imagined slipping it on her finger.

"If I were to punch someone…" She made the motion with the ring still in the evidence bag and then checked the position of the ring against that of the bruise. The resemblance was there. But would a jury see it? Maybe.

Her real hope, she knew, was what the lab would find. The grooves in the ring's design were so deep… She had to believe that the evidence would still be there. Unless Paul Townsend was telling the truth.

"I know. I understand. No, I—" The sheriff pulled the phone away from his ear for a moment. "Lloyd, I totally agree with you. But it's out of my hands. This came all the way down from the governor. I can't do anything with that woman." He listened to the man rant and rave and threaten to sue. "I don't know why she wanted your sons' rings. I know they're valuable. Nothing's going to happen to them. But at least Paul's not behind bars. Be happy about that. If she'd had her way…" He pulled the phone away again and looked up to find Ford Cardwell standing in his doorway. "Lloyd, I have to go. Do whatever it is you have to do." He hung up. "What do you want?" he snapped and then quickly apologized. "Sorry, it's been one of those days."

"I didn't mean to interrupt," Ford said.

"No, actually, I should thank you. What can I do for you?"

"I was looking for Hitch," Ford said.

Charley made a rude sound that went with the face he pulled. "Well, she isn't here. She was. I have no idea where she is. Probably starting trouble somewhere else. She won't rest until she has this whole town up in arms." He realized Ford was still standing there. "Try the morgue. I know it's late, but that's where she's been hanging out. You know where that is?" He didn't wait for an answer and quickly gave him directions. Big Timber was small enough that it was pretty easy to get around.

As Ford started to leave, the sheriff took his first good look at the man since he'd appeared in the doorway. "You don't look good," Charley said and frowned. "You look like someone punched you in the gut. You all right?"

"I've been better."

"You sticking around?"

"I'm not sure."

Charley nodded. "But you'll be back for the trial—if it comes to that. Rachel's going to need your testimony, so you'd best take care of yourself. Without you…"

Yes, without him, Rachel wouldn't have as strong a case. "Thanks again for the directions." As he left, the sheriff's phone rang. He heard him curse and say, "Who wants to chew off my ear now? On top of everything, I'm missing my supper, damn it."

So much had happened in the past seventy-two hours. Hitch had gone through all her notes again. She'd stuck her neck out bringing Paul Townsend in. There was pressure on the governor from both Bart Collinwood and Lloyd Townsend now. She had to wind things up and soon.

After pacing her hotel room floor, she knew there was only one way she could unwind. Drive. As she walked out of the hotel, she noticed something flapping in the breeze on her windshield. A piece of folded paper under the wiper of her SUV. She pulled on the extra pair of latex gloves she always kept in a pocket when on a case and carefully removed the typed note.

The message was much like the other one that had been slipped under her hotel room door.

You messed with the wrong people bitch.

Leave town or wish you had.

She bagged the note—just as she had the first one— shaking her head in wonder. It wasn't the first time she'd received threatening notes in her career. Nor did she suspect it would be the last. Such notes never made her want to leave town. On the contrary, it assured her that she was on the right track—and getting too close to the truth for someone's comfort.

Like the first note, this one had been written probably on a computer on plain white paper. She doubted it would have any fingerprints on it either, but she would have the lab check.

She'd been planning to go for a drive. It helped her to think. But the note had changed her mind. She decided that the walk to the morgue might be a better choice. Her assumption was that the note had been from Rachel's accomplice. But it could have just as easily been from someone in the Townsend family. Or even someone who believed Rachel was being treated unfairly. Her friend from college?

The walk to the morgue wasn't far, but it was off the main drag. The streets here lacked sidewalks, pavement and lighting. She walked along the edge of the packed dirt road, thinking about Paul Townsend. He was young and handsome and naive enough that he could have fallen for not just Rachel Collinwood but her alleged need to protect herself from her abusive husband. Paul could have thought he was saving her, being her hero, seeing the killing of Humphrey Collinwood as ridding the world of a monster.

Lost in thought, she didn't hear the vehicle coming up behind her until the sound of the engine roared. Hitch only had enough time to glance over her shoulder to confirm what she already knew. The driver was bearing down on her.

Chapter 19

Hitch wasn't at the morgue. Nor was she in her room when he called the hotel. Ford thought about what the sheriff had said about him taking care of himself. He couldn't remember the last time he'd eaten more than a few bites of anything.

As he drove through Big Timber, he looked for a place to eat. There weren't that many options this time of the night. He'd gone down a side street when he spotted red taillights disappearing in the distance. Closer, a person came stumbling out of a hedge along the road directly in front of him. He threw on his brakes. With a shock of recognition, he saw that it was Hitch and that she was injured.

Blinded by the headlights, Hitch jerked away from the man who ran toward her, thinking it was the same one who'd tried to run her down.

"Hitch, it's me." She felt a wave of relief as she recognized Ford's voice. She let him take her in his arms, because right now she wasn't steady on her feet. The pickup that had tried to run her down had come too close. She'd felt the brush of the bumper against the side of her thigh. She didn't think anything was broken from the contact or her dive into the hedge, but she hurt all over and was definitely shaken.

Whoever had been driving that truck hadn't just been trying to scare her. If she hadn't thrown herself into the hedge, the impact would have killed her.

"What happened?" He sounded scared. "That pickup that just went past? Did it hit you?"

"No. I'm all right." But her legs seemed to give out under her because of the shock that came with the realization of how close a call it had been. "I just need to sit down for a minute."

He caught her, scooping her up, her trembling in his arms as he carried her over to his truck. Reaching behind her, he opened the door and set her down on the seat. "I'll take you to the hospital."

"No hospital," she said quickly. "I'm not hurt. Just shaken up."

"Your cheek is bleeding."

She leaned back, eyes closed, until the dizziness passed as she tried to catch her breath and calm down. When she opened her eyes, she saw that he'd already dug out a first-aid kit. She smiled up into his handsome face, wondering where he'd been her whole life.

"This is going to hurt," he said as he wiped away the blood with an alcohol swab. She winced more from the cold liquid than the pain. "Sorry," he said, his fingers so gentle that she felt her eyes smart. She wasn't used to a man treating her as if she were made of glass. She was too independent, too strong, too determined. At least that was what most men she'd dated had said.

But not this man, she thought as she watched him open a sterile bandage and apply it to her cheek. "Thank you." Her voice came out a hoarse whisper, almost choked with an emotion that surprised her. She told herself it was just her brush with death and his gentle kindness. But as he finished bandaging her cut and looked down into her eyes, she felt a jolt clear to her core. Then his fingers were cupping her uninjured cheek. His rough thumb pad slipped under her chin to lift it as he leaned down and kissed her. The impulsiveness of the kiss, the surprise of it, the tenderness of it all caught her completely off guard.

His lips brushed hers, urging them open. They didn't put up much of a fight. As her lips parted, he cupped the back of her head, deepening the kiss. She grabbed a handful of his shirt, drawing him even closer as she lost herself in the startling passion of their combined kiss.

A groan rose from deep in his chest as he drew back a little to look into her eyes again. "I'm sorry. Here you are injured, and I…" His warm, strong fingers still holding the back of her head were buried in her hair. He seemed as shocked by the powerful kiss as she was.

Still bunching his shirt in her fists, she pulled him down for another kiss. He dropped his mouth to hers and deepened the kiss, this one even hotter than the first.

She loosened her hold on his shirt. His look mirrored hers. Wow. Everything about the kisses had been unexpected in so many ways.

"I've been wanting to do that for a very long time," he said, his voice sounding rough with emotion as he drew his hand from behind her head and straightened. "The timing, however—"

"Was perfect. I hadn't realized how much I needed that." She smiled at him and he smiled almost shyly back. "You don't find me too scary, then?"

"Oh, I wouldn't say that." He chuckled as he tucked her into the seat and closed the passenger-side door. She watched him walk around to the driver's side and slide behind the wheel.

"Any chance the truck driver just didn't see you?" he asked.

"No. Whoever was driving that truck wanted me dead," she said, leaning her head back against the seat and looking out into the darkness, thinking not about her near-death experience, but Ford and that kiss.

For a moment, he simply sat behind the wheel before he glanced over at her, drawing her attention back. "You feel better?" She could only nod. "You're probably not hungry."

"Starved," she said. Her stomach rumbled at the thought, reminding her she hadn't eaten all day.

He chuckled and started the engine. "Any chance you got the license plate on the rig that almost hit you?" he asked as he drove them to the local burger shop.

She thought of that glimpse she'd gotten before the headlights had blinded her. She could almost hear the roar of the engine as the driver bore down on her. "It happened too fast. Too dark to even make out a model of the pickup. All I really saw was the metal guard on the front. I think I would recognize it, if I saw it again."

"I think I know that grille guard," Ford said. "I didn't mention it because most trucks around here have the guards on them because of all the deer on the highway at night. But the truck that ran me off the road had a huge shiny metal guard on the front, as well. I think we're looking for the same man."

"If I were a betting woman, I'd say he's the same man Rachel Collinwood talked into helping her kill her husband."

* * *

It felt ironic, Ford thought as he and Hitch finished their cheeseburgers, fries and chocolate milkshakes and he drove her back to the hotel where they were both staying. He'd come here for Rachel. He would leave here missing Hitch. In a few days' time, he'd come to admire this strong, capable woman.

He scoffed, knowing it was more than that or he wouldn't have kissed her. He felt a fire again in his belly that he'd thought had been extinguished. Desire. He'd actually forgotten what that felt like. But Hitch had fanned the flames and now he burned inside for her and the passion he'd felt kissing her.

All during the meal, Hitch had seemed her old self— except for the bandage on her cheek and a few scratches and probably bruises from her dive into the bushes. They'd talked about growing up in Montana—skirting away from the investigation. It had been one of the most pleasant meals he'd had in a long time.

When he'd walked her to her door at the hotel, there'd been a moment when they'd both seemed to hesitate.

"Good night," he said and took a step back. As badly as he would have loved to be invited into her hotel room, he knew it was too soon. "I'm right down the hall, if you need me."

She'd nodded and smiled. "I'll keep that in mind."

His cell phone rang right after he'd stepped inside his hotel room. For a moment, he was hoping it was Hitch. She'd been just as surprised by what they'd shared. He'd seen it in her eyes, in the trembling of her lips. She wasn't one to leap blindly. At least not when it came to men. He wasn't sure how he knew that, just that he did.

Still, he tried to hide his disappointment. "Dad, I was going to call you. I'm coming home tomorrow."

"Good. You sound…good."

Ford had to smile. He and his father were both short on words in uncharted territory. He knew Jackson had been worried about him. Hell, Ford had been worried about himself.

"Coming over here has been good for me," he told his father.

"Did you resolve anything with Rachel?" Jackson asked.

He chuckled. "Did I get closure? Yeah, I did. I feel better about a lot of things." He envisioned Hitch for a moment.

"I can't tell you how glad I am to hear that," his father said. "It will be great to have you back."

As he disconnected, he saw movement on the street below the window and looked out. Hitch? It was just like her to go back out to the Collinwood Ranch tonight to see if she could catch the man she suspected of being the accomplice visiting Rachel again.

He'd been so sure that her brush with death would keep her safe and in her room—at least for tonight. He should have known better. As he saw her climb into her SUV, he reached for his coat. She had no business going out there alone—especially after what had happened to her tonight.

But at the same time, he wasn't at all surprised. She was one determined woman and he admired the hell out of her for that. Not that he was about to let her go alone.

As Hitch started to pull away, someone pounded on her window, startling her for a moment—until she saw Ford's handsome face. "Couldn't sleep again?" she asked.

"Felt like going for a ride. Looks like you had the same idea."

She studied him for a moment before she smiled. "All right. Get in."

He grinned as she unlocked the door and he climbed in.

"How are you feeling?" he asked.

"Fine."

"I thought you might have decided, after what happened to you, to stay in tonight," Ford said.

She glanced over at him as she pulled out and headed down the street toward the highway that would take them north. "No, you didn't or you wouldn't be here."

"Maybe I'd hoped you'd had enough for one day."

Hitch kept her attention on the road as they fell into a companionable silence until she turned off into the Collinwood Ranch. On the side of the mountain in the pines where they'd sat before, she cut the lights, pulled to the edge so there were no trees blocking their view and cut the engine.

"He wouldn't be fool enough to come back out here tonight," Ford said.

She chuckled. "Wanna bet?"

"I have a new twenty that says if he's the lover, he'll stay away."

Even in the dim starlight coming through the SUV's windows, she could see his smile. She liked that smile. "My twenty says the lover will visit tonight."

"Guess we'll see." He reached into his jacket pocket for his binoculars.

They sat quietly for a while. The pines stood in dark shadow next to the vehicle while the landscape beyond the mountaintop was cast in a silver glow from the magnitude of the stars out here so far from town. She heard an owl hoot from a nearby tree, and somewhere farther off a hawk answered.

She turned the key to let down her side window, needing the cool summer night's air. Earlier at the hotel, she'd been so close to asking Ford into her hotel room. If she had, they wouldn't be here now. They'd be wrapped up in each other's arms. The thought sent a ball of heat straight to her center. And she knew the real reason she hadn't invited him into her room earlier.

Most men she could take or leave. Ford wasn't like that. She told herself she wasn't ready for the kind of commitment even one night with him might take. She had to keep her mind on this case, but it was hard to do that with Ford just inches away and this spark between them like a live wire.

"Does it worry you that just a few days ago I was ready to drive over a cliff?" Ford said inside the dark SUV. He thought that would give any woman pause, even one like Hitch. He had to know because he didn't want any secrets between them if they were going to become lovers. And he was pretty sure that they were.

"No, because you wouldn't have done it," she whispered, not looking at him.

He chuckled. "How can you be so sure?" he asked, turning toward her, studying the outline of her face in the darkness.

She turned to meet his gaze. "Because you didn't want to go over that cliff."

"I wish I believed that."

"Doesn't matter now anyway," Hitch said. "You're not in that state of mind anymore. You're not that man."

He smiled at her. "You know that how?"

She held his gaze. "I see it in your eyes. I also felt it in your kisses." She turned back to her surveillance. "You want to live."

Ford realized that she was right. He tried not to stare at her, even though he loved looking at her face, staring into her eyes. She had mesmerized him in a way that he thought could never happen to him again.

The pain of what he'd been through was still there and always would be. But Hitch had made him realize that he could go on. He might even be able to find happiness in this world he'd only seen as too broken to repair.

He cleared his throat, changing the subject. "Other than you losing twenty dollars, what if he doesn't show tonight?"

"I haven't lost yet. He can't stay away from her and they both know that a phone call will show up on their bills."

"You think it will go to trial?"

Hitch continued to study the ranch house for a long moment before she lowered her binoculars and answered. "If she suspects that could happen, she'll run before she's locked up."

The answer surprised him. "But the bond she put up—"

"I suspect she already planned to lose that and the ranch. It isn't the only money she has—you can bet on that. If she was smart, and she is, she would have planned this for some time and taken into account all possible outcomes. This wasn't an impulsive act. Who knows how long she's been hiding money for the day when she might need it? She could have been planning this for years. She thought of *almost* everything. What worries me now is what she plans to do with her accomplice."

Ford shot her a look. "You think she'll kill him."

"She doesn't have much choice. He keeps going off script. She can't trust him. He's too much of a liability. She's already killed her husband. What's one or two more murders," Hitch said as the garage door at the ranch house suddenly rolled up and Rachel's SUV rolled out.

"One or two more?" Ford said.

Hitch met his gaze. "If she thought you might change your story about what you heard on the phone call, well, you'd be in the same boat. That's why the sooner you go back to Big Sky, the better off you'll be."

She started the patrol SUV's motor and took off down the mountain without headlights to follow Rachel—wherever she was headed at this time of the night.

"And you owe me twenty dollars," Hitch said as she raced after the disappearing taillights in the distance.

Chapter 20

Hitch had expected Rachel to turn toward town as soon as she drove off the dirt ranch road. To her surprise, the SUV turned right at the highway and headed in the direction of Harlowton.

"Where is she going?" Ford said, sounding as surprised as Hitch was.

"Wherever it is, she's going there in a hurry." By the time Hitch reached the end of the ranch road and turned onto the highway headed north, she could barely see Rachel's taillights in the distance. "I think she's trying to lose us."

Turning on her headlights and tromping on the gas, she raced after her. While it had been Rachel's SUV that had come out of the garage, Hitch hadn't been able to see the driver. What if it wasn't Rachel behind the wheel?

Clouds had moved in, cloaking the night. Ahead, she could make out the dim taillights. Rachel, or whoever, was driving fast as if she knew she was being followed. Hitch didn't want to lose her, but she also didn't want to come running up on her in the growing fog and careen into the back of her vehicle either. As the terrain became more hilly, she only got glimpses of the blurry red taillights ahead of her through the fog.

Hitch was going eighty-five when she came up a hill and saw brake lights off to the side of the road. She recognized the SUV. The driver had pulled off onto a wide spot.

As Hitch sped past, she glanced at the driver of the SUV. Rachel was behind the wheel. She caught a glimpse of the woman's face and the smug smile plastered on it. As Hitch kept going, she watched in her rearview mirror as Rachel turned back toward the ranch.

Over the next hill, Hitch hit her brakes and did a highway patrol turn in the empty road before heading back to Big Timber. Ahead, she could see that Rachel was no longer speeding. Hitch followed her until she turned into her own ranch road.

"Was that what I think it was?" Ford said.

"She tricked me. Got me to follow her while whoever was visiting her got away," Hitch said. She had to hand it to the woman. Rachel had been one step ahead of her from the beginning. The subterfuge only made Hitch more convinced that the woman was guilty of cold-blooded murder.

Hitch just had to prove it, and that was the problem.

It was late by the time they reached the hotel.

"I don't know about you, but I could use a drink," Ford said and glanced at his phone. "Bar closes in less than an hour."

She smiled. "I thought you didn't drink."

"Only on special occasions."

"And you think this is one of them?" she asked with a chuckle.

"It just might be." His look said he wasn't ready to go to his hotel room alone. She knew the feeling. Maybe tonight they needed each other. She realized with a start that she more than needed him. She wanted him, which was entirely different. This kind of want made her ache inside.

The bar was empty except for a few regulars watching TV at the other end of the room. She ordered herself a screwdriver. Ford raised a brow and laughed and said he'd take the same. Taking a sip of her drink, she slid off the stool, went to the jukebox and punched in a few of her favorite songs.

The bartender saw her and turned down the volume on the TV as she took her stool again and the first song came on.

"Seriously, why are you involved in such a dangerous job?"

"Someone has to do it. I would think you'd know better than anyone why I do this."

"That was war. This is…"

"Its own kind of war," she said and ran a finger down the sweating fog on her glass. "I'm sorry I suspected you."

"Thanks, since I take that to mean you no longer do," he said.

"Do you still love her?" She hadn't meant to ask the question, but once it was out of her mouth, she was anxious to hear his answer. She hated that she was hanging on his answer, knowing he would be truthful with her.

He took a sip of his drink and chuckled to himself. "No. I've realized that I've never been in love with Rachel. Not the real kind. I was in love with the idea of her." He met her gaze. "But I'm not even in love with that anymore."

"Good," she said as a new song began on the jukebox.

Ford stepped off his stool. "Dance with me." He reached

for her hand. His large one was warm and dry. A strong hand. It wrapped around hers as he gently led her out onto the small dance floor. A strong man, she thought as he took her in his arms.

They began to move to the slow country song. She breathed in the distinct male scent of him and was tired enough that she was almost tempted to rest her head on his shoulder.

She drew back a little to look into his face. "I'm serious about you leaving town."

He grinned. "Otherwise you won't be able to resist me?"

"Something like that. Ford, I'm serious. It's too dangerous. She saw us together tonight." She leaned back a little to meet his gaze. "Promise me that you'll leave in the morning."

"If that's what you want." He pulled her closer. This time she didn't resist. She rested her head on his shoulder, relishing being wrapped in his protective strength. What was it about this man that brought out such powerful feelings in her? It had happened so quickly that it had caught her off guard.

The song ended. When she raised her head from his shoulder, she met his gaze. Heat speed-raced through her veins, reminding her how long it had been since she'd even dated.

"Ford?"

"I know," he said. "Maybe when this case is over, if you—"

"I thought I'd find you here," said a deep male voice behind them.

Hitch turned to see the sheriff, thumbs hooked in the pockets of his jeans, his chest puffed out. "That lab of yours is trying to find you."

Chapter 21

When Hitch pulled out her phone, she saw that she had several messages from the DCI lab—and the governor. "I'm sorry. I have to go take care of this," she told Ford. Their gazes locked. "Thank you for the dance."

"We'll have to do it again sometime," he said with a slight bow of his head.

The look in his eye made her cheeks actually flush. "I hope so."

She rushed upstairs to the quiet of her room to listen to her messages. She desperately needed a break in this case and soon. She wanted this one over for more reasons than ever before.

After closing her door to the quiet of her room, she listened to the governor's first message. Bart Collinwood had been kicking up a lot of dust and so had Lloyd Townsend. If Hitch didn't find something solid on the case soon…

She listened to the DCI investigator's message and held

her breath. Maybe this was the break she needed. "I have news, just not the news I think you were hoping to hear. We found no blood or tissue evidence on the ring to suggest it had been used in a violent attack. Nothing on the ring matched Rachel Collinwood's DNA either."

Hitch let out the breath she'd been holding and told herself it had been a long shot. Still, when she'd seen the Townsends' rings, she'd thought she'd found a clue. Those grooves were so deep in that design that something would have been found. And Rachel and Paul had been lovers. She'd thought she'd found the key to breaking this case wide open.

"As for the design and the bruise left on Rachel Collinwood's face, we ran both the ring and photo through a variety of tests. Our conclusion? It doesn't match. There are parts of it that are close… Sorry. We have a unit coming out your way tomorrow. I'll have them return the ring to you."

Hitch tossed her phone on the bedside table. She couldn't help but feel even more deflated. She'd been so sure that she'd found the accomplice. The ring that had made the bruise wasn't Paul Townsend's ring—nor was it the husband's. All Hitch had to do was find the ring that matched that bruise. Talk about looking for a needle in a haystack.

Another dead end. All her instincts told her that her suspicions weren't wrong. But unless she found evidence… Worse, when she thought about it, Paul Townsend was too young and too undisciplined to be the accomplice. Wasn't that why a year ago Rachel had cut him loose? Rachel had realized that she couldn't count on him. So who had she turned to?

As she got ready for bed, her thoughts kept straying to Ford. She'd met few men who could occupy her thoughts as much. She thought about what he'd confessed to her about the day he'd gotten the call from Rachel. It hadn't been easy for him to admit. She could tell that he was embarrassed by even the foiled attempt to end his life. She couldn't imagine how low he'd been at that moment to even consider it. Ford Cardwell wasn't the impulsive type. If suicide had been his intention, then Rachel really could have saved his life.

If so, then Hitch now believed in fate.

She realized that she had no solid proof that Rachel had planned the killing of her husband. That was what frustrated her the most. She had the lack of fingerprints on the glass and pottery. She had the lack of the husband's voice on the call to Ford. She had the bruise. She had the cartridge casing by the kitchen door. She had the lack of bruises and abrasions on the husband's hands. But even with all of that, it still might not be enough to hold up in court.

Had she lost her perspective? Had she wanted Rachel to be guilty? "What if your instincts are wrong?" she asked herself in the empty hotel room.

"I'm not wrong." Whatever Rachel had been hit with, it also hadn't been with her husband's ring. So whose had it been?

Whoever had hit her had forgotten to take off his ring. But Rachel would have realized it at some point and had him put Humphrey's ring on. Which meant Humphrey was already dead.

But without that ring… This was the part of a case that she hated the most. Being so close she could feel it, but not being able to find that one crucial piece of evidence that would complete her investigation. She'd been here before. Usually, it was something small that she'd overlooked. Or a mistake the criminal had made or was going to make.

She needed the accomplice—and that ring.

She climbed into bed, telling herself she'd never get to

sleep, not with her roiling emotions—and her growing feelings for Ford Cardwell.

A few hours later, she was startled awake by the ringing of her phone. She picked up. "Good morning, Governor."

"Is it? What have we got on this investigation?"

"Nothing definite yet, but—"

"The sheriff seems to think that you're on some kind of crusade against this woman."

Hitch groaned inwardly. "I'm just trying to get at the truth like I always do."

"You have a great record at doing just that. But this case is…"

"Complicated."

"That's one way of putting it," the governor said. "I can't give you much more time on this. I have another case you're needed on. Not to mention the fact that you seem to have stirred up a hornet's nest."

"Give me forty-eight hours. If I don't have evidence by then, I'll leave it to the sheriff." Hitch knew what that would mean. Rachel Collinwood would get away with murder.

"Forty-eight hours."

The clock was ticking.

Ford was waiting for Hitch when she came out of the hotel. He pulled her aside behind a pillar at the edge of the building. "You okay?" he asked, his hand still on her arm. She nodded, but he could tell something was wrong. "It wasn't the ring, was it," he said.

She groaned. "You know about the ring?" Shaking her head, she said, "These small towns. No. It wasn't the ring I was looking for. I'd hoped it matched a bruise on Rachel's face." She described the bruise. "It didn't match close enough. So I'm back to square one, since I'm almost positive the bruise was made by a man's ring—just not her husband's."

Ford had heard about Paul Townsend being brought in. It had been his pickup that they'd seen leaving the Collinwood Ranch. But not his ring.

"I have an idea," he said, having given this some thought last night after they'd parted. He couldn't leave town. Not now. "Rachel trusts me. Put a wire on me and let me try to get the truth out of her."

Hitch was shaking her head before he could even finish speaking. "Not happening. I need to wind this investigation up in the next forty-eight hours, and quite frankly, you've become a distraction I can't afford."

"Is that what I am to you?" he said, grinning.

"I'm serious. Please go home so I know you're safe."

"I can't do that." He held her gaze. "I came here to save Rachel if I could. Instead, I find myself getting involved with you."

"I wouldn't say we're involved."

"Wouldn't you?" He cupped her cheek, drawing her face up to his own. "Tell me there is nothing between us and I'll walk away right now."

She parted her lips, but no words came out. He pulled her into his arms. He could feel her heart pounding in her pulse. "Last chance," he said.

Chapter 22

Hitch had flat-out refused to even think about his plan. She was determined that he leave and go back to Big Sky. Did she really believe that Rachel would harm him? Kill him? Even if she'd murdered Humphrey, Ford didn't believe that she would kill him.

But he could also be wrong about that. Wrong about a lot of things when it came to Rachel. He knew it was risky. The thought made him laugh. It wasn't that long ago that he was racing toward a cliff with only one thought in mind—ending his life as he knew it.

Now, though, his life felt precious. He didn't want it to end. He wanted to live—even if Hitch Roberts wasn't part of it. Not that he was ready to give up on the two of them. She needed this investigation over and so did he. He could tell that she'd hit a wall in the investigation. If he could move it along, he would do whatever he had to.

As he drove out to Rachel's ranch, he told himself that

maybe Rachel didn't trust him as much as she used to. But she didn't see him as a real threat. She saw him as naive and weak because of his feelings for her, which he'd more than demonstrated at her wedding. If anything, she found him dispensable, just as she had fifteen years ago. Now that he'd already given his statement to the sheriff, she wanted him gone.

But would she trust him enough to tell him the truth?

He had to pretend he was still blindly in love with her. That wouldn't be easy. Rachel had been his fantasy woman for years. Unfortunately, that woman had never existed, and it had taken her to show him that. Had Humphrey come to that same conclusion those last few seconds before she'd killed him?

Ford realized now that he'd used the fantasy of Rachel so other women never quite measured up and he didn't get hurt. As a boy, he'd seen the hell his father had gone through during the divorce. Ford's own mother had deserted them. No wonder he had commitment issues.

Until now. He'd never met anyone like Hitch before. She'd made him realize what he wanted in a woman— knocking Rachel off that pedestal he'd put her on.

As he pulled up in front of the ranch house, he knew this was going to have to be the acting job of his life. Rachel was smart. She was also leery of him after his last visit. If she spotted the lie… He pushed the thought away. He would just have to make sure she didn't.

As Rachel opened the door, he caught a whiff of familiar perfume. Her hair was pulled up, a gold necklace twinkling at her slim throat. She was wearing a slinky jumpsuit in a turquoise blue that brought out the blue in her eyes and hugged her curves. The woman was drop-dead gorgeous and she knew it.

"Ford, I was glad when you called. Come in."

She let him into the living room. "I hate the way we left things the last time you were here." Soft music played in the background. The lights had been dimmed. "Have a seat. Let me get us something to drink."

Still standing, he watched her walk into the kitchen, taken aback by this warm reception. Earlier when he'd called, he'd said the same thing. He didn't like the way they'd left things. She'd sounded wary at best on the phone but had said of course she wanted to see him before he left.

Now he felt a sliver of concern work its way under his skin. This could be a huge mistake. But he was already here, he told himself as he looked around. He spotted Rachel's phone on the table next to the couch. Hadn't the sheriff taken her phone? This must be a new one. He realized that she must have been looking at it when he knocked and put it down and forgotten it.

Ford quickly picked it up. She hadn't signed off. He wasn't sure what he was even looking for. Certainly not a confession.

After glancing at her emails, he opened her photos. He went to the most recent ones. He was scanning through them when one caught his eye. All the breath rushed from him. It was of Rachel. She was tied to an iron bed, wearing nothing but what appeared to be a fireman's jacket that barely covered her private parts. He zoomed in to make the logo larger. Sweet Grass County volunteer fireman's jacket.

Had Humphrey been a local volunteer fireman? Ford knew it would be easy enough to find out, but he doubted it. In the photo, Rachel was laughing and saying something to the person taking the shot. It was the gleam in her eyes that told him the photographer wasn't Humphrey. That and the fact that this photo had been taken on her new phone, so it had been shot recently.

He quickly switched to open Rachel's contact list, curious about whose number he'd find, when she called from the kitchen.

"I hope you still like dark beer."

"You know me," he called back and quickly looked around for a place to put the phone. He stuffed it between two of the large, heavy fashion magazines on the coffee table as he heard her coming back and sat down next to it.

"I was so glad I had a beer for you," Rachel said, returning to the living room with a bottle of dark beer and a frosted glass, which she put down on the table at the far end of the couch next to him. She sat down at the opposite end of the couch, picked up her glass of red wine and turned toward him. Her smile looked glued on and slightly crooked. He figured it wasn't her first glass of wine tonight.

"I'm so sorry we had to reconnect after all these years in such a tragic way," she said. "It appears that all of Humphrey's and my dirty secrets are now local gossip. I'm so embarrassed."

"You shouldn't be embarrassed," he said. "I'm sure you never expected to find yourself in such a situation."

"Exactly," she agreed. "People like Humphrey and I... Well, I never expected something like this to happen. Not to us. I know you were shocked," she said, leaning toward him a little.

He got another wave of her perfume. It made him nauseous. He reached for his beer and poured some into the glass. The cold made him shiver a little. "I *was* shocked," he admitted. "I had no idea."

"No one did. Shyla said I should have told someone. Called the police on him. Done something more before things got totally out of hand." She shook her head and took a sip of her wine. Cupping the glass in her hands, she looked at him. "I was so ashamed. I didn't want anyone to know. I especially didn't want you to find out. What you must think of me."

"You can't believe that I would think less of you because of this."

Tears welled in all that blue. She licked her lips and gave him a sad smile. "You were Humphrey's best friend, but I always felt you and I… I don't know. That we had a special connection."

There would have been a time when those words would have warmed him to his toes. Instead, he found himself comparing this visit to the last one, when she'd been trying to get rid of him. Apparently, she wasn't hiding her boyfriend in the back bedroom this time.

"Ford, there's something I have to ask you." She put down her wineglass and turned all of her attention on him. "There's a rumor going around. I'm sure it's not true. Some people saw you dancing with that woman, the medical examiner, and the other night I went for a drive and…" Her gaze locked with his. "I thought I saw you in her patrol car."

"It's true," he said and picked up his beer as he broke eye contact with her. This part had to be the most convincing, so he took his time. "That's another reason I wanted to see you before I left." He took a drink and set down his glass to turn to her. "Rachel, I don't know how to tell you this." He could see that she was nervous and trying very hard not to show it. "Hitch, well… I suspect you already know that she doesn't believe your story."

"It wasn't a story," Rachel said automatically and looked as if this wasn't news. She seemed to remember something.

He saw her look around and frown. She was looking for her phone. He saw her glance toward the kitchen.

"Hitch says she has solid proof," he said, drawing her attention again. "That's why I wanted to see you, because I want you to know. I would do anything for you. I don't think it's a secret how I've always felt about you." He looked down as if embarrassed by his confession. "I always thought you and I..." He heard her move before he felt her hand on his arm.

"Ford. I've been so stupid from the very beginning. You were one of the few people who knew about my background, how poor I was, how scared I was of not having anything to call my own. I can't tell you how many times I've wished it had been you instead of Humphrey."

He looked into her eyes. The woman was amazing. So beautiful with her lips trembling like that and her eyes shimmering in tears. He'd always been so taken with her, never looking too deeply below the surface. Otherwise, he might have realized what an astonishing liar she was, he thought as he pulled her into his arms.

Hitch caught herself pacing the floor as she read over the list of phone numbers she'd received from DCI of Rachel's calls to and from her cell phone as well as Humphrey's in the days that led up to the shooting.

No surprise, there were mostly calls to Humphrey's number and vice versa. Also, a lot of calls to her friend Shyla, who Ford had told Hitch about. She couldn't concentrate after Ford's message saying he was going out to the ranch. He would try to get Rachel to confess on his phone. Did he have any idea how dangerous that could be if he got caught? She'd called him the moment she'd gotten the text, but his phone had gone straight to voice mail.

She kept thinking of the danger he was putting himself in. She should have stopped him. Or at least tried harder to talk him out of what he was doing.

Rationally, she knew she couldn't have done either.

But she also couldn't sit around waiting to hear from him. After seeing all the calls to the same number, she'd realized that she should talk to Shyla Birch, allegedly Rachel's best friend. Not that she expected to get anything from the woman. But she had to do something.

Birch, who'd married a local deputy in town, lived in a small house just outside of Big Timber. As Hitch crossed the Yellowstone River, she caught sight of the house and a flock of geese etched against the evening sky. She hadn't called to see if Shyla was home, deciding to take a chance. She had, however, called to see if the woman's husband was working tonight. He was. She doubted Shyla would be forthcoming if there was a deputy in the room.

Parking, she got out and headed for the front door. She could smell the river. The night air had a wonderful summer-is-coming feel to it. In Montana, summer usually arrived somewhere before the Fourth of July and ended shortly thereafter.

The woman who opened the door wasn't what Hitch had been expecting. She was wearing a too-large T-shirt and shorts. Her red curly hair formed a halo around her head, accentuating large brown eyes. Her feet were bare and she was holding a bowl of what smelled like buttered popcorn.

"Shyla Birch? I'm state medical examiner Hitch—"

"I know who you are," the woman said, tucking the large bowl of popcorn against her hip.

"Ford suggested I talk to you."

Surprisingly, those words seemed to do the trick. Hitch

saw the woman hesitate and then sigh before she said, "Come on in, then."

The house smelled of stale cigarettes and popcorn. Shyla motioned to a chair by the couch as she grabbed the remote and muted the television before curling back under the blanket lying on the couch, with the bowl of popcorn in her lap. "Ford tell you that I'm Rachel's friend?"

"He said you were her *best* friend." That seemed to please her, Hitch saw, as she took the chair. "That's why I wanted to speak with you."

"I wondered when you'd get around to me." She shoved a handful of popcorn into her mouth.

"You probably know, then, what I'm going to ask you," Hitch said.

"Did I know he was abusing her? Did I see bruises? Did she ever talk to me about it?"

"And?" She waited for the young woman to answer.

Shyla pulled a face and put down the bowl of popcorn on the couch next to her as she picked up her cigarettes from the end table next to her. Hitch watched her light one and take a long drag before tilting her head back to let out a stream of smoke.

"She didn't tell me, but I saw bruises once or twice. She always had a story for how she'd gotten them. Looking back, though, oftentimes Humphrey would be there when she told me, so she was clearly covering for him and he was letting her."

"So you weren't surprised when you heard what had happened."

"Actually…" Shyla stared down at her cigarette for a moment. "I was shocked. I thought they were happy—in their own way. Did Ford tell you that I met my husband through Rachel?"

"No, he didn't. How did that come about?" she asked, trying hard not to sound like a medical examiner on a case. She must have succeeded, because Shyla seemed to relax a little, loosening up.

"Rick had gone out to the ranch after Rachel had called about a possible break-in. She'd come home and the front door was standing open. Humphrey was in New York on business and she was scared out of her wits. She called me to come out while she was waiting locked in her car." Shyla chuckled. "And the rest is history, as they say. Although I never thought I'd fall for a lawman." She rolled her eyes. "No offense."

"None taken. So had the house been broken into?"

"That's what's so weird. The door must have not been locked properly and had simply blown open. Rick had been going off shift when he got the call, so he stayed around to keep us company. Rachel made us some drinks. Humphrey came home and it kind of turned into a party. By the end, I was in love."

"Sounds like it was meant to be."

Shyla nodded, finished her cigarette and stubbed it out. "I heard that you think Rachel planned the whole thing."

There was something in the way she said it that made Hitch wonder if she also had thought the same thing. "I suspect she might have." She waited for a few moments before she added, "What do you think?"

Reaching for the popcorn bowl, Shyla took her time picking out a few kernels before she finally answered— instead of instantly defending her best friend.

"Rach is amazing. She really is. Did you know that she came from nothing? I mean, we were poor. Well, maybe not *poor* poor, but my parents both worked. They paid for my college, though, not like Rachel, who was on loans and scholarships. I don't blame her for wanting more than she got out of life, you know?" Hitch nodded. "But..." She looked down at the piece of popcorn in her fingers and tossed it back into the bowl, wiping her hand on the hem of her T-shirt, her thoughts clearly elsewhere. "I never thought she really loved Humphrey. Oh, she wanted him, but if you've ever been in love..."

Hitch remembered being in Ford's arms. It was an unexplainable feeling, an amazing, scary-as-hell feeling.

"But that doesn't mean she planned the whole thing," Shyla said, looking uncomfortable.

"No, possibly not," Hitch agreed. "I suppose you know about the prenuptial agreement she signed?"

"That was Humphrey's father's doing. Bart never liked Rachel. He thought she was a gold digger."

"Still, the agreement aside, Rachel could have divorced her husband and walked away with a lot of money."

Shyla let out a bark of a laugh. "Not near enough for that woman's tastes." She seemed to bite her tongue. "I shouldn't have said that."

"It's okay. I've seen her closet." An uneasy silence filled the room. "I have just one other question. I really appreciate your candor, and nothing you've said will go beyond this room. Is Rachel capable of putting together a plan to get rid of her husband and make it look like he was trying to kill her?"

Hitch knew she was putting the woman on the spot. Shyla's first instinct would be to protect her friend. And yet there was something refreshingly honest about the young woman.

"I'm not saying that's what happened," Shyla said carefully. "But Rachel... Well, she's always gone after what she wanted and not let anything stand in her way. She's definitely capable of doing anything she sets her mind to. She's got that kind of personality. But would she purposely kill her husband?" She gave a shake of her head. "Who does that?"

Someone cold-blooded enough that she wanted out but refused to give up the money, Hitch thought as she thanked Shyla and got to her feet. As she started toward the door, she heard a vehicle pull up. The front door flew open before she reached it and a handsome, broad-shouldered man in uniform came in and stopped dead at the sight of her.

"Rick, this is the medical examiner. She's looking into Rachel's case," Shyla said as she came off the couch. She sounded embarrassed and a little too anxious. "She was just leaving."

Rick Birch's brow furrowed. "Did you tell her that we're good friends with Rachel? With her husband, too, before all this?"

"Of course," his wife said quickly.

"Nice to meet you, Deputy Birch," Hitch said and started to step past him. He didn't move for a moment, blocking the doorway out. She continued toward him until he had to make a choice. He moved aside, but he didn't look happy about it.

On her way out the door, she heard him say, "What did you say to her?" before the door closed behind her.

Hitch walked to her car, thinking about everything she'd heard—and felt—from Rachel's best friend. Shyla had her doubts. Hitch wasn't the only one who suspected Rachel of far more than shooting her husband during a domestic dispute.

Climbing into her SUV, she started the engine and checked her phone, anxious to hear from Ford. She was getting even more worried after her talk with Shyla. She was about to pull out when her headlights glinted off something in the garage. She hit the brakes and stared at the small single-car garage attached to the Birch house. The garage door had a chunk missing where it appeared someone had driven into it. Through the opening, she saw what looked like the chrome of a cattle guard on the front of a pickup.

Putting the SUV into Park, she got out and walked to the garage door to look inside through the large hole. A pickup was parked inside. The large grille-guard bumper on the front was what had caught her eye. She stared at it, recognizing the design. It was exactly like the one that had nearly hit her the other night.

Chapter 23

Rachel hugged him, pressing her breasts against him. He felt her hand move across his chest around to his side, down to his hip. He realized with a start that she had checked him for a wire. Then her hand slipped into his pocket of his jacket. It came back out with his phone.

She drew back, looked down at it in her hand and touched the screen. "Oh, I'm sorry. This is yours. I thought my phone must have slipped down between the couch cushions." She didn't hand the phone back as she moved to the middle of the couch and reached for her wineglass with her free hand. She took a sip before she set his phone down between them.

She looked around again. "I thought I left my phone in here."

"Your phone?" He pretended to look around for it, and as he sat up, he kicked the leg of the coffee table. "Oh, there it is." He'd sent one of her fashion magazines sliding to the edge of the table, exposing the phone he'd put there. "Is that it?"

She stared at the phone. He could see her trying to remember where she'd laid it down and if it could have gotten covered by a magazine.

He took advantage of her momentary confusion to continue what he was saying. "Hitch has discovered incriminating evidence against you. I tried to find out what it is, but she wouldn't tell me. I'm just afraid it's going to get you sent to prison for the rest of your life."

She picked up her phone, pocketing it before taking another sip of her wine. She grimaced as if it tasted bitter on her tongue and put down her glass. "Has she taken this evidence to the prosecutor?"

"I don't know. Rachel, you know how I feel about you. Is there anything I can do?"

"Having you here, it's meant so much to me. I'm surprised you've stayed this long." She studied him for a moment. "I need more wine," she said, getting to her feet. She picked up his empty beer bottle. "Can I get you another beer?"

"Sure," he said as she headed into the kitchen. He realized that from here he could see her in the mirrored cabinets across from the sink. He watched her lean against the granite counter as if she needed it for strength. With a shaking hand, she refilled her glass and got another beer for him out of the refrigerator.

It was what she did next that stopped his heart cold. She opened the beer, poured some into a new frosted glass from the refrigerator's freezer, and then she took a small vial from her pocket.

He watched in horror as she poured something into his beer, holding up the glass to the light to make sure it had dissolved. Calling from the kitchen, she said, "You know me so well. That's why I'm glad you're here. I can tell you the truth."

She smiled as she picked up his beer and her wineglass. He watched her take a breath and then head into the living room.

In the living room, Ford quickly picked up his phone and hit Record. He put the phone back down where she'd left it and tried to still his breathing. His heart pounded so loudly, he feared she would be able to hear it. Of course Rachel was suspicious of his motives. But then again, he'd come running at the first sign that she was in trouble, reinforcing her belief that he adored her, that he'd always adored her, that he would always wish it had been him instead of Humphrey she'd fallen in love with. Did she think he was hoping for another chance with her, now that Humphrey was gone? Probably, knowing Rachel.

"Here," she said as she came back into the room and handed him the glass of beer.

He set the frosted glass with the doctored beer on the coffee table. Rachel quickly reached to put a coaster under it. "Thank you," he said but didn't touch the beer.

She returned to the kitchen to snag a full opened bottle of wine, then returned to her place at the end of the couch, facing him. "Humphrey loved a chilled glass for his beer, but I guess I don't need to tell you that. You probably remember."

He nodded. "I'm so sorry things turned out the way they did." She took a sip of her wine and didn't look at him. "I mean it, Rachel. If there is anything I can do… You know I'm here for you."

She looked up then, and their eyes locked for a few seconds before she said, "I wish there was, Ford. Having you here, it's meant so much to me. How will I ever be able to repay you?"

He thought about what he'd seen her put into his beer glass. Was it something that would kill him? Or just make him deathly ill? Gut-wrenching poison or truth serum? With Rachel, he had no idea.

One thing was clear. She hadn't bought his act.

"Remember the first time we met?" she was saying, a cheerfulness in her voice that didn't quite ring true. "I wish I could go back to that day. If you had left me alone, that squirrel would have eaten out of my hand."

He smiled in spite of himself. "Because you wouldn't have given up until it did. You were always like that. When you wanted something, you hung in until you got it."

"Like with Humphrey," she said, the cheerfulness gone. "You know he had second thoughts about marrying me, don't you? Of course you did. You were his best man, his best friend. He would have told you. He wouldn't have married me if it wasn't for the pregnancy. You probably thought that I got pregnant on purpose so he didn't get away. That's what his father thought. After we got married, when I lost the baby, Humphrey was devastated. He wanted that child so badly." She looked away as she took a sip of her wine. "I don't know why I'm bringing all of this back up. Bad memories."

"He loved you."

She met his gaze again. "Yes, he did. But he never forgave me." She let out a bitter laugh. "He would have left me, except that it would have proved his father right."

He frowned. "Forgave you for what?"

"I didn't lose the baby, because there never was one. His father hired a private investigator. I lied about the pregnancy. Humphrey didn't find out until we'd been married almost a year."

"What was the fight about the day he died?" Ford asked.

She looked away for a moment. "He found my birth control pills." She laughed. "Stupid me. I never kept them in my purse."

He stared at her in shock. "Why wouldn't you want his child? Wouldn't Bart have changed his mind about you if you'd given him a grandchild?"

"I wasn't anyone's broodmare," she snapped. "I wasn't ruining my figure, let alone having a child to take care of. That wasn't the life I wanted."

He didn't know what to say. His shock must have shown.

"Didn't I have the right? It's my body."

Ford couldn't help but wonder what his old friend would have done when he found out that his wife had been lying to him for years. "You could have adopted."

She let out a bitter bark of a laugh. "That's exactly what he said, telling me that we could adopt children no one else wanted because we had this amazing place to raise them." She looked horrified. "Children no one else wanted? Over my dead body."

Could her lies have led Humphrey to attack her? Maybe Rachel was telling the truth.

"Also, some money had gone missing from this foundation Humphrey had started. I was involved in it and he had the gall to ask me if I'd stolen it." She took another sip of her wine, anger pinching her classic features.

Ford let out the breath he'd been holding. Now he realized how little he'd known about their relationship or the lengths Rachel would go to get what she wanted. "Did he threaten divorce?"

Rachel laughed. "He said he needed time to think. That

he still loved me. But that he couldn't look at me right then. He took off into town to see his girlfriend at the café. It doesn't matter if they were actually sleeping together," she snapped before Ford could correct her. "The girl was all doe-eyed around him. Just the kind of woman he'd thought he'd married."

"That sounds like Humphrey," Ford said. "The part about still loving you. He told me at the wedding that he suspected you were lying about the pregnancy and even why you wanted to marry him so badly, but he said he didn't care. He loved you."

Tears filled her eyes. "I never knew that." She looked away again and downed more of the wine. "I hate to imagine what you must think of me." Her gaze went to his beer glass sweating on the coaster on the coffee table. "You haven't touched your beer."

"Did you do it, Rachel? Did you stage the whole thing to get rid of him so you didn't lose the money?"

Her head jerked around so she was facing him again. Color rushed to her cheeks, anger glinting in her eyes. "That's what you think, isn't it? You and the medical examiner."

He couldn't deny it. "Is it true? It's just you and me here, Rachel. Tell me so I can help you."

She glared at him for a long moment before she put down her wineglass and rose to her feet. "I think you should leave."

He nodded. "Just one more question." He motioned to the room, taking her in with it. "What did you hope to accomplish tonight with the dim lighting, the perfume, that silky outfit you're wearing and the chilled beer glass? Were you worried that you'd lost my undying admiration and love?"

She shook back a lock of her blond hair that had come

loose and fallen around her face. Her blue eyes were hard as ice chips and just as cold. "You have always underestimated me, Ford. If I wanted to seduce you, we'd be in my king-size bed right now."

He smiled. "No, Rachel, this time, you overestimated yourself." He picked up his phone. Turning off the recording, he looked up at her. "I came out here hoping you would tell me the truth. After all, you pulled me into this." He glanced at his beer glass. "I can't even imagine what you put into my beer, but I know now that you used me—just like you did Humphrey until you got tired of him. Was he going to divorce you? Is that why you killed him?" Her answer was that icy glare. "I wasn't kidding about the medical examiner being on to you. You thought your old life was bad? Wait until you get to prison."

With that, he turned to walk out. The wineglass hit the wall next to him and shattered, red wine droplets splattering against the white wall like blood.

He turned to look back at her seething angry face. Was this the last thing Humphrey saw before she pulled the trigger?

Hitch was so relieved when she opened her hotel room to find Ford standing there that she threw herself into his arms. He smiled as if touched by her concern and kissed her. They stayed like that for long minutes.

"She didn't buy it," he said as they moved deeper into her room. "But she did try to drug me."

"What?"

"I saw her put a powder substance in my second beer. But I did get something. She left her new phone in the room with me when she went into the kitchen. There was a recent photo taken of her tied to an iron bed. The only thing she was wearing was a Sweet Grass County Volunteer Fire Department jacket. It's her new phone, so the photographer wasn't Humphrey. She did it," he said quietly. "I know she did it. I saw it in her face." He sat down on the foot of her bed. "She killed him. She planned the whole thing right from the beginning fifteen years ago. I just don't know why she waited so long."

Hitch sat down next to him as he told her everything that had happened. Then he let her listen to the recording on his phone. When they'd finished, Hitch actually felt shocked. As long as she'd been in this business, she'd believed that she could no longer be shocked. "That woman is cold."

She got up and went over to the bed where the case notes were spread across the top. It took her only a moment to find what she was looking for. "The fingerprints found on the birth control pill package on the floor were Humphrey's."

He turned to her. "She admitted that's what they fought about. So maybe he didn't threaten her with divorce and she saw only one way to have it all. You have to stop her. No matter what it takes. She can't get away with this."

She smiled at him. "Don't worry. I'm working on it." She told him about her visit to Shyla Birch's house and meeting her unfriendly husband, the deputy, along with what she'd found in the garage.

Ford's eyes widened in alarm. "Are you telling me the pickup that almost killed you was driven by a deputy?"

"Or his wife. *Possibly.* The problem is the grille guard on the front of the pickup. When I got back, I found the manufacturer. The company sold nine in this area. *Nine.* But I can tell you one thing. Rick Birch and his wife are both with the Sweet Grass County Volunteer Fire Department. I saw one of their jackets hanging by the door as I left—not that it narrows it down. A lot of locals are also volunteer firemen. So tell me what you know about Shyla."

He raked a hand through his hair. "She was impulsive and a little wild, but I can't imagine her trying to run you down."

"I agree. Between the two? I would pick the husband."

Ford let out a curse. "You think he's Rachel's accomplice?"

"I think it's possible." She told him the story Shyla had related to her about how they'd met and fallen in love. "She credits Rachel for getting them together."

"You think Rachel knew him before then?"

Hitch shrugged. "I suspect he's protective of Rachel. He wasn't happy to see me with his wife. As I was leaving, I heard him demand to know what she said to me. He seems like the kind who went into law enforcement to bust heads. If he bought into Rachel's story about her husband, he might have seen helping her as a way to right a wrong. Or he could just be sleeping with her and agreed to do whatever she asked him to."

"He's *married* to Shyla."

Hitch rolled her eyes. "Right, Rachel's so-called best friend. You really think that would stop him?"

Ford shook his head. "How are you going to prove it one way or the other?"

"I wish I knew. The fact that he's a deputy makes it harder."

"But if you told the sheriff about the truck that tried to run you down…"

She saw realization sink in before he could finish. "Exactly. My word against his deputy. In the first place, I can't prove it was even him, let alone that he was trying to kill me. Nor did I get a license plate number. Just a metal guard like at least eight others like it around… So even if I could put his pickup on that street that night definitively, he could say that he never saw me. It is a very dark street."

"What are you going to do?" he asked, his voice softening as he looked at her.

She shook her head. "I'm just glad that you're all right."

"I'm sorry it didn't work. Rachel's too smart for me."

Hitch laughed. "She's not too smart for either of us and she's going to prove it. She has to be rattled right now. I would think she'll be contacting her accomplice."

"Another night on the mountain?"

"Not this time," Hitch said. "I have her phone tapped. We should be hearing something soon."

He tucked a lock of her hair behind her ear. "What should we do in the meantime?"

Rachel had stormed around her house after Ford left. Who did he think he was? That he'd come out to her house to try to get her to admit to something she hadn't done? What kind of friend was that?

She stopped to stare at the wall, still red from her wine, the broken glass twinkling on the carpet, and she felt all the anger rush from her. Stumbling back to the couch, she looked for her phone until she realized she'd put it in her pocket earlier. Frowning, she glanced at the coffee table. The magazines were no longer neatly displayed, but they had been before Ford arrived. So how could her phone have gotten under one of them?

It couldn't have.

She felt an icy chill run like spider legs down her spine and shuddered. He'd had her phone. She opened it. A photo came up of her on the bed and she dropped to the edge of the couch. With trembling fingers, she placed the call.

"Rachel, what's wrong?" Shyla said when she answered and heard her crying. "Do you want me to come out there?"

"No," Rachel said quickly. "It's... Ford was here earlier. He said some awful things to me."

"Like what? Rachel? Did I lose you? Are you still there?"

"It's my new cell phone. I don't know what's wrong with it. The battery keeps running down. I'm plugging it in. Just a minute."

"Rach," Shyla said when she came back on. "Rick is standing here. He wants to talk to you."

"Did I hear you're having trouble with your new cell phone?"

"I can't seem to keep it charged."

Rick let out a curse. "Rachel, they've got your phone tapped. The taps run down the batteries. Have you seen any apps that have suddenly appeared that aren't yours?"

She gritted her teeth and tried not to snarl. "I've had a little too much on my mind to be checking my *apps*."

"What about any weird text messages?"

Rachel opened her mouth to snap at him but closed it. "I got something about winning a prize that I had to redeem."

He swore. "Is your phone warmer than your old one? They often overheat if someone is using GPS to track your phone." She said it was. "Which means they're not just tapping into your calls—they're tracking you."

Rachel felt her skin grow clammy and cold. "What can I do?"

"Get rid of any apps you don't recognize, then update your phone and don't use it."

"And how am I supposed to hear from you?" she cried.

"I'll get you a burner. I'll have Shyla bring it out. But you have to quit running scared and acting like you're guilty.

Remember, you're the victim here. Humphrey would have killed you."

She nodded as she looked at the wine staining her wall. "Rick, I'm scared."

"Don't be. You did what you had to do. They're just trying to rattle you. Shyla wants to talk to you."

"Are you sure you don't want me to come out there?" her friend asked.

"No," Rachel said, looking at her phone where she'd plugged it in. "I'm fine. I'm going straight to bed. I think I just need a good night's sleep." She disconnected, and picking up Ford's beer where he'd left it, she walked into the kitchen and poured it down the drain.

For a moment, she stood at the sink staring out into the darkness before she walked down to her bedroom and began to pull out her luggage.

Chapter 24

"So you're really going," Hitch said the next morning when she woke up next to Ford. She'd been encouraging him to go for days. She'd seen the change in him, though, last night. He was finally free of Rachel Westlake Collinwood. She wished she was.

Last night after their lovemaking, Ford opened up to her. They'd shared stories, confided hopes and dreams and fears. Then they'd made love again and held each other like two lost souls caught in a storm.

"I need to go back and figure out what I'm going to do for a living," he said. "But I'm only a phone call away." He smiled at her and she felt the heat of it race through her veins. Last night had been amazing. Ford was a tender, thoughtful lover who took it slow—the first time. She smiled to herself, remembering the passion of the second time. Her cheeks heated at the memory.

"I'll miss you," she said, snuggling against him.

"No, you won't. You'll be too busy getting to the truth."

"I wish, but the forty-eight hours the governor gave me is almost up. On top of that, the sheriff told the governor about us. Not that I care," she was quick to add. "It just…"

"Complicates things. Another reason I need to leave."

Unfortunately, she had to agree, especially after what Ford had told her about Rachel trying to drug him. "This investigation has to break soon."

He laughed. "You'd know better than me, but I sure hope so."

"I have just a little more time before I have to put this one behind me. But just the thought of turning it over to the sheriff… As if he's going to continue gathering evidence between now and the trial. If there even is a trial." She shook her head. "So basically, nothing will be done, and Rachel will either get off entirely or receive a light sentence. There's nothing I can do about it."

Ford pulled her closer. "You still have a little time."

She chuckled. "At this point, I could have a month and I'm not sure I'd know exactly what happened on that ranch that day. And the worst part is that if I'm right that is exactly what Rachel is counting on."

He kissed her passionately before he let her go. "I'll call when I get back to Big Sky. Once you wrap it up—"

"The governor said there's another case waiting for me. But don't worry. I'll find a way to see you." Because she couldn't bear the thought of being away from him very long.

He pulled her closer. "I can't wait for you to meet my family."

She felt at a loss for words, wanting to tell him how she felt, but knowing that the timing was wrong. "We'll talk soon."

Ford knew it was time to go home. He could tell during his father's last call that he was getting worried. It was

Rachel. Jackson worried that he was too involved in this case—if not involved with Rachel herself.

Mostly, Ford knew he had to let Hitch do what she did so well and quit distracting her. She couldn't do her job if she was worried about him. He'd played amateur detective, and if he hadn't seen whatever Rachel had put in his beer, he would be buried now in the garden on the ranch.

He was on the edge of Big Timber leaving town when his cell phone rang. He saw it was Rachel calling and almost didn't take it. "Rachel?" For a moment, he didn't hear anything but crying. Then he heard the words that had him hitting his brakes and pulling to the side of the road.

"You're right about me. I don't deserve to live," Rachel said, her words slurred as if she were drunk. Drunk? Or drugged?

"What's going on?" he asked, his pulse jumping at her words.

"I can't do this anymore," she said. "I should have told you everything last night. I should have… I can't live with myself…" She began to sob again.

"Have you taken something, Rachel?" He heard her drop the phone, the rest of her words inaudible.

Swearing, he quickly turned around and headed toward the ranch. He debated calling 911 for an ambulance, but he was already on his way and would be there in a matter of minutes at this speed. Maybe she was just drunk. But if she'd taken something… He thought of that time in college when she and Humphrey had a fight and she'd taken a bottle of pills. Ford and Humphrey had walked her for hours until she came out of it.

He was just north of town near the creek when he caught lights in his rearview mirror. A highway patrol cruiser came racing up behind him, siren blaring, lights flashing. Ford swore but pulled over, planning to tell the officer why he'd been speeding and ask for his help. Rachel would hate that he brought the cops into it, but he had no choice now. He reminded himself that this was the woman who'd planned to drug him just last night. Still, he didn't want her overdose death on his conscience. Nor did he want Hitch's case to end like this.

When he started to pull over, the cruiser drew up beside him. The officer behind the wheel motioned for him to pull off the road onto a side road. He did as ordered, anxious to talk to the cop. He could feel the clock ticking and thought about calling 911 but knew it would take too much explanation. Pulling out his phone, he quickly called Hitch, but before he could speak, the officer tapped on his window.

Ford whirred down his window. "Officer, I know I was speeding," he said to the sandy-haired young cop. He saw that he was a deputy sheriff—not highway patrol as he'd first thought. "I just got a call—"

"Please get out of your vehicle."

"What? No, you don't understand." His pulse jumped. Something was wrong. His gaze went to the man's hands resting on the edge of the open window. A large ring on the officer's right hand caught his eye. Something about the design… He heard Hitch's voice far away and realized that she was still on the phone. "Officer, Rachel Collinwood called. I was on my way there before you pulled me over here by the creek—"

"I said get out of your vehicle now!"

"Okay, but this is highly unusual. Kind of like your ring…" He spotted the man's name on his shirt. "Officer Birch." His heart was now a hammer in his chest. Shyla's husband. The ring. The grille guard on the pickup that tried to run Hitch down. "I feel as if I've seen that ring before," he said, praying that Hitch was still on the line, that she was hearing this.

Movement in his side mirror. "Rachel? No wonder you weren't worried about her. She just climbed out of your patrol car."

"What the hell?" Birch said and spotted the phone lying on the seat next to Ford. The cop leaned in, snatched the keys from the ignition and, shoving Ford back, scooped up the phone. He swore and quickly ended the call, but hopefully Hitch had heard it all.

Hitch had been going through the evidence on the Collinwood case when she'd gotten Ford's call. "Hello? Hello?" She could hear Ford talking and realized he wasn't talking to her but to someone else. As his words registered and the call ended, she threw down the photos she'd been studying, grabbed her gun and her purse, and raced out to her patrol SUV, her heart in her throat.

Her mind whirred as she played what she'd heard over and over again. He'd been headed for Big Sky. But Rachel had called. Whatever she'd said had him headed for her ranch, where he was pulled over by Officer Rick Birch. Why had Birch pulled him over by the creek? And why was the deputy demanding Ford get out of the car? As Ford said, very unusual. And the ring...

She felt her pulse thundering through her veins. If she was right, Ford was in serious trouble. He'd passed as much of a message as he'd been able to before the call had been disconnected.

With her siren blaring and lights flashing, she sped out of town, across the bridge over the Yellowstone River, headed north. She had a pretty good idea of where Ford had been pulled over. He'd said by the creek. It was the turnoff to the Crazy Mountains. She zipped past several cars that had pulled over at the sound of her siren. She took a few curves and hit the brakes as she saw the turnoff ahead.

But she couldn't see if Ford's pickup and the deputy's cruiser were still parked down by the creek yet. It had taken her only minutes to get here, but what if she was too late?

"Let me handle this," Rachel said as she walked up to the driver's-side window and pushed the deputy aside.

"I see that you're feeling better," Ford said, wondering what these two thought they were going to do as he opened his glove box to take out his gun. With a sinking feeling, he saw that it was gone.

As he turned to look at her, Ford foolishly still believed that they weren't going to kill him. He heard the deputy come around to the passenger side of the pickup and open the door. They wouldn't kill him—not right here beside the main highway north. He turned back to Rachel, since she was clearly in charge, saw the expression on her face and knew that he was a dead man.

He had only a second to react. Way too little time to see the syringe in her hand before she stabbed the needle into the back of his shoulder. He tried to grab for it, but the deputy was on him, restraining him until she pulled the needle from Ford's flesh. By then, it was too late. He already felt the drug rushing through him.

"What the hell, Rachel?" he managed to say.

"Drag him over to the passenger side," Rachel said, reaching in to unsnap his seat belt. The deputy grabbed him. Ford tried to fight him off, but he could feel his muscles already going slack. "Now give me the keys and wait for me in your car for a moment."

Birch looked as if he didn't like taking orders from a woman, but with a grunt, he snapped Ford's seat belt in place, climbed out, slammed the passenger-side door and returned to his patrol car, parked behind Ford's pickup.

"Rachel?" He felt dizzy, his vision beginning to blur. Whatever she'd injected him with, it was fast acting. His fingers felt like they were no longer his own as he tried unsuccessfully to unhook his seat belt. He heard Rachel lock his door with the child safety lock system.

"Sit tight for a moment," she said and closed the driver's-side door. He could see her walking back to the cruiser in his side mirror.

Ford knew he had to do something, but with his coordination getting worse as the drug took hold, he realized even if he could get out of the pickup, he probably couldn't stand, let alone run.

At the sound of a gunshot, he flinched.

The driver's-side door of his pickup opened a moment later and Rachel climbed in.

"What did you do?" he asked, his words slurred. He tried to get his arms to move, thinking he would go for her throat, but both arms hung useless at his sides.

"*I* didn't do anything," she said as she wiped the pistol in her hand clean with a handkerchief. He recognized it as his own gun. "*You* did." Then, taking his right hand, she pressed his palm, then trigger finger into the cold steel. Using the handkerchief, she tossed his gun behind the pickup seat.

When had she gotten it out of his glove box? Or had it been Birch who'd taken it on one of the occasions Ford had stopped by the ranch to see Rachel? Had she been planning this the whole time?

She started the pickup and headed down the dirt road toward the Crazy Mountains. He didn't bother to try to ask what she planned to do with him. His tongue felt too large and useless in his dry mouth to waste speech on a question when he already knew the answer. She planned to kill him—just as she had her accomplice.

Hitch raced up to the turnoff. It wasn't until she dropped off the highway into the creek bottom that she could see the sheriff's deputy's patrol cruiser still parked there. But there was no sign of Ford's pickup. She could, however, see that Deputy Birch was sitting behind the wheel.

She quickly pulled up behind the cruiser and, gun drawn, stepped out to cautiously approach. The deputy was wearing his Western hat. He appeared to be looking down at something in his lap. He didn't move as she inched along the driver's side of his vehicle.

As she drew nearer, she could see that his window was down. The summer breeze coming up off the creek was warm. It made a slight whistling sound through the patrol cruiser's antenna. Hitch came alongside, the weapon pointed at the man's head, and grabbed the door handle and pulled. It took her a moment before she realized that she wouldn't be needing her gun. Officer Rick Birch had already been shot in the side of the head.

Slamming the door, she looked up the road and spotted dust boiling up some distance away between her and the Crazies. She glanced around to see if there were fresh tracks where someone had turned around. There weren't.

Her nerves were taut as she rushed back to her rig, jumped in and took off. As she did, she called DCI and gave them the information as to where they would find sheriff's deputy Rick Birch. Disconnecting, she drove, following the dust trail, praying she was right about the vehicle kicking up the dust being Ford's pickup. If she was, then Rachel was with him. Which meant that if Ford was still alive, it wouldn't be for long.

Chapter 25

"You wanted so badly to hear the truth?" She glanced at him before going back to her driving.

Ford saw the gleam in her blue eyes. She wanted to tell him. She wanted someone to know how clever she was.

Rachel suddenly hit the brakes so hard that even with his seat belt on, he flew forward. She caught him before his head hit the dash. "You're not wearing a wire, are you? Surely there wasn't time after my call." She tore open his shirt, checked under the waist of his jeans and then behind him before she sighed. "Of course you're not. And I have your phone. Even if I didn't, you wouldn't be able to record me." She laughed as she got the truck going again.

"You want my confession? You got it. I killed him. I set the whole thing up. It wasn't that hard," she said, warming to her story as she drove through the foothills toward the mountains. "I planned it for months, stashing away any money I could get my hands on. When he found the birth control pills… Well, I hadn't planned on that. He was so furious. I realized he really might divorce me. I followed him into town. I knew he'd go to that girl. I wanted to have the argument at her house. I wanted people to see it. Then I drove home. I'd already torn up the kitchen, breaking everything by the time he came home from town."

He thought about how Humphrey's fingerprints hadn't been found on any of the broken dishes on the floor—a red flag that Hitch had picked up on right away. If he had torn up the kitchen, his prints would have been on at least some of the shards. He wanted to tell her that it had been one of several mistakes she'd made, including killing Birch—and now him, but he could no longer speak. All he could do was listen and pray that Hitch had gotten the messages he'd tried to pass.

"You should have seen Humphrey's face when he walked into the kitchen and saw the mess. He actually looked at me as if I'd lost my mind. He really thought it was about that waitress at the café in town." She laughed. "He was going to help me clean up the mess. But before he could pick up anything, I jabbed him with the syringe—just like I did you." She chuckled. "It's fast acting, as you know, but he still managed to take a couple of steps toward me, so I pulled the gun. He looked dumbfounded for a moment, then demanded I hand the gun over." Her smile sent ice down his spine. It was worse than her laugh. "Oh, I gave it to him, all right."

"So you shot him before you pretended to be beaten by him." His words came out so slurred, he couldn't imagine how she had made sense of them.

"Pretended to be beaten?" she demanded. "Are you serious? You saw how badly I was injured." She sounded as if for a moment she believed her own lies. "Rick got a little carried away. I told him to make it look real. He certainly did that."

But he'd forgotten to take off his ring. Rachel must have noticed at some point. That would have been when they took off Humphrey's ring and the deputy used it to hit her. He'd seen the deputy's ring only minutes ago and recognized it from the bruise photo Hitch had shown him this morning, asking if he'd seen a ring that could have made that mark.

"That was the tricky part," Rachel was saying. "I needed someone I could trust. Rick was more than up for the job. But the fool actually thought that we would be together once I was exonerated."

Ford thought of Paul Townsend. How many other men had Rachel "interviewed" for the job before she got the deputy to help her?

She gave a slight shrug as if Birch had been dispensable, just like Humphrey. He felt his anger, once molten with rage, stir in him, cold as this woman. He knew he could kill. He had in the war. He wished he could get his hands around Rachel's neck right now. She hadn't given a thought to her best friend, Shyla.

"You probably are wondering where you came in," Rachel said to him as the foothills were behind them and he was looking out at the mountain road ahead.

Hitch saw the vehicle still a long way ahead of her slow and turn. She felt relief wash over her. It was Ford's pickup—just as she'd thought. Her instincts had been right. She called for backup, explaining that Deputy Birch had been shot and killed and that Rachel Collinwood appeared to have taken Ford Cardwell captive. They were now headed into the Crazy Mountains. She gave the dispatcher the name of the road they were on and disconnected as Ford's pickup disappeared into the pines as it headed up the mountainside.

She told herself that Ford was still alive. She had to believe that. Rachel hadn't killed him and wasn't only driving up into the mountains to dump the body. If she'd done that, she would have needed the deputy's help. So what was her plan?

The deeper they got in the mountains, the more worried she became. She felt helpless because no matter what she did, it might only put Ford in more danger. Rachel had already killed twice. There was nothing keeping her from killing again.

All she could assume was that Rachel planned to end it and take Ford with her. The woman couldn't possibly think that she could still get away with what she'd done, could she? Probably, Hitch realized, remembering Rachel's arrogance.

As she closed the distance between her rig and the pickup, Hitch worried that Rachel would spot her. The mountain road, bordered on each side by pines, climbed in a series of switchbacks up the steep peak.

Hitch had lost sight of the pickup as she drove up the road in the shadow of the mountain. Her heart was thundering in her chest. She could feel the clock ticking. If Ford was still alive… She sped up, realizing she couldn't be that far from the top.

Rachel's voice became an annoying drone in his ears as he listened to how cleverly she'd planned to kill her husband. "So Humphrey's lying on the floor dead. Rick has finished beating me when I call you, Ford. I scream and cry and finally grab the gun and fire a shot out the open kitchen door and disconnect, tossing it into Humphrey's blood and my own on the floor. I wait until Rick is gone before I call 911."

She didn't know about the cartridge casing Hitch had found just outside the kitchen door that had fallen through the deck slats. He made a disgusted, pained sound, thinking of his once best friend and this woman who'd come between them. She'd killed Humphrey, her deputy lover, and now she was about to kill him—unless somehow she was stopped.

He tried to ask if it was worth it, but nonsense came out of his mouth. She didn't seem to be listening anyway. What galled him was that she really thought she was going to get away with all of it—and she just might.

Unless Hitch had gotten the message he'd tried to pass to her. Hopefully she'd heard enough of the phone conversation to figure it out. If anyone could, it would be her, he thought, his heart aching. He'd found her and now would lose her. But he knew that Hitch wouldn't rest until she took Rachel down for all of it.

Rachel would never see the outside again. She'd told him that she'd worried about her next meal as a child. She wouldn't have to worry about it in prison. Nor about what to wear. And she deserved everything she would get and more.

"You probably want to know if I took the foundation money," she said as she drove up the mountain road. "I had no choice. Humphrey had cut off most of my credit cards and threatened to put me on a budget. I'm sure it was his father's idea. I had already lived hand to mouth. I wasn't going to do that again." She looked at him. "I suppose you'd say I could have gotten a job." She scoffed at that. "I was Mrs. Humphrey Collinwood and I wasn't giving that up without a fight."

She was quiet for a few minutes as the road topped the

mountain. Where was she taking him? He had no idea. But he knew how it would end. He could see how agitated she was. She wanted all of this behind her.

"Humphrey loved you like a brother and blamed me for you dropping out of his life," she said, shifting the pickup into four-wheel low as the road became more rocky and rough, the trees more sparse. "He saw us, Ford. At the wedding."

He had started inside, the bitter taste of regret in his mouth.

"I made sure Humphrey saw what he thought was you practically assaulting me. It worked just as I'd hoped. You couldn't stay in our life, Ford. I needed him dependent on me and no one else. If you'd been around, he would have seen through me so much sooner. He didn't want to believe it, but only the two of us knew the truth. I wasn't ever going to tell him, and you were gone from our lives."

But Humphrey had still tried to contact him several times. Had he seen through Rachel even back then? Or had he needed Ford to tell him the truth? Ford realized if he had, he might have saved the man's life.

As Hitch reached the top of the mountain, the pines seemed to open up, but the road still twisted and turned. She was forced to drive slowly over the rocks sticking up in the road. Each corner she came around, she feared she would suddenly come up on the pickup stopped in the road and have no time to react.

It was a relief when the trees opened up even more and she could see farther ahead. She came around the edge of a wall of rock and suddenly there was the back of the pickup. It appeared to be parked at the edge of the rocky peak. Beyond it, there was nothing but blue sky and empty air.

In that split second, she knew. Ford must have told Rachel what he'd been doing when he'd gotten her call. Hitch hit her brakes and quickly backed up so her SUV was hidden from view. She killed the engine and, grabbing her gun, jumped out. As she neared the pickup and the edge of the mountain, the wind howled, bending the branches of the pines. No wonder they hadn't heard her driving up the mountain behind them, she thought.

She moved quickly, staying at the edge of the trees as she kept her gaze on the two in the pickup. Rachel was behind the wheel—just as Hitch had suspected. Ford appeared to be half slumped in the passenger-side seat. For a moment, she feared he was dead. But Rachel seemed to be talking to him.

As Hitch drew closer, though, her heart dropped when she saw how close Rachel had parked from the edge of a cliff. The engine was still running. Hitch's stomach dropped as she realized what the woman planned to do.

Chapter 26

Ford couldn't feel his body. His mind, though, was sharp, and there was nothing wrong with his hearing. He tried not to think about what was going to happen or why living now meant so much to him. Hitch. They'd only just started, and now...

"I didn't want it to end this way, but you have to admit, you gave me the perfect way to get rid of you." Rachel chuckled. "If you hadn't told me about how I'd saved your life with my phone call... Well, I would have found another way, but you did make this easy. I appreciate that."

He made a sound deep in his throat as he looked out at the endless sky. He couldn't see how far it was to the bottom, which was just as well, he thought.

"The thing is, I can't trust you, Ford. If I thought you'd come back for the trial and tell them how much I loved Humphrey and how much he loved me and just keep it to the phone call... But you couldn't do that, could you? You kept digging. Just like that medical examiner. Once Humphrey found my birth control pills, he wouldn't listen to reason. Maybe I wanted him to find them. Maybe I just wanted it all to be over." She sighed.

"You brought this on yourself," Rachel said, as if working herself up to what she had to do. "You should have just told the sheriff what you'd heard and gone back to Big Sky until the trial. Instead, you got involved with that... woman." Her voice was rising. "You slept with her, didn't you. I saw the way you looked at me after that." He heard the jealousy, saw it in her blue eyes. "You betrayed me. You were the one person I thought I could trust. I trusted you with my life, Ford!" She looked at him as if she hated him. Her laugh was brittle. "She was just using you, and look where it's gotten you."

Rachel took a breath and seemed resolved. "Shyla will be driving up here soon to pick me up. Don't worry. She's coming from another road, so she won't see her husband. That marriage would have never lasted anyway. It's time to say goodbye, Ford."

He said nothing. Even if he could have spoken, he wouldn't have known what to say to someone so cold and calculating, so inherently evil.

Ford watched her as she picked up the winter scraper he kept in his truck to clean ice off the windshield in the winter. She leaned down and jammed it against the gas pedal. The pickup's engine roared. She pried the other end of the scraper against the back of the brake pedal.

This was it, Ford thought, wishing the drug she'd injected him with had knocked him out—not left him in this state where he could see and hear what was happening to him. But he figured Rachel had known what dosage to give him so he would at least mentally suffer until the end. Probably just as she had Humphrey.

As he looked at the drop-off in front of the pickup, he knew he would never have taken this way out. He would have stopped before the end of the road even if Rachel hadn't called.

What had saved his life, though, wasn't Rachel but Hitch. He was falling in love with her, which made dying now so much more painful. He desperately wanted to live to see where this relationship took the two of them. He knew she would be his last thought before the end.

Rachel looked over at him, the engine a roar, so she had to yell to be heard. "I'm sorry it had to end like this." He wondered if she'd said the same thing before she killed his best friend. She reached over and unsnapped his seat belt. Then she shoved the pickup into gear and reached for the door handle as the truck leaped forward.

Keeping low, Hitch crept up the passenger side of the pickup. There had to be a reason Ford hadn't moved, hadn't tried to stop this. She thought about Humphrey. Ketamine. Rachel knew how quickly it worked—and how just as fast it left the body, leaving no trace. If she'd used it on her husband, then why not Ford?

All she knew for sure was that she would get only one chance to pull Ford from the pickup as she heard the engine rev and Rachel struggling to get the sprung driver's-side door open.

Hitch moved fast the moment she heard the engine rev up. She knew she'd have only one chance. She grabbed the passenger-side door handle and yanked it open. As she did, she saw Rachel turn in her direction as she struggled to get out of the driver's-side door.

It all happened in an instant and yet time seemed to stop in that moment, suspended as if frozen. Rachel's expression was one of surprise, then realization as Hitch reached over to unsnap Ford's seat belt and practically throw him from the moving vehicle. Rachel was still struggling to get out, her mouth a perfect O, mimicking the saucer shape of her blue eyes.

Hitch fell from the pickup with her arms wrapped around Ford. She hit the ground hard, knocking the air from her lungs but not breaking her hold on him. She felt the back tire skim past them, felt the edge of the earth so close that one of her feet dangled over the precipice. For a moment, she wasn't even sure that they wouldn't still go over the edge of the cliff after the pickup.

Over the sound of the howling wind, the roar of the pickup's engine, came Rachel's screams. They seemed to go on forever, diminishing as she fell, until the cries finally stopped just moments before the boom of an explosion. The sky below the cliff turned orange and then black with smoke as Hitch dragged herself back from the precipice to stand.

Ford lay on his back staring up at the sky overhead. For a moment, she thought he was dead. But then he blinked. She saw his fingers move. She smiled down at him, then bent and kissed his lips. She felt them move under her own. Pulling back, she brushed his hair from his face as she picked up another sound. Sirens.

Chapter 27

Ford drove through the gateway opening between the mountain and into the Gallatin Canyon. He felt something release inside him as if he was finally coming home. He reached over to squeeze Hitch's hand. Her fresh scent mixed with the smell of new leather. He'd thought he would miss his old pickup when he'd had to replace it. But he'd been wrong about that. He seldom gave that truck a thought.

Anyway, the new-leather smell wouldn't last long, once he went to work on the ranch hauling hay and critters. He couldn't wait.

It was one of those cloudless Montana late-summer days, the sky overhead a bottomless blue. The afternoon sun shone on the pines and the rock rims over the sparkling clear green of the Gallatin River as it wound through the narrow canyon, the mountains rising high on each side. After everything he'd been through, he felt as if he was seeing it for the first time. It was the most beautiful sight he'd ever seen.

He glanced over at Hitch. "You sure you're ready for this?" he asked, grinning. He'd been waiting what seemed like a very long time to take her home to meet his family. The investigation had taken a while to complete even with his testimony about Rachel's confession—and the evidence Hitch had accumulated.

Shyla had been shocked to hear about her husband's death—and maybe even more shocked to find out that he'd been Rachel's accomplice. She had driven up the mountain road at her friend's request with Rachel's suitcases in her trunk. It had seemed a strange request. She'd thought she was taking Rachel to the airport. Little did she know that her best friend never planned for her to leave that mountain alive.

The story all came out over the months that followed. It had been the little things that Rachel had overlooked. All together, though, they painted a picture of a woman desperate to keep her level of living and at the same time get rid of her husband.

In the end, Hitch had put together enough evidence that the investigators almost didn't need his testimony about Rachel's confession. He tried not to think about her and the lives she'd wasted—her own included.

"Meeting your family can't be that scary," Hitch said now with a laugh. "Sounds like there are a lot of them?"

"Between the Cardwells and the Savages, uh-huh. My aunt Dana will insist on throwing a party to get everyone together. It's what she does. She's the matriarch of the family. Everyone pretty much does what she tells them to— even my uncle Hud. Then there is my father and stepmother and all my uncles involved in the Texas barbecue business and my aunts and my cousins…"

"I get the picture," she said with a shake of her head. "You've told them about me? About us? About what I do for a living?"

He nodded. "There are a few cops in the family and private detectives, and of course Uncle Hud is still marshal, although he's supposed to be retiring."

"Then I should feel right at home," she said, smiling.

"I hope so." He knew they would love her as much as he did. The woman had saved his life. If his aunt Dana had anything to do with it, they would welcome her with a brass band.

Hitch couldn't believe what they'd both been through together in such a short time as she looked out at the gorgeous summer day. It was hard to put it all behind her. She knew it must be even harder for Ford. She could tell coming home was the best medicine for him.

Fortunately, the drug Rachel had injected him with hadn't done any long-term damage. If the near-death experience had brought back his PTSD, it didn't show. He seemed to have come through it stronger and with fewer scars. He credited her with that, but he was strong and he was finding his footing on Cardwell Ranch. Ranching suited him. She loved seeing him happy.

But the fact that she'd almost lost him was never far from her mind. Rachel had proved to be more cold-blooded than even some of the worst male criminals Hitch had run across.

"The sad part," Ford had told her after it was all over, "is that I knew Humphrey. He wouldn't have divorced Rachel and left her penniless, no matter what the prenuptial agreement said. Even with all the lies she'd told him, he still loved her. He would have given her more money than she deserved."

"Not enough for her, though," Hitch had said. "She wanted it all."

"From what she told me, she knew that Humphrey loved her right up to the end. She seemed angry that he still did even when she shot him."

Hitch had wanted Rachel Collinwood to spend her life behind bars. She didn't even deserve a not-very-quick death. But often people didn't get what they deserved.

That thought made her smile, because a part of her thought she probably didn't deserve a man like Ford Cardwell, but she had Rachel to thank for bringing them together. Hitch had fallen in love with him, something that still surprised her, since she'd thought she'd never meet anyone like him.

"Brace yourself," he said now as he slowed the pickup after taking the turnoff to Big Sky. "I can't wait for you to meet everyone. It's just that they can be a bit overwhelming. Also, since I've never brought anyone home before, they're going to know I'm serious about you. Especially my aunt Dana. She'll spot how crazy I am about you right away. She'll be delighted and unable not to show it and get that wedding gleam in her eye. Then there is Uncle Hud—"

"The marshal." Ford drove over the bridge spanning the river. Ahead, she could see the ranch. To her surprise, she actually felt butterflies.

"Hud will be happy to have another person in law enforcement in the family. Not to mention my father. He's been worrying about what I plan to do with my life. He'll think this has happened too fast—"

"It probably has," she said.

He shook his head and smiled at her. "You know when it's right from the moment you feel it."

She nodded as he turned in front of a large two-story house. People instantly began to pour out onto the wide front porch and down the steps. Hitch laughed and couldn't help smiling.

"I wasn't kidding," Ford said. "Want to run now?"

Hitch shook her head. "Nope. You know me. I'm in it for the long haul."

"That's what I'm counting on," he said, and the two of them opened their doors and their arms to his family.

* * * * *

TWELVE-GAUGE GUARDIAN

This book is dedicated to mothers.
Please warn your children not only about strangers
but what to do if they are approached by them.
We need to keep our little ones safe.

Chapter 1

Cordell Winchester almost missed the Whitehorse Hotel. The old four-story brick building sat in a grove of cottonwoods on the far edge of town, the morning sun glinting off the worn structure.

More than a hundred years old, the place looked deserted. He took note of the vacant surroundings as he parked and went inside. The first thing that struck him was the aging smell, reminding him unpleasantly of his grandmother's lodge. It wasn't a reminder he needed this morning.

He'd been seven the last time he'd seen the Winchester Ranch—twenty-seven years ago—but he recalled the rambling old place only too well. He had always thought nothing could get him back to Whitehorse—let alone to the ranch.

The hotel lobby was done in overstuffed couches and chairs, the upholstery fabrics as dated as the furniture. At the unoccupied registration desk, he rang the bell, then turned to look toward the small parking area outside. No sign of his brother's black pickup.

Where was Cyrus? Not at Winchester Ranch. Cordell had called out there and their grandmother hadn't seen or heard from him. So where the hell was he?

Cordell took off his Stetson and raked a hand through his thick dark hair as he studied the small Western town in the distance. At a sound, he spun around to find an ancient man had appeared behind the counter as if out of nowhere.

"May I help you?" asked the stooped, gray-headed old man.

"My brother Cyrus Winchester is staying with you," he said, settling the Stetson back on his head.

The man nodded, showing no sign of surprise at seeing Cyrus's identical twin. Clearly this man hadn't checked in his brother last night. The clerk thumbed through a file with gnarled fingers. "412. Shall I ring him for you?" He'd already picked up the phone and dialed the room.

Just as Cordell had expected, Cyrus didn't answer. He'd been trying his brother's cell since late last night and gotten no answer and Cyrus's truck was missing. A sure sign Cyrus wasn't here.

Cordell wished now that he'd insisted his brother wait and they ride together, but Cyrus wanted to leave a few days earlier and stop to see friends in Wyoming. Cordell had been tied up with a case and couldn't leave until yesterday. He'd flown into Billings, spent the night and had driven the rest of the way this morning.

He and Cyrus had planned to go out for breakfast when he arrived, where Cordell had planned to make one last attempt to try to talk his brother out of this visit to their grandmother.

"I'm afraid there is no answer in his room."

"Did you happen to see him leave?" Cordell asked even though he figured that was doubtful. The parking area, he'd noticed when he'd driven in, was at the back of the hotel. The clerk couldn't see it from the front desk.

The old man's head wobbled back and forth. "I just came on duty."

"I'm worried about him." He couldn't put his finger on what had him so worried, but it was more than just being unable to reach his brother by phone since yesterday afternoon. "I'd like to check his room."

The elderly clerk hesitated.

Cordell took out his wallet, flashed his driver's license ID and Colorado private investigator license, explaining he was Cyrus's twin brother. He also laid a twenty on the counter. "I wouldn't ask except my brother hasn't been himself lately." Unfortunately true. Cyrus had been acting strangely since getting the letter from their grandmother's attorney inviting them back to the ranch.

The letter implied that their grandmother, Pepper Winchester, who'd spent the past twenty-seven years as a recluse, was dying and anyone who didn't come to the ranch would be exempt from a share of the legendary Winchester fortune.

Neither of them believed the fortune existed. And if it did, they weren't about to let their grandmother manipulate them with it. They'd seen the way their grandmother had used it to control their father and his brothers and sister.

But Cyrus had been insistent about wanting to go back to the ranch one last time. "Remember Enid and Alfred? I wonder if they're still alive. Come on, Cordell, haven't you ever wanted to see the ranch again?"

"No."

"Maybe I just want to see if that rambling old lodge is as scary as I remember it or the ranch is as vast as I recall."

Cordell didn't get it and said as much.

"You just don't want to go because Grandmother liked me best," his twin joked, a joke because their grandmother hadn't given a damn about any of her grandchildren even before she'd holed up at the ranch.

"I suppose it would be all right if you had a look in his room," the hotel clerk said now as he pocketed the twenty. He reached behind him and removed a key attached to an orange piece of plastic with the number 412 engraved on it and laid the key on the counter.

Cordell noticed that the other key to 412 was missing.

Rather than take the antiquated elevator, he ran up the stairs. He'd never liked small spaces. They reminded him of a room on the ranch that had been used as punishment when his father was a boy. The room had given him the creeps.

Just the thought made his stomach knot. What the hell was he doing here? Whitehorse, Montana, was the last place on earth he wanted to be. He had no desire to see his grandmother. Nor did he have any desire to return to the ranch and dredge up even some of the happier memories because, in his mind, the ranch was—if not haunted—then definitely cursed.

From the get-go, Cordell had had a bad feeling. That was why he hadn't been about to let Cyrus go out there alone. Cyrus and trouble just seemed to find each other.

And that was what had Cordell worried now. He should have heard from his twin by now.

At room 412, he knocked lightly as he studied the worn carpet under his boots. A warm breeze blew in through a window at the end of the hallway near the old-fashioned metal fire escape exit. The place smelled of decay and cleaner. It was just like Cyrus to pick a hotel like this to stay in, what his brother would have called "authentic."

He knocked again, a little louder this time just in case his brother had hung one on last night at the four bars in town and walked the half mile back from town, leaving his pickup wherever it had been parked.

"Cyrus," he called as he used the key and opened the door.

"He's not in there," said a female voice from down the hall.

Cordell turned to see an older woman with a cleaning cart.

"From the looks of his room, he didn't sleep here last night," she said and pursed her lips scornfully.

Cordell didn't like the sound of that and felt his anxiety multiply. He'd always "felt" his identical twin, sensed him on some cell-deep level even when they were miles apart.

He couldn't feel his brother. It was as if Cyrus was... The thought that his twin might be dead sent a gut-wrenching terror through him.

Pushing open the door to the room, he saw Cyrus's bag next to the undisturbed bed. The housekeeper was right. It didn't appear Cyrus had spent any time in the room other than to drop off his bag.

Moving through the small hotel room, he saw that his brother hadn't even dirtied a glass or broken the paper band on the toilet seat and his fear intensified.

Cordell pulled out his cell, saw that he hadn't received any calls from his twin, and started to call the ranch again when he spied Cyrus's cell phone on the table by the window.

Cyrus didn't go anywhere without his cell phone.

Heart pounding, he walked over and started to pick it

up when he saw his brother's room key lying on the floor next to the wall where it must have fallen. Next to it was a paper convenience-mart cup on its side on the carpet in the middle of a dark stain that looked like spilled coffee.

Cordell fought to remain calm as he surveyed the scene, noticing that the curtain was pulled back, the window opened a few inches as if his brother had heard something and looked out and seen...what?

The room was located at the back of the hotel. A strip of pavement made up the parking area. Beyond it was a stand of huge old cottonwoods that grew along what could have once been a ditch or creek.

Past that were piles of old lumber and scrap iron, and in the distance, Cordell could make out a weathered old rundown farmhouse. Several old cars were up on blocks and the yard was littered with toys. A bunch of sorry-looking kids were outside. They seemed to be hunting for something. He heard them calling for someone.

A large woman stood on the front steps of the farmhouse, her hands on her hefty hips. She appeared to be giving the children orders in a strident voice.

Cordell turned his attention back to the parking lot below the window. He could see the glitter of glass on the patched pavement under the only light post. When his brother had arrived last night, it would have already been dark—especially in the parking lot without a light.

What could he have seen?

There were two cars parked between the faded painted lines, an old brown sedan with local plates and a blue VW bug with California plates. The VW had a flat tire on the left rear.

He stared at the flat tire unable to shake the bad feeling that had settled over him. Cyrus must have seen something down there last night. Something that had made him drop everything and run down to help?

He picked up his brother's cell phone and checked to see if he'd gotten any messages other than Cordell's this morning, then checked Cyrus's outgoing calls.

Fear settled like a boulder in his belly when he saw that the last number his twin had called was 911.

Chapter 2

As Cordell started to look for a phone book to call the sheriff's department, he saw his brother's pickup coming up the road. Relief flooded him and yet at the same time he wanted to throttle his twin for scaring him like this.

He watched the pickup come in from a back way and wondered why he couldn't feel that connection that had always been there between the two of them.

It unsettled him and made him more anxious as he glanced at his watch. Cyrus was more than three hours late. Not only that, he'd also apparently spent the night elsewhere. It wasn't like his brother to have met a woman and been tom-cattin' around all night.

Cordell couldn't throw off the feeling that something had happened.

As the pickup pulled into the back lot and parked, he watched anxiously, just needing to see that his brother was all right.

The door of the pickup opened and with a start Cordell watched as a woman wearing a baseball cap over her short bluntly cut black hair climbed out. She was dressed in jeans, a jean jacket over a T-shirt and sneakers. Not really Cyrus's type, he thought.

Then she did something that sent a jolt through him.

She glanced nervously around the parking lot before her gaze shot up to the window where he stood. Cordell stepped back at the same instant and watched from behind the edge of the curtain as she opened the VW, took out something and seemed to stuff it under her jacket before heading for the back door of the hotel.

He quickly pocketed his brother's cell phone and room key and stepped into the closet, leaving the door open just enough that he could see most of the room.

It wasn't long before he heard voices out in the hallway, both female. He knew without hearing all the conversation that the young woman driving his brother's truck had conned the maid into opening Cyrus's room for her.

He heard the door open, then close and lock. For a moment, she stood perfectly still as if listening, as well. Then she quickly moved to Cyrus's overnight bag on the end of the bed.

Cordell had a good view of her backside from where he was hidden. The woman appeared to be five-six or seven, slim with an athletic build and enough curves to fill out her jeans nicely. Had this woman been in trouble, Cyrus would have jumped to her defense without a second thought.

She unzipped the bag and hurriedly rummaged through it. He wondered what she was looking for. She definitely hadn't come to get something for his brother. So what was she doing with his pickup?

That was when he got a glimpse of the pistol stuck into

the back waistband of her jeans. It peeked out from the hem of her jean jacket as she bent over the bag. Was that what she'd gotten out of the car?

Cordell moved swiftly, knowing the minute she heard the closet door roll back, she'd reach for the weapon.

She was fast, faster than he'd anticipated. Just not as fast as he was. He came out of the closet, diving for her and the weapon. At the sound behind her, she spun around, her hand going for the gun and coming out with it in her left hand.

As she swung toward him, leading with the weapon, he grabbed her wrist, driving her back and onto the bed. He wrenched the gun from her hand, tossing it across the room. It skittered to a stop near the door.

The woman got in a kick that only missed his groin by a couple of inches. Her right hook, though, caught him squarely in the jaw, surprising him by the force of her punch, before he could grab both her wrists and pin them and her to the bed.

Her eyes widened in alarm. *"You?!"* she cried, looking at him as if she'd seen a ghost and confirming that she'd at least seen his twin before she took his pickup.

"Where is my brother?" he demanded, holding her down on the bed.

"Your *brother?*" She stared at him as if dumbfounded.

"You're driving his pickup. You're in his room going through this stuff. Where is my brother?"

"I thought you—"

"I asked you a question." He knew what she thought. Few people could tell him and Cyrus apart.

Cordell pulled her arms up over her head, secured both wrists with one hand and reached for his cell phone. "You want to tell me or the sheriff? Your choice."

"Could you get off me? I can't breathe."

He studied her face. She was pretty but she hid it well with too much eye makeup along with a small silver nose ring and dyed black hair cut in a sleek bob that made her pale porcelain skin even paler.

"Come on. You're hurting me. Let me up and I'll tell you everything."

"I don't think so," he said, seeing something in her blue eyes that warned him this woman couldn't be trusted. "Let me say this again. My brother, where is he?"

As he started to dial 911, she said, "The last time I saw him, he was being taken to the hospital."

"The *hospital?* What happened to him?"

"I'm not sure. I think he was struck by a vehicle in the parking lot last night," she said, motioning with the snap of her head toward the back of the hotel.

The open drapes, the spilled coffee, Cyrus's cell phone on the table and the 911 call to the sheriff's department. Cordell felt his heart drop. "Is he all right?"

"I don't know."

Cordell shook his head in confusion. "Why did he go down there unless… You! You didn't just witness this. You were involved somehow. How else did you get his pickup?" He could only assume his brother had rushed downstairs to save her. But from what?

She seemed to relent. "I was crossing the parking lot. I stopped, surprised to see that I had a flat tire on my car. Just then I heard an engine rev and this van came roaring out of the darkness."

"My brother saved you." It was the only thing that made sense. Cyrus must have seen the van and realized it was waiting for her.

"He shoved me out of the way. I fell. When I came to, a man who looks a lot like you was lying nearby." Her gaze skidded away. "I heard sirens. I didn't know what had happened. I was afraid the van would come back. I saw your brother's keys lying next to him and took his pickup."

"The sirens—"

"It was an ambulance," she said.

"Did you happen to notice while you were taking his keys if he was still alive?" Cordell asked with sarcasm that she seemed to ignore.

"He was still breathing from what I could tell."

Cordell couldn't hide his relief. "Nice of you to stick around and make sure he was all right."

She glared at him. "I'd had a scare. I didn't know your brother from Adam. For all I knew he was with the guys in the van."

He studied her. This whole mess sounded just like Cyrus. Maybe he'd even seen the driver of the van flatten her tire. The moment the man went back to his van to wait for her to come out of the hotel, Cyrus would have started to call 911. How, though, had the man in the van known she would come back out again last night?

"You'd just returned to the hotel? Wasn't it late?" he asked her. She looked surprised he'd figured that out. "So why leave again so soon?"

"I came back to check out. I'd changed motels."

"Why?"

"Isn't it obvious? I didn't like the feel of this place, too far from town and it's old and crumby."

Maybe she was telling the truth, though he had his doubts. He was still shaken by the news that his brother had been taken to the hospital after possibly being hit by a van to save this ungrateful woman's neck.

Fortunately Cyrus was tough. He would be all right. He had to. And yet that foreboding feeling was still with Cordell.

"So my brother saves you, first you take off and just leave him lying there and then you come back here to go through his belongings?"

"I'm not a thief," she snapped, her blue eyes darkening.

"What's your name?"

Again her gaze shifted away. "Raine Chandler."

"I'd like to see some identification."

She shot him a disbelieving look that said she couldn't show him anything with him on top of her.

He eased off and she reached as if to get something out of her hip pocket. The blow took him completely by surprise, knocking him back. As her fist connected with his nose, the pain radiating up through his skull, she wriggled out from under him. His vision blurred as his eyes filled. Blood poured from his nose as he reached for her.

But she was too fast. Through the film of tears, he saw her vault over the bed to the spot where he'd tossed her pistol by the door. She came up with the gun.

For a split second he thought she'd turn it on him. But then she was out the door.

He didn't try to stop her. A few moments later he heard her rev his brother's pickup engine and tear off, tires spitting gravel. No reason to give her chase. He was more concerned right now with getting to the hospital and seeing his brother.

Cyrus could deal with retrieving his pickup, Cordell thought as he went into the bathroom to clean himself up. He couldn't wait to hear his brother's side of the story. Downstairs, the hotel clerk gave him directions to the hospital.

"They're in the process of moving from the old hospital to the new one," the clerk told him.

It wasn't hard to find since the entire town of Whitehorse was only about ten blocks square. The new hospital was on the far east side of town in the opposite direction from the hotel where Cyrus had gotten a room he hadn't used.

When Cordell walked into the small reception area, the nurse behind the desk looked at him as if she'd seen a ghost. He'd gotten used to being an identical twin and often forgot about the effect it had on other people. They always did a double take when he and Cyrus were together.

When they were younger they played tricks on their teachers and even their girlfriends. The tricks often backfired, landing them in hot water.

Now as private investigators in Denver, he and Cyrus used being identical to their benefit. It was almost as if they could be in two places at one time.

Their grandmother had never been able to tell them apart, he remembered, then chastised himself for letting her creep into his thoughts. He knew he was just trying not to worry about Cyrus.

"I'm Cyrus Winchester's brother. Twin brother," he said to the nurse now as if that wasn't obvious.

"Oh," she said, both hands going over her heart. "You did give me a start when I saw you standing there." She patted herself as if trying to still that heart. "I thought, 'It's a miracle.'"

His stomach dipped. "A miracle?"

She seemed to realize what she'd said. "I'm sorry. Hasn't anyone told you? Of course not. Until you walked in here we didn't know the patient's name so we haven't been able to notify his next of kin. Your brother is in a coma and has been since he was brought in last night."

Someone had been in her room.

Raine realized it the moment she opened the motel-room

door and saw the tiny piece of cardboard from the coffee cup she'd stuck in the jamb lying on the floor.

She froze, her gaze taking in the cheap motel room. She'd put the Do Not Disturb sign on the door and it was clear that the maid hadn't been in.

The bed was rumpled from the few hours of sleep she'd managed to get the night before and her towels were on the bathroom floor where she'd dropped them after a quick shower this morning.

She glanced behind the door, then at the open closet. She didn't like surprises and almost laughed out loud at the thought as she stepped cautiously in, pulling the pistol and closing the door and locking it silently behind her.

The room was small. Lumpy double bed, bathroom, closet. Not a lot of places for a person to hide. She checked under the bed, in the closet and behind the bathtub shower curtain. Empty.

Tucking the pistol back into the waist of her jeans, she checked her overnight bag. Someone had gone through it. What had they been looking for? Evidence, she thought. Or identification? She'd left neither in the bag.

Walking over to the window, she saw how they'd gotten in. The latch was broken on the sill. She'd planned to go to another motel tonight anyway. The window looked out on the alley, a stand of trees and an old house that had once been painted white.

Raine felt her pulse thrum in her veins and her heart began to pound at the sight of the aging house. She could almost smell the rank mustiness. She hated old houses.

Closing the curtain on both the window and the past, she quickly packed up the few belongings that she hadn't put in storage when she'd left home, then placed a call to a local car repair shop and made arrangements to have her flat tire fixed and her car brought into town, saying she would pick it up later.

She knew it was just a matter of time before that cowboy came looking for her. She was still shaken by her run-in with him at the hotel. He'd looked so much like the man she'd seen lying in the parking lot last night that it had taken her completely off guard.

Glancing around the room, she made sure she hadn't left anything, then walked to the door with her overnight bag in hand. She opened it a crack to look out. The hallway was empty.

She pulled the gun from her waistband and, unzipping her overnight bag, laid it on top, making the weapon more accessible should she need it.

As she pushed open the outside door, she scanned the parking lot. The lot was empty except for the pickup she was driving and a large, luxury car with Texas plates parked at the opposite end.

Trying not to hurry, she walked to the pickup, tossed in her bag and climbed in after it. For a moment, with the doors locked and the gun handy, she just sat, not sure what to do next.

Run. Just drive in any direction and get the hell out of here. She could dump the pickup somewhere down the road. Early this morning, she'd dug in the pickup's glove box looking for information on the man who'd shoved her out of the way of the van last night and had pulled up short when she'd seen who the truck was registered to. Cyrus Winchester of Winchester Investigations of Denver, Colorado.

What were the chances that the man who'd come to her rescue just happened to be a private eye?

She started the pickup but still didn't hit the road. She was kidding herself if she thought she could leave. Even if she had her car and had left this pickup where Cyrus's twin brother could find it, she couldn't run. She'd hate herself the rest of her life if she didn't follow through with this. Wasn't it time she learned the truth—not to mention got the justice she deserved?

Last night the parking area behind the old hotel had been too dark to see the person driving the van. But Raine figured he had to be the same one who'd slashed her tire. He'd been waiting for her.

You were set up, girl.

It certainly looked that way. But why had someone gone to the trouble of luring her to Whitehorse? Surely not just to run her down in the hotel parking lot. They could have killed her in L.A. since at least one of them obviously knew where to find her—and where to send the messages that had gotten her here in the first place.

Why, after all these years, try to kill her? It made no sense. They had no reason to believe anyone was after them. But now the sheriff's department would be looking for the dark-colored van because the driver had put Cyrus Winchester in the hospital.

And his brother would be looking for Raine. Finding her in a town the size of Whitehorse would be child's play—for both the cowboy *and* the attempted killer.

Any woman in her right mind would hightail it out of town and not look back.

But Raine Chandler wasn't just any woman, she thought with a curse.

Chapter 3

Cyrus looked pale, his head bandaged and a series of tubes and cords running from his lifeless body.

Cordell took his brother's limp hand in both of his and sat down hard on the chair next to the hospital bed. No wonder he'd felt the connection broken between them.

"Cy, I'm here," he said, his voice breaking. "I'm going to find out who did this to you and take care of it. In the meantime…" He glanced away from his brother's face, trying to compose himself. He didn't want his brother to hear the fear in his voice. "I just want you to rest so you can wake up soon."

He heard the scuff of a shoe sole behind him and turned to see the doctor standing in the doorway. He squeezed his brother's hand and, reluctantly letting go, rose.

"Tell me about my brother's condition," he said, motioning for the doctor to come out into the hallway with him. He didn't want to talk about it in front of Cyrus. He'd heard that comatose patients could hear what was being said to them and around them, and from the doctor's grave expression the diagnosis wasn't good.

"I'm Dr. Hanson," the elderly man said, searching Cordell's face. "Identical twins. You certainly gave my nurse a start." He grew more sober. "As she told you, your brother is in a coma. He was already comatose when he was brought in so we were unable to get any information from him."

"What caused the coma?"

"Blunt force trauma to the back of his head. There was also some bruising around the hip and left leg as if he'd been struck."

"Like being struck by a vehicle?" Cordell asked. "Apparently he pushed a woman out of the way of a speeding van. She didn't see what happened to Cyrus, but found him lying on the pavement."

The doctor nodded. "That would be consistent with his injuries."

Cordell had thought he would get the whole story from his brother once he reached the hospital. Now he saw that if he wanted to know any more about the accident he'd have to ask the woman. But first he had to make sure Cyrus was going to be all right.

"What can we do for him?" he asked the doctor.

"There appears to be no bleeding or swelling of the brain that requires surgery, but we will continue to monitor your brother closely. Right now he is stable, his vital signs strong. A coma rarely lasts more than two to four weeks."

Others last for years, Cordell thought. "I know my brother. He's a fighter. He'll come out of this." Soon, he prayed.

The doctor gave him a sympathetic smile. "We certainly hope so. Some patients recover full awareness. Others require some therapy." His look said some were never the same. "We won't know the full extent of your brother's injury until he regains consciousness."

If he ever does. Cordell kept hearing the words the doctor *didn't* say. He felt helpless. But there was one thing he could do while he waited for his twin to come back and that was to get the bastard who'd done this to him.

That meant finding Raine Chandler, and getting the truth out of her.

As Raine drove through a residential neighborhood in Whitehorse, she pulled out her cell phone and hit a speed dial number, realizing she was calling in late.

"I was just about to call out the cavalry," Marias drawled.

"Sorry, I've been a little busy."

"Uh-huh." Her friend had been against her coming to Whitehorse from the get-go. "What happened?" Marias knew her too well.

"I ran into a little trouble last night, but I'm fine."

"They know you're there *already?*" Marias let out an unladylike oath. But then there was nothing ladylike about the biker-turned-cop-turned-P.I.

"Not a huge surprise under the circumstances. I'm not sure where I'm going to be staying so I might not be able to get Internet or cell phone coverage. Seriously," she said when Marias snorted in disbelief. "Whitehorse is in the middle of nowhere and once you get outside the city limits, all bets are off when it comes to high-tech devices."

"You're leaving?" Just like Marias to latch on to that.

"No, just maybe staying outside town if I can find a place." Up the block, Raine spotted a tan sedan like the one she'd seen behind the hotel this morning. The car was parked in front of the new hospital. Of course he would go see how his brother was doing and his brother would tell him everything.

He would find out she'd been telling the truth. She hoped that would be the last she'd see of the cowboy.

Unless, of course, he and his P.I. brother were somehow involved. What if the plan last night hadn't been to kill her but to save her? She would have been indebted to Cyrus Winchester. Maybe something had gone wrong and instead of saving her, he'd ended up in the hospital.

And now his identical twin was putting the strong arm on her.

A little paranoid, are you?

No, just covering all her bases, Raine thought. "I promise to try to stay in touch." She hung up before Marias could argue that this trip was nothing more than a suicide mission. If she only knew how complicated this had become.

Raine pulled over under a large tree next to a house just down the block from the hospital. This might be the perfect opportunity to check out the car—and the man driving it.

She was about to get out of the pickup when she saw the twin come out and climb into the tan mid-size sedan. It had rental car written all over it. At least she'd been right about the car being the same one she'd seen parked behind the hotel this morning.

Sliding down in her seat, she peered through the steering wheel as he pulled out and headed toward downtown. Where was he going? She decided to follow at a safe distance and find out.

She was surprised though when the trail led to the sheriff's department. If last night's attack had been a ploy, then this cowboy wouldn't be going to the sheriff about it. He would want to keep all this as quiet as possible—and handle it himself.

She pulled over again and dialed information for Winchester Investigations in Denver, Colorado. The phone rang three times before a woman picked up and from the brisk way she answered, Raine guessed it was an answering service.

"I'm calling for Cyrus Winchester."

"I'm sorry, he's not available. Both Cyrus and Cordell Winchester are out of the office. If you'd like to leave a message—"

Raine hung up. *Both* Winchesters were private detectives? No way would a P.I. go to the cops unless he was on the up-and-up.

So what *were* they doing in Whitehorse?

The Whitehorse County Sheriff's Department was located along the main drag in an old brick building. As Cordell climbed out of the rental car, he scanned the street.

In the diagonal parking spaces were a half-dozen trucks in front of the various businesses from a couple of bars and a café to a clothing store, beauty parlor, hardware and a knitting shop. None of the pickups were his brother's, though.

Inside the sheriff's department, Cordell spoke first to the dispatcher.

"I'll see if the sheriff is busy," she said.

He watched the street while he waited, feeling anxious. His fear was that the woman who'd called herself Raine Chandler would flee town. Her VW had California plates on it. What was she doing in Whitehorse? Apparently not just passing through. He'd had the good sense to take down the car's license plate, assuming it wasn't stolen. He wouldn't put anything past the woman given that she was toting a gun and clearly involved in something more than a near hit-and-run.

"Yes?"

He turned at the sound of a female voice to find an attractive dark-haired woman in a sheriff's uniform. Her head was cocked to one side as she perused him, her lips turning up into an amused smile.

"Which one are you?" she asked.

"I beg your pardon?"

"I'm sorry. I'm McCall Winchester, acting sheriff. I recognized you from some photographs my grandmother showed me of you as a boy."

He caught her name and couldn't help frowning.

"Trace Winchester's daughter," she said.

He felt his eyes widen.

She let out a laugh. "Yes, I did turn out to be his daughter no matter what my grandmother said at the time. I'm the true black sheep of the family."

Cordell smiled at that. "It's a family of black sheep."

"Why don't we step back to my office?"

He followed her down the hallway, surprised that his cousin was the acting sheriff. She took a chair behind her desk and he settled into one of the others facing her. "My brother and I are up here because of our grandmother's letter."

McCall nodded. She didn't look happy about it.

"I'm guessing she isn't dying and wants something from us."

"That would be my guess," McCall agreed.

Cordell hadn't come here to talk about his grandmother and didn't give a damn what she was up to. He was too worried about Cyrus.

"Do you know about my brother's accident?" He saw that she didn't, probably because Cyrus hadn't had any identification on him. Which meant either the woman took

Cyrus's wallet—or the van driver had stopped long enough to take it.

"Cyrus was attacked last night behind the Whitehorse Hotel. He's in a coma at the hospital."

"I'm so sorry. I'd heard a man had been injured and taken to the hospital but I had no idea it was your brother. The deputy on duty last night talked to the clerk who'd apparently called for an ambulance, but he said the only vehicle in the lot belonged to a woman."

Cordell nodded, thinking of the woman he'd tangled with earlier at the hotel. "The woman took my brother's pickup. She told me a crazy story about almost being run down by a person driving a dark-colored van. Her tire was flat on her VW, she said she was scared and saw Cyrus's keys on the ground and took off."

"So you talked to her?"

He looked away embarrassed that he'd let her go. "I was about to check her identification when she got away."

McCall raised an eyebrow at that. "I suppose that explains the blood on your shirt. It's yours?"

He looked down, not realizing some had dripped onto his sleeve. "She said her name was Raine Chandler, but I really doubt—"

"The VW bug with the flat behind the hotel is registered to a Raine Chandler of Los Angeles, California."

So she had been telling the truth—at least about that.

"Do you have some reason to doubt her story?" the sheriff asked.

Did he? Just a gut feeling that she was leaving out a whole lot of it. "I'm not sure. But with Cyrus in a coma, she is the only one who knows what really happened last night."

McCall frowned. "I heard that you and your brother are private investigators, but I hope you're not planning to take this matter into your own hands again. I'll put out an APB on her and your brother's pickup since she apparently didn't have permission to take his truck and she left the scene of an accident and possible crime last night."

"When you pick her up, I want to talk to her."

His cousin seemed to consider that. "I think we can work something out. I take it you haven't seen Grandmother yet."

"No."

"I'll let her bring you up to speed on everything that's been going on out there." His cousin shook her head as if whatever it was wasn't good.

Cordell rose from the chair, not bothering to tell her he had no intention of seeing Pepper Winchester. He had to find out who had injured his twin. He knew it was his way of dealing with Cyrus's coma. He told himself that by the time he found the bad guys and at least saw that they were behind bars, Cyrus would be all right again.

"It was nice meeting you." He reached into his wallet and took out his card. "My cell phone number is on there, but I'll check back with you."

Raine called Marias again. "I need your computer expertise. Can you check on a couple of private investigators out of Denver? The name is Winchester, Cordell and Cyrus Winchester of Winchester Investigations. See what you can find out."

"Anything special you're looking for?"

"Why they're in Whitehorse, Montana, would be helpful."

"I see. If you want to hang on... Do you happen to have a license plate number?" Marias asked.

"I can do better than that. I have Cyrus's pickup registration."

"I don't want to know, right?"

"Right." Raine reached over and opened the glove box. "Hold on, he's about to move again."

"He?"

"Cordell Winchester." From down the street, he had just come out of the sheriff's department. Raine leaned over out of view as she dug through the glove box, found the registration, then peered out cautiously as he climbed into his car.

Where to now? she wondered as she watched him start his car and pull away from the curb.

"What information would you like?" she asked her friend, then read what Marias asked for from the registration form as she waited for two cars to go by, then followed Cordell Winchester.

"Two brothers apparently," Marias said into the phone. "Same birth dates?"

"Identical twins."

"Really? Handsome?"

"As sin."

"This is a professional request, right?"

"Strictly business," Raine said and winced as she remembered the way her fist had connected with his nose. "No love lost between us."

"Oh, so that means you've 'met,'" her friend said with a laugh. "I hope it was romantic."

"If romance is him holding me down in the middle of a queen-size bed."

"Sounds good to me," Marias quipped. "Hell, sounds damned good now that I think about it. Hmm, that's interesting."

"Are you going to tell *me?*" Raine asked as she tried to keep Cordell's rental car in sight.

"I just did a little familial search. Father's name Brand. Mother a Karla Rose French. Divorced. Grandfather Call Winchester, deceased. Grandmother Pepper Winchester, still living. Got to be a nickname, wouldn't you think?"

"That's what you thought was interesting?"

"No, it's the part where Pepper Winchester's address is Whitehorse, Montana."

Cyrus and Cordell Winchester's grandmother lived here? Pepper Winchester. "Why does that name sound so familiar?" Raine said more to herself than Marias. Up the street, Cordell Winchester made a quick turn at the corner two blocks ahead of her. He'd tagged her. "Gotta go."

Cordell couldn't believe it. He'd glanced in his rearview mirror and seen his brother's pickup a dozen car lengths behind him. The woman was following *him?!*

He made a quick turn, then another down an alley. Unfortunately, he met a delivery truck coming in and had to back up and take another street.

Around the next corner…

No sign of the pickup.

Cursing under his breath, he searched each side street. She couldn't have gotten away that quickly. No way.

Then he got lucky. Down a side street he spotted his brother's truck go past a few blocks away. She was headed out of town!

Unfortunately, he had a stop sign, then several cars pulled out that he had to wait for. But the second he'd gotten the chance, he'd gone after her, not surprised to see the pickup hightailing it out on one of the secondary roads south.

He had to floor the rental car to keep the pickup in sight. Cyrus would have had a heart attack if he saw the way this woman was driving his truck. The thought brought a stab of pain.

The pavement ran out. Dust boiled up behind the truck. She took a curve, throwing up gravel from the tires. Cordell backed off a little after getting the windshield of the rental car pelted, several bits of gravel pitting the glass.

He fished out his cell phone to call the sheriff's department, but found there was no cell phone service. It was just as well. At least now he could say he'd tried to call. The truth was he wanted to talk to Raine Chandler alone. He didn't want her pleading the Fifth and getting locked away behind bars where he couldn't get the truth out of her.

The narrow dirt road wound south over the rolling prairie, a roller coaster ride at this speed. He just prayed they didn't meet another vehicle coming up the road. There was barely enough room for one car. Going this fast, Raine would never be able to get far enough over to let another car pass.

At first he was convinced he would come up over a hill and find Cyrus's pickup wrecked at the bottom. But this apparently wasn't her first time driving on roads like these. He wondered what part of California she was from that she'd learned to drive on narrow dirt roads rutted with washboard.

He gave her a little space, confident that with all the dust she was throwing up, she wouldn't be able to lose him.

They left Whitehorse long behind them. As the country began to get more rugged, he realized they must be nearing the Missouri Breaks. He'd driven through the Breaks on the way to Whitehorse, crossing the Missouri River as it cut a deep gorge through this desolate, isolated country.

The country was familiar, too familiar, since he'd spent his first seven years living out here in the middle of nowhere on the Winchester Ranch. Unless he was mistaken, they weren't that far from the ranch.

Cordell was beginning to worry he'd never be able to catch her if she cut across to Highway 191. But then he saw the pickup fly over a cattle guard and come down hard, the right rear wheel hitting loose gravel on the edge of the road. He got on his brakes to keep from going airborne off the cattle guard, as well, and saw the rear of the truck fishtailing.

He could see her fighting to regain control. She almost pulled it off. Then she hit a stretch of deep washboard. The pickup tires lost traction and the next thing Cordell knew the truck was headed for the ditch adjacent to the road.

Fortunately, the ditch wasn't deep, but it was filled with water and mud which streamed up and over the truck before the vehicle finally came to a stop bogged down in the gumbo. Raine Chandler wasn't going anywhere.

Cordell was already out of his car and running toward the pickup before the driver's-side door swung open. He grabbed her and dragged her out, this time not giving her chance to go for her weapon.

Taking the gun from her jacket pocket, he stuck her pistol barrel against her temple, forcing her to her knees in the dirt next to the ditch as he held both wrists behind her. "Who put my brother in the hospital?"

"I told you—"

"I swear I will drown you in that ditch if you don't start telling me the truth."

He heard her take a deep breath and let it out slowly. She was shaking, no doubt from the adrenaline of the chase—certainly not from fear of him. There was a determination in her eyes that he'd misjudged before. He wouldn't make that mistake again.

"If you let me up, I'll tell you everything."

He let out a bark of a laugh. "You think I'm going to fall for that again?"

"I already told you. I was crossing the parking lot behind the hotel when someone tried to run me down. Your brother shoved me out of the way, I fell and that's all I remember. I must have blacked out for a moment because when I came to, your brother was lying there on the ground and I could hear sirens."

He pushed her down harder, pressing the gun barrel into her temple. "Why didn't you stay and tell the sheriff's deputy what had happened?"

She shook her head, making him want to throttle her. "I told you. I was scared. I panicked."

"Bull. You didn't want to be involved. Why?"

"I was scared."

He couldn't imagine anything scaring this woman. He also didn't believe she'd come back to the hotel this morning to find out Cyrus's name. So what had she been looking for?

"Do you have a permit to carry this gun?"

She hesitated a little too long. "Not in Montana."

"Why are you carrying a gun anyway?" he demanded.

"I live in L.A. You'd carry a gun, too."

Cordell didn't know what to think. Was it possible Cyrus had just been in the wrong place at the wrong time? Or was this woman lying through her teeth?

"Why would someone want to run you down?"

"How would I know? Maybe they mistook me for someone else. Or maybe it was an accident. Now would you please let me up?"

"Like your tire on your car just happened to be slashed?"

He sighed. He was getting nowhere with her. He let go of her hands, standing back in case she came up fighting, which he half expected. To his surprise, she got slowly to her feet.

"How is your brother?" she asked quietly.

"He's in a coma." Cordell had to look away. Just saying the words made it all too real.

"I'm sorry." She sounded surprised and sympathetic.

"Good," he said. "Because you're going to help me find the person who did this to him."

"I told you I don't know who was behind the wheel of that van."

That, he thought, might actually be the truth. But he suspected she knew damned well why the person had cut her tire and then tried to run her down. Cyrus couldn't have gotten downstairs from the fourth floor fast enough, unless he'd seen the man knife her tire and then go wait for her in the van with the motor running.

Cordell stepped to the open door of the pickup and took out her purse, an overnight bag with a small laptop computer tucked in the side and a large leather satchel. Laying each in the grass, he began to go through them, keeping the gun within reach should he need it.

"Please, that's my personal—"

"Stay right where you are," he warned her.

She stopped moving toward him, looking resigned as he opened her purse and quickly searched it. A little over two hundred in cash, most in crisp new twenties probably straight from the ATM machine. A California driver's license. He glanced at the information on it. Twenty-six.

Nothing unusual in her overnight bag.

He was beginning to wonder if she might really be telling the truth when he opened the large leather satchel. *"What the hell?"*

Chapter 4

Raine was still reeling from what he'd told her. His brother was in a coma? She felt sick to her stomach even before Cordell opened her satchel.

"I asked you what the hell this is," he demanded, taking a step toward her, shock and disbelief contorting his handsome face.

"I'm a journalist." The lie didn't come easily even though it was the one she'd been using for her cover. She hated lying to him. She'd inadvertently gotten his brother into this. She felt guilty enough. Lying didn't make it any easier. But she still couldn't be sure she could trust this man....

"A *journalist?*" Cordell grimaced as he glanced again at the photographs in the satchel. "This is about some *article?*"

"Are you going to question everything I say to you?" she demanded, going on the offensive.

"I am until I hear something I can believe."

She tried a little truth on him. "I'm working on an old

missing person's case, a child who was abducted sixteen years ago from Whitehorse. Her name was Emily Frank."

Cordell studied her openly before pulling out the stack of photographs from the abductions. As many times as she had looked at the photos, she never failed to be moved to tears by the piles of charred bones, the rusted fifty-five-gallon barrels where the remains were found or the faces of the children still missing—and presumed dead.

Cordell shoved back his Stetson, looking shaken and uncertain, as he pulled out all the research material she'd gathered. "All *this* is related to the article you're working on?" he asked in disbelief.

She nodded.

"This child, Emily Frank… Tell me you aren't here looking for her remains."

"No. I'm interviewing the people who knew her."

He was watching her closely as if he knew she was leaving out some key piece of information—and wondering why. "So how many people have you interviewed?"

She knew where he was headed with this. He was trying to decide if her article research was connected to his brother's accident.

"None. I only got to the town yesterday," she said. "I haven't had a chance to talk to anyone yet."

He frowned. "Someone knows you're in town."

He was right about that, she thought and added truthfully, "I have no idea how they might have found out."

Cordell sighed. "What newspaper or magazine do you work for?"

She tried not to glance away from his black bottomless gaze. "I'm freelancing this one."

"How about a home address, a former newspaper or magazine, someone who can verify your story."

She felt her eyes narrow as she met his gaze. "My mother took off when I was a baby. I never knew my father. I've been on my own since I was eighteen. I put all my things into storage before I left California. I wasn't sure how long I'd be gone. So, no, I don't have a home address or anyone who can verify what I'm working on."

"*Someone* knows," he snapped and pulled off his Stetson to rake his fingers through his hair. "Chucking it all for a story, that's some dedication to your work. Why Montana? I'm sure there are missing children in California. There must be hundreds of stories you could have done there, if not thousands. Why this particular case?"

She was forced to look away. "I saw a picture of her. There was just something in her eyes..." She swallowed back the lump in her throat.

"I'm going to have to go through all of your notes, everything you have on this case."

She balked, just as she was sure he'd known she would.

"I should mention," he said, his words like thrown stones, "I went to the sheriff this morning. She just happens to be my cousin. I told her you stole my brother's pickup and might have been involved in the attack on him. She's already put an APB out on you because you left the scene. Unless you want to go to jail, I suggest you reconsider."

"I've told you what *I'm* doing here," she said, shaken to hear that his cousin was sheriff. "Why don't you tell me what brings two private investigators to Whitehorse, Montana?"

His eyebrows shot up. He hadn't expected her to find out who he was. Along with surprise though, there was grudging admiration in his gaze. "Not that it's any of your business but my brother and I came here to see our grandmother, Pepper Winchester. She's...dying."

She flinched as a shaft of guilt pierced her conscience. She believed him. Just as she believed his shocked reaction to the photographs in her satchel. This man wasn't working for a sexual child predator. At least she hoped not.

"Come on, we need to go somewhere so I can go through all of this," he said. "Or are you going to lie to me and tell me that all of this doesn't have something to do with you and the article you're writing?"

She wasn't.

He nodded, seeming relieved for once she wasn't going to argue the point. "Since my brother's pickup isn't going anywhere until a wrecker pulls it out, you're riding with me."

"I'd like to speak to the nurse at the hospital first," she said.

He turned back to look at her.

"I just want to verify what you've told me about your brother."

"I've heard that journalists don't take anyone's word on anything without at least a backup source, but do you really think I'd lie about my brother being in a coma?" Even under the shade of his cowboy hat, she could see the piercing black of his gaze. He was angry and she really couldn't blame him.

He shook his head in obvious disgust. "Fine. When we get to a place where my phone works, you're welcome to call the hospital." He swore under his breath. "Are you always this paranoid?"

"Only when people really are after me."

He sighed and pulled out his cell phone. "No coverage. Or do you want to check yourself?"

"I'll take your word for it until cell phone service is available."

He shook his head. "That's real damned big of you. Let me make something clear, I'm not sure what happened last night but I have a pretty good idea. You and your article got my brother into this. If guilt or the threat of jail doesn't work, then I'll use whatever methods I have to, but you *will* help me find the people who did this to him, one way or another."

Cordell couldn't believe this mess. Cyrus in a coma and him saddled with this journalist and her paranoia.

Now what the hell was he going to do with her? he asked himself as he studied Raine Chandler. The cool breeze stirred the hair at the nape of his neck and he turned to see a dark bank of clouds on the horizon to the west. Great, just what he needed. A thunderstorm and him miles from a paved road.

He remembered as a kid how the roads would be impassable until after a storm when the wind and sun dried things out.

He considered making a run for town, but he could tell by the way the clouds were moving in that he would never make it before the storm hit. The rental car would be worthless and his brother's pickup was buried in the mud and not going anywhere. He swore under his breath again.

There was only one place to go.

As much as he hated it, he knew it was the best plan given the storm and the fact that he needed to take Raine somewhere so he could go through all of her research materials. His brother might have stumbled onto trouble last night, but Raine Chandler was up to her neck in it.

All he had to do was find the people after her.

That meant going to a private spot where she didn't try

to get away from him until he found out what he needed. Cordell groaned at the thought though. "Come on."

"Where are we going?"

"To my grandmother's ranch. It's closer than town." He saw something flicker in her eyes. "Or would you rather go to jail?"

"Maybe I'd be safer there."

He stopped to give her his full attention. "If you think your virtue might be at risk coming with me, then let me set you straight. You aren't my type and I have much more important things on my mind than sex. That blunt enough for you?"

"Quite. Did I mention that I believe Emily Frank was taken by someone in one of Whitehorse's more prominent seemingly upstanding families?"

Cordell let out a hoot of laughter. "Like the *Winchesters?* Think again. We've never been upstanding. Not even seemingly."

"You might be surprised how money and power tip the scales toward upstanding."

"No, actually I wouldn't be surprised." He eyed her, realizing she'd researched his family. Before or after Cyrus had crossed her path? "Winchester is just a name to me. I haven't been back here in twenty-seven years and if there were any money or power, my father and brother and I have never been a part of it."

She cocked a brow at him. "What about your grandmother?"

"Not that it is any of your business, but until recently my grandmother was a recluse who hadn't left the ranch in all those years. None of the rest of us had seen her in all that time or lived anywhere near here. Even if she hadn't been locked away for twenty-seven years, I can assure you she wouldn't abduct a child."

"If you haven't seen her, then you have no way of knowing—"

"My grandmother," he interrupted, "is so fond of children she doesn't even know how many grandchildren she has. She had to pay her lawyer to try to track us all down. I won't even go into how she treated her own children, even her favorite son."

"And this is where you're taking me? To see this grandmother?" She sounded incredulous.

"It wouldn't be my first choice, but you've left us no other option." Thunder rumbled in the distance. "You know anything about storms up in this country? Unless we get moving and damned soon, that storm is going to catch us and we are going to be stuck, literally, out here until someone comes along and that could be a damned long time. Once it starts raining, this road will become gumbo. We'd never be able to get back to town before the storm hits so we're going to wait out the storm at the Winchester Ranch. And believe me, I'm much unhappier about that prospect than you could ever be."

What in her research was she trying so desperately to keep from him? he wondered. Well, he'd soon find out. Once they reached the ranch, he'd go through everything in that satchel. She was his only possible connection to the men who'd put his brother in a coma. She was going to help him even if he had to wring her pretty little neck.

It would make it easier if she trusted him though, but he didn't take it personally. If he'd learned anything from his first marriage and subsequent divorce, it was that trust is a fragile thing that once broken badly is impossible to get back again.

He wondered, though, who had broken Raine Chandler's trust. Whoever it was had done a bang-up job.

Raine realized she had little choice but to go with him to the Winchester Ranch. Fighting Cordell would be futile since right now he held all the cards.

Also she wanted the man who'd hurt his brother just as badly as he did. If it was true and Cyrus Winchester was now fighting for his life, she owed him for his chivalry in saving her last night.

Cordell Winchester was another story. He didn't have a chivalrous bone in his body and she balked at being forced into anything, especially by him.

But she also realized it couldn't hurt having an obviously high-priced private investigator now helping her find the person who'd been driving that van last night—the same person she'd come to Whitehorse to find.

As she started to gather up her things he'd dumped in the grass, Cordell stopped her. "I'll take care of this."

"I'd prefer to carry my own things."

He smiled. "I'd prefer you not bloody my nose or kick me in the groin or pull a gun on me."

"That's right, you have my gun. I'd like that back."

"I'm sure you would. But you don't need to worry. From now until we're finished with this, I will keep you safe."

She lifted a brow questioning whether he thought he really could handle that job. Fortunately she'd learned to take care of herself. "I'm not sure you won't need my help."

He gave her a look that said she was pushing her luck. She heard him swear under his breath as he walked away. She watched him, trying to gauge what kind of man he really was. One thing was for sure—he had no idea who the woman he'd just taken captive really was.

As she watched him, for the first time, she took a good

look at Cordell Winchester. She was suddenly aware of the man on some primitive level. He looked like an ad for Montana, a cowboy who was just as comfortable in the wild outdoors as in a large city or a boardroom.

She must have been blind not to have noticed before this how his jeans hugged his tight behind, the legs long, the hips slim. His shoulders seemed broad enough to block out the sun.

Raine felt desire warm her blood. It had been a long time since she'd been even remotely aware of a man. She'd been too busy with her career. She'd apparently forgotten what it felt like to want a man so much it made her ache. Or maybe she'd just never known a man like Cordell Winchester, a man who could unleash that kind of primal need even when she couldn't stand the sight of him.

This was a man who had to be used to getting what he wanted from women. She was glad she wasn't that type of woman. But the thought also came with a little regret that she wouldn't be finding out if Cordell was as sexy as he looked.

As he started to the car with her things, he saw her eyeing him. "Something wrong?"

She scoffed at that. Everything was wrong. She couldn't wait to see the last of this Winchester and, judging by the expression on Cordell's face, he felt the same way.

Cordell hated the idea of dragging this woman out to the ranch with him as much as he hated going there in the first place. He knew he had no business taking her prisoner and the last person he wanted to see was his grandmother.

But the storm had given him no other option other than being trapped in the small rental car with her. That, he thought, could definitely be worse than the ranch. At least at his grandmother's they should be able to get something to eat and drink and, if they were stuck there overnight, a place to sleep.

He didn't trust Raine Chandler as far as he could toss her and needed this time to find out everything he could about her—and this article she was writing.

As it was, he'd have to watch her 24/7. At least at the ranch, she was far enough from Whitehorse that taking off would require she hoof it forty miles. Or take a horse. He couldn't see that happening.

"This is just temporary," he said as they climbed into the car. Once he found the person who hurt his brother, Raine Chandler was free to do whatever the hell she wanted.

"So," he said and started the car, "why don't you tell me about this article you're working on."

She sighed. "Her name, as I already told you, was Emily Frank. She was ten when she was taken as she walked home from school. She was never found. Neither were her abductors."

He shot her a surprised look. "You said abductors? Are you saying there was more than one person who took her?"

"A man and a woman."

"How do you know that?"

She seemed to hesitate. "I have something of the girl's."

He felt a chill trot the length of his spine. "It's just hard to imagine a woman—"

"Sometimes a woman in these situations is more dangerous than the man. She often goes along with it to make him happy but resents it—and is hateful to the child because she is jealous. In a few cases, it is her idea."

Cordell gripped the steering wheel tighter as he drove, sickened by the things she was telling him. "These people are monsters."

"A common misconception is that they are recognizable psychos," she said, as if warming to her subject. "Look at the famous cases. The neighbors always say, 'They seemed like such a normal family.' They hide behind the facade of being upstanding citizens. Often they are very involved in their community, do a lot of good deeds and are high profile. Money and power masquerading as the wholesome family next door. They're people you could pass on the street and never suspect. These people appear so normal that the good people of Whitehorse have no idea that these child abductors live right among them."

Cordell looked shocked and sick to his stomach. She saw him grip the steering wheel tighter.

"You said Emily was taken sixteen years ago," he said after a long moment.

She knew what he was asking. "Who knows how many more children they have taken since that time."

"Come on, residents would become suspicious if a bunch of kids went missing from a small Montana town."

Raine shook her head. "These people are serial child abductors. They don't stop. They don't have to. They're bulletproof because they're so deeply rooted in the community and the children they take are on the remote edge of society."

He frowned over at her.

"Children from families with few resources or connections to the town. Foster children."

"These children are still going to be reported missing."

"Missing and presumed runaways. Because of that the foster parents often don't alert the authorities right away. Even when they do and the child isn't found, the victim is considered a runaway until her body is found."

Cordell didn't say anything for a long time. "Isn't that going to make the abductors nearly impossible to find?"

"That's why they haven't been caught. These people will do anything to keep their twisted secret." She felt his gaze on her.

"Including making another run at you?"

Cordell Winchester was smart. She liked how quickly he'd understood the situation.

She started to argue that the hit-and-run last night had nothing to do with her—or her reason for being in Whitehorse. She saved her breath. "They'll send someone after me again," she said simply.

If they haven't already, she thought, studying the cowboy sitting next to her. "That is, if they can find me at some isolated ranch in the middle of nowhere."

He chuckled as the car sped down the narrow dirt road. "We're just sitting out the storm at my grandmother's. Don't worry, I'll make sure you can use yourself as bait if that's your plan."

"What a relief." Raine stared out at the rolling prairie. He'd also been right about the storm. It moved in quickly, the first drops of rain splattering against the windshield. Ahead the land seemed to break up into badlands and she knew they must be nearing the Missouri Breaks. On her way to Whitehorse, she'd dropped down into the Breaks to cross the winding river as it made its way through Montana.

She'd never seen such wild, isolated country. Now she realized just how far they were from civilization. Normally, she felt she could hold her own. But Cordell Winchester outweighed her and was obviously much stronger. He also had her gun. And now a storm had blown in, one that he swore could strand them out here.

So why wasn't she terrified? She glanced over at him,

studying his expression and seeing nothing but pain. She could see that he was worried sick about his brother. And he'd been visibly shaken by the photographs of the abducted children.

Was it possible he was in town just to see his grandmother, and his brother had just been in the wrong place at the wrong time last night? It was beginning to seem that way.

She studied him, realizing he was much harder to read than most people. He must make a damned good private investigator. And like her, she suspected he didn't let most people in.

There was something about him that made her also suspect he'd been hurt by someone. She felt that, rather than saw it, a built-in empathy for others you recognize because they've gone through something akin to what you have. A sixth sense. Who had hurt him? she wondered.

Raine heard Cordell swear as rain pinged off the hood, falling harder and faster. The car swerved several times in the mud forming on the surface of the road. Ahead she spotted a huge log arch over a narrow, weed-choked road. The sign on the arch read, Winchester Ranch, and Cordell seemed to relax as he slowed the car to make the turn.

She felt her heart beat a little faster as he drove down the road, the weeds between the ruts scraping loudly along the undercarriage to the beat of the pouring rain. She could feel the tires spinning out as the ranch lodge came into view.

Out of the corner of her eye, she saw that Cordell's expression was one of dread. "So you really haven't been here in twenty-seven years?"

"Not since I was seven. This is the first time I've been invited back."

"You must have been a pretty awful kid."

Through the rain and the sweep of the wipers, she stared at the ranch buildings nestled against the hillside. The place looked very Western and rustic. A sprawling log structure, it ran out in at least a couple of wings and climbed to three stories on one of what appeared to be an older wing.

"About my grandmother... She's..." He seemed at a loss for words. He let out a sigh. "You'll see soon enough."

Raine sat up straighter as they dropped down the slippery slope to the massive ranch lodge, not surprised that she was anxious to meet Cordell's grandmother.

"How do you plan to explain me?" she asked.

He gave a devastating smile that made the interior of the car seem too intimate and definitely too close. "I'm going to tell her you're a car thief."

"That should impress her," she said as he brought the car to a stop in front of the log mammoth. A curtain moved on the second floor. An old blue heeler hobbled out into the rain to growl next to the car. Other than that, nothing moved.

"Didn't I hear something about a couple of murders on this ranch a month or so ago?" Raine asked as it suddenly hit her why the name Pepper Winchester had sounded so familiar.

Chapter 5

"I'm sure it won't be the last murder out here, either," Cordell said as he stared at the ranch lodge. If it hadn't been for the rain, he would have turned around and left. But the roads had already begun to turn to gumbo.

Now he would have to see his grandmother when he hadn't been the one who'd wanted to come here in the first place. Cyrus had been the one determined to see this place and now— Just the thought of his brother brought a wave of pain. The twin connection that had comforted him since they were born was still gone. He felt as if a part of him had been ripped out.

He'd left his number with the hospital along with instructions that they were to call if there was any change at all in his twin's condition. Unfortunately, there was no cell phone service out here. He checked his phone anyway. No messages. He didn't know whether to feel relieved or more concerned. He just had to believe that Cyrus would come out of this.

"Looks like we'll have to make a run for it," he said, noting that the rain didn't look as if it planned to let up.

As he got out of the car, Cordell realized it had probably been a mistake to bring Raine here. Next thing he knew she'd be doing an investigative piece on the Winchesters and who knew how many more secrets were hidden in these old walls?

The front door opened as he and Raine ran toward the lodge. He was taken aback to realize the small, broomstick-thin elderly woman in the doorway was Enid Hoagland. His brother Cyrus would have gotten a kick out of the fact that the mean old woman was still alive.

"Which one are you?" Enid demanded as she stepped back to let them into the small foyer.

Before he could answer, his grandmother appeared. "He's Cordell," Pepper Winchester said. "Enid, why don't you make something hot to drink for our guests? They're soaked to the skin."

Enid didn't look the least bit happy about being sent away. For a moment, Cordell thought she would refuse to go. But with a huff, she turned and disappeared into the dim interior.

He was shocked that his grandmother had recognized him. She hadn't been able to tell him and Cyrus apart when they were younger. Why now? Unless maybe she'd heard about Cyrus's accident.

"This must be your wife," Pepper said, turning her gaze on Raine.

Cordell flushed, realizing of course his grandmother hadn't heard about his divorce. He'd just assumed everyone for thousands of miles around would have heard since it had been such an ugly one.

"No, this is Raine Chandler," he said. "My wife and I are divorced."

His grandmother raised a brow. "So like my attorney to get it wrong. I'd fire him if he was still in my employ." She smiled as she shook Raine's hand, her old eyes seeming to bore into the younger woman.

"Raine is an investigative reporter," he said.

Pepper winced.

"Don't worry, she isn't investigating the Winchesters." He took a breath and let it out slowly. "At least not yet," he said under his breath. "So you've heard. Cyrus was attacked last night outside his hotel room in Whitehorse and is in the hospital in a coma."

Pepper's hands went to her chest. "I hadn't heard. Is he…"

His grandmother's concern surprised him. That and the fact that she really had been able to distinguish him from his brother apparently. Had she always been and just hadn't bothered?

"It's too early to know his prognosis," Cordell said. "The doctor is hopeful he will regain consciousness soon. We all are."

"Yes," his grandmother agreed. "I'm sorry." She glanced out at the rental car. "You'll have to bring in your own bags. Alfred…"

"Yes, I heard. But we won't be staying," Cordell said.

"Why ever not?" his grandmother demanded.

"We're just here to wait out the storm," he said.

She raised a brow. "You were just in the area and decided to drop by? Enid has already made up two rooms anyway."

Cordell started to argue, but realized this might be for

the best. He and Raine would have the privacy they needed if they had rooms away from his grandmother and Enid. And if the storm let up…

"So this investigative piece you're writing…" Pepper said, turning to Raine now that the lodging was settled.

"It's about child abductions, one in particular. You might remember it. A ten-year-old girl named Emily Frank. She was abducted on her way home from school sixteen years ago in Whitehorse."

Pepper frowned. "I'm sorry, I *don't* remember." But clearly she also didn't want to hear any more about it. "I'll make sure Enid has your rooms ready while Cordell gets your bags." With that she turned and left them.

The phone rang as Pepper Winchester started down the hall. She picked up one of the extensions before Enid could. "Hello."

The news about Cordell's twin had shaken her. But given the information, she wasn't surprised to hear the voice on the other end of the line.

"Mother?" She hadn't heard her son Brand Winchester's voice in twenty-seven years. It surprised her that it could fill her with such a landslide of emotions. "Have you heard about Cyrus?"

"Yes, just now when Cordell arrived. He's out bringing in his bags."

"He's staying there?" He sounded both surprised and disapproving.

"Don't worry, there hasn't been a murder here in weeks," Pepper said, unable to contain her annoyance.

"I heard about that. I'm going to be coming out."

Her daughter, Virginia, had said it would take a gun to Brand's head to get him to ever come back to the ranch even for a visit. Pepper couldn't wait to tell Virginia how wrong she'd been. It had taken his son's accident to get Brand back here.

"I hope you'll stay here at the ranch." She didn't mention that his old-maid sister Virginia was also here. She didn't think Virginia's presence at the ranch would be a draw for her brother, but just the opposite.

Brand hesitated so long Pepper found herself getting irritated and had to squelch saying something she would regret.

"All right," he finally agreed and Pepper heard the telltale sound of Enid replacing the extension in the kitchen. "I'll be there tomorrow after I see Cyrus at the hospital."

"Plan on having supper with us," Pepper said. "The roads should be dry enough by then." She hung up and stood for moment thinking that her plan had worked in ways she hadn't expected.

After twenty-seven years, they were all wandering back to the ranch. She found little satisfaction in it, though, as she walked down the hall and shoved open the kitchen door. She'd thought that letting them believe she was dying would do the trick—that and greed. Surprisingly only one had fallen for that—Virginia.

Pepper shoved her annoyance with her only daughter away and considered that things might work out after all. With luck she would discover which of her spawn was a traitor and a murderer.

"My grandmother wasn't being insensitive about the story you're working on. Although she *can* be insensitive without much effort," Cordell said, seeing Raine's expression when he returned with the bags from the car.

He shook off the rain from his jacket as he set down the bags in the entryway. She hadn't packed much for a possible extended stay in Montana. He wondered how long she'd planned to stay.

"As I told you, my grandmother's been a recluse for the past twenty-seven years," he continued when she didn't say anything. "I'm sure she didn't hear about anything that's happened during that time."

"What made her become a recluse?" Raine asked, looking into the dim interior of the house beyond the entryway.

"Her youngest son had disappeared, believed to have run off," he said, keeping his voice down. "Apparently it was more than she could bear." Cordell hesitated as a thought struck him. "Funny, but she seems to be taking his murder better than his disappearance. Odd, huh."

"He was *murdered?*"

Cordell nodded. "Twenty-seven years ago. So what do you think she did? She invited the rest of her family back to Winchester Ranch, a family she hadn't seen in all those years."

"Maybe she wants to try to make up for it before she dies."

He shook his head. "She's up to something, something no good."

"But you still came back."

"I only came back because of my brother Cyrus. You and I are here only because of the storm and I needed someplace where I can keep an eye on you."

"You're not very trusting, are you?"

He didn't bother to answer. "You couldn't get me within five hundred miles of this place and that old woman in there if I had any other choice." He saw Raine's reaction. "Do you believe in evil?"

She seemed startled by the question.

"I don't know if it is this place or what this place does to people."

"Places aren't evil. People are," she said with conviction.

"Are you going to spend the rest of the day out there talking or let me show you to your rooms?" Enid demanded as she suddenly appeared, startling them both.

"Speaking of evil," Cordell said under his breath.

Raine looked around the ranch lodge, wondering about the Winchesters, especially Cordell Winchester, as she followed Enid up the stairs.

Divorced. She should have known. That could explain the coldness she'd felt in him. His ex had broken his heart, she'd bet money on it. He had all the classic symptoms of a man who had been betrayed by the woman he'd loved.

She dragged her gaze away from him and considered his weird family and this place where they lived that he thought evil. The Winchester Ranch lodge looked as if it had been dropped from an old Western movie set. The log walls, a rich patina, were covered with Native American rugs, dead animal heads and Western art that looked old and expensive.

Enid was faster than she looked and Raine had to hurry to catch her, Cordell coming slowly up the stairs behind them.

Enid opened a door into a large room with a sitting room and huge bed and private bath. "This is your room," she said as if she thought Raine planned to sneak off and find Cordell's as soon as the lights went out. "Cordell's room is across the hall." Enid glanced down the stairs as if to make it known that anyone on the lower floor would be able to see her if she left her room for any reason.

"Thank you," Raine said, wishing she was in some nondescript motel room. She'd never liked staying with strangers and the Winchester family and the hired help seemed about as strange as anyone could get.

As she glanced at Cordell, she was reminded of his brother. She could see the worry on his face and felt overwhelmed with guilt at the knowledge that the twin brother who'd saved her life was now fighting for his. She had no choice but to help Cordell.

"Your room is across the hall," Enid said to Cordell.

"Thank you," he said. "That will be all."

The elderly housekeeper gave him a withering look, spun on her heel and disappeared down the staircase.

Cordell stepped through the open door to his equally large suitelike room and set down Raine's overnight bag, purse and satchel on the table. He glanced at the fire going in the fireplace, then at the open-curtained French doors that led out onto the small balcony.

"I'm not going to try to escape," Raine said, entering his room. "I'd like my things in my room."

He nodded toward her overnight bag and purse. "They're all yours. I still need to go through the satchel."

Her gaze went to the double bed on the ornate iron frame. It was identical to the one in her room and would take a footstool to climb into it. Several homemade quilts were piled onto the end of the bed, making her wonder how cold it got out here at night.

Enid had made a point of letting them know she thought they were already sleeping together and that being forced to get two rooms ready only made more work for her. The old woman wasn't as sharp as she thought she was, Raine thought. But the grandmother…well, Raine thought everyone probably underestimated her.

Cordell dumped the contents of her leather satchel onto

the table by the window and Raine closed the bedroom door behind her. She didn't want him going through everything without her here. Nor did she want everyone in the household to know what they would be discussing. Cordell didn't seem to notice she hadn't left.

She liked the sound of the rain as she stepped to the French doors, opening them a crack. She felt as if she needed the fresh air. She'd never liked being closed in. She looked out over the ranch, feeling antsy and wondering how long they would have to stay here. There was something about the place that made her uneasy. Or was she just anxious about what was going to happen next?

"Hopefully the rain will stop soon and it will dry up enough that we will be able to leave later tonight," Cordell said behind her.

Raine watched the pouring rain thinking his grandmother was probably right. They were stranded here at least for the night.

She closed the door and stepped back into the room. Cordell had sat down at the table and was gingerly looking through the photographs and other information she'd gathered. She took a chair across from him.

"If you're just writing about Emily Frank, why do you have all these other photographs of missing children?" he asked.

She could tell the faces of all those missing children were taking their toll on him. It was impossible to look into all that innocence and know horrible things had been done to those children before their bodies had been dumped or buried or, in the case of the people Raine was looking for, burned like trash when they were finished with them.

"Because this isn't just about Emily," she said. "There are serial child abductors out there. Some keep the children a short period of time and kill them. Others keep them until the child is too old, then they get rid of that one and get another one the right age."

Cordell swore under his breath. "These statistics can't be right. About eight hundred thousand children are reported missing every year or two thousand a day?"

"Over fifty thousand of those are victims of abductions by strangers. The others are taken by family members or people they know."

"I had no idea," he said, clearly upset.

"Few people do unless it hits closer to home for them. Almost all of the ones abducted by strangers are taken by men."

"I don't understand how this can happen."

"In eighty percent of the abductions by strangers, the first contact occurs within a quarter mile of the child's home. In many cases, so does the abduction. Most strangers grab their victims on the street or try to lure them into their vehicles. About seventy-four percent of the victims are girls."

Patiently, she stood and picked up a map. Opening it, she spread the map of Montana out on the table and saw his eyes widen when he noticed the dozens of colored stars.

"Don't tell me that is where children have gone missing," he said.

"The blues ones are believed to be runaways. The yellow ones are considered solved cases based either on a suspect's confession or the discovery of remains. The red ones are unsolved missing children cases."

He stared down at the map, a look of horror on his face. "And the green stars?"

"Those are only the cases a man named Orville Cline

confessed to in this state. In only one study, child molesters averaged over a hundred child victims per molester."

Cordell pushed back his chair and walked over to the fireplace. She watched him grab the mantel and lower his head. "This Orville Cline, where is he now?"

"Serving time at Montana State Prison in Deer Lodge. He confessed to taking Emily Frank and killing her."

Cordell spun around in surprise. "Wait, if—"

"He lied. I have evidence that he couldn't possibly have taken Emily Frank." She picked up the folder on Orville Cline and handed it to Cordell, who read it standing up. She watched him read the confessions Orville had made during the trial. Raine had read this so many times, she could have recited the man's confession to Emily Frank's abduction and murder verbatim.

Cordell snapped the folder shut and looked up in surprise. "Why would he confess in horrific detail about an abduction and murder he'd didn't commit? Maybe he confused her with another little girl."

Raine shook her head. "They don't forget or mix up their victims. That's part of the high they get out of it, remembering. He knew he didn't take Emily Frank."

"Then why confess?"

She rose and walked over to the French doors again. The rain had stopped and now a cool breeze swept across the balcony smelling sweet and summery. "I think he made some kind of deal with the couple who really abducted Emily."

"But you don't know that for a fact."

"No, but I do know that he lied about it," she said, turning back to him. "Open the small manila envelope." She opened the door wider. The breeze felt soothing against her cheek as she listened to him sort through the items on the desk. She heard him open it, heard his sharp intake of breath, then the silence that followed broken only by the rustle of the sixteen-year-old spiral notebook pages.

"My God," Cordell said behind her. "Emily wrote this?"

"She kept a diary of the days she was imprisoned after her abduction. Her handwritten notes contradict what Orville Cline said happened. He lied."

Cordell frowned. "Where did you get these?"

"They were sent to me recently."

That surprised him.

"I don't know from whom or what their motive is, but I believe they want me to find out the truth about Emily Frank's abduction."

"Orville Cline?"

"Doubtful. I think it was one of the people who abducted Emily."

"Why would… Are you telling me you think one of them wants the truth to come out?"

She shrugged. "That's what I thought until someone tried to run me down last night."

"Exactly. It looks more like they just tricked you into coming up here. If you're telling the truth, someone tried to kill you last night. That was no accident behind the hotel." He was frowning again. "But why? If Orville Cline confessed to Emily Frank's killing, they are in the clear. So… why contact *you?*"

"Journalists are often targets," she hedged. "Especially ones who might have some new information on the case."

"Can you prove this Orville Cline couldn't have taken Emily?"

"Not yet," she admitted. "But that diary Emily kept proves he lied about the details."

Cordell looked down at the pages with the heartbreaking words neatly printed on them. Like her, he had to be awed by the girl's courage, her hope and faith in a world that hadn't been kind to her, her perseverance in such a horrible situation. Emily believed she would be rescued.

"The person who sent you these has to be involved," he said quietly as if the full weight was just now making an impact on him. "If you're right and Emily wasn't the only child they abducted and there is even a chance that this person wants the abductions to stop…"

"Now do you understand why I'm here, why I'm willing to risk my life?"

Enid had a scowl on her face when Pepper walked into the kitchen. Nothing new there. She studied her housekeeper, considering giving her hell for eavesdropping on her private conversation. But Enid had been eavesdropping for years. It was one reason she was still employed here. She'd overheard too much.

"Brand is coming," Pepper said. "Please make a room for him. I told him to plan on having supper with us."

Enid grunted unhappily and Pepper had to wonder why the woman stayed. Then grimaced at her own foolishness. Enid was here only for one thing: the Winchester fortune. She planned to get her share. One way or another.

An uneasy truce had hung between them since the latest secrets had been uncovered at the ranch. Though no bargain was made, it was assumed that Enid would stay on at the ranch as housekeeper and cook. But she would be rewarded for her loyalty.

The elderly Enid never spoke of her husband's murder nor did she seem to grieve for his loss. If anything, Alfred appeared quickly forgotten by his wife.

Pepper understood such behavior, though she secretly

believed she'd been grieving for her own lost husband for years.

"Did you see what your latest grandson dragged in here?" Enid said, raising her eyes to the ceiling where she'd made up rooms for Cordell and the young reporter. "We'll be lucky not to be murdered in our sleep."

Pepper laughed at that. She'd put money on herself and Enid being much more dangerous than that young woman upstairs. She watched Enid make a vegetable beef soup for their lunch. It had been days since the elderly cook had attempted to drug her.

For months after her son Trace's disappearance, Pepper had welcomed the drugs Enid surreptitiously slipped her. She had welcomed the oblivion. She hadn't even considered why Enid was doing it.

But once Trace's murder had come to light, everything had changed. Pepper now wanted her wits about her. She was in search of the truth about her son's murder and suspected there had been an accomplice—right in this house.

It was why she'd gotten her family back here. Also why she dumped most cups of tea her housekeeper brought her down the drain.

Enid was no fool. She had to know. Which made her wonder what Enid would do next.

One thing Pepper knew for certain. It was just a matter of time before the aging housekeeper would demand payment for keeping Pepper's secrets.

"I'm going to find Cordell," Pepper said, gripping her cane.

Enid shot her a disapproving look. "I hope you're not planning to ask another one to stay on the ranch."

"With Alfred gone, we need Jack here," she said of her grandson Jack Winchester. Jack had promised to come back. He and his new bride, Josey, were on an extended honeymoon, but Pepper was hoping when he returned that he would take her up on his offer to turn Winchester Ranch into a working ranch again.

"That new bride of his isn't going to want to come back here," Enid said.

"It can be lonely and sometimes the wind..." She shook her head, remembering how the sound of the wind had nearly driven her crazy when her husband had brought her here after their honeymoon. "It can be a harsh, unforgiving place."

Enid huffed at that. "Life is what you make it." Her gaze met Pepper's. "But I guess I don't have to tell you that. You've managed fine, haven't you?"

She heard the insinuation in Enid's words. Keeping secrets was a dangerous proposition, Pepper wanted to tell her. Enid thought she had her right where she wanted her. But Pepper had a plan.

Actually, she felt it was her duty not to leave this world without first making sure this mean, old bitch was sent straight to hell ahead of her.

Chapter 6

Cordell started at the knock and quickly put all of the documents back into Raine's satchel.

At the door he found the housekeeper. "Your grandmother wants a word with you down in the parlor," Enid said. "Also dinner will be served tonight at six sharp. Don't be late."

Cordell had been waiting for the other shoe to drop since receiving the letter from his grandmother's lawyer. He glanced back at Raine, hating to leave her alone.

"Do I have time to take a bath?" she asked, getting to her feet. When she reached to take the satchel with her to her room, he stopped her, saying, "Leave that. I'd like to look at it again. I need to go see what my grandmother wants."

She nodded and scooped up her computer. He didn't say anything, pretty sure she couldn't get Internet service out here and what difference would it make if she could?

"We'll leave as soon as we can. Believe me, I'm more anxious to get out of here than you are."

Cordell waited until Raine disappeared into her room across the hall before he stepped out, closed and locked his own room. Enid saw him pocket the old skeleton key. He knew he'd only managed to increase her curiosity.

Pepper was waiting for him, standing at the window leaning on her cane in what Enid had called the parlor. It was a nice-size room with leather furniture, a stone fireplace and a single large window that opened to the front of the house. Even though it was June, a blaze burned in the fireplace, but did little to do away with the chill in this house.

When she heard him enter the room, Pepper turned and took one of the chairs. He sat across from her in a matching leather chair. It creaked under his weight and he realized this was the same furniture they'd had when he was a kid living here. In fact, little about the lodge had changed over the past twenty-seven years. Everything was more worn, but the memories were still fresh.

"I had hoped you would have answered my letter to let me know when you would be arriving," his grandmother said reproachfully.

"The letter wasn't from you, but your attorney, and I didn't see any reason to answer it. Truthfully, I'd hoped I could change Cyrus's mind about coming out to the ranch. I don't have a lot of good memories of this place."

"You don't like me."

"No."

She smiled. "You and your brother look so much like your father."

His jaw ached from clenching it. "I don't really think you want to talk about that, do you?"

"Brand called. He'll be here tomorrow and will be staying on the ranch."

Cordell couldn't help being surprised. He'd called his father after he'd received the letter from his grandmother, figuring Brand had gotten one, as well. He had. He'd been adamant about not coming back except for his mother's funeral and, even then, he wasn't sure about that.

Cordell's father never talked about the ranch or his childhood here. He'd thrown himself into raising his boys after their mother had taken off when they were babies. Brand never said it, but he blamed Pepper. She couldn't stand any of the women her sons brought home and made their lives hell until they couldn't take it anymore and bailed.

After the twins left home, Brand threw himself into work. To Cordell it seemed his father had spent his life running away from the past.

"I know everyone blames me for their unhappiness. Do you think it is fair though, blaming me for what your grandfather did?" There was an edge to his grandmother's voice, a blade of both anger and pain.

"You were the *mother*. Mothers are supposed to protect their children."

He was instantly reminded of photographs of the children who'd been abducted from this area. "You didn't protect my father."

"No, I didn't. I let Call discipline them."

"Until Trace came along. What was it about him that made you protect him and not the others?"

She actually looked uncomfortable. "I was older. I felt as if I'd lost the others a long time ago. I guess you could say I drew a line in the sand."

Cordell laughed. "Is that what you call it? I'd always heard that my grandfather rode off one day and just never returned. Apparently that wasn't the case, huh. And, no,

I don't believe for a moment that Alfred Hoagland killed my grandfather."

"His wife, Enid, swears that is the case."

He shook his head. "Why don't we cut to the chase? What do you want? You didn't invite me and Cyrus back here out of the goodness of your heart. Or because you're dying. You don't have a sentimental bone in your body."

She lifted her chin, body erect, and he saw a steely gleam in her dark eyes. She was still a beautiful woman, graceful and elegant, but cold and unfeeling, no matter what she said. "You might be surprised. Jack has already told me that you boys were in the third-floor room the day Trace was murdered," she said, her voice strong. "I need to know what you saw."

He wasn't sure what he'd expected her to ask him. Not this. That awful room was where his father and aunt and uncles had been sent as punishment. He and his brother had been forbidden to go to the room so of course they'd sneaked up there. *"Saw?"*

"Jack told me that you and your brother had a pair of small binoculars that you were arguing over."

Jack, the nanny's son? "Why would you believe anything Jack—"

"He's my grandson." She smiled wryly. "Those rumors about the nanny and my son Angus? They were true."

Cordell shook his head. "What a family."

"Yes, isn't it?" She lifted her cane and pointed toward the window. "See that ridge over there? That's where Trace was murdered."

His eyes widened. He'd had no idea his uncle had been killed within sight of the ranch. No wonder she was asking about this. From the third-floor room with a pair of binoculars was it possible one of them could have witnessed the murder? Apparently his grandmother thought so.

"I didn't see anything."

She nodded solemnly. "What about your brother?"

He shrugged. "You're going to have to ask him." He felt that awful pain and fought the thought that if Cyrus had seen something, they might never know. Cyrus might never regain consciousness. "What is it you think he might have seen? I thought Uncle Trace's killer was caught."

"Yes, but died after suggesting there was a co-conspirator."

That took him by surprise. "If Cyrus had seen a murder, he would have said something."

His grandmother didn't look convinced. "Not if he'd seen someone from this family on that ridge that day."

"If you think my father—"

"I didn't say it was Brand. Cyrus might have been so shocked that it was a family member he might not have dared tell. I know there were more children in that third-floor room than just you and Cyrus and Jack. Who else was up there?"

Cordell shook his head. "I just remember the three of us." He could feel his grandmother's gaze boring into him. She knew he was lying. He wasn't sure why after all these years he was still keeping the secret.

Because he'd promised. It was that simple.

The question was, how had his grandmother found out? Had Jack told that there had been two girls, one a year younger than him and her kid sister? They had ridden their horses over from the ranch down the road and he and Cyrus had sneaked them up into the room.

His grandmother would have gone ballistic had she known they were in the house. Pepper had never liked any of the neighboring ranchers—not that any of them were close by. But she'd especially disliked the McCormicks.

When she didn't come out and ask about the girls, he realized Jack hadn't told.

That made Cordell feel better about his "cousin" Jack.

"I called the hospital," his grandmother said. "There is no change in Cyrus's condition."

Cordell said nothing. He'd checked his cell phone on the way downstairs. There'd been no messages. That meant no news.

"Is that all?" he asked, getting to his feet.

His grandmother nodded, though she didn't look pleased.

Now at least he knew why she'd invited them all back to the ranch. She was looking for a traitor in the Winchester family.

Cordell smiled to himself at that as he headed back upstairs. Didn't she know that you couldn't throw a rock around here without hitting someone with traitorous motives?

Raine turned on the tub water and poured in a shot of bubble bath, waiting until she was sure Cordell and the old housekeeper had gone downstairs before she pulled out her cell phone. No service. Tossing it back into her purse, she opened her small laptop. It only took a moment to get online via satellite.

Just as she suspected there would be, there was an email from Marias.

"Get in touch."

She replied through instant messaging. "No cell service. What's up?"

A few moments later. "Winchesters squeaky clean, good rep, tough and damned good-looking from their photos on their website."

Raine shook her head, smiling as she got up to turn off

the water in the tub. It was just like Marias to check them out to see just how handsome they were.

"So nothing to worry about, right?" she typed when she returned to her computer.

"Doesn't look that way."

They'd apparently taken time off from work to come visit their grandma. Except Cordell hadn't wanted to and couldn't wait to get out of here. She wondered how things were going downstairs with the two of them.

No reason to be suspicious of the Winchester brothers apparently.

"But you did get another package from Montana."

Raine jumped, startled by the tap on her door.

"Raine?"

Cordell.

She typed, "I assume you opened it."

Marias typed a smiley face.

"What's in it?"

"A crude map. Almost looks like a kid drew it. I think it might be a map to the house."

Raine felt her heart clutch in her chest. "Can you email it to me?"

"Could take a few minutes."

Cordell tapped again, then she heard the creak of the hardwood floor as he went across the hall. She listened to the sound of a key in the lock, his door opening and closing, then silence.

In the bathroom, she tested the water. Still hot. The room was steamy. She closed the door and stripped off her clothing before gingerly stepping into the tub and sinking down in the scented bubbles.

She felt confused and unsure. Trust came hard for her. But in her job she'd become good at reading people. Did she still believe Cordell and his brother had been hired by someone to set her up?

She sank down deeper in the tub. She was starting to trust him and that scared her more than she wanted to admit. What if she was wrong?

That answer was simple. She would never leave White-horse, Montana.

In the other room, she heard the sound of another email alert.

The map? With a chill she sank deeper in the water, terrified of what might be waiting for her at some remote house used by the child abductors.

Sheriff McCall Winchester wasn't surprised when Cordell called to say he'd found Raine Chandler and gotten his brother's pickup back. She was surprised, though, to see he was calling from a landline—at the Winchester Ranch.

"I still want to question her about your brother's assault," she told him, suspecting that her private investigator cousin had already done that.

"It sounds like it was an accident. Cyrus was just at the wrong place at the wrong time," he said.

"Uh-huh. Still… Do you know where I can reach her?" She heard him hesitate.

"We're waiting for the roads to dry out," he said finally.

"Oh?" McCall said. So there was more to this story, just as she'd suspected.

"After what happened last night, Raine was upset. I thought coming out here would get her mind off it."

Raine, huh? "Did Ms. Chandler say what she's doing in Whitehorse?"

"She's a journalist. Doing a story up this way."

"Know what about?"

"Didn't really get into that much."

McCall bit her tongue. "Could you ask her to stop by my office when you get back to town? Or better yet, let me ask her."

"She's in the bathtub across the hall in her room," he said, making McCall smile at how careful he was to make it clear she had her own room.

"Well, then why don't you have her stop by my office," McCall said. "I heard your father is coming to the ranch tomorrow. Grandmother invited me out for dinner. I hope you'll be there. I assume Aunt Virginia is still there?"

"Haven't seen her."

"Dinner should be interesting."

"More like pure hell. I wouldn't count on me being there. Is there anything new on the dark-colored van and the man driving it?"

"We found the van. It had been stolen from Havre. Forensics will be coming in tomorrow to see what they can find. I'll let you know if they come up with anything." McCall hung up, irritated with her cousin but sympathetic.

Earlier she'd stopped by the hospital. Cyrus was still in a coma. She picked up the report the deputy had given her on the altercation in the parking lot behind the hotel, anxious to talk to Raine Chandler.

Something was definitely wrong. McCall hoped her cousin knew what he was doing taking Raine to the ranch. She feared he didn't have a clue who the woman was—or what she was capable of, for that matter.

After all, he believed she was a journalist up here on a story.

Impatient after his call to the sheriff, Cordell turned on the television but he couldn't find a channel that could hold his attention so he just left it on the news and turned down the volume.

He began to go through the information again that Raine had collected on missing children. It was shocking and he suspected it was only the tip of the iceberg.

He found an article from a psychologist who dealt with the children who were recovered from child molesters. "Trust is devastated. Often the victim is made to feel responsible for what happened. They feel powerless, trapped. That sense of learned helplessness can last a lifetime." He skimmed the rest, words jumping out at him. *Humiliation. Alienation. Trauma. Vulnerability. Psychological shock. Postvictimization.*

He got to his feet. He couldn't read anymore. He had so many questions he wanted to ask Raine. What was taking her so long? She hadn't seemed like the kind of woman who would lounge around in the bath this long.

Picking up the Emily Frank file, he saw that she'd been a foster child. He realized he knew nothing about foster care. Sitting down, he began to read.

A line jumped out at him. "Children in foster care live in an uncertain world. They lack the stability and permanence that other children take for granted and are often moved at a moment's notice, all of their belongings fitting into no more than a plastic grocery bag."

He could relate to that. He and his twin had moved constantly from the time they were seven until they were able to go away to college. His father, Brand Winchester, was a quiet, taciturn man who worked as a ranch manager, moving like the wind from one job to the next. He'd never remarried after the twins' mother had left them when the boys were babies.

Brand never blamed his mother for the failure of his marriage or his life, but it was unspoken.

Cordell and Cyrus had been old enough to remember the day their grandmother had kicked them all off the ranch where they'd lived since they were born. He and Cyrus had learned at an early age to give their grandmother a wide berth, spending their days outside as much as possible with the horses or playing in the barn or outbuildings.

The family had scattered like fall leaves after that, none of his father's siblings keeping in touch except once in a long while. At least he and Cyrus had each other and had never been abandoned by their father.

Looking back though, Cordell realized how they could have ended up in foster care if things hadn't worked out for his father once they'd left the ranch and the only life his father had known.

His gaze settled again on the words in front of him. "Foster children's lives are about leaving behind things and friends and places they know, their lives haunted by neglect and child abuse. In foster care they often lose their sense of identity."

He picked up a grainy newspaper photograph of Emily Frank. The girl was wearing a dress that was too big for her. She looked gangly and a little too thin, but she wore a beatific smile.

He saw something he hadn't noticed before. A tiny silver horse pin. Even in the photograph he could see that it was in an odd place because of a small tear in the fabric that not even the pin could hide.

His heart ached for the little girl. According to the foster home paperwork, Emily had been kicked around from one foster home to another since she was two and had only been at the new foster home in Whitehorse one night. Before that she'd run away from her last foster home.

He could see how the foster parents might have thought she'd run away this time, too. They wouldn't have acted right away, a huge mistake.

He wondered how she'd ended up in foster care to begin with. Maybe Raine would know. He glanced toward his door, wondering how long before she finished her bath. He was anxious to find these monsters and hoped to hell Raine had a plan other than using herself as bait.

The tap at his door startled him. He quickly put everything back in the satchel and went to answer the door.

Raine stood out in the hall, her hair damp, her face glowing from her bath. She hadn't taken the time to put on that awful white makeup or the dark eyeliner. He marveled at how young and clean and fresh she looked without it. Like a different woman.

It struck him that she used the makeup almost like a mask—or a disguise. Was it possible Raine had known this girl Emily Frank? He felt his pulse quicken. Was it possible she'd been a foster child at the Amberson house when Emily was taken?

That, he realized in a flash, would explain why she wrote about these abducted children, why she knew so much about foster children, why she'd come all this way to do a story on Emily Frank.

"Is everything all right with your grandmother?" she asked, and he realized he must have been frowning as he wondered about her. "Is she upset about me staying here?"

"No, she is more interested in the past than the present. I don't want to talk about her, if you don't mind." He sighed and motioned for her to come in, reminding himself that it didn't matter if Raine had a connection to Emily Frank or not.

All that mattered was finding the bastard who'd put his brother in a coma.

The moment the door closed behind her, he demanded, "How do we find these people?"

Raine had seen the way he was looking at her and regretted that she hadn't taken the time to put on her makeup.

But she wrote off his behavior as impatience the moment he spoke. He just wanted to find the man who'd hurt his brother. On that they could agree.

"Emily had just come to Whitehorse the night before so only a limited number of people knew about her," she said. "From her diary, I think it is clear that her abductors knew she was a new foster child. They might even have been tipped off by the foster parents or possibly the social worker."

"You can't really believe they were in on this?"

Did she? "Everyone is a suspect and they knew Emily had run away from her last two foster homes. Emily Frank had unknowingly made herself the perfect abduction victim."

"Last *two* foster homes? I only read about one that she ran away from."

Raine sighed. He'd been studying the material while she was gone and was just looking for discrepancies. "The other foster family kept it quiet. It reflects poorly on the foster family if the children run away, but you'll find it in the social worker's report." She stepped to the table and pulled it out of the stack of papers to hand it to him.

He looked chastised. "How did she end up in foster care anyway?"

"The way a lot of them do. Single mom. Dad never in

the picture. Mom deemed unfit. The state takes the girl in the middle of the night and puts her in foster care with complete strangers."

"Why was the mother deemed unfit?"

"All it said on the report I was able to get was child endangerment. Could have been anything." She glanced from him to the television and froze.

"I have to admit I knew nothing about foster children until I started reading the material you'd gathered..." His voice trailed off as he finally noticed that she was no longer listening. "Raine?"

She groped blindly for the remote, unable to take her eyes off the newscaster and the words streaming across the bottom of the television screen.

Cordell saw her reaching for the television remote and turned to look at the television screen. A woman newscaster was standing in the Whitehorse Hotel parking lot. He thought it must be a story about last night's hit-and-run—until he caught the words running along the bottom of the screen and felt as if he'd been punched in the stomach.

Raine turned up the volume an instant later, the news commentator's voice filling the room.

"The girl disappeared from her home last night."

Out of the corner of his eye, Cordell saw Raine drop onto the edge of the bed with a sound like a wounded animal.

"Lara English had been playing hide-and-seek with her foster siblings at the time of her disappearance behind the Whitehorse Hotel. One of the children reported seeing a dark-colored van leaving the area shortly before hearing sirens."

"What the hell?" Cordell said under his breath. It couldn't be a coincidence that a child had been abducted from behind the hotel—the same area where Raine had nearly been run down and his brother struck by someone driving a dark-colored van.

"The foster mother, believing the child was hiding or had run away, didn't call the sheriff's department until late today."

An angry-looking woman came on the screen. "You don't know this kid. I do. So of course I thought she was just hiding from the other kids and refusing to come out or that she'd run. What was I supposed to think? You have no idea what some of these foster kids are like. No idea."

Lara English's photo flashed on the television screen.

"Hell," Cordell said on a shocked breath. He stared at the photograph that came up on the screen. The girl was blonde, blue-eyed and grinning into the camera. He felt his heart drop like a stone. The girl looked enough like Emily Frank to be her sister.

The news report ended with the usual. "If anyone sees this nine-year-old girl, please call the sheriff's department." The number flashed on the screen.

His cousin McCall came on in uniform and encouraged anyone with information to contact her immediately.

As the news changed to the construction of a new bridge in Great Falls, he took the remote from Raine's trembling fingers and turned off the television.

"Okay, no more lies. What the hell is going on?" he demanded even though he could see she was in as much shock as he was. "And don't tell me it doesn't have something to do with you."

Raine stared at the blank television, her heart racing as if she'd just had to run for her life. She tried to breathe but couldn't seem to catch her breath.

She could still see the little girl's face that had only moments before been on the television screen. Emily Frank. No, she thought with a mental shake, only a child who looked enough like Emily to—

"Raine? *Raine!*"

She blinked and dragged her gaze away from the now blank television screen.

Cordell handed her a paper cup half full of cold water. "Here, drink some of this." She took a sip, hating how weak and afraid she felt, how helpless. He motioned for her to finish it.

She did and he took the empty cup from her trembling hand. Her mind seemed scattered as she watched him ball up the cup and throw it into the trash. He came back to kneel in front of her.

"These are the same people who took Emily Frank, aren't they?" he said, taking both of her hands in his.

She was aware of the warmth of his hands and how her cold ones seemed to disappear in his. She looked up into his dark eyes and wondered how she'd ever thought them cold and unfeeling. There was heartbreak in them.

Raine wanted to pull back from the pain she saw there. It too closely mirrored her own.

"Talk to me," he said quietly. Of course he'd seen the resemblance between Lara English and Emily Frank. He knew it had been no coincidence they looked so much alike.

Raine felt sick to her stomach. Cordell knew, just as she did, that this was about *her.* It had been from the moment she'd received the lined pages torn from Emily's school notebook. "They took that girl because of me."

"Why would they do that?" Cordell asked. "It can't be because of some magazine article. You were a foster child, weren't you?"

With her gaze locked to his, she knew she didn't have to answer. He'd seen the answer.

"You knew Emily Frank?"

Raine shivered and dragged her gaze away to look toward the French door she'd left partially cracked open earlier. A cool breeze blew in. She watched it stir the row of tall old cottonwoods flanking the massive log lodge. Beyond them was a huge red barn and horses in a summer-green pasture.

Not even that picturesque scene, though, could lift the horrible weight resting on her chest. How was it she could feel for these lost children, but she couldn't appreciate beauty or feel love? Because something had died in her sixteen years ago the day Emily Frank was taken.

She turned back to Cordell, surprised at the tears that brimmed in her eyes and the sobbing ache that hitched in her chest. "I am Emily Frank. That's why they took that girl. Because of me."

Chapter 7

Cordell stared at her in disbelief. "That can't be. Emily Frank is dead."

"That's what a lot of people believed especially after Orville Cline confessed to her abduction and murder," she said, slipping her hands from his as she rose to go to the window.

Cordell shuddered as he recalled the graphic description in Orville's confession as to how he killed her and what he did with her body.

"Emily escaped," she said, her back to him. "They never found her. Then a week ago I got the pages from Emily's notebook."

He rose to his feet, unsure what to do or say. He couldn't help noticing the way she was talking about Emily as if she was a separate person from her. He suspected that was the way she thought of her. But now, at least, he knew the connection.

Outside, a fierce warm wind howled across the eaves. In this part of the country, the weather changed in an instant, often with huge ranges in temperature, as well.

The roads would be drying out. For once, luck was with them, he thought, since this latest news had changed everything.

"Emily was one of those foster kids bounced from home to home from the age of two," Raine said. "She never knew her father. She could barely remember her mother, a teenager who dumped her at strange people's houses so she could go out partying with her friends. From such a young age, it makes a kid resilient."

"Still—"

"It's amazing the way we're able to accept what happens to us," she said. "We don't know any differently. It isn't as if we have that much contact with kids from normal families."

Cordell couldn't believe that. She would have seen other children at school or in the neighborhood who had a father and mother, families, secure lives that didn't change in an instant.

He frowned as it all began to sink in. "You're not a journalist on a story."

She shook her head, her gaze settling on his. "I'm a private investigator in L.A."

"A *private investigator?*" Small world. But that explained a lot, including the gun she carried and how she'd managed to get away from him at the hotel this morning.

"If you don't believe me you can call my partner, Marias Alvarez."

"I believe you." He realized he did. Just as he'd believed her confession about being Emily Frank. "How did Emily get away?"

She stood silhouetted against the afternoon light, her

back to him. Earlier she'd looked defeated, but now there was a new strength to her, a new determination as she turned suddenly to face him.

He wondered how many times this woman had been forced to find that strength. Cordell couldn't bear the thought of what she'd been through.

"When Emily was found more than two hundred miles from Whitehorse, she was near death. No one knows how she got there. She didn't speak for two months and when she did, she had no memory of what had happened to her."

"My God," Cordell said and hoped with all his heart that she would never have any memory of what had happened to her. "We have to go to the sheriff."

"If we do, he'll kill Lara right away. You have to trust me on this. If you go to the sheriff, it will cost Lara her life and I fear it will be the last I hear from the person sending me the information."

Cordell didn't doubt she knew what she was talking about. But what if she was wrong? "What are you saying? The person who sent you those pages just got you back here to kill you."

She shook her head. "Why would they do that? Orville Cline had already confessed to Emily's murder."

"Maybe they're worried that your memory has come back and are afraid you can identify them."

Raine hesitated, then said, "I still believe that one of them wants this to stop and is helping me to bring the child abductor down." She told him that her friend and partner Marias Alvarez called the person CBA or Crazy Bastard Abductor. "I think Crazy Bitch Abductor might be closer to the truth. I believe it's the wife sending me the information and that she got me back here because she knows she can't stop him without help."

"That's some theory. I hope it doesn't get you killed."

"What choice do I have? There's a little girl out there missing. I have to find her before it is too late," she said, her voice breaking. The news about the latest little girl had chilled her to her very bones. She knew exactly what Lara English was going through.

But she couldn't give in to her emotions. She had to be strong. "I have to put all my energy into finding Lara."

"And you believe this CBA will help you do that," he said, sounding more than a little skeptical.

"Now that he's taken Lara, I have to believe it," she said.

Cordell studied her for a long moment and she could see he was considering her argument. "You do realize that he knows someone leaked you the information. That's how he knew where you'd be last night when he took Lara."

She nodded solemnly. "That means the woman could be in as much trouble as Lara. Another reason we have to find them and Lara before it's too late."

"How do you suggest we do that?"

"The Crazy Bitch Abductor sent us a map."

"I hope this map makes more sense to you than it does to me," Cordell said as Raine stared at her computer on the way to Whitehorse.

The wind dried the top of the road bed. As long as he avoided the mud puddles, the rental car got enough traction to keep them out of the ditch.

Before they'd left the ranch, he'd called to have a wrecker pull out his brother's pickup. He planned to pick it up in town. For these Montana roads, a truck worked much better. He'd also called the hospital. There was no change in Cyrus's condition.

"I would assume it's a map to the house where my abductors took me sixteen years ago," Raine said.

The map was crude at best, hand-drawn as if by a child. He felt a chill the first time she'd showed it to him back at the ranch. He'd had to agree with her when he'd seen it. Maybe someone was trying to help her. Or not.

"I still think we should go the sheriff," he'd argued when he'd seen the map. "McCall needs to know what's going on."

"Your cousin is already searching for Lara. She's a cop. Don't you think she's already considered that Lara might have been abducted? Especially after what went down behind the Whitehorse Hotel last night?"

He'd agreed that she was right and he didn't want to take a chance with Raine's life any more than he did Lara's. The problem was he didn't trust whoever was sending her this information.

Raine was the only one they knew of who'd gotten away from her abductors in this area. Orville Cline had confessed to her murder. Raine was living proof of his lie—and knew that he hadn't taken her.

Wasn't that more than enough motive to get her back to where it had all happened to tie up the loose end in the cruelest of all ways? By making her relive her abduction through Lara English?

His heart broke for the child Raine had been just as it did for Lara. He swore he would see that these people paid— or he'd die trying.

"You don't think this house is where he took Lara, do you?" Cordell asked.

"No. The CBA would be too afraid to give that up—if she even knows. No, I think there is something at the house on the map that she wants me to find, though."

He glanced over at her, hearing the fear in her voice she was trying hard to hide. "You never told me what happened after you were found miles from Whitehorse," he said, not comfortable with his own thoughts right now.

But he needed to know everything about Emily Frank if he planned to help Raine. When she didn't answer, he glanced over at her. "I'm sorry, if you'd rather not tell me—"

"No. I want to tell you. If I had come forward before this, maybe Lara English wouldn't have been abducted."

"You can't remember what your abductors look like," he pointed out. "And as you said, these people are chameleons, blending in with society. All you would have done was put yourself in the line of fire earlier."

Raine couldn't argue that, but the truth was she hadn't been ready to face this. She wasn't sure she was now.

But she knew she had to be honest with Cordell if they hoped to find Lara before it was too late. Together they might stand a chance, a slim one, but at least a chance. And she knew he had a lot of questions. Anyone would.

"I told you Emily didn't remember anything. That wasn't true."

"Raine, you don't have to—"

"I don't remember what they looked like. Either I didn't see their faces or I didn't want to remember them. That night while the thunder and lightning boomed around me, I wrote the pages in my notebook to keep myself calm. I guess that's when the idea came to me how I could escape."

"You didn't try before that?"

She shook her head and smiled over at him.

"I can't imagine having the presence of mind to do that. Not at age ten. I would have cried and screamed myself hoarse."

"You never know what you would do in a situation like that," she said. "I was a foster child. I'd been thrown into so many uncomfortable situations, I don't think I was as terrified as a child who'd never known adversity. Also I was used to being alone and pretty much taking care of myself."

"What happened after you escaped?"

"I found my way to the highway, followed it until I came to a farmhouse. It was early in the morning. I hid in the back of a pickup that was running in the yard. After the truck pulled out of the yard, I fell asleep curled under an old tarp and when I woke up I was in a town I had never seen before.

"As it turned out, I was in Williston, North Dakota, not even in Montana any longer, hundreds of miles away from Whitehorse. When the driver went inside a store, I climbed out of the back of the truck. I must have been a real mess when a nice woman found me. I was running a fever, sick and weak. They were afraid I wouldn't survive."

"They didn't know you and how strong you are," he said, his voice filled with admiration.

Raine felt her face heat from it and hurried on with her story. "The Chandlers took me in. It was Mrs. Chandler who'd found me and got me medical attention. They say I didn't speak for months and by then I was smart enough to make up a story so I never had to go back to that foster home in Whitehorse. I think I knew I would be abducted again or sent away to possibly somewhere worse."

"The Chandlers were nice to you?"

"Tom and Minnie Chandler were in their forties. Their only son was away at college. I think they were thankful to have a child under their roof. They adopted me after a time. They let me choose my own name. Raine seemed appropriate since the storm was what had saved me."

Cordell shook his head, awed by her story. "They never put it together that you were Emily Frank, this girl missing from a town just across the hi-line a few hundred miles?"

"Emily was believed to have run away. There wasn't much of a network for missing children sixteen years ago. That was before Amber Alert. And as I've said, from my experience, foster children often run away or fall through the cracks. I'd only been with the Ambersons in Whitehorse one night. They didn't know anything about me except that I'd run away from the last two homes I'd been in."

"You're saying they weren't invested in looking for you." He couldn't believe what he was hearing. "So there wasn't much of a search for you. Still you would think that someone in Williston would have heard about the missing girl. The Chandlers had to wonder why no one was looking for you."

She smiled. "When Minnie found me, I was wearing a hand-me-down worn dress that was too big for me and no shoes. I think she realized when no one came looking for me that I was better off with her and that's why she didn't try to find out where I came from."

Cordell's thought exactly. "I'm glad they were good to you. They must have been relieved when Orville Cline confessed to abducting and killing Emily Frank. They probably thought you were safe."

"We all did," Raine said. "I was at college when I read about Orville Cline's arrest and his confessions. I wanted to believe he was the one. It was easier than believing that the people were still out there, still taking little girls. I thought he lied about killing..." her voice caught "...Emily because he didn't want anyone looking for me. It never dawned on me that he could have made a deal with my abductors."

Cordell heard the pain in her voice, the guilt. "You can't

blame yourself. After what you'd been through, you had to know that if you did anything, they could find you."

"But they still found me, didn't they?"

"How? That's what I don't understand," he said.

"I've been asking myself that. I assume someone put two and two together in Williston."

"Is it possible the truck driver saw you when you got out of the back of his pickup?"

"Maybe. I jumped out and ran and hid. But wouldn't you think he would have told someone?"

"Maybe he did. Maybe he told your foster parents back in Whitehorse, but since it appeared you'd merely run away…"

Raine nodded. "I've known all along I would have to talk to them eventually. But first I have to see where this map leads me."

Cordell could hear how anxious she was as he looked down the road they'd just turned down and wondered where they were being led—and, more to the point, by whom?

He saw Raine glance at her watch. She'd told him that if Lara could be found within seventy-two hours, she stood the best chance of being found alive.

They'd already lost precious hours. He could almost hear the clock ticking.

Chapter 8

Cordell looked out at the growing darkness, his anxiety growing.

"According to the map, it's just a little farther," Raine said in the pickup cab next to him. "He wouldn't want the house to be too far from town and yet far enough away and remote enough that he knew no one would accidentally stumble across it."

Cordell had insisted they stop in Whitehorse long enough to trade the rental car for the pickup. The moment he'd realized the roads would be passable that they could leave the ranch, he'd called a towing service in town.

The wrecker had gotten to the pickup in the ditch, just minutes before they did. They'd followed the tow truck driver into town and made the switch, losing only a little daylight.

From Highway 2 they'd turned off a dirt road, then another, each road getting smaller and less used until now they were in a creek bottom of narrow ravines, rocky bluffs and twisting juniper-choked coulees.

"The next turn should be up here on the right," Raine said.

"I don't see a road," he said, squinting through the twilight. Deep shadows hunkered in the underbrush along the creek.

"There it is." Just then a whitetail deer bolted from the brush and ran directly in front of the pickup, startling them both. He hit the brakes. Raine let out a breath as the deer swept past unhurt.

Cordell didn't like the closed-in feel of this river bottom. Nor did he trust that whoever had sent Raine the map was interested in confessing and ending this. Ending this, maybe. But with someone dying and he feared that someone the informant had in mind was Raine Chandler, aka Emily Frank.

The road dropped down into a thicket of stunted aspen trees along the creek bottom. A perfect place for an ambush, he thought as he pulled a pistol from under his brother's seat, checked the clip and rested the weapon next to him as he turned down the road.

He noticed that Raine had apparently thought the same thing as she already had her gun resting in her hand, no doubt loaded and ready to fire. It made him feel a little better to realize that she wasn't putting all of her trust in this CBA.

She'd tucked away the computer and lowered her window. The air smelled of summer, the grasses tall and green. A wisp of cloud floated along on the breeze against the pale twilight.

It was one of those perfect Montana summer evenings. He wanted to breathe it all in, to stop by the creek and watch stars come out in the awe-inspiring big sky. He wanted more than anything to not go around the next bend.

Instead, they were on the hunt for monsters, the worst kind, the kind who hurt children. Just knowing the man and woman who'd hurt Raine were so close by made him homicidal. He feared if he didn't get them first, they would get Raine.

As he drove around the bend in the road, he saw the house. Raine saw it, too. She let out a heartbreaking sound. This, he knew, was where her abductors had brought her sixteen years ago.

Raine thought she was prepared. For so long the abduction had been buried deep enough that she really hadn't been able to remember anything. Parts of it had come back over the years.

But there were still holes in her memory, holes she wasn't so sure she shouldn't leave empty and dark.

Unfortunately, her instincts told her that the only way she'd be able to find Lara was if she remembered everything.

As the pickup's headlights swept over the abandoned old farmhouse, the past washed over her, taking her breath away, sending her heart hammering as she smelled the dank darkness, felt the aching cold, heard the sound of the door opening. And closing. She knew this house.

"Stop!"

Cordell hit the brakes as she threw open her door.

She heard him call to her to wait, but the house pulled her to it, metal to magnet. It was as if she no longer could hold back the nightmare. Sixteen years ago she'd believed she would die in this house.

Behind her, she heard Cordell running after her.

As she neared the house, she thought she tasted blood.

The cut lip. She'd forgotten about that, but not about the woman who'd smacked her and told her she'd better do everything the man told her if she knew what was good for her.

The door to the old place was partially open, a sliver of darkness gaping behind it.

Cordell caught up with her, shoved a flashlight into her hand. She looked over at him, grateful. He wasn't going to try to stop her. He knew nothing could, not even him.

He played the light over the front step with his flashlight, then into the dank musty interior. She turned hers on and moved up the creaking steps. Her fingers ached as she touched the door. It swung open with a creak that sent a blade of ice into her heart. A blast of cold, putrid air rushed out at her.

"Let me go in first," he whispered as he stepped past her.

The door yawned all the way open. The smell triggered thoughts and feelings and fears that made her pulse pound in her ears and legs weak beneath her. She clutched her gun in one hand, the flashlight in the other and told herself she could do this. She was the little girl who'd survived. She was Emily Frank.

She'd put off facing this all these years. Now she had no choice. The clue to where they'd find Lara English was here. Why else lead her here?

To kill you?

No, she thought as she followed Cordell inside the house. Taunt her, maybe. Terrify her, absolutely. But ultimately, the answer was here.

The house seemed full of whispers and skittering sounds, creaks and groans. One dark room after another appeared in the beam of their flashlights until she reached the stairs that dropped down into the partial basement.

"Hell, no," Cordell said beside her.

Pepper Winchester stood in the third-floor room in the dark. She didn't want to turn on the lights. This evening she wasn't up to reading what her children had scratched in the walls.

She'd been coming up here for weeks now. As some form of punishment for her sins? Or just because she had nowhere else to go?

In this room was where she'd let her husband, Call, send their children. It was small and always made her feel closed in. There was a window that faced out toward the ridge where her youngest son had been murdered.

She looked out it now, barely able to make out the ridge in the growing darkness. It came to her why, after so many years, she'd begun to frequent this horrible reminder of her failure as a mother. It was also a reminder that one of her children had betrayed her in the worst possible way.

One of her children had helped with the murder of his— or her—youngest sibling. And to make matters worse, she feared one of her own grandchildren had witnessed it from this very room—and kept quiet all these years.

A rustling sound startled her. Her hand went to her throat before she realized it was only the party hats that had ended up huddled in the far corner. There must be a breeze coming up from the elevator shaft.

It was the party hats that had clued her into the fact that her grandchildren had been in this room the day of Trace's murder. Trace, her youngest, her most precious, her favorite. He had died on that far ridge the day of his birthday.

Pepper blamed herself, this house, this life, her long-dead husband, Call. Trace's alleged killer was dead. But in her heart she believed that her son's true killer remained free and unknown. At least for the time being.

At the sound of a car engine, she turned to see lights coming up the narrow ranch road. Brand. She hadn't seen her son for twenty-seven years, had yet to speak to him since the day she'd sent him away and all the others when Trace hadn't shown for his birthday party.

She knew her children had reason to hate her. She'd taken away their birthright: Winchester Ranch.

But that was the least of what she'd deprived them of over their lives.

In the last of the day's light, she fumbled for the elevator button. The door opened, she shoved aside the gate and stepped into an even smaller space. Heart pounding and her breath coming in gasps, she descended to the ground floor and hurriedly got out, her cane tapping on the wood floor.

She knew the kind of reception she would get from her son Brand. Like his son Cordell, he hated her, blamed her, wanted nothing to do with her.

Pepper had only one hope as she hurried to greet him. Out of her five children, she hoped Brand wasn't the one who'd betrayed his brother.

"I have to go down there," Raine said as she took a step down the stairs.

Cordell heard both pleading and determination in her tone. The message was clear: *Please don't try to stop me.* He doubted he could even if he tried.

He shone his flashlight into the cold damp darkness below the house and cringed. He wouldn't have kept a dog down there, let alone a child.

He'd done his best not to imagine where Lara English

was being held. But seeing this partial basement, which in truth was nothing more than a crawl space, he could imagine the horrible place that little girl was in right now. Alone? Or were they with her?

He shuddered at the thought and followed on Raine's heels into the pit below.

She stopped suddenly, the beam of her flashlight flickering over a pile of old lumber. Raine played the light over the boards, then the wooden slats of the wall behind it. Cordell kept his flashlight pointed at his feet, trying to stay out of her way. He didn't doubt that this was something she needed to do. He couldn't imagine what thoughts and emotions were going through her head right now.

Suddenly she seemed to sway on her feet. He reached for her and saw in the ambient glow of their flashlights that her eyes were as vacant as this old house.

"Raine?" He couldn't help the fear that gripped him. *"Raine?"*

She didn't answer, but blinked and her face contorted in a mask of pain. Dear God, she was reliving what had happened to her down here.

"Raine!" He grabbed her arm and shook her. Her eyes fluttered and he watched as she fought her way to the surface, gasping for breath, a high keening sound coming from her lips.

He could see the memories trying to pull her back under, a riptide wanting to take her, drown her.

He dragged her into his arms, holding her, saying her name over and over. "Raine. Raine." But he feared she was Emily Frank again and there was no bringing her back.

A few moments later she surfaced and seemed surprised to find herself in his arms. "What happened?"

Cordell shook his head. He didn't have a clue.

She closed her eyes and for a moment, he thought he'd lost her again.

"I remember," she said in a hoarse whisper. "I wasn't molested. Only because I fought back. Only because I would have preferred to die than let that man touch me again." Her eyes opened and he'd never been so relieved to see that sea of clear blue. "I bit him. Cordell, are you listening to me? I bit the man who abducted me. I bit his left hand so hard there is no way I didn't leave a scar."

He was too busy thinking how relieved he was that she was her old self again.

The realization of what she was saying finally sank in. A scar. It might be a way to identify the man. If they ever got that close to him.

Raine stepped toward the wall behind the small pile of old lumber. Her flashlight beam scoured the boards, then froze on a spot.

He stepped closer.

It had been sixteen years so the letters scratched in the wall were almost too faint to read. When he did make them out, he wished he hadn't. His insides seemed to liquefy and he knew he would remember those words until the day he died.

There carved in the wood was, *Emily Frank died here*.

Chapter 9

Emily Frank's former foster family was just finishing dinner. The night breeze carried the scent of boiled chicken and root vegetables.

Cordell noticed that Raine seemed to hang back as they neared the large rambling farmhouse even though he doubted the couple would recognize her—not after sixteen years. Also she'd changed her appearance from the blonde little girl they would remember, having dyed her hair dark.

The only thing about her that was recognizable from the girl she'd been was her eyes. They were that incredible sky-blue, so clear they seemed infinite. He'd gotten lost in them enough to know just how unforgettable they were.

He could tell she was nervous about seeing her former foster parents again even though she'd spent only one night there. He knew she feared they might have been in on the abduction.

"The abduction was planned. It wasn't spur-of-the-moment," she'd told him on the way to town. "The couple who took me knew who I was. That means they'd known the Ambersons were getting a foster child."

"And not just any foster child," Cordell had said. "One who'd run away from the past two homes she'd been placed in."

Raine had looked over at him as if impressed that he was beginning to understand how this had gone down. Either that or she was wondering why it had taken him so long to figure things out.

"You all right?" he asked now. They'd parked down the road from the house, deciding to walk up the narrow lane that ended at the front door. Cordell had thought it would be easier on Raine.

The question seemed to jerk her out of her thoughts, her gaze going to the house's second story where a pink curtain billowed out the open window on the breeze.

"I was just wondering what makes people become foster parents," she said.

A love for children would have been his first guess—at least before he'd met Raine. A more cynical answer would be the money, though he couldn't imagine that foster parents were paid enough per child to make it worthwhile taking on children who often had problems—and were a problem.

"I would imagine there are some who are wonderful and feel they are called to do this," he said.

She nodded and gave him a wry smile. "I'd just like to know who called the Ambersons," she said under her breath.

As they neared, the screen door swung open and a man stepped out onto the large porch. He smiled in greeting, squinting a little as he studied first Cordell and then Raine as if he thought he should know them. That was the thing about Whitehorse. Most everyone did know each other.

His eyes seemed to narrow before his gaze returned to Cordell.

"Good evening. Can I help you?" he asked. He had a deep, rich voice. His hands were large and callused and he looked strong and solid. A man who did physical labor, Cordell guessed.

"Abel Amberson?" The serious man was in his late fifties, graying at the temples, lines around his eyes and mouth more from being out in the sun than from laughing, Cordell thought.

Abel gave a slight nod, looking instantly wary.

"I'm Cordell Winchester. This is Raine Chandler. We're here about one of your former foster children."

The man arched a brow. "You aren't with Social Services."

"No. We're looking into the disappearance of Emily Frank," Cordell said.

"Emily?" he repeated, clearly taken aback.

"We hoped we could ask you some questions. I'm sure the local sheriff will be speaking with you as well about the latest abduction."

"Latest abduction?" asked a woman coming through the screen door. Grace Amberson was a small woman with a kind face and eyes. "Why would you be questioning *us?* She's not our foster child."

"No, but Emily Frank was," Raine said.

The woman's gaze swung to Raine and held there long enough Cordell thought she might have recognized her. "Emily wasn't abducted," Grace said. "She ran away."

"A child molester now serving time in prison confessed to taking Emily Frank," Cordell said.

Grace Amberson clasped both hands as she cried, "Emily wasn't taken by a child molester. What are these people talking about, Abel?" Her voice broke and tears welled in her eyes.

"The man's name is Orville Cline," Raine said. "Maybe you've heard of him."

Cordell knew she was watching for a reaction. She must have been disappointed.

"Who?" Abel asked. His wife showed no sign of recognition, either.

"Orville *Cline*. He confessed to abducting and killing Emily Frank."

"No, that's not possible," Grace cried, her voice filled with horror.

"Why don't you let me take care of this, Grace," her husband said quietly. Behind them a half-dozen children from about five to thirteen peered out from the screen. "Take the children in and give them some ice cream. I'll be in shortly."

"I'm sorry if we upset you," Raine said to Grace and smiled through the screen at the children. "Would you mind if I used your bathroom?"

Cordell could see that the woman wanted to say no but it wasn't in her nature.

"Of course." Grace held the door open behind her as Raine entered.

"I think you'd better show me some identification," Abel said the moment the women were gone. "You've upset my wife."

Cordell took his driver's license and P.I. license from his wallet and handed it to the man. "We're investigating the Emily Frank case for a client. Ms. Chandler and I are both private investigators."

Abel Amberson's eyes widened in surprise as he handed

back the licenses. "This comes as a terrible shock. We were told she ran away."

"Who told you that?"

"Social Services and the sheriff at the time. She'd run away from two other foster homes. Was she really taken by this man?"

"According to him. His confession is very...detailed," Cordell said, putting his ID away and pocketing his wallet.

"Is that what they think happened to this other girl, Lara English?" Abel looked stricken. He glanced back toward his house as if worried about his family inside it. "Why hasn't someone warned us?"

Cordell shook his head. Probably because the local news media hadn't picked up on it. Emily Frank's abduction was one of a dozen crimes Orville had admitted to committing. Cordell wondered how many more the man had lied about.

The screen opened and Raine came out. She looked pale. "Ready?"

He nodded. "Well, thank you, Mr. Amberson, for your time." He held out his hand and Abel shook it. "If you think of anything that might help." Cordell handed him his business card. "My cell phone number is on the back."

As he and Raine walked down the narrow road to where they'd parked the pickup, Cordell could feel the tension coming off her like a live wire.

"Abel Amberson didn't have a scar on his left hand," he said once they were out of earshot.

"No, but I found something in the house," she said. "I was admiring the children's drawings tacked on the refrigerator when I saw an invitation to the Whitehorse Summer Gala. Apparently it is invitation only. That means only the cream of Whitehorse crop will be there tomorrow night."

Raine looked over at him as they reached the truck. "And

care to guess who the guests of honor are this year? Abel and Ruth Amberson for their years of foster care. Do you think your grandmother can get us an invitation?"

From the window, Pepper saw not just one son, but two climb from the car in front of the lodge. Both men were tall and handsome like their father.

Brand glanced toward the window where she stood and she braced herself. From his expression this was the last place on earth he wanted to be.

She shifted her gaze to her older son Worth, or Worthless, as Call had called him. It surprised her how old he looked. Both of her sons were in their fifties.

That was hard for her to accept, that, like her, they had aged. She remembered them as being strong and determined, wild as this land. She could see them riding across the ranch, young and free.

Guilt wedged itself into her heart as sharp and painful as a knife blade. What had she done to them? Turned them out, took away what they thought was their legacy: the Winchester Ranch.

Pepper straightened, setting her expression as she headed for the front door leaning more heavily than usual on her cane. Facing her sons would be harder than anything she'd ever done, she realized.

If only she was the cold, uncaring bitch they thought she was. It would make this so much easier.

As she reached the top of the stairs, she saw Virginia go to the door. She could tell by the set of her daughter's shoulders that she thought Brand and Worth were only here for the money, money she felt was owed to her.

Her old maid daughter, her oldest child and only girl, wore her bitterness like a shroud. That, too, Pepper thought, was her fault. Was it fear that made Virginia so greedy? Or did she really not care for anyone but herself?

Maybe she thought that with the Winchester fortune she wouldn't feel so alone. Of course, she was wrong. Her mother could attest to that.

At the door, Virginia gave her brothers awkward hugs, then the three of them turned and looked up the stairs as if they'd sensed their mother watching them.

Pepper put steel in her back as she slowly descended the stairs. She could feel their gazes riveted on her, each of them wondering just how frail and close to death she was.

She kept her chin up. She wouldn't let them see the mountain of regret that lay on her chest, making it nearly impossible to draw a breath.

"Mother," Brand said.

"Brand," she said with a nod. "Worth." Her oldest son didn't meet her gaze. Up close he looked even older and in poor health. It broke her heart.

"Any news on Cyrus?" Pepper asked of her grandson.

"The same," Brand said, the pain evident in his expression. He glanced around the lodge. "The place hasn't changed." His gaze settled on her again. "Neither have you." He didn't make that sound like a good thing.

Enid appeared, giving them all a start and making Brand smile to himself.

"I suppose you want me to show them to their rooms," Enid said.

"I can do it." Virginia took hold of Brand's arm. "But maybe Enid could get them something to drink before dinner."

Enid shot Pepper a look that said she didn't take orders from Virginia especially with Virginia talking as if she wasn't even in the room.

"I think that is a wonderful idea, Virginia. I'll help Enid and meet you all back down here in the parlor before dinner."

Enid turned on her heel and with a huff took off for the kitchen.

"She *really* hasn't changed," Brand said, sounding amused.

Virginia snorted. "I don't know why you haven't fired her a long time ago, Mother."

Pepper watched the housekeeper disappear down the hall. "Oh, I suspect Enid will die here."

Virginia led her brothers up the stairs and Pepper listened to the three of them whispering among themselves, joining ranks against the enemy. And she knew only too well who the enemy was.

Cordell didn't have to call his grandmother about tickets to the gala.

When Raine checked her cell phone as they left the Ambersons, there was a message from Marias that her CBA had sent her something.

Raine felt her stomach drop. "What now?"

"The message I got was that there will be two tickets for you at the door with your name on them for the Whitehorse Summer Gala. You've been invited to some exclusive party."

"What is it?" Cordell whispered, no doubt seeing Raine's expression.

"Apparently we're going to the dance," she said. "My benefactor left us tickets at the door. Anything else?" she asked Marias.

"Not that you want to hear," her friend and partner said. "I just keep wondering who's pulling your chain and why."

"Yeah. Me, too. Maybe they just want to see if I can dance."

Marias laughed. "Aren't they in for a thrill."

Raine hung up and looked over at Cordell. "What?" she asked, seeing his frown.

"At least if they're at the dance, then Lara is safe," he said.

She certainly hoped so. It felt as if time was running out. The last thing she wanted to be doing was going to some socialite dance in this wide spot in the road of a town while knowing Lara English was out there somewhere, scared and alone.

But she had to hold fast to her theory that the CBA wanted the truth to come out. As hard as it was for her to believe it was the same woman who'd kicked her over to the side of the floorboard as she'd gotten into the car sixteen years ago. The same woman who'd helped her husband abduct that terrified ten-year-old.

Suddenly a set of headlights flashed on. The next moment Raine heard the roar of an engine as what appeared to be a large truck ran right at them.

She saw Cordell swerve, the truck missing them by only inches as it sped past, and they crashed into the bushes at the edge of the road, breaking through and dropping down a small hill to come to an abrupt stop just feet from a narrow creek and in a stand of cottonwoods.

"Are you all right?" Cordell cried.

All she could do was nod. She was shaking all over after almost being run down for the second time in two days.

He turned to look back. She did the same, but she could see nothing but darkness. She could only think that she'd almost died on the road that she'd been abducted from so many years before. Was that how this was supposed to end?

She was to die here sixteen years ago and had cheated the grim reaper—but only until now.

"That was no accident," Cordell said. "That means the driver of that truck knows that we went by the Ambersons. They must have tipped him off. Or whoever they called about Emily tipped the driver off. The Ambersons were upset. Of course they would call someone to see if it was true about her abduction by Orville Cline and tell the person that we'd been by."

Raine felt his gaze on her.

"Are you sure you're all right?"

She was trembling, still shaken by the near accident and that horrible feeling that this was where she was meant to die.

Cordell unhooked his seat belt, then reached over, unhooked hers and pulled her to him. The night was dark as a cloak around them. "It's going to be okay," he whispered against her hair.

Raine drew back and looked up at him. "You are such a terrible liar."

He smiled, eyes crinkling in the faint glow of the dash lights, and suddenly it was as if they were the only two people left in the world. She leaned into him, wanting desperately to believe him. The night and the cottonwoods closed around the warm cab of the pickup like a cocoon.

She looked into his dark eyes and willed him to kiss her. She wanted to forget everything for just a while, to lose herself in this man's strong arms.

As if in answer, he lowered his mouth to hers. She snuggled against him, relishing the heat of his mouth, his body. He pulled her closer. Her body melded into his as he deepened the kiss. His tongue brushed over her lips, the corner of her mouth.

Her nipples hardened against the thin sheer fabric of her bra. She swore she could hear the quickened beat of his heart in sync with her own.

She encircled his neck as he trailed kisses along her jawbone and down the column of her throat. A shiver of naked desire moved through her. Raine could feel her pulse throb under his touch, a primitive beat like drums in her ears.

A moan escaped her lips as she felt his fingers unbutton her shirt. His mouth dipped to the tops of her breasts. She arched against him, felt his thumb flick over her aching-hard nipple. She bit her lip to keep from crying out as his mouth rooted out her naked breast from the sheer fabric of her bra.

The windows steamed over even on the warm summer night. Raine lost herself to the sound of their combined frenzied breathing, the rocking of the pickup, the feel of Cordell's body as he cradled her to him.

Her release came with a cry of pleasure that echoed through the cab, followed shortly by Cordell's own. They clung to each other, naked, breathing still ragged.

"I didn't mean for that to happen," Cordell said after a few minutes. "At least not in the pickup."

Raine kissed him. "I did," she said as she reached for strewn clothing.

Her cell phone rang as she was pulling on her jeans. "Hello," she said, still sounding winded.

"You all right?" Marias asked. "You sound funny."

"I'm fine." She glanced over at Cordell. "More than fine. What's up?"

A beat of silence that sent her heart off again, then Marias asking, "Then you haven't seen the news?"

"Have they found Lara English?" Raine asked, hope filling her.

"Orville Cline," Marias said. "He walked away from a work release prison program yesterday morning in Deer Lodge and hasn't been seen since."

Chapter 10

Pepper Winchester studied each of her adult children as Enid served supper.

None of the three looked in the least bit happy to be here. So why were they here?

She could understand Brand coming. His son was in the hospital in a coma. But then if he was so miserable here at the ranch, then why not stay in a motel in town?

He could have easily come to Whitehorse without seeing her—or setting foot on the ranch.

"So has it changed that much from when you were last here?" she asked into the weighty silence.

All three seemed to be startled out of their thoughts.

"What?" Worth said. He was large like his father but without the extraordinary good looks that the other Winchester men had inherited.

"The ranch," she explained. "I was wondering if you'd missed it."

She saw Brand's jaw tense. He looked back down at the food on his plate, his fork suspended over a piece of dried-out roast beef.

Pepper felt oddly sad to see that he had missed the ranch. The sting of being sent away all those years ago was still there in his expression.

They'd all been so vocal about getting away from the ranch and her, but they'd never left. She'd assumed they'd been waiting for their share of the infamous Winchester fortune.

Now she saw, in at least one case, she'd been wrong.

"You missed the ranch?" The question was directed at Brand.

He put down his fork, clearly refusing to look at her. His anger when he finally spoke was edged with disappointment.

"What do you expect, Mother? That we wouldn't miss this place?"

Not her, but the ranch.

She glanced at Virginia, who merely looked confused by the conversation, then shifted her gaze to Worth.

"What does this ranch mean to you?"

Virginia frowned. Worth opened his mouth, then closed it before looking across the table at his brother.

"We *were* the ranch," Brand said through gritted teeth. "It was us. We lived and breathed this place from the time we could sit a horse."

Pepper remembered all of them, Brand, Worth, Angus and even Virginia, working the ranch—and complaining about it. Back in those days even Enid and Alfred saddled up to help with branding and moving cattle.

"Don't you remember the cattle drives?" Brand asked, finally looking at her. "I thought you actually enjoyed them."

She had. She felt tears well in her eyes and turned her attention to her plate as she reminded herself that one of these people at this table—or even all three—might have been in on their youngest brother's murder.

Acting Sheriff McCall Winchester had her hands full. Everyone was out looking for Lara English. Fortunately it was June and the warm weather was holding. If Lara was just hiding somewhere, she should be fine.

And if she wasn't... That was what had McCall worried, especially after she'd been advised that Orville Cline had escaped. The child molester had confessed to abducting and killing a ten-year-old girl just outside of Whitehorse sixteen years before.

McCall would have been about the same age as Emily when the girl was taken. So why hadn't she heard about it?

She made copies of Orville Cline's mug shot and called in the deputies and leaders of the volunteers on the search parties.

"Pass this around," she'd told her deputies when she'd given them photos of Orville Cline. "Make sure everyone is on the lookout for him."

The girl's disappearance had made her cancel dinner at her grandmother's as well as her talk with Raine Chandler. It bothered her that Raine had apparently let both McCall's cousin and grandmother believe she was a reporter.

What that might have to do with Cyrus's attack she had no idea. Maybe nothing. Maybe it had been as cut-and-dried as Cordell believed. Or not.

Suspicion came with the job, McCall thought as she nodded for the deputy to send in another of the children. She'd commandeered a room in the large farmhouse where the children lived with their foster mother. The foster father was a long-haul truck driver and on the road.

McCall had wanted to talk to each of the children. She had a feeling that one of them might know more than they told their foster mother.

A moment later, a skinny boy who looked to be about twelve came in. The first thing she noticed was how nervous he appeared. According to her list, his name was Clarence.

"So what is it you'd like to tell me, Clarence?" she said, smiling.

He started to say something, but she stopped him.

"I know you saw something. Don't worry, it's just between you and me and you'll feel better if you tell me. You liked Lara, didn't you?"

He nodded and swallowed, before choking out the words, "It was the bogeyman. He took her."

McCall leaned back. "The bogeyman?"

He nodded excitedly. "I saw him when we were playing hide-and-seek."

"What did he look like?" she asked casually.

"He was really big. I'd seen him in the trees before."

"You say he was big? Fat or tall?"

"Tall and big and strong."

"What color was his hair?"

Clarence shook his head. "He always had his hood up."

"Did you see his eyes? Were they dark or light?"

He shook his head. "I didn't get that close because he saw me. If he finds out I told—"

"He won't. I promise. Did you happen to see what he was driving?"

The boy looked confused. "He wasn't drivin' nothin'. He was hiding in the trees."

"He must have had a vehicle, though, right? Maybe parked over behind the hotel."

Clarence frowned and looked down. When he raised his gaze, she saw that he'd thought of something. "I guess that old brown van could have been his."

McCall felt her heart beat a little faster. "Did you see it last night when you and Lara and the other kids were playing hide-and-seek?"

"I was the only one who saw it when it hit that guy." The moment he'd let the words out, she could tell he wanted to snatch them and stuff them back into his mouth. "I wasn't supposed to say anything about that."

"Who told you not to say anything?" McCall asked, though she could guess.

He looked toward the door.

"I'm sure your mother had a reason for telling you to keep it to yourself," she added.

"She didn't want no one knowin' we were outside playing that time of the night," Clarence said.

Understandable. So he'd seen the van being driven by the bogeyman hit Cyrus Winchester.

"And you didn't see Lara after that?" she asked.

He shook his head. "She probably ran away after seeing the bogeyman hit that guy."

McCall figured that was exactly what his mother had thought, as well.

She showed the boy Orville Cline's mug shot, but he only shook his head. Even though he couldn't identify Cline as the bogeyman, she had a bad feeling Orville was already in town.

"There isn't anything else we can do tonight," Cordell said as he shifted the pickup into four-wheel drive and drove down the creek to a spot where he could get back on the road above them.

Raine knew he was right. She was sure that the person who'd just run them off the road was more concerned with them than Lara. If Lara survived tonight she should be safe until after the Whitehorse Summer Gala tomorrow night.

Unless, of course, you added Orville Cline into the mix.

She told herself that something was going on between him and the couple who'd abducted her sixteen years ago.

Raine could only hope it was a falling out and not some kind of deal.

But as Cordell said, there was nothing she could do about it tonight. Who knew where Lara might be hidden. With all the old abandoned farmhouses and sheds around she could be anywhere.

All Raine could do was pray that Lara was still all right. She had to believe that whoever had gotten her would finally make contact tomorrow night at the dance.

They drove over to the hospital to visit his brother. Cyrus's condition hadn't changed. Raine could see the toll this was taking on Cordell and wished there was something she could do. Finding the person who'd done this was the only thing she could do. Tomorrow night at the dance, she promised herself. Someone would contact her. She had to believe that.

"Are you all right?" she asked Cordell as they left the hospital.

"Every hour, every day, that he doesn't wake up..." He took off his Stetson and raked a hand through his hair. "I keep telling myself that Cyrus is strong and no one has more determination. If anyone can come back from this it's him."

Raine took his hand as they walked out to his brother's pickup.

"Let's get something to eat. No way am I going back out to the ranch. Want to take our chances at a motel?"

She nodded and squeezed his hand. They needed each other. She didn't kid herself that their lovemaking earlier had been anything more than that. But they had made love, tenderly and sweetly, and just the thought of being in his arms again warded off the chill of their circumstances for a while.

Cordell pulled into the drive-thru at the Dairy Queen and ordered them dinner, then drove to a motel on Highway 2. They ate sitting in the middle of the bed, eating and talking about anything but what was going on right now.

He told her about growing up on ranches, moving from one ranch to another as the jobs changed with his father and brother. Raine told him about growing up in North Dakota, fishing with her adopted father.

They watched the late news. Nothing new about Lara. Also no sign of Orville Cline, but law enforcement officers across the state were looking for him.

They showered together, then made love, lying afterward spent in each other's arms, and fell asleep comforting each other.

Cordell woke to find the bed beside him empty. He sat up with a start. Raine stood silhouetted against the open curtains of the window. Stars and moonlight glittered around her.

He could see that she was hugging herself, staring out at the night. He could well imagine her thoughts. Lara was never far from his.

Rising from the bed, he stepped up behind her to wrap

his arms around her and look out into the night. She leaned back into him with a sigh and he felt the intimacy of this moment more strongly than even their lovemaking.

She turned in his arms to look up at him. "I don't know what I would have done without you and if it hadn't been for your brother…"

He kissed her gently.

"Do you believe in fate?"

Cordell smiled at that. She sounded like his brother. Even under the circumstances, Cyrus would have believed this was meant to happen. Cordell couldn't accept that. "I don't know why this has happened but I'm glad that you're safe."

She smiled and closed the curtains, letting him lead her back to bed. They lay side by side, both staring up at the ceiling.

"Who was she, the woman who hurt you?" Raine asked, turning to lean on an elbow to study him in the dim light of the motel room.

"Who said…" His voice trailed off as he met her gaze. "My ex-wife."

Raine nodded. "She broke your heart."

He smiled at that. "Let's just say she made me gun-shy when it comes to trusting women."

"I've noticed." She pushed a lock of his hair back from his forehead. "How long has it been?"

"Four years."

She let out a low whistle. "She really must have done a number on you."

He nodded and dragged his gaze away. "She wasn't who I thought she was."

Raine lay back again to look up at the ceiling. "Neither am I."

"You're Raine Chandler," he said, pushing himself up

on an elbow to gaze into her wonderful face. "One of the strongest, most determined women I've ever met."

She smiled at that. "I don't feel very strong right now."

"You came back here even though you had to have suspected it was a trap," he said.

"As corny as it sounds, I wanted closure. I thought if I could get justice, as well, then..." She shook her head. "Now I couldn't quit if I wanted to."

No, and neither could he.

"What will you do when we find the person who hit your brother?" she asked, looking concerned.

Cordell shook his head. "If you're asking me if I will want to kill him, hell, yes. Will I? No."

"It will be enough for you to just turn him over to the sheriff?" she asked, surprised.

"It will have to be. I don't take the law into my own hands."

She said nothing.

"Raine? Is there something you're planning to do that I should know about?"

She met his gaze. "What if I was planning to kill the person responsible for Emily Frank's abduction?"

"I wouldn't blame you if you wanted to."

"But you wouldn't try to stop me."

He studied her for a long while before he said, "No."

She looped her arms around his neck and pulled him down to her. The kiss was filled with passion and heat. He felt the fire catch flame inside him. This time their lovemaking was fierce.

They weren't so different, the two of them, Cordell thought later as they lay spent in each other's arms. Both of them were afraid to trust, especially when it came to the opposite sex. And both of them wanted justice but could easily take vengeance.

He feared that after tomorrow night there would be no going back for either of them.

Chapter 11

The next evening Cordell looked up and saw Raine standing at the top of the stairs at the ranch lodge. His breath rushed out of him. She was beautiful. The gown his grandmother had given her fit like a glove, running over her curves like flowing water.

She hesitated, looking shy. But as their eyes met, she smiled and came down the stairs to take his outstretched hand.

"Wow," he said as he closed her hand in his. Something was changing between them. He could feel himself falling for this woman and it scared the hell out of him. With a start, he noticed she was wearing a tiny silver horse pin—the same one she'd been wearing the day she was abducted.

"You look beautiful," his grandmother said to Raine. She looked older and Cordell had picked up on the tension on the ranch with his father and aunt and uncle under the same roof.

"And you look very handsome," she said to him and reached out to touch his cheek. It was the most loving she'd ever been to him and it surprised him. "You look lovely together."

Raine looked away as if embarrassed. Or maybe, like him, for a moment she'd forgotten why they were dressed like this.

Cordell hoped her embarrassment wasn't because they weren't really together, not a couple, no matter how much Enid and his grandmother suspected they were. This was about catching monsters. He didn't doubt that Raine would hightail it back to California once it was over.

They didn't say much on the ride into town. For Cordell, the gravity of this evening had set in. Raine seemed lost in her own thoughts.

The moon came up, a huge golden orb that climbed up over the horizon into a vast sky studded with glittering stars. A warm breeze sighed among the leaves of the trees along the street as they parked outside the large old school where the dance was being held.

"You're sure about this?" he asked her as he cut the engine. Silence fell over them, the warm summer night making the inside of the pickup cab intimate. Cordell wanted to hang on to this moment, sitting here with Raine. It felt like a high-school date, both of them nervous and expectant. And for a moment he could pretend that was all this was.

Dinner could have been much worse, Pepper Winchester thought halfway through the meal, although she couldn't imagine how.

The food was Enid's usual tasteless fare, Virginia hit the wine hard right away and her sons were more morose than ever.

She was counting down the minutes, hoping to put this meal and this night behind her when Brand tossed down his napkin before dessert was served and demanded, "What is it you want from us, Mother?"

"I don't want any—"

"She thinks one of us is responsible for Trace's death," Virginia spat out, sloshing her glass of wine as she put it down. "And she thinks one of her grandchildren saw the whole thing from the third-floor room."

That definitely answered the question of whether or not Virginia had done some eavesdropping of her own, Pepper thought.

"Well?" Brand demanded. "Is that true?"

There seemed no reason to deny it.

"You think one of us *killed* our own brother?" Brand was on his feet now, his face twisted in anger. "Have you lost your mind?"

Enid appeared then in her usual fashion—sneaking up on them. "Does this mean you won't be having dessert?"

"I'll have dessert," Virginia said, refilling her wineglass.

Pepper waved Enid back into the kitchen. "I have reason to believe that someone in this household conspired with the killer to have Trace murdered within sight of the lodge, yes."

"Someone in this household?" Worth asked.

"Don't you mean someone in the family?" Brand snapped.

"I suspect it was a member of this family because if I'm right, one of my grandchildren saw the murder—and covered for that person."

Brand was shaking his head. "So that's what this invitation back to the ranch was about." His rueful smile broke her heart. "I should have known. But for a moment there,

I thought maybe, just maybe, you had changed. That you regretted what you did all those years ago. That you wanted to make amends. Or at least bring your family together to say goodbye."

His gaze bored into her and she felt his disappointment in her like a knife to the heart.

"Brand—"

"Don't, Mother. You want to know who killed your beloved son? You did. If one of us conspired with a killer to get rid of Trace, then you have only yourself to blame for pitting us against him." With that he stormed out of the dining room.

In the silence that dropped like a wet blanket over them, Enid appeared with a chocolate cake. She set it down in front of Virginia, along with a knife. Before Enid could turn to leave, Virginia picked up the knife and looked at the only other brother left at the table.

"Worth, are you going to have some cake with me?" Virginia asked. "It has to be better than dinner was."

"Sure," Worth said, his gaze going to his mother's.

Pepper felt a chill snake up her spine at the look in her son's eyes. As Virginia cut the cake, she watched her, realizing that either of these two could have been behind Trace's death.

But then they weren't the only ones at the table who were capable of murder, she thought as Virginia handed her a piece of cake.

"Who says you can't have your cake and eat it, too?" Virginia said with a laugh. "Isn't that right, Mother?"

This was it, Raine thought as Cordell parked the pickup. She could feel it. "They'll be here tonight," she said as she watched a group of laughing couples enter the building for the Whitehorse Summer Gala.

Music escaped as the front door of the school opened and died just as quickly as the huge doors closed.

She hoped this wasn't a mistake. All those people inside the school, all the noise… How would they find her? Or her find them.

But in her heart, she believed she would recognize the couple when she saw them. And if all else failed, recognize their voices. Some things she remembered only too well.

Still she felt torn, feeling they should be out looking for Lara instead, even though she knew their chances were next to impossible of finding the girl without help.

She met Cordell's dark gaze. What a gorgeous man both inside and out. She'd come to trust him, trust him with her life—and her secrets. That said more for his character than his good looks.

At his gentle, caring expression, she felt her heart kick up a beat.

"Raine, I just want to say—"

"I know," she said quickly, afraid of what he was going to say. They'd grown close too quickly. She didn't trust the feelings she had for him and certainly wouldn't trust his for her right now. This was too emotional for both of them. Maybe when this was over…

Raine refused to let her thoughts go there. "Let's do this."

He nodded, though looking disappointed she hadn't let him say what was on his mind, and reached for his door handle.

Outside the pickup, the warm summer breeze caressed her skin. She looked up at the stars in the midnight-blue canopy overhead and breathed it in, memorizing all of it.

The feel of the breeze, the smell of summer, the awareness of the man beside her, knowing this could be the last time.

Cordell took her hand and squeezed it as they started up the steps and Raine took one more look at the summer night—a night made for lovers—before he opened the door and they slipped inside.

As they walked in, Raine felt as if everyone turned to look at them. Cordell pulled her closer, his hand warm on her waist, as they worked slowly through the crowd gathered around the dance floor.

She took strength in his touch and tried to relax. The couple who'd abducted her were in this room. She could feel it more strongly than ever.

Groups of people stood around talking, drinking and eating the food that had been laid out along several tables. The school gymnasium was decorated as if for a prom with glittering lights and a dark blue backdrop.

The voices, laughter and music blended together in a din. How would she ever be able to distinguish any one voice?

Fear seized her. This had been a fool's errand. She and Cordell should be out looking for Lara—not here at a dance.

As if seeing her panic, Cordell whispered next to her ear, "If they're here, they aren't with Lara."

She nodded. Lara was safe. At least until the dance was over.

They worked their way around the large room, picking up bits of conversations, looking for one couple, listening for a voice she recognized. After they'd made the loop twice, Cordell asked with a slight bow, "May I have this dance?"

Raine took his hand and let him lead her onto the dance floor. The band was playing a slow song. She laid her head on his shoulder and pretended they were merely a man and a woman dancing on a warm summer night.

But being in Cordell's arms sent her senses soaring. She loved the smell of him, the feel of him, and when he danced them into a dim corner, the taste of him as he kissed her.

He pulled back to look in her face. His gaze caressed her face, then settled on her lips an instant before he lowered his mouth to hers again. She melted into his embrace, into the kiss, and then he was dancing her back into the crowd, holding her closer as if they really were lovers.

Raine closed her eyes, wishing they had grown up in this town, been high-school sweethearts who'd settled on the ranch and went every year to the Whitehorse Summer Gala dance.

But instead she'd been abducted on the edge of this town and Cordell had been exiled from the ranch and his brother Cyrus now lay in a coma because of what had happened all those years before.

Earlier, she'd heard Cordell on the phone with the hospital. His twin's condition hadn't changed. She reminded herself that he was only helping her to get the people who'd injured his brother and find Lara and save her from these monsters.

But it was good to remind herself what they were doing here tonight and not let desire or emotion make this more than it was.

"Are you all right?" he asked, looking worried. "If you're right, the person will contact you."

She smiled and nodded. The song ended. "I'm going to find the ladies' room." She started to step away, but he grabbed her hand.

"Hurry back."

Her smile broadened as she saw the concern in his expression. She nodded and he released her, but she could feel his gaze on her as she wound through the crowd and away from him.

She studied the faces she passed. How different her life would have been if she'd known these people all her life. If she and Cordell really had been high-school sweethearts and there wasn't a child molester about to kill a little girl if they didn't find her.

Suddenly she was blinded by regret and rage, disappointment and determination. Life had not been kind to her and yet she'd survived it all. She'd never thought about being happy. She'd just been glad to be alive, not to be hungry, to have a roof over her head and a job.

She'd asked little of life.

But tonight she yearned for more. She wanted Cordell. She wanted happily ever after. And yet she feared that wasn't the destiny that awaited her and hadn't from the moment that car pulled up beside her sixteen years ago.

The music drifted on the air, growing fainter as she finally found a ladies' restroom deep in the building without a line. This one was empty. Her heels echoed on the tile as she rushed to the sink.

Turning on the cold water, she cupped it in her hands and splashed it on her face to wash away the hot angry tears that flowed down her cheeks.

Her heart ached at the memory of being in Cordell's arms on the dance floor, the way he'd looked at her when she'd come out in the dress, that amazing kiss and the look in his eyes just moments ago—

She grabbed one of the cloth towels and began to dry her face. Her makeup was ruined, her eyes red and swollen, and she could practically hear the clock with Lara's name on it, ticking down the minutes.

She knew what had her so upset and felt guilty for it. All her thoughts should be with Lara. But she was falling for Cordell Winchester. Last night in the pickup and again in the motel, it had been about lust and comfort and the need not to be alone with their thoughts and fears.

Tonight, though, in his arms on the dance floor... She couldn't bear the feelings he'd evoked in her. And she'd seen something in his gaze—

At the sound of the bathroom door swinging open she hurriedly rushed to the end stall.

The voices of two women melded together as they came through the restroom door. Faint music swept in with them, then the door closed and everything grew quiet.

Raine leaned against the stall wall, her face feeling hot. She was tired, completely drained, both emotionally and mentally. She knew she couldn't trust her emotions and had to pull herself together.

She'd hoped by now that one of them would have made contact. She had to believe that her theory was right—even though by all appearances the person had only gotten her back here to kill her.

No, she told herself. It was the man who'd taken Lara and tried to run Raine down. Just like tonight with that huge truck that had run them off the road. It was the man. The woman had to be the one who Marias called CBA and she would contact her. Why else leave tickets for the dance at the door for her and Cordell?

But as she stood, her back against the stall wall, she felt as if this was hopeless. She would go back out there and mill until it was over and pray that she spotted the couple. After that...

She didn't have a clue what to do after that. A stall door down the line creaked open, then closed and locked.

"I can't believe what Nancy Harper is wearing," the woman in a far stall said.

"Ghastly," the other woman said from somewhere over by the long row of sinks. She sounded as if she was standing at the mirrors no doubt checking her makeup.

The woman flushed the toilet, the door unlocking and opening. Raine heard the woman's heels on the tile floor as she joined the other woman.

Neither seemed to realize Raine was in the last stall at the end of the long line. She thought about flushing the toilet and letting them know they'd been caught gossiping and might have, if the woman at the mirror hadn't spoken again.

"Do you think you can talk Frank into coming over for a drink after the dance?"

Raine froze at the sound of the woman's voice.

"It's going to be awfully late."

"I know but I picked up a bottle of wine I think you and Frank will like."

"Honey, is everything all right with you and Bill?"

"Of course." She laughed, a laugh that sent a blade of ice up Raine's spine. "It's just that he'll be tired and I'll be all wound up and not wanting the night to end."

"Well, I can ask Frank…" Their voices started to trail off.

Raine could barely hear the other woman's reply her heart was pounding so hard. The woman's voice, the one who'd stayed by the sinks. That was her! That was the voice of the woman who'd helped abduct her sixteen years ago.

Cordell had watched Raine head for a ladies' restroom in the far recesses of the building. Now he felt anxious as he waited for her to reappear. The crowd kept obstructing his view of the hallway just enough to set his nerves on edge.

For a while with Raine in his arms on the dance floor, he'd forgotten that someone had made certain that she was here tonight by seeing that they got an invitation. But he hadn't noticed anyone taking any particular interest in either of them.

Oh, there were always a few men who couldn't help but notice Raine. But he hadn't seen anyone watching them and no one had made contact.

He was beginning to wonder if all of this wasn't just a way to torment Raine. The dance was almost over. If this woman, the one Raine's friend Marias called CBA, had gone to all this trouble to get Raine to Whitehorse and to this dance, then what was she waiting for? Had the woman lost her nerve?

As his cell phone vibrated in his pocket, Cordell began to move in the direction Raine had gone. He pulled out his phone and checked caller ID.

He was jostled by the crowd and forced to step outside one of the open doors. Standing on a small landing in the darkness, he snapped open his phone.

"How did you get this number?" he asked, still watching the hallway Raine had disappeared down.

A woman's chuckle. "Didn't Raine tell you? I'm amazing." Marias quickly turned serious. "I've left a dozen messages on her cell. This couldn't wait."

Cordell felt his blood run cold as he listened. "What did you just say?"

Raine quickly bent down and looked under the stalls. She saw two pairs of women's high heels. A pair of bright red strappy sandals and a pair of classic black high heels.

She didn't know which ones belonged to CBA. As the

outer door closed, Raine quickly stepped from the stall and hurried after them.

Several more women were coming in as she reached the door and she had to wait as they passed before she could exit. By then, the two women had dissolved into the crowd.

She looked around frantically for Cordell, then at the array of shoes on the dance floor. She'd never find the woman before the dance ended and all she had was a name: Bill. There must be dozens of Bills in this town.

Raine moved along the edge of the crowd as quickly as she could, searching for Cordell and the woman with the strappy red heels. There were too many black heels on the floor. She'd never find that woman.

As she passed an open door, she felt the cool summer night air beyond the darkness and wondered if Cordell had stepped out for some fresh air.

"Raine."

At the sound of her name, she turned back to step out into the dark. She blinked, trying to get her eyes to adjust, and saw no one. Had she just imagined someone calling her name?

She turned to look back into the huge glittering room. That was when she saw Cordell across the dance floor. He'd just stepped in from outside. He appeared to be searching for her, his cell phone to his ear. But it was his expression that turned her blood to ice.

There was a sound like the scrape of a shoe sole on the concrete behind her as she started to go back inside hoping she could reach Cordell before she lost him again in the crowd.

She was grabbed from behind. The cloth clamped over her mouth brought it all back. She was ten again on a dirt road in a strange place and terrified of what was about to happen to her. Only this time, she knew.

Cordell didn't think he'd heard Marias correctly over the music and the din.

"Orville Cline was sighted yesterday—just miles from Whitehorse. Do I have to tell you where he's headed?"

Cordell stepped back into the gym and began to push his way through the crowd in the direction Raine had gone. "You think he's the one who got Raine up here."

"Don't you?"

"He couldn't have done it alone. The van that tried to run her over, the tickets for this dance, the map. Raine is positive it's the woman—"

"Don't you get it? Raine needs to believe that. I'm catching the next plane out of here—"

"No, she needs you there in case she gets any more messages and there is nothing you can do here," Cordell said as he hurried down the hallway, the restroom door in sight. "I'll have Raine call you."

He reached the door, slammed it open. Several women at the sinks jumped, startled by his abrupt entrance—and the fact that a man had just burst into the women's restroom.

"Raine?" No answer. *"Raine?"* He bent to check under the stalls. Only one pair of heels, the wrong ones.

He turned and rushed out, his gaze frantically searching the crowd. No Raine. Cordell told himself not to panic. She was here somewhere. The dance had begun to thin out as the band wound down for the last song.

Raine, where the hell are you?

He bumped into a man, registering the man's conversation as he did.

"Don't be ridiculous, Adele," the man was saying.

Cordell's gaze went to the woman as he mumbled, "Excuse me," to the man. The man had backed her into a corner. She had tears in her eyes, her lipstick was smudged as if he'd just kissed her hard on the mouth.

The crowd didn't move and for a moment Cordell was unable to move, either. Next to him the man took the drink the woman was holding. "Are you trying to get me drunk, Adele?" He tilted his face toward her, moving in closer, dropping his voice as he gripped her jaw in his large hand. "Do you really think that will keep me home tonight?"

Cordell heard the anger in the man's words and saw fear in the woman's face—or was that open defiance? The crowd moved but Cordell stood rooted to the floor. What had stopped him cold was the hand gripping the woman's jaw—and the scar on the man's hand.

The bite mark was a perfect child-size half moon.

Chapter 12

"When was the last time you saw her?" Sheriff McCall Winchester asked.

Cordell rubbed a hand over his face. "No more than thirty minutes ago. I called you as soon as I found her pin out on the steps by one of the open doors."

They were sitting across from the school and had been watching everyone who came out of the building. No sign of Raine.

McCall picked up the tiny silver plated horse pin. "You think she dropped this on purpose?"

He nodded. "I knew the moment I saw it on the outside step glittering in the moonlight."

The sheriff eyed him. "Sorry, what is the significance of the pin?"

"She was wearing it when she was abducted here sixteen years ago."

"Abducted?" McCall sighed. "I think you'd better start

at the beginning." She listened, taking notes only when necessary, as he told her about Emily Frank.

It was only after he'd finished that she demanded to know why he hadn't come to her the moment he'd heard about Lara English being abducted.

"Raine said he would kill Lara if we did."

"Raine?" So that was the way it was, McCall thought, hearing the way he said the woman's name revealed just how involved his cousin was with her.

"But you called me now."

He gave her a tortured look. "I didn't know what else to do, especially since Orville Cline has escaped."

McCall nodded. "So we don't know who has Lara or Raine."

"But I do know who took Raine sixteen years ago." He told her about the bite scar. "I followed him to his car and got his license plate number." He handed her the gala napkin he'd written it down on. "I would have followed him and his wife home but I had to find Raine."

"And when you didn't, you found the pin and called me." She looked at the local license plate number. It wouldn't take long to run it. "You realize a scar on the man's hand isn't enough proof to arrest him."

"No, you need Raine to identify him. That's why we have to be careful. If Raine is right and his wife is the one who got her here…"

"What are you suggesting?"

"If this man took Lara English, then he will lead us to her."

"Us?" McCall said.

"I know you don't have the law enforcement officers to watch his house 24/7."

It was true.

"But I'm going to be watching him. I'll let you know the moment he makes a move."

McCall chewed on her cheek for a moment. "If you saw the man with the bite scar after Raine vanished…"

"He could have hidden her somewhere and returned to the dance. Or Orville might have her."

McCall didn't like the sound of that. "But why take Raine?"

"She was the only one who got away," Cordell said.

"I suppose it could be that simple." She ran the plate number and felt her pulse take off like a wild stallion.

The name Bill and Adele Beaumont came up on the screen.

"Do you know them?" Cordell asked, glancing over at the screen.

"Yeah," McCall said. "They own half the town."

"Raine said they would be above suspicion."

"So far the only thing you have against them is that they were at the dance tonight, they are prominent citizens and Bill has a scar which could be from a human bite—but may not be," McCall said.

"I also know that he's rough with his wife," Cordell said. "What about matching the bite scar with Raine's teeth prints? I realize she isn't ten anymore but I thought bite marks were like fingerprints, no two exactly alike?"

"Even if the crime lab could match Raine's bite with that of the marks on Bill Beaumont's scar, that doesn't prove that he abducted her. It would be hard to even prove that Raine is Emily Frank."

Cordell groaned. Clearly, he hadn't thought of that. "There has to be something we can do. Raine said the man who took Lara will keep her alive until tonight. If he thinks the sheriff is suspicious of him…"

McCall had to agree. Moving on Bill Beaumont if he was guilty would only cause him to get rid of the girl and Raine—if he had them both and if he hadn't already killed them.

"Okay, I'll put you on surveillance on the Beaumonts," McCall said, realizing she had little choice. She couldn't trust that if she used one of her deputies, it might get leaked to the Beaumonts. No one in this town would believe Bill was a child molester. Everyone would be ready to protect the local family against some weird-dressed California private investigator here stirring up things—and even more so against a Winchester.

"But the minute anyone makes a move, you call me. Don't you go playing Lone Ranger on me, cuz," she said.

"You got it." He reached for the door handle. "Raine's tough. She's gotten through a lot."

McCall nodded but knew he was just trying to convince himself because the fool had fallen in love with the woman and he couldn't bear the thought of her being with some sick monster. McCall couldn't, either.

If Cordell was right and Bill Beaumont had abducted Raine again, then he couldn't have taken her far. After she left her cousin, she began to search the area around the school, looking for an old house or shed, somewhere he could stash her.

If whoever grabbed her had seen that she got tickets to the gala, then he would have made prior arrangements.

As McCall drove around the area behind the school, she called her mother. "What do you know about Bill and Adele Beaumont?"

Most people when asked something like that would respond, "Why do you ask?"

Not Ruby. Her trade was gossip, she served it up with every order she delivered at the diner. It made up for the bad tips days.

She heard her mother take a long drag on her cigarette, turn down the television as she exhaled and ask, "Beaumont? Are they squabblin' again? I'm not surprised."

"Why do you say that?" McCall asked.

"You ever meet Bill, talk to him for two seconds, and you can see what a chauvinist he is. He's a jackass or worse."

"Worse?"

Ruby sighed. "Look how he treats Adele."

McCall pictured the slight petite woman. Every time she'd seen her, Adele was dressed to the T and made up as if she lived in a metropolitan area instead of Whitehorse, Montana.

"He doesn't seem to treat her too badly from what I've seen," McCall said, thinking of the big new SUV Adele was driving.

"He has his thumb firmly on that woman. He says jump. She says, 'How high?'"

"Are you saying she's abused?"

"Depends on what you call abused. She lives in the nicest house in these parts, wears the best clothes money can buy, drives the nicest car, everyone in town treats her like she's royalty."

"And this is bad how?"

"I'll bet you this week's paycheck that once the two of them are alone inside that big house of theirs things are a whole lot different."

"What are you getting at?" McCall asked.

"Just a feeling I have," her mother said, usually not this noncommittal. "Let me tell you this. There are a handful of men who run this town. They all have coffee in the diner mornings, sit at the same table, even sit in the same chairs. Sometimes another man or two will join them. No one ever sits in Bill Beaumont's chair."

"Bill and Adele never had any kids," McCall remarked. "He would seem like a man who would want to leave his genes behind."

"They couldn't have any," Ruby said. "Her fault," she added before McCall could ask. "I heard he almost left her over it."

McCall shuddered. If Cordell was right, this could explain in some warped sick way why Adele went along with Bill's horrible "hobby."

"They could have adopted," McCall said.

"Bill? Are you serious? Why are you so curious about the Beaumonts?"

"I thought I saw them squabblin' outside the dance tonight." It wasn't exactly a lie. Cordell had seen them, even overheard them.

"He'll never leave her and he'll never let her leave him," Ruby said with authority. "He'd have to give her half his money. But I'll bet he makes her pay dearly for what she gets out of this marriage."

Cordell sat parked down the street under a large weeping willow tree and watched Bill Beaumont's house.

He and his wife, Adele, hadn't come home alone. Another couple had followed them from the dance and were now inside.

He could see the lights through the sheer drapes, catch glimpses of people moving around inside the house. He glanced at his watch anxiously.

Raine had been gone now for almost two hours. He

wouldn't let himself think about what could have happened to her in that length of time.

She was smart and capable and stronger than any woman he'd ever met. He had to believe that she was all right and would survive this, just as she'd survived being a foster child and her abduction at ten.

His cell phone rang, startling him out of his thoughts. He checked the caller ID. Marias.

"I told you I would call you when I heard something," he said into the phone.

"Another message just came through from the CBA." Marias took a breath and let it out. In that breath he heard her anger—and her fear. "This one, though, is for you. It says, 'Unless you want to end up like your brother and your girlfriend, back off. This has nothing to do with you.'"

"Like hell," Cordell said under his breath and hung up.

Just after 2:00 a.m., the couple who'd been visiting the Beaumont house walked out to their car. They appeared to be arguing, their voices carrying on the cool night air.

Cordell whirred down his window.

"I'm telling you she didn't want to be left alone with him," the woman said.

"It's two in the damned morning, Theresa. You want to go back in there and babysit her, fine, but I'm going home and going to bed."

The woman looked toward the house, clearly conflicted. "She's afraid of him."

The man scoffed as he opened his car door. "Yeah, Bill's a real scary guy," he said sarcastically.

The woman seemed to make up her mind. She opened her car door, glanced back at the house once more, then joined her husband, closing the door behind her.

Brake lights flashed, the engine turned over. Inside the

house someone moved behind the sheer drapes as the couple drove away down the street.

Cordell glanced at his watch again twenty minutes later. The dial glowed. He could feel the minutes ticking by. What if he was wrong? What if the real monster was with Raine right now?

There were two vehicles parked in front of the Beaumont home. A pickup and a large SUV. When the porch light snapped off, Cordell felt his heart drop. Was it possible Bill Beaumont wasn't going anywhere tonight?

He couldn't bear the thought of Raine in some horrible place any longer. He started to open his door, not sure what he planned to do, but he was going up to that house and if he had to, he would beat the truth out of Bill Beaumont.

Through a crack in the drapes he could see movement. Someone was pacing back and forth and appeared to be having a heated argument.

He eased his door open and climbed out. Working his way through the shadowed darkness of the trees, he neared the house. He could hear muted voices, the man's more strident, the woman's meek.

Along the side of the house, he found an open window and eased it open wider. He could hear snatches of the argument.

Bill was worked up, yelling at his wife, who seemed to be trying to console him.

Cordell was about to go in the window when he realized everything had gone silent.

At the sound of the front door opening and slamming shut, he rushed to the edge of the house. Bill was climbing into his pickup truck. An instant later, the engine turned over and Bill threw the truck into Reverse and roared out of the yard, the tires spitting gravel.

Cordell waited a moment to make sure he wasn't seen before sprinting to his brother's pickup and following.

For the first time all night, he felt hope that he might actually find Raine before it was too late.

Out of the corner of his eye, he saw the drapes part on the front window of the Beaumont house. He had only an impression of a woman watching him as he drove off.

"See if you can find any connection between Bill Beaumont and Orville Cline," McCall said into the phone.

"The child molester in Montana State Prison?"

"There have to be phone records or even visits." Would Beaumont be so stupid as to visit Orville Cline in prison?

McCall hung up and glanced at the clock. She hadn't heard from Cordell and could only assume that Bill hadn't left his house.

She'd known Bill since she was a kid. He was one of those do-gooders, as her mother Ruby called him.

"A terrible tipper though," her mother had always been quick to point out. "He and his cronies come in to the café, drink gallons of coffee for hours and leave a measly tip for one cup of coffee. His wife is worse. You'd think they were headed for the poor farm the way they pinch pennies. That's the rich for you."

Ruby Bates Winchester measured everyone in town by how generous they were with her at the diner. McCall wondered if it didn't have more to do with the service they got from her mother than how tight they were with their money.

For a moment, she thought about her mother and how much she'd changed since she started dating Red Harper. McCall had never seen her mother truly happy before and now that she was, it was a beautiful thing. She hoped it lasted.

Her mother had taken the news about her husband Trace Winchester's murder twenty-seven years ago in her stride. At least on the surface.

But McCall had happened to see her mother at the cemetery one evening just before dark. Ruby was sitting beside the huge ornate tombstone Trace's mother, Pepper, had insisted on. But Ruby had won the battle about where her husband and the father of her daughter would be buried.

"I want him in town so I can visit him," she'd told Pepper on one of the few occasions the two women actually spoke to each other.

Pepper had wanted Trace buried in the family plot on the ranch. It was one of the few times her grandmother have given in.

McCall had been touched by Pepper's generosity in letting Ruby have this small victory, especially since Pepper had tried so hard when Trace was alive to split them up.

McCall told herself that was all water under the bridge. Her father was dead and buried. Any doubts she had about who had killed him, she'd tried to bury with her father.

That evening, though, when she'd seen her mother sitting on Trace's grave in the cemetery, McCall had stopped and watched Ruby gently touching the gravestone, talking to the husband she'd lost when she was pregnant with McCall.

Maybe they would all find peace, she'd thought that night. Someday.

It was one reason she'd agreed to have her wedding with Luke at Winchester Ranch. Even with the animosity between her mother and grandmother. She hoped the two could call a truce—at least until the wedding and reception were over.

McCall had reluctantly accepted her grandmother's generous offer to host the wedding at Winchester Ranch on

Christmas. She knew Ruby was excited about finally setting foot on the ranch after all these years.

McCall just hoped the wedding went off without any bloodshed. With the Winchesters, you just never knew.

Her phone rang. She picked it up thinking it would be Cordell with an update on what was or wasn't happening at the Beaumont house. She feared letting him run surveillance might be a mistake.

But the call was from one of her deputies letting her know that they hadn't found Lara English and were calling it a night. They'd begin again in the morning.

"Thanks, Nick. Please thank the volunteers and make sure everyone gets home safely." McCall had spent hours earlier as part of the search party and knew how emotionally draining it could be when you might be looking for a body instead of a little girl.

Unable to wait any longer, McCall called Cordell's cell. The phone rang four times before going to voice mail.

She frowned and hung up, her anxiety growing. She waited a few minutes and tried the number again. Still no answer.

Grabbing her hat and keys, she headed for her patrol SUV.

Chapter 13

McCall drove by the Beaumont house and didn't see Cordell's pickup anywhere on the street—nor any sign of him. Didn't mean that he wasn't still watching the house, she told herself.

Before driving over here, she'd gone out to her cabin on the Milk River and changed into dark jeans, boots, a dark long-sleeved T-shirt. She'd left the patrol SUV and took her pickup instead.

Now she parked and walked down the deserted street watching for any sign of her cousin. As she neared the Beaumont house she caught a glimpse of Adele through the sheer drapes at the front window.

Like McCall, she'd changed her clothing since the dance and now wore jeans and a shirt. She seemed to be pacing. McCall slowed at the edge of the yard and stepped into the shadows of the trees that lined the property as Adele suddenly froze, then hurriedly picked up her cell phone. She glanced at caller ID, then took the call.

McCall moved closer, never taking her eyes off the woman. Adele looked upset and Bill's pickup wasn't in the driveway. Could be in the garage.

Peeking in the garage, McCall found it empty. No Bill. No Cordell. She didn't even have to venture a guess where Cordell had gone. Wherever Bill had headed. She silently cursed him for not following her orders.

As she moved away from the garage, she saw that Adele was still on the phone. But if the woman had been upset before the call, now she seemed to be in a panic. She moved one way then another, appearing frantic as if looking for something.

McCall saw her snatch up her purse from where she must have dropped it earlier and, snapping the phone shut, headed for the door.

Ducking back into the shrubbery and trees, the sheriff stayed hidden as Adele, wearing a black jean jacket, got into her car and backed out. The headlights flashed over McCall, then darkness closed in again.

As she hurried to her truck, McCall wondered where Adele was headed this time of night and what had her so upset. Who had been on the phone? Bill? And if so, where was Cordell?

Cordell had known that tailing anyone in a town this small was tough. At this time of the night with no traffic at all, and Bill Beaumont looking for a tail, it was nearly impossible.

His heart was racing at the thought that the man driving the truck in front of him was about to take him straight to Lara English and Raine.

But where was Orville Cline? He and Beaumont had to be in this together.

He thought about the fight he'd overheard between the

Beaumonts. By her tone, Cordell knew Adele had been pleading with her husband, but Cordell hadn't been close enough to hear what she was saying. But earlier Bill had accused her of trying to keep him home tonight.

Apparently Adele Beaumont had lost the argument since her husband had left the house.

Cordell drove up a few blocks and pulled over, cutting his lights as Beaumont continued down the main drag, then turned right through the underpass. From where he'd pulled over, Cordell could see the street on the other side of the underpass. Beaumont turned left.

Cordell went after him, through the underpass and up onto Highway 2. He saw no sign of taillights. He should have been able to see him, Beaumont didn't have that much of a lead. Cordell swore. Maybe he'd taken a right on Highway 191 and was headed for Canada.

But as he pulled out, he saw Beaumont's pickup parked in an empty dirt lot at the turnoff. He appeared to be on his cell phone.

Cordell drove past and pulled into the open-all-night Westside gas station. He got out, and watching Beaumont across the road, paid with his credit card and filled up his tank. Beaumont got off the phone. A few minutes after 3:00 a.m., a car came up the highway. The driver slowed, glancing over at Beaumont. As the car headed north, Beaumont fell in behind it.

Heart in his throat, Cordell climbed back into the pickup. His hands were shaking. He'd only gotten a glimpse of the man in the car—but it had been more than enough to know that the driver was Orville Cline.

Orville was now leading Bill Beaumont north out of Whitehorse.

* * *

McCall got the first call just after she turned off the road. Keeping Adele Beaumont's SUV taillights in her view, she slowed and picked up. "Winchester."

"I'm following Beaumont north," Cordell said without preamble. "He just picked up Orville Cline."

McCall didn't waste her breath giving him hell for not calling her sooner. "Stay on them, but don't make a move against them. I mean it, Cordell. You call it in when they stop. Got that?"

She waited for a reply but realized she'd already lost him. She cursed under her breath. Adele wasn't headed north but south out of town. McCall had hoped that Raine and Lara were being held together. Now that didn't look as if it was the case.

Ahead Adele was turning off onto a side road. McCall followed slowly, not about to use her headlights or brakes and cause Adele to know she was being followed. The moon was bright enough that she could see the road well.

McCall knew this area south of town. There was an old farmhouse down in a hollow, the same hollow Adele's big SUV had just dropped into. She drove only a little farther up the road and pulled off far enough that her pickup couldn't be seen from the road.

When her cell vibrated again, she jumped and realized how tense she was. Everything about this had her on edge. Three civilians' lives were at risk. Her first thought was to call in the troops, but she immediately changed her mind. She couldn't be sure who was waiting in that farmhouse and what they would do if backed into a corner.

She was on her own, she thought as she took the call.

"I got the warden up at the prison out of bed," Deputy

Shane Corbett said. "He said to tell you that you are on his mud list for getting him up at this hour."

"I can live with that. What did you find out?"

"He had the information handy since every law enforcement officer in the northwest is looking for Orville Cline right now. He'd already checked on Cline's visitors, especially recent ones. Bill Beaumont wasn't one of them."

McCall had been hoping for a connection. Right now she had nothing against the Beaumonts except a scar and a suspicion—both flimsy at best.

"But Cline did have another visitor two days before he escaped," Shane was saying. "The two got into an argument and the visitor was asked to leave."

The sheriff couldn't hide her shock as Shane told her the name of the prisoner's visitor.

"Adele Beaumont visited Cline?"

"She was supposedly there to deliver some books as part of an inmate reading program Cline was involved in."

A cover. Her heart was beating so hard she could barely make out Shane's next words.

"Orville Cline was worked up good after that. The warden said he didn't think too much about it when he was told about the encounter. Now though…"

"Yeah," McCall said as she continued to follow the faint glow of taillights into no-man's-land. "I might need some backup. I'm going after Adele Beaumont right now. We're about fifteen miles south of town on Alkali Creek Road."

She heard Shane let out a breath.

"The Beaumonts may be involved in the abduction of Lara English," she told the deputy. "It's a long story, but one of their alleged victims got away sixteen years ago. She's back in town but has disappeared. Better call Luke and bring in the rest of the deputies. My cousin Cordell was watching the Beaumont house earlier tonight and is now following Bill Beaumont and Orville Cline. They are headed north out of town."

Shane swore under his breath. "Is there anyone who's not missing?"

"Don't do anything until I call," she said, afraid that if they all went in like gangbusters, it would jeopardize both Lara's and Raine's lives. "Just be ready."

"You got it," Shane said.

McCall checked her gun, grabbed another clip and her shotgun, before stepping out into the summer night to begin walking across country toward the old Terringer place.

Cordell saw the two vehicles in the distance turn off the highway onto a side dirt road that led back toward the Milk River.

He noted the way they slowed and knew they were waiting to see if the car they'd spotted behind them slowed, as well. He kept going, driving past, keeping his speed up. He could see them waiting and had to drive another five miles up the highway before the road turned and his taillights disappeared from view.

Hitting the brakes, he pulled over. For the past five miles, he'd been looking for other side roads that headed down to the river. There was one about two miles back. It wasn't ideal. He couldn't be sure it would take him in the direction he needed to go, but he could be sure that Cline and Beaumont would be watching the road they'd taken.

Turning out his headlights, he flipped a U-turn in the road and headed back to where he'd seen the other road. In the distance, he couldn't see any lights from the two vehicles and assumed they'd driven down into the river bottom. There must be some kind of old building down there. They sure as heck weren't going fishing at this time of the morning.

He had to believe that the two would lead him to Raine and Lara.

Taking the side road, he drove down until the dirt track ended at the river and he saw that it was nothing more than a fishing access. He parked and checked his gun, then got another clip out of the glove box, before he sprinted south along a game trail that ran parallel to the river in the direction Cline and Beaumont had gone. Even in the moonlight it was hard to run along the uneven path.

But Cordell could feel the minutes slipping away. He had to get there in time.

Lara pulled the old blanket around her not sure what had awakened her. When she'd heard the door open, her only thought had been food. But she was also cold. Maybe the woman was bringing her dress back after washing it for her.

She reminded herself to thank the woman and not make her angry. But she was so tired and cold and hungry that it was hard to concentrate. She just hoped whoever was coming would bring her food and something to drink.

Too late Lara had realized she shouldn't have eaten all the food they brought the last time or drunk all the water. It had been hours now that her stomach had ached for something to eat.

Lara felt a gush of cold air as someone entered the room she was in. She shivered and sank deeper into the blanket wrapped around her.

As badly as she wanted food and water, she was filled with dread at seeing the people who had taken her again. She'd tried not to think about why they were keeping her here or what they wanted. But after all this time, she couldn't help but worry.

She caught the scent of perfume and the single beam of a flashlight, her dread deepening as she realized the woman had come alone. The woman set something down. A moment later the room was filled with light.

The lock scratched open and the door of the box swung out. Lara closed her eyes against the glare of the light, huddling in the blanket, shivering from more than the cold as she sensed the woman standing over her simply staring down at her.

"Little girl," the woman finally snapped. "Your new mommy is here."

Lara swallowed the lump in her throat and parted the blanket to peer up at her. Her new mommy?

The blanket was suddenly jerked away. Lara cowered, afraid the woman was going to hit her. Instead, all she did was stare at her for a long time before she said, "Stand up."

Lara did as she was told even though her legs threatened to fold on her. Weak and cold, she stood shivering, hugging herself.

"Put your arms down," the woman snapped.

She did. Then the woman did something that surprised her. She reached out and brushed a lock of her hair back from Lara's face.

Lara looked up at her expectantly. Maybe the woman wasn't going to hurt her. But she didn't seem to have brought her anything, either, no food, no water, nothing to wear, and she'd thrown the blanket in the corner of the rotting floor of the old house as if she no longer needed it.

For just an instant, there was something almost kind in the woman's eyes. Or was it regret?

"I'm hungry," Lara said and instantly wished she hadn't.

She felt her heart begin to pound under her skinny chest as she saw the woman's expression change.

"You're just like all the others, aren't you? No matter what we do for you, it's just never quite enough."

"I'm not hungry," Lara said quickly. "I'm not."

The woman shook her head as she reached into the pocket of her jacket and drew out a knife.

"You're a bad girl. A very bad girl. Mommy is going to have to punish you."

Chapter 14

"She's still alive?" The voice if not the words sent a cold blade of terror through Raine. It was the man who'd abducted her sixteen years before. She would never forget that voice.

"I'm not trying to do your dirty work for you again. The deal was I get her for you and you get me what I want. What you do with her is your business. I've done my part."

"You're sure it's her?" asked the man whose voice she recognized.

"I got her to town for you. If you don't believe it's her, have a look for yourself. But don't be questioning if I know what I'm doing, all right?"

"Sorry, Orville."

Raine froze as the beam of a flashlight flickered over the box she was in. She'd gotten the tape off but now left a piece loosely wrapped over her bare ankles. She hoped it would appear she was still bound, but she couldn't see her ankles well enough to know if it worked or not. She put her hands behind her and wrapped the tape as best she could on her wrists.

Raine had no plan, just a determination to survive. She thought of Cordell as she heard what sounded like a bolt being slid back on the top of the box. Earlier tonight Cordell had tried to tell her how he felt about her but she'd stopped him. She silently cursed herself for doing that. Now she might never hear those words.

The door swung open with a loud groan. She blinked as the light fell over her. Two men stood in the glow of the ambient light from the flashlight. One was tall, thin, his face angular and narrow giving her the impression of a fox. Orville Cline. She recognized him from his mug shot.

The other was handsome, square-shouldered, blue-eyed with a head of thick black hair. It was no wonder he'd gotten away with this for so long. Who would ever suspect a man who looked like that?

Sheer terror filled her. She'd told herself all these years that she didn't remember what either of her abductors had looked like. Their faces had been lost in the other memories, the ones she'd refused to let surface.

But the memory came back in a rush. It felt as if she'd been kicked in the stomach. She remembered him.

"Emily?" He stepped closer.

It took every ounce of her self-control to remain still as he knelt down beside her and, holding the flashlight in one hand, grabbed her jaw between his fingers to force her to look into his eyes.

She cringed, remembering his hands on her. Her mind went numb. She lay there unable to move, hardly able to breathe.

His eyes searched hers and then he laughed and let go of her. "Oh, yeah, you're Emily. My sweet Emily."

Anger stirred in her. Raine felt her heart begin to pound wildly as rage raced through her veins hot as lava. He was still kneeling in front of her, this horrible man. Last time he'd touched her, she'd been only a child, defenseless. But she would no longer be his victim. She felt her hands fist behind her. The past seemed to shed from her like snakeskin.

He rose as if seeing something in her gaze that warned him.

But he didn't know she was no longer bound. All she had to do was kick out at his ankles. She could be on her feet in an instant. She'd spent years studying martial arts for just this moment.

"Come on," Orville Cline said behind him. "I gave you what you wanted. Now you give me mine, Billy Boy. Take me to mine and then you can come back to your sweet Emily," Orville Cline said mockingly.

"I'm not going to tell you again that my name is Bill."

"Whatever you say, Billy Boy," Orville said, amusement in his voice.

Raine realized with a jolt what Bill-Billy-Boy had done. He'd made a deal with Orville and that deal was Lara English. She'd been wrong. She'd thought for sure it was the woman who'd gotten her here. Now she saw her error.

But where was the woman?

Realization came with a flash.

The woman was with Lara.

Raine knew that if she attacked the man now, she would be jeopardizing Lara's life. As furious as she was, she knew she could take him and would stand a decent chance of taking Orville Cline, as well.

But what if the woman was waiting for a call from Billy Boy?

Common sense won out over her fury. She lay perfectly still as he slammed the lid on the box and turned to leave.

He'd forgotten to slide the bolt!

Raine held her breath, praying he wouldn't remember as the beam of his flashlight headed for the stairs, Cline following him. She listened to their heavy tread on the stairs, then start across the floor upstairs.

She couldn't stand it a moment longer. As quietly as possible, she lifted the lid of the box and, stripping off the ripped tape from her wrists and ankles, she got to her feet in the pitch blackness. She felt dizzy and her legs were weak from being in such a cramped position for so long.

She realized it would have been folly to have tried to attack him. A mistake that would have gotten her killed—if she was lucky. She hated to think what he had planned for her.

Carefully she stepped out of the box into the pitch blackness. She recalled where the door to the room was and moved cautiously toward it. Beyond that was the bottom of the stairs. She was halfway up the stairs when she heard the sound of footsteps coming back across the floor toward the top of the stairs.

One of them was coming back.

Lara wondered what the woman was going to do with the knife. She stared at the shiny blade in the glow of the flashlight beam, hypnotized.

A whisper of a sound behind her new mommy with the knife made her look toward the darkness. She caught movement and for just a moment she thought it was the man.

All hope that he'd brought her food and something to

drink evaporated as she saw that it was another woman and the only thing she had in her hand was a gun. The second woman put her finger to her lips for Lara to be quiet.

Lara was always quiet. She brought her focus back to the knife. Her new mommy had a grip on her wrist, her nails biting into her flesh, but Lara didn't cry out. She bit back on the pain the same way she did the fear.

Her stomach growled and her throat was so dry she could barely swallow. She felt dizzy and weak and just standing took all her energy.

Lara saw that the other woman was dressed in a uniform. The woman again touched her fingers to her lips and Lara nodded and felt tears fill her eyes. She wondered if she should tell her new mommy.

As if sensing something wrong, her new mommy looked up at her. "Don't you dare start blubbering."

Lara hurriedly shook her head and made a swipe at her tears with her dirty hand.

But the tears wouldn't stop. It was as if a dam had broken. Her body began to tremble, then shudder with the sobs.

"I told you—"

The slap came as no surprise to Lara. It rang out in the empty house like a gunshot as she tried desperately to quit crying, knowing that what was coming next would be much worse.

Cordell saw the flicker of light through one of the glassless windows of the old house ahead. He slowed to catch his breath and scope out the scene.

There was a car and a pickup parked outside. As far as he could tell that meant that only Bill Beaumont and Orville Cline were inside the house.

Beside the car, he caught a small flash of light, then

something glowed for a moment in the darkness. The smell of cigarette smoke drifted on the night breeze. Orville Cline leaned against the side of the car waiting.

Cordell moved cautiously around the other side of the house, the side by the river. No light now shone in the house. Had Bill come back out? Nearing the corner of the building, he peered around it.

Orville was still smoking over by his car. No one else was in sight. That had to mean Bill was still inside the house. With Raine and Lara?

Cordell backtracked to the first large glassless window opening and hoisted himself up onto the sill. He knew he would be a perfect target against the moonlit night and quickly lowered himself to the floor as soundlessly as possible.

The worn floorboards creaked under his weight as he took a step, then another as his eyes adjusted to the darkness inside the old abandoned house. As he moved deeper into the house, he saw light coming up from a stairway that led down to what must have been a partial basement.

That was where Raine and Lara had to be. The thought sent a shaft of fear through him as there was no sound coming from down there except for the heavy tread on the stairs.

Weapon ready, he moved toward the stair opening.

The board under his boot heel creaked loudly and he froze as a male voice yelled up from below, "I told you to wait. I just need to take care of something and then we'll go."

A sound outside, then the flicker of a flashlight beam as it headed his way. Cordell had a split second to make the decision whether to fire, kill Orville and then take care of Bill Beaumont in the basement.

He couldn't risk what Beaumont would do to Lara and

Raine before he could get to them. He ducked around the corner into a small room as Orville Cline entered the house.

In the glow of lantern light, McCall edged up behind Adele Beaumont. She was so filled with disgust that her heart was pounding. Lara huddled in the corner of the dirt floor, a filthy hand covering the red cheek that Adele had slapped.

Adele seemed to be alone. McCall made sure before she stepped closer. That was when she noticed the knife in the other woman's hand.

The girl had seen her and burst into tears no doubt with relief.

Just the sight of the girl huddled there naked, shivering from cold and fear, broke McCall's heart. She'd known Adele and Bill Beaumont, not well, but had seen them around for years. How could they do something like this?

She had never felt such fury. It was all she could do not to rush at the woman. She wanted to hurt her like she'd hurt Lara.

Timing it, McCall shoved the barrel of the pistol into Adele's back and knocked the knife out of the woman's hand.

"You touch that child again and I will blow your brains out," McCall said through gritted teeth.

She felt Adele freeze, then begin to cry. "I was trying to save her. I—"

McCall started to call in her location when Adele made a lunge for the knife.

She swung the gun, catching Adele across the side of the face. She howled as she fell over onto the dirt.

"Are you crazy?" Adele screamed. "I was trying to rescue—"

"Get up and take off your jacket."

"What?" Anger flared in Adele's gaze.

"Take off your jacket and give it to the girl. Now!"

Adele shoved herself up into a sitting position, glaring angrily. "I will sue the sheriff's department for everything it's worth. You have no idea what you've done. Your career is over. I will destroy you."

"Shut up." McCall snatched the jacket from Adele's fingers and tossed it to Lara. "Put that on, sweetie. Everything is going to be all right now."

"Where are this child's clothes?" she demanded of Adele, the weapon aimed at her heart.

"You're making a huge mistake, Sheriff," Adele said with venom. "You will live to regret this."

McCall looked down at her and felt her finger caress the trigger of the pistol. Why waste taxpayers' money with a trial or letting this woman live for years in prison or a mental hospital? What if Adele pulled strings, hired the best lawyer money could buy and got out one day to do this again?

She glanced over at Lara, who'd pulled on the jacket. "It's going to be all right." McCall smiled over at the girl, keeping an eye on Adele, the gun pointed at the woman's heart.

Lara took a shuddering breath and nodded, not looking all that sure.

McCall eased her finger off the trigger. It was the hardest thing she'd ever had to do. And she again started to make the call for backup.

Adele came flying at her with a piece of broken chair leg McCall now remembered seeing nearby. The blow knocked the gun from McCall's hand. It skittered across the dirt floor out of her reach.

Adele hit her again, knocking her to the floor. McCall got an arm up to ward off the next blow, but Adele was relentless. As McCall lunged for her gun, she saw Adele scoop up the knife from the floor.

McCall snatched up her weapon and swung around but too late. Adele had Lara and was holding the knife to her throat.

"Drop the gun, *Sheriff,* or you know what I'll do to this precious little girl, don't you?"

In the darkness, Raine backed down the stairs as quickly as possible as a flashlight beam played on the steps above her. She'd just reached the bottom when she heard Bill stop, turn back and yell at Orville.

Like Bill, she'd heard the other set of footfalls on the wooden floor overhead. She'd hoped that it was Orville being impatient enough that Bill wouldn't come back down. Why was he anyway?

"What the hell is wrong with you?" It was Orville. She heard him come storming into the house.

Her mind raced. The other footfalls couldn't have been him then.

Bill had stopped at the top of the stairs. "I told you to wait out by the car."

"What do you think I was doing? Then I hear you yelling…"

Raine backed up, stumbled into something that teetered and threatened to topple over. She spun around and grabbed for a small wooden crate that someone had stood on end. She could barely make it out in what little light spilled down from the stairs from Bill's flashlight.

But as her hand closed on it and she heard the footsteps lumbering the rest of the way down the stairs, she hefted it up and pressed her back to the wall. There wasn't time to close the lid on the box, which meant that within just a few seconds Bill would shine his flashlight beam into the box and realize she was gone.

Not gone. Since there was no way she'd had time to leave this room. Which meant—

The flashlight beam flicked over the box.

"What the hell?!" Bill cried.

Behind him, Orville said, "What is it?"

Raine stepped around the edge of the wall and swung the crate with all her strength.

The sound of the wood splintering as it connected with her abductor's face couldn't drown out his scream. It surprised her that she took no pleasure in the sound.

His flashlight fell to the floor, the light cutting a swath through the empty room toward the far wall. As he reached for her, Raine kicked out at him, catching him in the knee.

He slammed into the wall next to him as the knee gave way.

But before she could strike again, she saw the gun and heard the click as he snapped off the safety and aimed the barrel at her heart.

"I should have killed you sixteen years ago."

Cordell moved fast. He had no idea what was happening down in the basement, but something was definitely happening.

He came up behind Orville Cline swiftly and jammed the gun into his back. "Downstairs," he ordered, forcing Orville ahead of him.

The basement was a partial one just as Cordell had thought. The ceiling was low, the air dank, the space dark and claustrophobic. He'd feared that the moment they reached the basement, Bill Beaumont would see them.

But Cordell couldn't take the chance that Beaumont would hurt Raine and Lara if he waited. He kept the gun in Orville Cline's back as he quickly assessed the situation.

No Lara. And Beaumont was holding a gun on Raine.

"Got a problem here," Orville said.

"Well, I'm about to end this problem," Beaumont said.

"I wouldn't do that," Cordell said.

Beaumont swung around in surprise, leading with the barrel of his gun. He got off a shot before Raine attacked him. That shot caught Orville Cline in the chest. He let out a grunt and started to fall forward.

Cordell shoved him out of the way, Orville crashed through an open doorway and into a coffinlike box, as Cordell scrambled to get to Raine. Raine and Beaumont were on the floor, fighting over Beaumont's gun.

Just as Cordell grabbed for the gun, Beaumont pulled the trigger. Fire shot through Cordell's arm. Then he was knocked back, his gun wrested from him, and Beaumont had an arm locked around Raine's throat and the gun pointed at Cordell's head.

"Emily and I are leaving," Beaumont said, sounding winded. "If you follow us, I will kill her."

Cordell looked into Raine's eyes. One of them had started to swell where Beaumont must have hit her.

"Do as he says," Raine said. "I'll be all right." She was looking at his bleeding arm with concern.

"Listen to her. Emily was always the smart one," Beaumont said. "The only one who got away."

Cordell watched him drag Raine up the stairs, the gun to her temple. He didn't dare try to stop Beaumont.

Just as Beaumont reached the top, he swung the gun barrel away from Raine's temple and fired back down the stairs. Cordell dove, but not fast enough.

Bill made Raine drive, all the time holding the gun on her. She'd known when he hadn't killed her the moment they stepped out of the old house that he was taking her to where he'd hidden Lara.

She thought she would die at just the thought of Cordell lying, bleeding in that basement. She'd called his name as she was being dragged out of the house, the gun again to her head, but Cordell hadn't answered.

He's not dead. She would know if he was, she would feel it.

Of course, he hadn't answered when she'd called his name because Bill might have gone back to finish him off.

Think of Lara. Once Lara was safe…

As she drove down to the highway and, following his instructions, turned onto it, Bill pulled out his cell phone. She could hear the phone ringing. Once, twice, three times before it was finally answered.

"I need you to meet me. You know where." He swore. "You're what?" He swore again and barked into the phone, "Damn it, Adele. Don't do anything until I get there. We're on our way." He snapped the phone shut and glared over at her. "This is all your fault."

Did he really believe that? Apparently so. She wanted to argue the fact, but she feared he'd lose his temper and kill her beside the road. He'd already gotten in a few punches. She could feel her left eye threatening to swell shut and her ribs hurt where he'd gotten her with an elbow.

Bill looked worse than she did, she thought. His face was scratched and bleeding where the slats of the crate had connected with it. His nose looked broken. He kept wiping it with his sleeve, glaring at her since it must have hurt.

Raine drove down the deserted highway, trying to focus only on saving Lara and getting back to that house by the river. *Hang in there, Cordell.* It was the wee hours of the morning and there didn't seem to be another soul alive in the entire world.

As she drove, though, Raine memorized the way so she could return as soon as Lara was safe.

But Bill's phone call troubled her. The woman he'd called Adele was obviously with Lara—just as Raine had suspected. So why had Bill been surprised by that?

Because if Cordell hadn't shown up when he did, Bill would be taking Orville Cline to Lara now. Adele wasn't supposed to be there. Was it possible she had gone there to free the girl?

"So is Adele your wife?" she asked.

He didn't answer for a moment and she was thinking of asking another question when he said, "Thirty-six years of marital bliss."

Raine shot him a look to see if he was serious. She must have looked surprise to find that he seemed to be because he demanded, "What?"

"I just thought you must not be happy in your marriage if you have to steal little girls and—"

"I don't molest them," he snapped. "What do you think I am?"

She thought he really didn't want to go there. She checked her words. "Then I guess I don't understand why you—"

"No, you don't understand. I love children. I only take the ones who need me." He swore, seeing that she still wasn't getting it. "I wanted children but Adele couldn't have any. I didn't want someone else's child so adoption was out of the question."

"So you pick up children to satisfy your temporary need for a child." Raine couldn't believe what a sick bastard he was.

"You make it sound dirty," he snapped. "But it's not. I'm good to them. I show them probably the only love they get. It's not my fault that it is only for a short time. They become demanding after a while. They no longer appreciate what I've done for them. They want to go home." His tone had turned nasty.

Raine stole a look and saw that he'd become angry. She didn't dare open her mouth for fear of what she might say.

He glanced behind them as he had several times since they'd hit the highway and mumbled that he should have made sure that bastard was dead or at least disabled the car Orville Cline had stolen.

Raine hadn't dared look back. But from Bill's satisfied expression she knew there were no headlights behind them. That, however, didn't mean that Cordell wasn't alive and following them at this very moment with his headlights turned off.

She prayed that was the case because she needed it to be so. She needed to believe that Cordell was all right—because once they reached wherever Lara English was being kept, Raine knew she was going to need all the help she could get.

Chapter 15

From the floor, the sheriff stared for a moment at the woman holding the knife to Lara English's throat. There was a wild, inhuman look in Adele's eyes that glowed in the lantern light.

McCall slowly dropped her gun.

Adele smiled. "Now don't get up. Just kick the gun over here."

She did as she was ordered and kicked the gun over to Adele. McCall had left her shotgun outside against the door. She hadn't wanted to scare Lara. She looked at the little girl. She seemed calm again. Earlier she'd cried when it looked as if she might be saved. Now she seemed to know better.

"Lara, sweetheart," Adele said as the pistol came to a stop at her feet. "I'm going to put you down. I want you to hand the gun to Mommy. But be really careful."

"Yes, Mommy," Lara said in a robotic voice that tore

out McCall's heart—the same thing she wanted to do to Adele Beaumont.

Lara knelt down slowly, the blade pressing against her small throat, and picked up the pistol. "Here, Mommy."

"Thank you, sweetheart. You are such a good girl," Adele said, as she took the gun in her left hand. She made the exchange from the knife to the gun too quickly for Mc-Call to do anything more than watch. The gun was now pointed at the back of Lara's head.

Lara gave a small brave smile.

"Now," Adele said, holding Lara's arm and the gun to the child's head, "the first thing we are going to do is walk over and take the sheriff's pretty handcuffs. Don't move, Sheriff. You don't want this poor child to die, do you?"

McCall pulled out her handcuffs and handed them to Lara.

"Snap one on the sheriff's wrist. That a girl. Now let me." Adele grabbed the handcuffs, letting go of Lara just long enough to snap the other end of the cuffs to a pipe protruding from the wall.

"Now we're going to walk out to the car and Mommy is going to take you someplace nice for dinner. Are you hungry?"

Lara nodded enthusiastically.

"That's my girl."

The exchange turned McCall's stomach. She couldn't stand the thought of Adele leaving with that child. "Adele, don't do this."

Lara looked concerned again. The prospect of food was too much for her and McCall wondered how long it had been since she'd eaten.

"Do what? Sheriff, I'm a hero. I found Lara and now

I'm taking her back to town for a hero's welcome. I tried to tell you that's what I was doing, but you wouldn't listen."

McCall felt sick to her stomach. But as long as Lara was safe.

Adele's smile could have ripped flesh. "In fact, I think I might tell everyone that I caught you here with the little girl. You were about to do something horrible to her. If I hadn't stopped you…"

"No one will believe that."

"Of course they will. I'm Adele Beaumont. Do I look like a woman who would hurt a defenseless child?" She backed toward the front door, still holding the gun to Lara's head. "And by the time I get this child back to town, I know Lara will back up my story. Won't you, Lara. Didn't Mommy come to save you?" The girl nodded obediently. "The poor child has been through so much. She seems to think I'm her mommy. Isn't that sweet?"

"Turn here."

Raine slowed and turned down the narrow dirt lane. Ahead she could make out a house sitting in a stand of old cottonwoods. The house looked even more run-down than the one that she'd been held in but a light glowed inside.

There was a large newer model SUV parked on the back side, Raine saw as she pulled in front of the house and stopped. Bill shut off the engine and took the keys. He glanced back over his shoulder. Still no sign of anyone behind them.

He turned back around just in time to see what Raine saw: a woman coming out of the house with a little girl. Raine barely recognized the child as Lara English. Her hair was matted, her face smudged with dirt and she was wearing a jean jacket that swam on her and apparently little else.

In the light that spilled from the open door of the house, Raine looked from Lara to the woman holding the girl's hand and felt her heart drop. *You can call me Mommy.* Her earlier fear seized her at the sight of the horrible woman who'd been part of her abduction sixteen years ago.

Beside her, Bill swore. "Damn that woman. She's going to mess everything up." He threw open his door, then seemed to remember Raine. "Get out," he ordered, brandishing the gun.

Raine climbed out and when she did she saw something that made her heart soar. A glint of light from the moon reflecting off what had to have been a vehicle. It disappeared over a rise in the road Raine had just driven up. She listened for a moment but didn't hear the sound of a car engine. Could she have just imagined—

Bill grabbed her arm and shoved her toward the house. "Get back inside, Adele. Now!"

Adele had stopped beside her car. The door was open and she'd apparently just dragged out a jacket from the back. As she slipped into it, she watched her husband thoughtfully. Raine could tell the woman was thinking about trying to make a run for it with the girl. Would her husband of thirty-six years shoot her?

"Adele." The warning in his tone seemed to force Adele's decision. She grabbed Lara more roughly and pushed her toward the house.

Lara entered with Adele behind her. Raine followed, Bill with his gun on her.

He seemed to notice the sheriff handcuffed to a pipe about the same time as Raine. "What the hell, Adele?" he demanded. "What is the sheriff doing here?"

Raine watched Adele seem to shrink under Bill's anger.

"She must have followed me from town," she said in a small, childlike voice.

"You think?" He turned on her and Adele shrank away from him. "You just never learn, do you, Adele? Now I'm going to have to clean up the mess you made. Just like I always have to do."

Cordell had bandaged his side as best he could but it was bleeding again as he got out of the car. He'd searched Orville Cline's body for the keys the moment he'd heard Beaumont's truck engine turn over.

Now he followed a small gully toward the house where he'd seen Beaumont's truck stop. He had to stop once to adjust the makeshift bandage he'd constructed out of an old sweatshirt he'd found in the car. The sweatshirt said Montana State University across the front. Now it was wet with blood.

He moved through the trees that once sheltered the house in time to see a woman and child go inside, followed by Raine with Beaumont close behind holding a gun on her.

As he neared the edge of the house, he saw something by the door glint in the moonlight. Stepping closer, he saw that it was a shotgun.

Inside the house, he heard Beaumont's raised voice. He seemed to be hollering at his wife.

Cordell plucked up the shotgun and moved quickly back from the open doorway to check to make sure it was loaded.

It was.

Then he moved toward the door again. The last thing he'd heard Bill Beaumont say was something about cleaning up his wife's messes. Life, Cordell thought, was all about timing.

He knew he would have the advantage of surprise, but

he would also have only an instant to assess the situation and act. He would be jeopardizing Raine's and Lara's lives. Unfortunately there was no one else here to rectify things and he was losing blood and wasn't sure how much longer he'd be standing.

He prayed for perfect timing as he rounded the doorway, leading with the shotgun.

Raine was never so happy to see anyone come through that doorway. She felt such a well of emotion to see that Cordell was alive. If she'd ever doubted it, she knew now. She loved this man.

Bill had taken his eyes off her just moments before to go over and berate his wife. Raine had taken advantage of his inattention and pulled Lara over to her. The girl came willing enough. She seemed dazed, lost, and Raine recognized that look and felt sick inside that this child had had to go through what she'd experienced.

And suddenly Cordell appeared in the doorway with the shotgun. Adele saw him and let out a cry to warn Bill.

Raine acted on instinct, shoving Lara in the direction of the sheriff as Bill spun around. McCall grabbed the girl and covered her head as the sound of the shotgun blast boomed.

The boom reverberated through the old house. Bill made a gurgling sound, stumbling backward. Cordell suddenly seemed to be having trouble standing and Raine realized he'd been shot earlier just as she'd feared.

He took a step toward her, then dropped to one knee. A wadded-up piece of clothing fell from inside his jacket. Raine's heart dropped at the sight of the blood-soaked material.

As she started to rush to Cordell, she saw Adele trying to get the gun from her jacket pocket.

"Cordell, watch out!" she cried as she dove for Adele, slamming her back against the wall.

Adele had managed to get the gun from her pocket. Raine grabbed the gun, trying to wrench it from the woman's hands, but Adele was much stronger than she looked.

McCall held the girl to her as she worked with her foot to get the pistol that Bill Beaumont had dropped when he was shot. She finally got a boot toe around it and dragged it back toward her.

She could see Raine trying to wrest the gun from Adele, but she knew only too well how strong Adele was. That strength came from that inhuman part of her, McCall thought, as she dragged the gun to her.

Letting go of Lara, she grabbed up the gun with her free hand and fired two quick shots. Neither seemed to have any effect on Adele for a few moments.

McCall prepared to fire again when she saw Adele's fingers slip from the gun she was fighting to keep from Raine. The woman glanced over at her, a horrible hateful look in her eyes, before she looked down at where the bullets had torn through her jacket. The cloth blossomed red as Adele Beaumont slowly slid to the floor.

Leaning back, McCall laid the gun next to her and pulled Lara close again. Past Lara, Raine rushed to Cordell to press the wet cloth to his side.

Lara sat up as if sensing it was over. "I'm hungry," she said.

McCall started to tell Raine to go down the road to her patrol SUV to call for backup but before she could two deputies burst in followed by one very good-looking game warden.

"Adele has the key to the cuffs in her pocket," McCall said as Luke Crawford started to rush to her.

He went to the fallen woman and came back with the key. As he unlocked the cuffs, he sat down next to McCall on the floor and pulled her to him.

"How did you—?"

"Shane told me where you were when you called in the last time," Luke said. "I remembered this old farmhouse. I know we were supposed to wait for your call, but when we didn't hear from you..."

She smiled up at him, then pulled him down for a kiss. What would she ever do without this man?

Across the room, one of the deputies was seeing to Cordell as they waited for the ambulance to arrive. Another deputy had given Lara a stick of gum, promising her a candy bar once they reached his patrol car.

McCall leaned into Luke, absorbing his warmth. "I should have followed my first instinct and shot her right away. I sure wanted to."

Luke pulled her closer. "But you didn't."

No, she thought as she looked across the room to where Adele Beaumont lay, all the crazy wild gone from her blank eyes. "But I'm not sorry she's dead. I'm not sorry they're both dead. How is Cordell though?"

Luke shook his head. "He's apparently lost a lot of blood, but the ambulance is on the way."

Chapter 16

Raine stepped into Cordell's hospital room. It was right down the hall from his brother Cyrus's. Her relief and joy at hearing that Cordell was going to pull through was tempered with the news that Cyrus's condition hadn't changed.

As she neared his bed, Cordell opened those wonderful dark eyes of his and smiled. His face, though pale, seemed to light up and she felt weightless and silly and ecstatic. Tears welled in her eyes as he reached for her hand and pulled her closer.

She leaned her face against his and tried not to cry.

"Hey," he said. "I'm okay."

She nodded through her tears.

"You were amazing."

Raine didn't feel amazing. She'd endangered all of their lives.

"How's Lara?" he asked.

"Good." Drying her eyes and pulling herself together,

she told him about the deputies taking her out for breakfast at the Great Northern. "She put down pancakes, eggs and bacon without blinking an eye. It turns out that the girl's grandmother saw the story on the news. Apparently, she'd lost contact with her daughter and granddaughter. McCall is helping her get custody. Lara is very excited since she has happy memories of staying with her grandmother when she was younger."

"That is good news," Cordell said.

She heard the change in his voice. "Cyrus is still stable."

He nodded. "I know. I'd hoped that by the time this was over, he would be back with us."

"I'm so sorry," Raine said, her voice breaking. "This is all my fault."

"Baby, this is the Beaumonts' fault and Orville Cline's. But they are all gone now, may they never rest in hell." He stroked her hair. "If it hadn't been for you, Lara would have been another casualty of those monsters."

Raine laid her head on his chest and listened to the steady beat of his heart.

"I need to tell you how I feel about you, Raine."

She lifted her head, afraid of what he was going to say, afraid he didn't feel the way she did.

"No, I won't let you stop me this time," he said before she could speak. "I love you. I know this is sudden and you probably don't feel the same way but—"

Raine smiled through fresh tears as she touched a finger to his lips. "I feel the same way."

He laughed, then grimaced at the pain. "You do?"

"I do."

He grinned. "Those are words I'd like to hear you say one of these days real soon."

Epilogue

McCall was amazed how quickly life had gone back to normal. Her first calls had been the usual Whitehorse crimes: complaints about barking dogs and loud teenagers, requests to make checks on the elderly and giving rides home from the bars to those who weren't able to drive.

She'd come down from the shock of the events of the past few weeks. Cousin Cyrus was still in a coma, but he was stable and they were all holding out hope he would regain consciousness at any time.

Fortunately her cousin Cordell had recovered nicely, Lara had been placed with her grandmother until a permanent custody could be arranged and even the gossip had died down somewhat about the Beaumonts.

Other than that, life seemed to be getting back to normal, well, as normal as it could in Whitehorse, Montana.

Then her cell phone rang and she saw that it was her grandmother.

"Good morning, Grandmother," McCall said. It still seemed strange to call Pepper Winchester Grandmother. She'd gone all twenty-seven years of her life with Pepper denying her existence.

But all that was behind them and even McCall's mother, Ruby, was starting to come around. Ruby was actually looking forward to her daughter's Christmas wedding at Winchester Ranch.

"I just talked to the local florist," her grandmother was saying. "She said you hadn't been over to look at flowers for the wedding. Tell me you've at least ordered your dress. You do realize the wedding isn't that far away?"

"It's June and the wedding isn't until Christmas."

"Exactly. You can't keep putting this off. Tomorrow I could have Enid drive me in—"

"That's not necessary," McCall said.

"I know, but I'd like to help you. That is, if it's all right with your mother."

She heard the plea in her grandmother's voice. "I would love it if you'd come with me to pick out the flowers."

There was a lightness to her grandmother's voice that McCall hadn't heard before. "When's a good time?"

"We could meet at Jan's Floral at noon," McCall suggested. "Would that work for you?"

"That would be perfect. Maybe we could have lunch afterward. That is if you don't have to get back to work right away."

McCall smiled, listening to how formal they sounded. "That would be nice."

"Thank you. Would Luke like to join us?"

"To pick out flowers?" Her game warden fiancé would have no interest in picking out flowers for the wedding.

Luke had been great, though, about having the wedding at the ranch.

"You deserve to have your wedding there," he'd said. "You're a Winchester and it's high time everyone accepted it. Also I suspect it's your grandmother's way to try to make amends."

McCall hoped that was the case and that her grandmother wasn't using the wedding as part of one of her hidden agendas.

"Luke's working down in the Missouri Breaks," she told her grandmother now. "It's fishing season, you know. Lots of licenses to check."

"All right then. I will see you tomorrow." Pepper sounded as if she wanted to say more but McCall got another call and had to let her go. Whatever it was, McCall figured she'd find out soon enough. Hopefully *before* the wedding.

Cordell sat down next to his brother's bed and took Cyrus's hand in his. That twin connection that had always been there was still gone and he felt such a weight on his chest that sometimes he couldn't breathe.

"We got the bad guys," he said quietly. "Just as I promised. I sure could have used your help though. Now it's time for you to come back."

The only sound in the room was the beep of the monitor.

Cyrus was still alive. That meant there was hope. Cordell latched on to that slim thread and held on for dear life.

"I can't wait to tell you about Raine. You're going to love her. The two of you met already." He swallowed, feeling the burn of tears and fought them back. "She's a lot like you. Brave to a fault and she's a private investigator. Can you beat that?"

Cordell realized how foolish he'd been to think that once he caught the people responsible that Cyrus would wake up.

It had been crazy. Cyrus's condition hadn't changed since the accident. It might never change.

He shoved that thought away and stood as the doctor came into the room. Cordell knew he had to make a decision. He followed the doctor out into the hall.

"You have to face the possibility that your brother might never recover from his injury," the doctor said again.

Cordell nodded, though he doubted he could ever accept that.

"I would suggest moving him to a long-term care facility that specializes in these kinds of cases."

"I want to take him back to Colorado. Is there a problem with transporting him in his condition?"

"He is breathing on his own, his vitals are strong, I see no problem with that and there are some fine facilities in Denver."

Cordell nodded. "I'll make arrangements right away then."

"Are you leaving?" Pepper Winchester asked in surprise.

Her daughter Virginia turned from packing clothing into her suitcase, her expression sour. "There is no reason to stay here under the circumstances."

"The circumstances being that your mother isn't dying quickly enough?"

"Mother, don't start," Virginia said. "You don't want or need me here. You have Enid. She is more like a daughter to you than I am."

Pepper couldn't hold back the laugh. "Enid?"

"Fine. If not Enid then definitely Brand and the others."

"Oh, Virginia, must you always come back to this?" Behind her, Pepper heard Brand and Worth come up the hall. They were carrying their overnight bags. Apparently they were all leaving.

What surprised her was how hollow that made her feel. She didn't want them to go. She realized how incongruous that was since she still believed one of them was an accomplice to murder.

"I'll let you say goodbye to your brothers," Pepper said and, cane tapping, went down the hall where she found Enid eavesdropping. She stopped next to the elderly housekeeper, who didn't seem the least bit upset about being caught.

Even though she knew what would be said about her and how much it would hurt, Pepper stayed there by Enid to listen.

"Why *did* she get us back here?" Virginia demanded in her shrill voice. "She really can't believe that one of us had something to do with Trace's death."

"I don't know," Brand said and sighed. "Maybe she needs us."

Worth swore. "A little late, don't you think?"

"He's right, Mother never needed anyone but Trace," Virginia said, close to tears.

"I think you're smart to leave," Brand said, always the sensible one. "Being here just seems to bring back all those old resentments."

Pepper could almost hear her daughter bristle.

"Don't pretend I'm the only one who can't forgive Mother."

"Virginia, I really don't want to get into this," Brand said. "I have one son recovering from gunshot wounds and another in a coma. I'm much more concerned about the future than I am the past."

"At least you have children," Virginia spat.

In the silence that followed Pepper could hear what none of them could bring themselves to say. Pepper knew they were all thinking about the child Virginia had given birth to and lost.

"Virginia," Brand said, clearly trying to be diplomatic. "You didn't have anything to do with Trace's—"

"Is that what you think? That I had something to do with killing him?" Virginia let out a laugh.

"You knew the woman who confessed to killing him."

"So did you. So did Worth and Angus, not to mention Enid and Alfred. Who said it had to be one of us?"

"She's right," Worth spoke up. "Alfred might be dead, but Enid doesn't appear to be going anywhere and any fool can see that something is going on between Enid and Mother. If I had to guess I'd say blackmail. I wouldn't put it past Enid for an instant."

Beside Pepper, Enid let out a snort and whispered, "I never liked that boy."

"I'm sure it will all sort itself out," Brand said. "Who says the woman didn't lie about one of us being involved?"

"Oh, that is so like you, Brand," Virginia snapped. "You always just put your head into the sand and pretend everything is fine. Sort itself out. In other words, you're not going to do a damned thing, are you?"

"What would you like me to do? I can't change Mother and I can't change the past. What is it you want me to do, Virginia? Just tell me and I'll do it."

Virginia was crying again.

Pepper heard Worth and Brand start down the hall. She and Enid hurriedly took the servants' stairs to the kitchen.

"Mother?" Brand called when they reached the front entry.

Pepper came out of the kitchen to tell her sons goodbye. Virginia joined them, sans suitcase. Apparently she'd changed her mind about leaving.

"Are you coming back for the wedding at Christmas?" Pepper asked them after she'd given her sons both awkward hugs.

Worth merely nodded, expressing what Pepper knew to be true of him. He would come back if the others did. It was as if he didn't have a mind of his own and never had. She sighed inwardly.

"Are you sure it's a good idea to have the wedding here?" Virginia asked. "I know McCall's the sheriff and her fiancé is some kind of law enforcement, but they aren't bulletproof and Winchester Ranch doesn't seem to be the safest place."

Pepper ignored her as she looked to Brand. The others would do whatever he did. Until that moment, she hadn't realized just how much this meant to her to have them all here. Sentiment aside, there was still a murderer among them. If it was on her last dying breath, she would know which one it was.

"I'll be here," Brand said as if he had a bad feeling he'd better come home for Christmas this year.

Raine had just picked up her VW bug at the garage when Cordell drove up in his brother's pickup. It was one of those Montana summer days, not a cloud in the brilliant blue sky, the sun bright and warm, the breeze scented with freshly mown grass.

She watched him from the shade of the building as he climbed out, still taken aback that this gorgeous man loved *her*.

Raine realized for the first time she wasn't worried about the future. For sixteen years, she'd lived with the knowledge that there were people out there who would kill her if they knew who she really was. She hadn't been able to forget for even a minute that she was Emily Frank, the victim of child abductors.

But as Cordell Winchester came toward her, she realized she was Raine Chandler, a woman who could finally dream of a happily ever after.

"Hi, beautiful," Cordell said now as he took her in his arms and kissed her. He held her tight and she could tell he didn't like even a temporary separation. But he had to take care of his brother and she had to discuss with Marias selling her half of their investigative business in California.

Last night, lying out on a blanket under the Montana midnight sky, Cordell had asked her to marry him. She'd told him it was too soon. He'd argued that some things you just knew for certain and this was something he just knew and more time together wouldn't change his mind.

So she'd made him a deal. They would get married when Cyrus was able to be the best man at the wedding. Cordell's eyes had filled with tears. He'd started to ask but what if Cyrus never—

Raine had stopped him. "That's the deal," she'd said. In the meantime, they would take care of business and see each other as often as they could.

"Promise me I'll see you in Colorado soon," Cordell said now as the kiss ended.

She gazed into his dark eyes, felt her heart fill to overflowing with love for this man, and whispered back, "I promise."

* * * * *

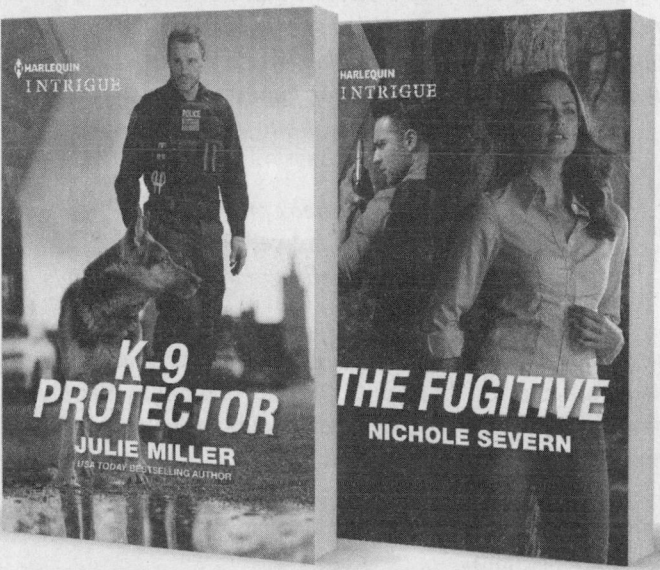

A grisly discovery leads detective Waco Johnson to Cardwell Ranch—and a thirty-year-old unsolved homicide. When evidence points to Ella Cardwell's mother, Waco knows he'll need the rancher's help to find her. But as family secrets are uncovered, Ella and Waco are thrust into a killer's sights.

Read on for a sneak preview of
Cold Case at Cardwell Ranch,
by New York Times *bestselling author B.J. Daniels.*

The wind whipped around him, kicking up dust and threatening to send his Stetson flying. Cold-case detective Waco Johnson cautiously approached the weatherworn boards that had blown off the opening of the old abandoned well.

The Montana landscape was riddled with places like this one, abandoned homesteads slowly disappearing along with those who had worked the land.

He hesitated a few feet from the hole, feeling a chill even on this warm Montana summer afternoon. Nearby, overgrown weeds and bushes enveloped the original homestead dwelling, choking off any light. Only one blank dusty window peered out at him from the dark gloom. Closer, pine trees swayed, boughs emitting a lonely moan as they cast long jittery shadows over the century-old cemetery with its sun-bleached stone markers on the rise next to the house. A rusted metal gate creaked restlessly in the wind, a grating sound that made his teeth ache.

The noise added to his anxiety about what he was going to find. Or why being here nudged at a memory he couldn't quite grasp.

He glanced toward the shadowed gaping hole of the old well for a moment before pulling his flashlight from his coat pocket and edging closer.

The weathered boards that had once covered the opening had rotted away over time. Weeds had grown up around the base. He could see where someone had trampled the growth at one edge to look inside. The anonymous caller who'd reported seeing something at the bottom of the well? That begged the question: How had the caller even seen the abandoned well's opening given the overgrowth?

Waco knelt at the rim and peered into the blackness below. As the beam of his flashlight swept across the dust-dried well bottom, his pulse kicked up a beat. Bones. Animals, he knew, frequently fell into wells on abandoned homesteads. More often than not, it was their bones that dotted the rocky bottom.

Shielding his eyes from the swirling dust storm, Waco leaned farther over the opening. The wind howled around him, but he hardly heard or felt it as his flashlight's beam moved slowly over the bottom of the well—and stopped short.

A human skull.

Don't miss
Cold Case at Cardwell Ranch *by B.J. Daniels,*
available August 2021 wherever
Harlequin Intrigue books and ebooks are sold.

Harlequin.com

Love Harlequin romance?

DISCOVER.

Be the first to find out about promotions, news and exclusive content!

- Facebook.com/HarlequinBooks
- Twitter.com/HarlequinBooks
- Instagram.com/HarlequinBooks
- Pinterest.com/HarlequinBooks
- YouTube.com/HarlequinBooks

ReaderService.com

EXPLORE.

Sign up for the Harlequin e-newsletter and download a free book from any series at **TryHarlequin.com**

CONNECT.

Join our Harlequin community to share your thoughts and connect with other romance readers! **Facebook.com/groups/HarlequinConnection**

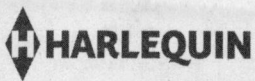